D0513481

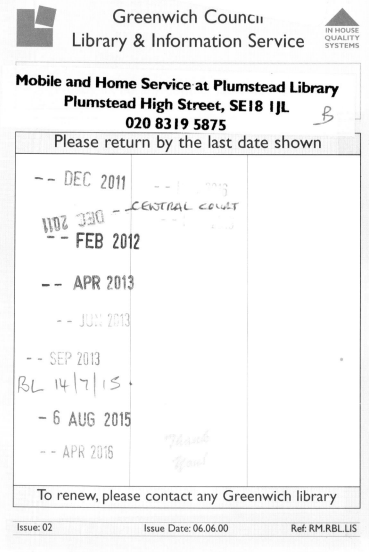

SARAH

SARAH

Charlotte Hardy

SEVERN HOUSE LARGE PRINT
London & New York

This first large print edition published in Great Britain 2007 by
SEVERN HOUSE LARGE PRINT BOOKS LTD of
9-15 High Street, Sutton, Surrey, SM1 1DF.
First world regular print edition published 2006 by
Severn House Publishers, London and New York.
This first large print edition published in the USA 2007 by
SEVERN HOUSE PUBLISHERS INC., of
595 Madison Avenue, New York, NY 10022.

British Library Cataloguing in Publication Data

Hardy, Charlotte
    Sarah. - Large print ed.
    1. Abused wives - Fiction 2. Governesses - England - Whitby
    - Fiction 3. Widowers - England - Whitby - Fiction
    4. Whitby (England) - Social conditions - 19th century -
    Fiction 5. Love stories 6. Large type books
    I. Title
    823.9'14[F]

    ISBN-13: 9780727876072

Printed and bound in Great Britain by
MPG Books Ltd, Bodmin, Cornwall.

One

Standing in the lee of the deck house she was protected from the worst of it. Above her, flurries of snow whirled and danced round the sails, billowing and flapping in the furious rush of the ice-cold wind, as the ship rose and then unexpectedly dropped into the hollow between the waves. Clouds massed solid, white, driving low over the masts.

The brig made a sudden dip, lurching to one side, and the sea rose grey-green, tipped with white as the wind took the spume and carried it film-like through the air. Sarah gripped the handle at the corner of the deck-house as the brig, groaning as if every timber in her was bruised, stopped momentarily and then, drawing breath, heaved herself up again. The sea disappeared and the vista was filled with sky.

As the ship righted herself Sarah fixed her eyes on the cliffs a mile away, took a deep breath, and huddled closer into her cloak. She could make out green along the cliff top and a small cluster of cottages.

The door opened behind her and the big man came out. She had been conscious of him earlier, had watched him, but now shrank into herself, still staring at the distant cliffs.

As the ship lurched again she lost her grip, would have shot down the companionway and very likely been washed over the side if the man had not caught her arm and righted her. Her heart pounding, she gripped the cold rail and looked round at him.

'You'd better get inside, miss. You may not be so lucky the next time.'

His voice was impersonal, off-hand, curt. She glanced up into his face as she tried to regain her breath. She was uncertain what to say. It was a striking face – large, with thick eyebrows, deep-set eyes and a strong jaw; he had a natural frown, as if he were thinking deeply. He looked at her as if he were looking into her, or indeed right through her.

'There would be little loss,' she muttered, turning away.

'What did you say? I didn't hear you.'

She was taken aback at his harsh tone, and glanced up. 'It doesn't matter.'

'If it doesn't matter, why say it? You seem to take damn little care of yourself, young lady. Get inside.'

'Thank you, sir, but I shall remain here a little longer. I cannot stand the smell of coke. Besides,' she added unexpectedly, 'I like this weather.'

He turned to her, surprised. There was no reply for a moment, as he gripped the rail beside her; then he spoke again, thoughtfully, as he looked away towards the cliffs. 'Like it?

Aye, so do I. It suits my temper. It is harsh maybe, bitter too.' He glanced at the rigging overhead. 'But it's bracing weather, honest weather.'

There was little she could say to this. In a way she agreed with him. At this moment, it suited her temper too, but he was not inclined to ask her opinion, she thought.

The ship lurched into a wave with a jarring shudder which ran all through her, a shudder which Sarah thought should have broken every timber in her, and spray dashed across the deck. She held tightly to the handle at the corner of the deckhouse, but felt the man's hand on her arm, steadying her. She could not help looking up at him again, and murmuring 'Thank you' – but the words were carried away on the wind.

Moored at London Bridge, the brig had looked large and sturdy, its rigging rising high above the quayside, as she flung herself aboard. But now here with the sea all about them she seemed small and insignificant, a dirty little collier, very alone and very fragile in the great wash and surge of the sea.

But Sarah was glad of the sea; glad of the wind whipping spume from wavetop to white wavetop, glad of the waves, impenetrable, icy, steep and rich in glaucous colours, blue, grey, green, white. Something in her exulted in the violent power of it; on its mighty bosom, and by its eternal power, the sea would save her and for the first time her heart lifted and she felt there was hope yet.

'Have you any idea when we arrive, sir?'

'Where are you travelling to?'

'Er – I'm not sure.'

'What do you mean? You don't know where you are going?'

'I've forgotten—'

'Forgotten?'

'I, well—'

He turned to her in astonishment. He was a terribly forceful man. 'You are on a ship, and you don't know where she's bound?'

'The captain did tell me,' she stuttered, 'but then—'

He gave her a very strange look. 'She's bound for Newcastle. But she'll be putting in at Whitby first.'

'Whitby? What is that? I was never there.'

'It's a fishing port – and coaling station. With luck we should be in before dark.' He glanced round the corner of the deckhouse. 'You can see the ruins of the abbey.'

She followed his finger and saw, far away on the cliff top, an irregular outline. Her mind was working quickly. 'It is a small town? Not well known?'

'Not well known? Who says so?'

'Oh – well, it is no matter. It is not important. Thank you for your information.' She turned sharply away.

An hour later as dusk was falling the collier nosed her way between the breakwaters at the river mouth. The wind softened in the lee of the cliffs and as the sailors bustled about her, taking in sails, shouting and heaving at ropes, Sarah stood at the rail staring up into the town, which rose sharply on either side of the river. Even at dusk on this December afternoon, even in the irregular snow-flurries, there was activity on the quayside. In the many little fishing boats, lanterns were alight and men were scrambling about, arranging ropes and nets and piling baskets. On land too lights had come on in many windows and flickered a welcome to her, mild, golden.

'Captain!' She made a sudden decision. 'I shall disembark here.'

The quay had a reassuring steadiness, though for a while after it seemed occasionally to rock and heave beneath her feet. Her face glowed from the wind but she was chilled in her very self with cold.

The quayside was busy with stalls where women were selling fish, even at this late hour in the fading light. There was a constant shouting of fishermen in their boats, and she narrowly missed a horse and cart lumbering past.

A trap pulled up with a well-wrapped groom holding the reins. She was still debating which way to go when she heard the voice behind her again.

'Josiah! Hi there! I'll be with you in a moment!' The big man in his voluminous ulster, tall hat clamped down over his brow, came down the gangplank, passed her and tossed a large bag into the trap. As he was about to climb in he looked round, saw Sarah and stopped.

'Can I offer you a lift anywhere?' he called over.

She silently shook her head. He paused and then came across and stood looking down at her. 'Is anyone meeting you?'

'Thank you, but I shall be quite all right.'

'Will you? You didn't seem to know where you were going just now. Do you know anybody here?'

'Your groom is waiting, sir! I shall be perfectly comfortable, but thank you for your concern.'

He shrugged and turned back to the trap, but as the groom was driving away he looked back once more to where she was still standing by the ship, her bag at her feet.

'Excuse me, sir,' she stopped one of the sailors as he came off the collier. 'Can you recommend a hotel here?'

The man, wrapped in a thick tarpaulin, grinned. 'Depends. There's the Angel; that'll very likely suit a lady. Or there's the White Horse. That's cheaper.'

'Could you find a boy to carry my bag?'

'Aye, ma'am.'

Not long afterwards a boy appeared with a wheelbarrow and heaved her grip into it. Together they set off along the quay, where the fish market was now lit by flaring pine torches, with planks laid on barrels. Fish lay everywhere in wicker baskets, and fishwives well wrapped against the cold called to each other in an accent she could not understand.

Panniers were being loaded on donkeys' backs. She lifted her skirts to avoid the puddles that lay everywhere.

They turned off the quay across a bridge and into a narrow alley leading steeply up into the town; on either side doors opened into taverns and grog shops, crowded with sailors and working men and women, and a warm breath, laden with tobacco and beer, would sometimes waft out. The boy turned into a wider street running parallel with the quay where there were more shops open, and people hurrying past bent against the wind, which swirled and buffeted along the street. There was a constant clattering of boots and wood-soled clogs over the cobbles.

After a few minutes, the boy stopped before a brightly lit inn. He carried her grip up the steps and deposited it in the hallway, and following him she felt the intense relief of warmth after the weather outside. She fished in her reticule for a penny, and the boy went out.

There was no one about but through a door she saw a fire in the parlour and going in she huddled over it to warm herself. She removed her gloves and was throwing back her cloak when a man hurried in behind her. 'Sorry to keep you waiting, ma'am. What can I get you?'

'A room.'

He called behind him, 'Sally, light a fire in number five! If you'd like to wait here for a few minutes, ma'am, while fire is lighting.

Will you require a room for your servant?'

'I have no servant,' she said quietly.

'Very good, ma'am. And would you care to order dinner?'

'Thank you, I am not hungry.'

Half an hour later she was shown into a room looking down into the street. Her bag was standing on a dressing table; the fire burning in the grate had not yet begun to thaw the room. She stood for a little staring down into the street where people still bustled to and fro, bending into the wind and gusts of snow, hurrying in and out of a shop opposite. But at last she turned back into the room, uncertain, and began to undo the drawstring of her cloak. Then, shivering, she sat at the end of the bed, and taking out her reticule, opened it and turned it out onto the counterpane. Some gold coins and paper notes fell out and she took them up, smoothing out the notes and counting the coins. Arranging the notes in a pile, she stared down at the money for some time motionless and at last drew a long breath.

No longer able to help herself she uttered a little groan and, falling forward onto the bed, burst into tears.

Two

A door slammed below her and there was the heavy noise of feet on the stairs. He was shouting, and as she cowered in the corner of the room the door flew open and he was there, loud, his face distorted, enormous, red, as if he might explode. She screamed as he lunged towards her, snatched her by the wrist and swung her round, flinging her bodily across the room so that she crashed against a chair, fell across it and onto the floor. As she regained her feet he came for her again and she was screaming and screaming as he took her arm and with a mighty swing caught her with his fist full on the side of her face. She whirled round, out of balance, tripped in her skirts and fell heavily again. He was shouting down at her but she was too terrified, cowering as he pulled her by the arm and jerked her sharply up. He was so strong, she had never known him so strong, he seemed inflated, his face engorged with hatred, his eyes blazing. He was still shouting, and again he thrust her across the room. She crashed against the wall, so hard that the breath was knocked right out of her. As she collapsed to the floor, she thought, I must surely die; he's going to kill me. She heard herself screaming, screaming, 'Don't! Don't! No—'

With a start she opened her eyes and could not think where she was. Breathing hard and quickly, turning her head from side to side on the pillow, she stared up into the darkness. In her terror she reached for the heavy old damask hanging and wrenched it back. Across the room at the window, the bleak, silver-grey light of snow clouds indicated the dawn. She fell back on the pillow, still breathing fast, and remembered.

She closed her eyes as her breathing steadied. Thank God, she was here; thank God he could not find her here, thank God— She waited, feeling her heart calmer, waiting, and staring up at the grey light, the blank of the morning. Now everything came back, her flight, the ship at London Bridge, the voyage, and her sudden decision to disembark in this little fishing port. The room turned about her and she twisted in the bed, fell back, staring across at the jug on the washstand, trying to think out what she had done. There was no going back, that was certain. Never would she go back. Never. Never. But what she was to do at this moment she had not the faintest idea. She was alone and there was not one person in this town who knew her or knew of her or who cared a farthing whether she were alive or dead. If she had slipped off the ship yesterday who would have known? The captain had taken her money but did not bother even to ask her name.

In the reticule on the dressing table, barely visible in the dim light, lay a few sovereigns and banknotes, the only things in the entire world that lay between her and utter ruin. For a moment a swimming, dissolving feeling flowed through her, loosening her inside, the dizzy, capsizing motion which she recognized as fear. And again in a spasm she turned in the bed staring unseeing at the dusty curtains of the bedstead. She was alone. Breathing quickly, she started up onto one elbow.

She had to do something.

She had counted her money; she could live a few months, if she was very careful. But that was not enough. If she couldn't go back, she would have to find employment. She took her cloak, wrapped it round her shoulders and going to the window looked into the street. The rooftops opposite were thick with snow and beyond them she saw the sea and could make out the breakwaters at the harbour mouth. The pearly light bleached everything so that there was no dividing line between sea and sky; beyond the breakwaters there was only a white blank.

Below in the street a few passers-by made fresh tracks in the snow. Smoke rose from several chimneys. Restlessly, her mind turned over the possibilities: was it wise to have disembarked in this little town? Shouldn't she have gone on to Newcastle – or Edinburgh? Surely in a larger city there would have been better opportunities for someone like her to earn her bread? Biting her lip, she strained to think it all out.

With a shudder she threw off her cloak and nightdress, huddled into her clothes, and shortly afterwards made her way down to the parlour, where to her relief a girl was lighting a fire.

'Wilt tha have summat to thee breakfast?'

'I beg your pardon?'

'I'll be gettin' breakfast in a moment. There's two of t' regulars'll be down soon and they'll be in a hurry to be off.'

'Thank you.' She made sense now of the girl's speech. 'Yes. I didn't eat last night.'

'Tha mun be fair frozen. Not eat thee dinner?'

Sarah turned away, and was silent. The girl finished lighting the fire and went out. The parlour had a chill rancid air, stinking of tobacco smoke. But now she heard a clattering on the stairs and men talking volubly.

The door opened with a crash and two middle-aged men entered, thickly dressed against the cold, one of them rubbing his hands vigorously, and both talking earnestly at once. 'Sally!'

'Comin', Mr Birtwhistle!' The girl popped her head through another door. 'The usual? And for thee, Mr Hardcastle?'

'Aye, lass, and a pot of tea as soon as you like.'

Sarah remained at the window looking out and somewhat embarrassed by the evident familiarity of the two men with the ways of

16

the establishment.

The kitchen door burst open again and the girl bustled in with a large teapot, clattering it down on the table where they sat and assembling cups and knives and forks.

As one of the men was pouring the tea, he glanced over at Sarah. 'Wilt tek a cup o' tea, young lady?'

'Thank you,' she said faintly. 'I will. It's very cold this morning.'

'It is that! Fair freezing. By – is that time? Sally! Where's that breakfast or I'll miss the eight forty! It's reckonin' day in Leeds! Dost tha want me to lose me situation?'

Sarah took the cup the man offered and sat a little further along the table. She sat silently, holding the cup in both hands, sipping the hot tea and staring down at the old oak surface with its myriad marks and cuts, scratches and carvings, memories of the countless guests who had passed through the inn.

Not long after, the girl reappeared with breakfasts for the two men, who set to with unabashed relish.

'Shall I serve thee breakfast too, young lady?' the girl said with a free and casual manner which Sarah found disconcerting. Sarah glanced at the heaped-up plates the two men were attacking. She was at that moment ravenous.

'Thank you.'

Not long after one of the men rose, having demolished his breakfast with extraordinary speed, took a last mouthful of tea, snatched up a heavy leather grip and dashed out. As he was about to disappear through the door, he called back, 'Sally! I'll see thee day after Christmas!'

Again she heard the girl's voice from the kitchen. 'Right you are, Mr Birtwhistle!'

Mr Hardcastle seemed to have more time to spare. Once he had finished his breakfast he turned to give his attention to Sarah, who was now devouring her own. The plate was piled high with sausages, eggs and bacon, together with several other things she did not recognize, and which, but for her ravening hunger, she would have avoided. Enormous wedges of bread and butter sat on a side plate. She was awkwardly aware of the spectacle she must be presenting.

'On thee way 'ome for Christmas, young lady?' he said with easy familiarity.

'No.'

'Art travellin' alone?'

'Yes,' she said quietly.

'Young lady like thee shouldn't be travellin' alone. Hast far to go?'

She said nothing and tried to continue with her breakfast. After a moment he went on, 'Does thee family live hereabouts?'

'No.'

'A reet mystery, eh? What'll thee do for Christmas, then?'

'I shall stay here.'

'Here?' he echoed. 'Christmas in a hotel? Hast run away from home?'

Sarah turned on him, exasperated with his

18

impertinent questions, but he was sitting comfortably with a cup of tea in his hand, looking her over from beneath heavy tufted eyebrows with a sardonic half-smile on his face. He was man of fifty or sixty, bald with a plump, choleric face. Something about his cool manner irritated her.

'What I choose to do is of no concern to any one else.'

'Suit theeself.' But he did not move, neither did the smile disappear. He was perfectly at his ease. 'Th'art a lady by the sound of thee. Does thee father know th'art here? What does he say to it? Hastn't a brother or cousin might accompany thee? Or even a maid?'

'Will you please stop these questions. I hope if I choose I may stay in a hotel without being questioned by a complete stranger!'

'Don't tek on, lass,' he said easily, still failing to rise to her provocation. 'I were only thinking of thee. I don't like to think of a pretty young thing like thee alone in a strange town over Christmas. Folk might talk, that's all. Where dost come from?'

'London.' She paused, then in a lower voice, 'I beg your pardon, sir, if I offended you.'

'Well,' he said, then drew a breath and stood up. 'If th'art staying here over Christmas, I'll see thee again. 'Cos I am, an' all. Eeh – is that time?' He stood up quickly. 'Sally, is Mr Empson there? Tell him I've got to go.'

He turned to Sarah, looked down at her and gave her a wink, then made for the door. 'Oh, and Sally! I'll be in to dinner!'

When the girl came back to clear the table Sarah told her she was going to stay on for a few days over Christmas.

But thinking over her few words with Mr Hardcastle, she realized she had told him all the wrong things and he was certain to get the wrong impression – that she was some kind of adventuress, or worse. And he seemed just the kind of person to go gossiping about her. Annoyed with herself, she returned to her room for her cloak and bonnet, and set out into the town.

The streets were busy and she made her way over the snow, now uneven and dirty, back down to the harbour. The ship had gone, and staring at the green-black water she understood that there was no going back.

Wrapping her cloak round her she made her way thoughtfully along the quay, taking in the animated life, the busy morning market and the fishing boats where fishermen were arranging their nets. There was a weak sun, little more than a faint orange glow, but the wind had dropped.

As she stared across the river at the little houses rising steeply from the quayside, with their snow-covered roofs packed together and the outline of a church above them, she was thinking. Was this the best thing, or should she move on? Try somewhere else? A big city – go on to Newcastle or Edinburgh? Perhaps she should have crossed to Calais instead of making her way up this bleak and inhospitable coast? In France she might get work teaching English – and she could easily cope there. Her French was quite adequate. She could teach here too. In fact, as she stopped to think about it, there was nothing else she could do; she would have to advertise herself in a newspaper.

Feeling her spirits stiffening as her future began to clear she saw there were two things she must do: find lodgings, and place an advertisement in the local newspaper. In a shop she asked whether there were a news-paper in Whitby, and the assistant directed her to an address further down the street.

Sitting in the dark office, with the noise of printing presses coming through from the shed behind and the peculiar smell of printer's ink in her nostrils, she composed an advertisement.

'A lady recently arrived in Whitby is desir-ous to offer her services to any family of good standing who may require tuition for their children in French, pianoforte, grammar—' She chewed her pencil as she thought. What else could she teach? The fact was, she had never taught in her life and had looked down her nose in a very snooty fashion at gover-nesses and such like. That was neither here nor there. She chewed the pencil again, and hastily continued: 'elocution and deport-ment.'

She read it through. Recently arrived – weren't they bound to ask why had she recently arrived? What was she doing there?

She read it through again. 'Of good standing': that was a clever touch, and would flatter the reader.

There was one thing more: she must change her name. Glancing through the window she noticed a butcher's shop opposite. Without thinking, she wrote down 'Miss Shaw', handed the notice to the clerk, paid for it and was out into the street before she could change her mind.

As she was threading her hand into her glove she glanced for a moment at her wedding ring. She pulled it off and put it in her purse.

Nothing was likely to happen before Christmas, only a couple of days away. In the meantime she could think about lodgings.

However, though she asked about the town, in the newspaper office, and anywhere else she could think of, Christmas came and she had not found anything.

The White Horse appeared to be deserted but for herself and Mr Hardcastle.

Three

Christmas Day wore away in utter misery. She had never been so depressed in her life. Surely anything was better than this? As she wandered through the town she caught glimpses everywhere, glancing into little cottages or through the windows of larger residences, of families united round the dinner table, heard gusts of laughter from taverns, smelled the Christmas geese or sides of beef, the punch, lemons, rum, smells savoury and sweet, invigorating hearty smells; the town was suffused with good cheer and she wandered through it like a ghost, thought she must be accursed, and did not know whether she could make it through the day. As night fell she found herself face down on her bed, her feet frozen cold and her face bathed in tears.

Eventually hunger drove her to the dining room. Before going down she took a deep breath, straightened her back and looked long at herself in the mirror. Whatever the future held, she told herself, there was going to be a future. Somehow everything would work out all right and it was only the fact of Christmas which had cast her into such a suicidal frame of mind.

She splashed her face with cold water, combed her hair, straightened her dress and went down into the dining room.

It was empty except for Mr Hardcastle. At the door she stood undecided for a moment as to where to sit. He gave her a friendly greeting, however, and, with a flourish of his hand, motioned her to the table before him. Slightly unsure of herself, but crazy for some company, she sat facing him.

From the kitchens at that moment there came a burst of hysterical laughter, and the clashing of metal.

Mr Hardcastle looked at her and raised his eyebrows. 'Do'st think we're goin' to get fed tonight?'

Mr Hardcastle obviously enjoyed his food and drink; a bottle of claret stood open on the table and he did not hesitate to fill her glass before his own.

'Merry Christmas! Miss – eeh, I don't believe we've been introduced. Not proper, like. Hardcastle's the name! And—'

'Miss Shaw,' Sarah remarked with a small cough.

He sipped his wine, then took a larger draught. 'Eeh, I've drunk worse. Sup up.'

Sarah tasted the wine. It was rich, full of flavour and strong. After a day in the freezing cold...

'Thank you,' she said politely, and then jumped as he bellowed unexpectedly,

'*Sally, where's that dinner!* Now!' He turned

again to Sarah. 'Let's get cosy. I don't believe th'art from around these parts? Up from London?'

'Near London, sir.'

'Oh aye? Wheere?'

She looked down. 'It doesn't matter.'

He made a face. Then after a moment, 'Nay, I dessay not.'

The kitchen door opened, and Sally came in precariously holding two bowls of soup. There was a rich meaty smell from them.

'Eeh, that's summat like!' Mr Hardcastle took up his spoon. 'Merry Christmas! And another bottle o' this, Sally.'

As she drank the soup and sipped at her second glass of wine – he had not hesitated to replenish her glass – Sarah began to be more curious about Mr Hardcastle. And in a lull in the flow of his talk, warmed by the wine, she said, with a smile, 'You haven't told me why *you're* not at home for Christmas, Mr Hardcastle.'

He looked down and puckered his mouth, as if he had tasted something sour. There was a pause, then he drew a long breath. 'Nay, lass.'

'Are you married?'

'Oh aye.' Mr Hardcastle frowned. There was another pause. For once his ebullience deserted him. Sarah was unsure whether to press him further, when he said, 'I suppose th'art wondering why I'm not at home, then?' He grimaced, took a mouthful of wine, and went on, 'Oh aye, I'm married reet enough.

Tha can thank thee stars th'art not, young lady.'

'What do you mean?'

'What do I mean?' he echoed. 'I mean, I'm married and I'm not married.'

She waited. Then he continued: 'Oh aye, and what kind o' marriage is that? That's what tha's askin', ain't it? A pretty cold kind, that's what.' He gestured towards the window. 'It's cold enough out theere, ain't it? Snow, sleet, all sorts. Well, I tell thee, I'd rather be out in that than back home with my missus.'

Sarah was embarrassed at this vehement outburst but Mr Hardcastle had started and couldn't be stopped. He took another large mouthful of wine.

'Eatin' me Christmas dinner in a hotel? Pretty shameful for a man like me, eh? At my time o' life – nigh on sixty?' He had become lugubrious. 'Better this, though, than goin' home to *her*.'

There was another shriek of laughter from the kitchen, and he looked across at the door. Then he took a grip on himself, picked up the wine bottle and found it was empty.

'*Sally, tha lazy hussy!* Where's that claret?' He made an effort to seem more cheerful. 'Well, I'll tell thee this, young lady, it's a real treat havin' thee on t'other side o' table. Somethin' I didn't expect.'

Soon after Sally appeared with the wine, and then roast beef. They ate for a while, then Sarah, fortified by her third – or was it her fourth now? – glass of claret, couldn't help going on, 'So – are you separated, Mr Hardcastle – living apart?'

His cheerfulness left him again. 'No such luck. Livin' apart? We're married. For better for worse, for richer for poorer. Till death do us part. If only it would.'

'I'm very sorry – I shouldn't have mentioned it.'

'Nay, lass, it's reet friendly of thee. It's not often I can talk about it. Never, really. It's just summat I have to carry about wi' me.'

'Where is your home?'

'Bradford. I'm a commercial traveller, in case th'aven't guessed. Sheet music: all sorts – light airs, schottisches, galops, the latest valse; light-opera selections, piano transcriptions, band parts. Sacred too, hymn books retail and wholesale. I'm known all over t'West Ridin', as far north as Newcastle, as far south as Sheffield. Every music shop, every bandmaster, every organist, every choir master in t'North knows me, always pleased to see me, good old Hardcastle, genial sort of feller, always a laugh when he's around.'

Sarah was very interested. 'And is there a music shop in the town?'

'Oh aye – Tompkins in Flowergate. Dost tha play?'

'Well, just a little, you know ... And do they sell pianos – and musical instruments and so on?'

'Oh aye, all sorts.' He took another sip of wine. So did Sarah; the mention of a music shop cheered her. There might be a possibility – in the candlelight, and with the genial countenance of Mr Hardcastle, now sunk in perplexity, before her, she was relaxing and feeling more hopeful, her own troubles receding as she sympathized with his.

'I'm – very sorry, Mr Hardcastle. It must be very hard,' she said softly.

He reached across and touched her hand. 'Nay, lass, it's good of thee to listen to me troubles.' He perked up. 'Eeh, but this is reet convivial, eh? I don't know when I've had such a merry Christmas. Sup up!' And he took another large mouthful. She took the opportunity to extricate her hand from his.

She raised her glass, and then, for no reason at all, but prompted by his large expressive face, she repeated in an imitation of his accent, 'Sup up!' But in putting it down, she missed her aim, and spilled some of the wine on the tablecloth. She giggled. He laughed too as he took his napkin and dabbed at the puddle.

She lifted her glass again and said, in a silly, half-drunk voice that didn't sound at all like her, 'And here's to Mrs Hardcastle – let's hope she's having a Merry Christmas too.'

Mr Hardcastle giggled too. 'She's gone to her sister's, the old witch. I can just see the two of 'em, cacklin' over her witches' brew of a dinner – and mekkin' up spiteful gossip about me, no doubt!'

The image of the two old ladies as witches released something in Sarah and she became

28

almost hysterical. He had to come round to pat her back, as some of her wine went down the wrong way.

'Here's to the old witches!'

As Sarah was still gasping and spluttering, half choking but giggling too, Sally appeared with the Christmas pudding. Mr Hardcastle was bending over Sarah with his hand on her back, as Sally put the plates down on the table.

'Mr Hardcastle, behave theeself!' Sally said playfully. 'An old man like thee!'

'Less of the old, if tha don't mind!' He swung unsteadily to her. 'This young lady – ' he endeavoured to achieve a sober posture, and straightened his face – 'this young lady and I were sharin' a joke – weren't we, Miss – Miss—' He giggled again. 'Bless me, I've forgotten thee name already!'

'You're drunk, Mr Hardcastle!' Sally steered him back to his own chair and sat him in it. 'Now eat thee Christmas pud! Sorry about this, miss.' She caught sight of Sarah's face, tears in her eyes as she at last regained her breath. 'Eeh, I believe th'art as drunk as he is!'

Sarah endeavoured to straighten herself, wiped her eyes and drew two deep breaths. 'Well, if I am it's no matter.'

After that momentary lapse, and in her clouded mind, she took a grip on herself.

Mr Hardcastle, his spoon in his hand, bent over his Christmas pudding. 'An old man like thee!' he muttered. 'Aye, says it all, don't it?'

He shook his head. 'An old man like thee!' A tear now appeared in his eye. 'I'm nigh on sixty, and what am I doin'? Eatin' me Christmas dinner in a hotel, while me witch of a wife sits at home! Eeh, it's no life.' He sighed, and the tear dripped slowly down his cheek. Sarah tried to take control.

'Don't take on, Mr Hardcastle. Eat up your Christmas pudding.'

'Call me Marmaduke,' he said after a moment. As he put down his spoon, the plate clear, he looked across at her. 'Tha'st been very good to me, Miss—'

'Shaw. Sarah.'

'Sarah. Very good. We've had a very merry Christmas, haven't we?'

'We have.'

'Aye, we have. Th'art a reet good sort. One o' the best. Aye.' He reached for her hand. 'Sarah—'

She withdrew it quickly before he could reach her.

She finished her pudding in silence and a little later, as he offered to order another bottle, she said, 'Come on, you're tired. We'll get you into bed.'

'Into bed?'

She knocked at the kitchen door and Sally appeared.

'Give me a hand to get him into bed, please. I don't think he can take any more.'

'It won't be the first time. Art up to it? He's a weight.'

'Yes,' Sarah said quietly. She was completely sober by now. And taking Mr Hardcastle between them, one under either arm, they began to steer him upstairs.

As they were negotiating the narrow staircase, Sally a step above and Sarah below, Mr Hardcastle turned, his arm round her neck. He slumped down onto her and even between them it was difficult to support him.

'Eeh, Sarah, but th'art a lovely girl, a really, lovely—' and he kissed her, his lips greasy with food and wine. In the confined space it was difficult to avoid him, but she attempted to twist her face away. Just then, some deep inner instinct surfaced in her, some primitive revulsion, and with a strength she did not know she had, she forced Mr Hardcastle up and away from her. 'Don't!'

By the time they had got him as far as his room and steered him to his bed, where he collapsed in a heap, Sarah was suddenly very tired. She went to her own room, but she had barely undressed and got into bed when she heard steps stumbling on the old wooden staircase and a fumbling at the door. She started up in bed.

'Who is it?'

She heard a belch. She climbed out of bed and stood behind the door.

'Sarah!' Mr Hardcastle wheedled.

She opened the door. 'Mr Hardcastle, go back to bed,' she said, stone-cold sober, with her lips set firmly.

He lurched towards her. 'Sarah, th'art lovely, th'art beautiful.' He stumbled, lurched to

31

one side, and then righted himself.

She went quickly past him to the door and shouted down, 'Sally! Come here quickly, please!' She turned back into the room. 'Mr Hardcastle, go back to your room immediately.'

He came towards her again. 'What dost do that for? We were so friendly, so – wish I was married to thee, Sarah; tha'd mek a champion wife. Tha understands a man – tha can—'

He lurched to her and put one arm round her. She twisted in his grip, and shouted again, 'Sally!' But all she could hear was a burst of laughter from far below.

'Mr Hardcastle, if you don't let go immediately and return to your room, I shall get very angry.'

'Don't be angry,' he wheedled, his weight slumping on her again. 'Nay, lass, let's be friends. Can't we be friends?'

'Mr Hardcastle, if you don't let go of me immediately, I shall be very angry indeed. And I certainly shan't be your friend.'

Mr Hardcastle now turned resentful. He swayed, still holding her with one arm. 'Nay, that's very unfriendly. And I only want to be friendly. Not unfriendly. And th'art very unfriendly. Very unfriendly.'

And then without warning, he had pushed her a step and she found herself falling across the bed, with his enormous weight on her, breathing heavily. 'Don't be unfriendly, Sarah. Th'art a lady, I can tell, tha mustn't be unfriendly—'

'*Sally!*' Sarah screamed, as she struggled beneath him. She was trapped. She shouted again, and struggled to free herself. Mr Hardcastle's movements were awkward, clumsy. She looked about for a weapon, stretched out to the brass candlestick on the bedside table but could not reach it.

'Sally!' she shouted again, but now as she tried yet again to free herself, she realized Mr Hardcastle was asleep.

Four

The following morning, when she finally dragged herself downstairs, there was no one about and no sign of Mr Hardcastle. She had no stomach for food and wanted only to get out for some air in the hope of clearing her head.

There had been another fall of snow during the night and it was still bitterly cold, but she could not bear to remain indoors, so, wrapping herself in every piece of clothing she possessed, she went out into the town. It was still quiet and she made her way through deserted streets, stepping carefully over the uneven and rutted snow, up to the market-place. A little further she found a long narrow flight of steps. Taking up her skirts, and dragging painfully for breath, she found herself clear of the town, looking down again across the snowy rooftops and the chimney pots smoking in the bright still morning to the ships crowded together in the harbour, with their confusion of masts and rigging. She had passed the parish church, crossed through the graveyard, and now was standing amid some medieval ruins – the abbey, she supposed. For a long time she wandered among the old stones, looking up through sightless windows and half-shattered columns, where a lonely crow or two would wheel and caw, and then out to sea, following one sail which could be distantly made out. She tried to collect her thoughts, and eventually, taking deep breaths, was able to ponder on the phrase 'an unprotected female'.

Mr Hardcastle had been a drunken boor, but that did not excuse her own conduct. God only knew what they were saying to each other in the White Horse at this moment. She had exposed herself to every kind of innuendo, left herself prey to every kind of nod and wink, of nudge and chuckle. What a fool she had been! In a town where she knew nobody, where she should have been on her best behaviour – on her very best behaviour – on guard against the slightest shadow of impropriety. It was all very well for Mr Hardcastle to get drunk, it was a man's prerogative; all right even to make a lewd or improper suggestion to a woman, to lunge at her even. Men did such things – they just shrugged it off afterwards; laughed about it.

But for a woman. To get drunk in a public hotel; what desperation had driven her? She pulled her cloak about her and, drawing another long breath, stared up among the ruins of the abbey.

Eventually she returned to the hotel, still apparently deserted, and in the afternoon, after ignoring as best she could the raised eyebrows and amused smiles from Sally whenever they passed, she found herself in the parlour, in a half-awake state of empty misery, curled up in an old high-backed armchair staring out of the window. She was too tired to eat, too tired even to go to bed, her mind a complete blank. The afternoon was already fading into an early dusk and her life seemed to have come to a dead stop.

She heard the door open behind her then voices.

'Oh, Frederick, I'm so frightened. I told them I was going shopping.'

'Where's your maid?'

'I left her at the Town Hall. But if anyone saw me coming in here—'

'Do you think they did?'

'I don't know.'

'Listen, Chrissie – have you thought over what I said. Have you?'

There was a pause and some movement, and Sarah thought they might be kissing. Her first instinct was to get up and leave but already it seemed too late. She sat, tense, waiting for more.

'Oh, Freddy, if only you had spoken to Papa.'

'I've told you before, I know just what he'd say. It'd never do. Listen to me, Chrissie. I've been thinking – and there's one way, one certain way to make him listen to sense.'

'What?' It was a timid whisper.

'Run away!'

There was a long pause. At last the girl whispered again, 'Do you mean it?'

'Confound it, Chrissie, that'd bring him to his senses. We'd come home man and wife – think of it!'

'Run away – to Scotland?'

'Damn it – where else do you think?'

'I mean – just run away, and not tell anyone?'

'Just imagine the look on their faces! Think, Chrissie – to walk in the door and tell Samson to announce us – Mr and Mrs Frederick James. God, what a sight that would be! The old man would have a fit, I should think.'

Another pause, then, 'But think how Mamma would feel – not knowing where I was—'

His enthusiasm only increased. 'You'd be all right – and it would only be for a few days – just time enough to get married.'

'And then come straight back?'

'Of course. The deed would be done – and we'd be together for ever!'

'Oh my darling!'

Sarah could hear sighs, whispers and the scuffling of clothes. She sat stunned, rigid, staring out of the window; it was impossible

36

to move now.

After a moment, he spoke again, in an urgent undertone. 'Will you do it?' Then a moment later, 'That's my girl! Now – we'll have to think how we're going to work it out. Your house is so stuffed with people, it's going to take the devil to plan.'

'I've arranged to go to Susan's for the night on Thursday. They usually send Sanderson with the carriage. But if you—'

He chuckled. 'The carriage will be there – and I'll be inside! Arrange to leave after dark, so no one will see the carriage outside in the darkness, and if anyone notices anything I'll tell the man to say he's been hired for the evening because their regular carriage is in use – or something like that – it'll be easy, and once we're away – we'll just be together, my darling, us two together. Think of it! Do you love me?'

'Oh, Frederick!' More scuffling and sighs.

'Will you do it?'

'Yes.'

'Good girl. Let's say, Thursday at six – that'll give us time to get a good distance – say to Scarborough for the night. Then the next day we'll be on our way to Edinburgh! Think of it!'

'I must get back. I told Polly I was going to look at ribbon. Oh, Frederick, you are sure—'

'Sure? As a rock, Mrs James!'

'Kiss me.'

Then a moment later, he spoke. 'Listen, I'd

better go first. Give me a few minutes to get clear, then you can leave.'

'Very well.'

The door closed and now Sarah dared to glance round her chair. She saw the girl, her cloak thrown back from her shoulders, her bonnet still on, staring at the door, her shoulders hunched and her hands clenched together. But before she could make a move, Sarah was out of her chair and had her by the arm.

'Young lady!'

The girl gave a small scream as she whirled about. Sarah grasped her other arm. 'I beg you don't be frightened, but I couldn't help overhearing. I didn't mean to, I swear it. But I must speak to you, it is imperative.'

The girl was wriggling now in her grasp. 'Who—'

'Don't worry, I'll tell you everything. But you shall not leave this room until you hear what I have to say.'

After a moment the girl, in shock and scared, allowed Sarah to lead her quietly back to the fire.

'Forgive me, I would not for the world have listened to your conversation had I known – but you had gone too far before I could speak. Young lady, you must sit quietly and hear what I have to say.'

She took Chrissie's hands in her own as they sat together on the settle. Sarah looked carefully into her eyes.

'I have heard what you said. It's too late

38

now – I cannot unhear it, and you must hear what I have to say.'

Chrissie was recovering from her shock. 'You had no right.' She drew herself up, and pulled her hands away. 'It was a private conversation.' She rose. 'I don't know who you are. You must excuse me, but I have business to attend to.'

'No!' Sarah took her firmly by the arms again and made her sit down. 'You are not going anywhere until you have heard me.'

'It is no business of yours!'

'It has become my business! You were on the point of committing a monstrous and terrible folly, something you would regret for the rest of your life. I cannot allow you to go ahead until you have heard me.'

In the force and certainty of Sarah's words, Chrissie became quieter, and seemed prepared to listen. 'Who are you?'

'My name is Sarah Shaw. A few days ago I fled from my husband.'

'Why?'

'Why?' Sarah shook her head slightly and went on almost absently, 'Oh – I suppose I was no longer prepared to tolerate his brutality.'

'What?'

Sarah saw the incredulity in the young girl's face. She went on hurriedly, 'That is what I want to say; I want to tell you about my own marriage. You see, I did exactly what you are proposing – I ran away to get married. My parents disapproved of my husband, they

39

tried to reason with me, they pointed out all his shortcomings and weaknesses – his carelessness with money, his drinking, the absence of any prospects, career or position in his life – all the things which at the time, amazing as it sounds, made him seem so attractive, as if he was unlike other men and didn't need to be tied down by all the frustrating rules and decencies of life—'

'Frederick isn't like that!'

Sarah gave her a long look. 'Let me finish. It is so much easier for someone else to see what you cannot. Why are your parents opposed to your young man? Have you asked yourself that? Is your father stupid? Or vicious? Is he too mean?'

'No! He is the soul of goodness!'

'Well, then. I ran away and we were married. And when we returned, my parents refused to speak to me. My sisters refused to speak to me. None of my relations would speak to me. My friends were extremely em-barrassed. It was *very* difficult. We were cut off from almost everybody I knew. Mind you, *his* friends didn't mind. They crowded round to the lodgings we had taken in London: a couple of rooms over a stable, noisy, smelly, inconvenient. They were very agreeable, in and out at all hours, ready to open a bottle. We had a slatternly housekeeper who robbed us blatantly, charging for things we hadn't eaten or used. So we lived for a few months as the gilt wore off our marriage, and the sight of my husband in bed at midday every day began to bring home to me the reality of what I had done. I was so lonely for the sight of my parents and my sisters, and all my friends and relations, I thought I would go mad sometimes. Only one sister used to steal round to visit me from time to time to give me news of the family. And when I saw the expression in her eyes – the pity, and the distaste at the sight of the confusion and muddle in our squalid lodgings – it turned my heart over. Eventually after some months, I screwed up my courage, or humbled myself – call it what you will – and went to my parents' house. I stood on the doorstep, dreading what they would say.

'At last the door opened, and my father stood before me. I shall never forget as long as I live the look on his face, the words he said. He was on a step above me, so he really was looking down on me, as if I were crouching at his feet. "You have chosen your path – in spite of everything we said. So be it." This was my father, the man who was all in all to me, whom I loved even without being able to put it into words, my playmate, my friend, my counsellor. His face, his voice were without expression. "Henceforth you are no daughter of mine." And he closed the door. I will never forget that moment. Never. Never. I was cut off from all my past. From everything I had known. I was on my own – with my husband. And there was no one else – from now on we must rely entirely on each other.

'I dragged my way back to our lodgings. I just couldn't stop crying. In the omnibus people looked at me, but I simply couldn't help myself.

'When I got home my husband was entertaining a few friends, a bottle stood on the table, they were in a merry mood. I looked at them, and thought, this is my life from now on.

'A few days later my sister came to see me. She brought a letter from my mother. She said she was heartbroken at the way things had turned out but she was powerless against my father's wishes. She enclosed a few pounds and on the strength of this we moved into new lodgings, a little better than our previous rooms. But it didn't really change anything. Relations were always difficult with everyone. No one could forget that we had run away to get married. It was a stain on our marriage, that there was something not right; nothing was ever the same again. I was wretchedly lonely, starved of affection. As for my husband, everything my father had said was, of course, true. He had no regular livelihood, drifting in and out of employment. Much of what he had told me before our marriage was a lie – that he had been in the law, a rising barrister and so forth, and had expectations of high things at the bar. It turned out he was not qualified, had not even sat his exams, but had merely devilled for various lawyers on an occasional basis. And as the reality of it all became clearer, so things became more and more strained between us, the love went out of our marriage until there was nothing left but silence, tears, debts, drinking and violence.'

Chrissie started.

'Oh yes, that was when he started beating me. The first time he hit me, I was so outraged, I thought, I shall never tolerate this. I shall leave. But I did not leave, and I did tolerate it. He would come to my bed the next morning, contrite, saying it was the drink, and all his problems, and that he really needed me, couldn't live without me – all that. But at last...' she paused, and added, as if surprised, 'last Saturday, as it happens – he attacked me so violently that I realized that if I did not leave that very night he might kill me.'

She stopped, looking carefully into Chrissie's face. The young girl had been listening with a bewildered, horrified expression. There was silence between them.

'And do you think it will be different for you?' Sarah said softly.

Chrissie had been about to open her mouth, but stopped. Sarah took her hands again.

'Promise me you won't do anything tonight. Wait at least a little until you have had time to think. I know you love him, I heard it in every word you uttered—'

Again Chrissie was about to burst out, but Sarah went on, 'You do! And perhaps he may be a very honourable young man – but you

43

must ask yourself what your parents have against him. Has he spoken to your father?'

'No—'

'Why?'

Chrissie looked down and chewed her lip.

'Was it for the reasons I mentioned? Or like them?'

For a moment Chrissie nodded faintly, and then burst out, 'Papa would never understand! Frederick cannot get his money yet, and he has still to take his degree. But he is going to distinguish himself, I know it!'

Sarah thought for a moment. 'Is there anyone else in your family – an uncle or grandfather perhaps you could talk to in confidence – who would be able to explain to you what your father thinks?'

'There is someone – my uncle. I have always been able to talk to him,' Chrissie said uncertainly.

'Take him into your confidence – put it to him, and ask his advice. You will see what I say is true.'

Chrissie looked down, thinking.

'Promise me you will talk to him before you do anything.'

At last she spoke in a low voice. 'Very well.'

'Thank you. Now you must go. Your maid will be waiting.'

After Chrissie had gone Sarah was left staring at the fire. As she thought over their conversation, she sank even further into depression. What was this fatal generosity in women, she wondered, this need to give themselves to a man? To believe in him, to serve him, to abase themselves before him so completely, to entrust themselves to him so blindly? Why did they abandon all sense, even when the truth was so blatant before them, why refuse to see what everyone else could?

She thought back over the first days with George. She had been unable to believe her luck! That this godlike man, so handsome, so quick-witted, always laughing and teasing, until her wits were in a whirl, confused and excited together, that he should like *her*! Prefer *her* to her sisters, to Emma and Beth. She remembered when they had gone on the river and George took off his jacket and rolled up his shirtsleeves, and in the fun and horseplay among the boats, when they were splashing water all over each other and the shirt was plastered to his back so that all the shape of his body was clear, how it triggered something in her – she knew not what – but it caught at her breath, she felt a tightening in her chest and couldn't drag her eyes from him – and then later that evening, when they were home and she made punch and every-one was laughing and talking at once, he caught her eye through the crowd, as if there were a secret understanding between them, and she felt a warmth all through her. And then at last as the evening was growing dark, when the French windows were open and they strolled out into the garden, she found herself alone with him in the darkness. He

45

was talking – she didn't mind what he said, it was all clever and funny – and he leaned over her to break off a sprig of myrtle; then he was looking down at her, toying with the myrtle and looking deep into her eyes, serious now, breathing words into her – all flattery of course, outrageous even to remember it – and then simply bent and kissed her. She was suffocating, breathless, faint with desire; she thought she would die as she reached her arms behind his beautiful head and returned his kiss greedily.

She drew a breath, frowning to herself, and for the first time wondered what George was doing at this moment. He would have been to her parents by now, of course, and to Beth's too. Probably to her uncle and aunt Browning. That was why it would have been quite impossible for her to go to any of them, impossible even to write to them. Once they knew where she was – as she thought it over, she saw that she had had no choice but to come here. At least here she was safe for the time being.

But then, had it been so wise to tell the girl her own story either? She did not know her, had no idea who she might pass it on to. She frowned again.

Much later, however, after she had eaten her dinner and was going to bed, her courage began to revive a little and she decided that, with all her follies and mistakes, she didn't have to be an absolute doormat and she determined to accept insults and sarcasm from no one, least of all Mr Hardcastle – if and when he should deign to reappear.

Five

She was still waiting for him to speak. Mr Hardcastle was sitting further along the table attending to the large breakfast in front of him and had not yet acknowledged her presence. She watched him, waiting for him to return her look; he would not and the more she watched him, the angrier she got.

'Good morning, Mr Hardcastle,' she said loudly, and then added, her voice loaded with irony, '*Marmaduke*.'

He looked up at last, grunted, and turned again to his breakfast.

'Did you say something?'

He carried on eating.

'I beg your pardon,' she enunciated clearly, 'I thought you were going to say something. I thought you were going to apologize for your disgraceful behaviour on Christmas Day.'

Silence.

'You see, I took you for a gentleman. I realize now I was mistaken.'

He dashed his knife and fork down. 'Aye, and I was mistaken an' all – for I took thee for a lady!'

'What do you mean?'

47

'What do I mean? It's pretty obvious, en't it? Travellin' on thee own – and then mekkin' eyes at a feller, a stranger in a hotel – aye, leadin' him on, and then when he thinks tha likes him, goin' all hoity-toity and screamin' the 'ouse down. Lady? Hah – I could think of another name for thee.'

She stood up. 'How dare you!'

'How dare I? I tell thee what, young lady – if th' *art* a lady – ' he pointed his knife at her – 'I'm goin' to have a word with Mr Empson. He's particular about the sort of company he accepts 'ere at the White Horse.'

Sarah stared as he returned calmly to his breakfast.

Before she could think of a reply, Sally came in. 'Letter for thee, young lady.' She placed it on the table beside her plate. Her heart still hammering, Sarah sat abruptly, turning her back on Mr Hardcastle, and looked at the letter. It was postmarked in Whitby, and for a stupid moment she could not imagine who might want to write to her. She ripped open the seal and unfolded the sheet.

Dear Miss Shaw,

With reference to your notice in the *Advertiser*, I should be obliged if you would wait on me this Tuesday the 29th in the forenoon, or if that should not suit, be so kind as to name another day convenient.

Yours faithfully,
J. McMaster

Thank you, Mr McMaster, she breathed to herself, whoever you are! Thank you, for you have saved my life. She rose, went quickly into the parlour and rang the bell. When Sally appeared she asked for a sheet of paper and a pen. Ten minutes later she had framed her reply; she folded the sheet and wrote out the address on the back. As she sealed it she felt a mighty surge of confidence. After the episode with Mr Hardcastle it was imperative to gain a situation as quickly as she could. Now she had this letter in her hands she felt stronger; with any luck she might not be in the White Horse much longer.

She looked again at the address. West Cliff House: clearly Mr McMaster was a gentleman. Perhaps he was a kind gentleman with lovely children? She allowed her imagination to float free for a moment. A lovely house, with a spacious garden overlooking the sea. Two charming golden-haired children, a delight to be with, polite to their elders, full of fun and childish pranks, and eager to learn. They would go for walks along the cliff top in the summer, collecting wild flowers and looking out for ships; they would sing nursery rhymes at the piano while a benevolent pater-familias beamed down, they would make up amateur theatricals together— She reined herself in – well, perhaps better not to run too far ahead.

She tied on her bonnet and went out to post the letter.

When she returned to the hotel she found the manager waiting for her; he asked her to step into the parlour. He was not smiling, and after a couple of opening sentences made his meaning clear.

'It is not ordinarily the policy of the hotel to admit single females,' he said bluntly.

'I beg your pardon?' She had been on the alert since Mr Hardcastle's threat. 'You said nothing of this when I arrived.'

His expression did not alter. 'The management reserves the right to ask guests to leave if they are causing offence.'

'Causing offence?'

'Reports have come to my ears—'

'Are you referring to the night when Mr Hardcastle tried to force his way into my room?'

'Reports have come to my ears,' he repeated stonily, 'of improper behaviour. I was unfortunately unable to be in the hotel over Christmas, otherwise I would have dealt with the matter on the spot.'

Sarah was bereft of words. But she forced herself. 'So you are taking Mr Hardcastle's word for what happened? Does a lady have no rights—'

'Mr Hardcastle is a regular. As I said, the hotel does have a reputation to think of. So I would be obliged if you would secure lodging elsewhere from tomorrow.'

He turned away without speaking further.

Sarah was speechless. She turned in the

room, seeing nothing, trying to control her breathing. What could she say? She was helpless.

She made enquiries and found out where the house was; West Cliff House did indeed stand on the West Cliff, a little apart from the town. After some thought she decided that poor as she was, it would be wise to take a cab; she had to make a good impression and if she were to arrive in wet boots after dragging her skirts through the snow, her nose red with the cold ... no, a cab would be best.

The house, a large square grey-stucco building, was newish, as far as she could tell: ugly, dowdy, but a gentleman's residence. There was a forlorn air about it, all the same; it was unkempt, and the garden looked neglected under the snow. Many of the blinds were down and it seemed shut and deserted for the winter – as some other of the houses were, she had noticed. For a moment she thought she might have the wrong one, but the cabby assured her that this was it. She paid him off from her little store and turned to the house. She drew a breath, pushed open the gate and made her way up the snowy path. There were footprints in the snow and wheel tracks too. Clearly someone was at home.

At one side of the door there was a brass bell-pull, long in need of a polish. She paused to straighten her collar, adjust her bonnet, push back a stray hair and collect her thoughts. This was the only answer she had received to her notice; she had to get this job, whatever it was. Uttering a silent prayer, she reached for the bell. There was a distant jangle from within and the sound of a dog barking; at last a bolt was drawn and a tall middle-aged man in servant's uniform looked down at her. 'Yer to see Mr McMester?'

She nodded. He unfastened a chain and opened the door just sufficient to admit her.

The hall was poorly lit from the half-light over the front door. The servant crossed a few steps to a door, once painted black, now faded to a sort of green, and knocked. There was an indistinct shout from within; the tall man nodded to Sarah and opened the door.

The room she now entered was high and, after the gloom of the hall, positively blazing with light from a window facing the sea. It was lined with shelves crammed with books, journals and papers. A fire burned brightly beneath a marble mantel, and standing before it a black Labrador watched her curiously. Under the window stood a spacious scroll-top desk, overflowing with papers and documents, some rolled up, some tied in bundles with red ribbon, some lying on the floor. In the midst of this confusion stood a tall broad-shouldered man whom she instantly recognized. A large-headed man, with a strong chin, thick abundant hair starting up from his forehead and lightly peppered with grey and deep-set penetrating eyes.

He raised a powerful eyebrow. 'Hm! So

you're Miss Shaw. I had half an idea.'

He had a strong, rich voice, like an actor's. He crossed behind her and closed the door. He turned again, took up a chair and placed it opposite his own.

'Sit down – here.'

She found herself sitting with the light in her face while he stood before his desk looking down at her with his back to the window. In her confusion and uncertainty she found time to notice all this and to understand that it was a deliberate arrangement. He signalled to the dog, which now settled itself again before the fire; he took up the newspaper from the desk and studied it for a moment. She knew he was rereading her advertisement.

'You have French?' he asked abruptly.

'As it says,' she said quietly but she hoped with dignity, gesturing towards the newspaper.

He reached a book from the mantelpiece, opened it where a sheet of paper had been marking the page, and thrust it towards her.

'Be so good as to translate this, starting from there.' His thick finger stabbed at a paragraph. Something in Sarah reacted. There had been no introduction, no civilities, no mention of the weather or enquiries as to her health. One moment she had been standing on the doorstep, the next she had this book in her hands and was staring at a blur of print. She looked up at him.

'May I ask whether I am speaking to Mr

McMaster?'

He was leaning slightly, his knuckles on the desk, his other hand on his hip. He seemed very relaxed. 'What's the matter? Too difficult for you?'

She looked down quickly, confused. After a moment however the print began to come into focus, and after another, the sense began to filter into her brain. She turned the book over to see the spine.

'This is a textbook of Roman law.' She looked up at him, mystified.

'Indeed. Translate, please.'

She struggled to grasp the sense of the text, scanning the first few lines, and at length began to pick out the meaning. He let her go on, watching her closely, as she was well aware. After a few sentences she began to recover her confidence and to go on more boldly. In the next moment, however, the book was taken from her hands and replaced on the mantelpiece.

'That'll do.'

He studied the newspaper again, and then looked up. 'Have you any letters of introduction?'

She was prepared for this. 'Unfortunately they were spoiled by sea water during my voyage from London.'

'Hmm.' He stroked his chin for a moment, still staring down at her. 'Who were you last with?' he asked suspiciously.

'Mr Thompson – of Croydon in Surrey.'

'How long were you there?'

'Two years and seven months. I had charge of two children, a boy and a girl.'

'Good. Well, I can write to Mr Thompson.'

'Oh – no – well, er,' she stuttered hurriedly, 'Mr Thompson isn't there now – he has gone to India. That is why I left.'

He threw her a suspicious look. 'Is that why you were going to – *Newcastle*?'

'No, I – that is, London was too expensive, and I was hoping to find something less—' She felt like a criminal undergoing a cross-examination, and something in her rebelled. 'Mr McMaster—'

'What?'

'May I ask why you have summoned me here today?'

'All in good time. For the moment I'll ask the questions. Now...' He scanned the newspaper advertisement again as if searching for inspiration. 'Can you cast accounts? How is your arithmetic?'

Her heart sank. Arithmetic was not her strong point. 'I usually left that to my housekeeper.' She tried to sound distant and vague as if such things were beneath her.

'Really? And she cheated you right and left, I'll be bound.' He paused, thinking, and went on, biting the side of his forefinger, and then jabbing it towards her. 'You say "housekeeper". You have had your own establishment, then?'

'No – that is, I meant, Mrs Thomas left it to the housekeeper.' Her heart was racing. She wasn't sure how much longer she could keep this up.

'Thomas? You said Thompson just now.'

'I meant Thompson, of course,' she stuttered. She could feel her face reddening.

'Hmm.' He stroked his chin again, still looking down at her consideringly. Sarah wondered whether it wouldn't be simpler just to take up her skirts and run. Every reply she made only seemed to dig her deeper into the pit. She had never met such an overbearing man in her life.

'Then there's handwriting. How is yours?'

'You have my letter, Mr McMaster,' she said as drily as she could. 'You may judge for yourself.'

Among the many papers scattered on his desk, he picked hers out. He glanced at it for a moment and then grunted. At least he didn't seem to find fault with that and her heart rose slightly.

He was in thought once more. He turned abruptly. 'Do you have a follower?'

She was mystified.

'A follower,' he repeated harshly, 'a sweetheart.'

'That is my business.'

'Not if you are working for me. I shall need your full attention. I don't want some lovesick girl mooning about the place and spending half her time writing letters, or sneaking out of the house at all hours.'

She was so angry that she could not muster a reply, but at last muttered, 'I am not a girl, lovesick or otherwise.'

He seemed oblivious of her mood, however, and strode across the room and threw open the door. 'Well, let's hear your piano playing. Follow me, please.'

She followed him across the hall and into a spacious drawing room, looking out through long windows in two walls over snowy gardens. The furniture looked comfortable, there were thick plum-coloured velvet curtains, old portraits on the walls, but there was no fire alight; the room was cold and felt unused. In one corner stood a grand piano.

He gestured to it. 'Play anything you like.'

At the sight of the piano her confidence rose at last, and in her anger and confusion she suddenly thought, Now I will show him. Sarah was an accomplished pianist, and beside the genteel ladylike pieces she performed for the benefit of after-dinner guests there were others she played to satisfy herself, the pieces her husband had begged her to stop, the noisy, dramatic pieces that woke up the whole house.

She lifted the lid, looked down at the keys, and tried out a few chords, partly to find out if it was in tune, partly to test the responsiveness of the keys, partly to check whether any were broken. It appeared to be in order though probably had not been played in a long time. She glanced up at him and without further delay struck into the opening chords of Beethoven's Opus 111 – his last sonata. The room rang with a clashing, thunderous burst, a clattering of thick chords, great fistfuls of music. Sarah did not spare herself or the piano. She was sick of Mr McMaster, and now had the chance to put him in his place. She thrashed that piano, lashing it through its paces, clattering through the harmonies, missing a few notes and misplacing others; she didn't care. Now she had a chance to get back at him, to get back at Mr Hardcastle, at Mr Empson, at all of them, to get back at her desperate situation, to assert her place in the world. She whipped that piano up and down, stamping on the pedals; even when she lost her place – for she played from memory and it was weeks since she had last sat at the piano – even when she lost her place, she didn't slow, jumping to the next place she could remember and driving on.

For the first time since she had run away from home she felt a release, a fierce satisfaction, and forgot the man standing in the centre of the room, his arms crossed, his head slightly on one side as he watched her.

Suddenly her memory failed again and she stopped abruptly.

She sat motionless looking down at the keys, her hands crossed in her lap, feeling the blood in her face and a buzzing in her limbs, but curiously relaxed, as if she had undergone some purification and was made clean. Purged of her anger, her fear, she sat waiting.

When he still had not spoken, she turned to where he stood watching her, a curious, interested look in his eyes.

'I haven't my music with me,' she murmured.

'Did the sea water get that, too?'

Six

At that moment she heard from somewhere above in the house a violent burst of childish screams and McMaster turned, looking up. A second later there was a rapid patter of feet on the stairs and a woman rushed in.

'Oh, Mr McMaster – if you could come!'

The screams were shrill, agonizing, and the dog joined in, barking furiously. McMaster ran out of the room and she just caught, 'Wait here,' as he disappeared. She heard his heavy tread taking the stairs two at a time. There were more confused shouts, the woman's voice again, McMaster's voice, the dog barking, as the screams continued. Sarah waited appalled and a moment later, unable to help herself, ran after him up a wide staircase to a landing which ran round the open well of the hall. She stopped at the threshold of an open door and saw McMaster on his knees struggling with – she wasn't quite sure what it was, wriggling and squirming in his arms – but after a moment she saw it was a child and as he struggled, his face turned towards her and she recoiled. It was bright red, and the child was screaming as if it might burst.

'God damn it, will you be silent! *Silence!*' A woman was beside him, unable to help, and not far away, beside a table, Sarah noticed a child's high chair lying on its side.

'Get the chair up, you fool!'

The woman hastily righted the chair, McMaster rose to his feet still grasping the screaming boy and attempted to seat him in the chair. 'Now sit there!'

But in a moment the boy had flung himself forward onto the ground and was writhing. 'I won't! I hate you! I hate you! I want Miss La Touche!'

'Don't be such a damn fool – haven't I got Miss Shaw to look after you? Now stop this row – what will she think?'

The boy was momentarily stopped and looked up at Sarah standing in the doorway.

'That's right—' He glanced up at Sarah. 'Here.'

She knelt beside the boy lying on the floor.

'Now here's Miss Shaw – she's going to look after you while I'm away—'

'I hate her!'

'Will you be *silent!*'

The boy was still.

'Don't be afraid,' Sarah said uncertainly, 'jump up now.'

The boy glanced to his father, who now scooped him up effortlessly and sat him in his chair again. He straightened his jacket, breathing heavily. 'Hudson – has he had his breakfast?'

The woman gestured to the carpet, where a plate and fragments of food lay scattered about. 'I were about to clear it up, sir, when tha come in.'

Sarah knelt beside the chair, where the boy was watching his father. He was about eight or nine, though slight for his age, and very beautiful, with curly golden hair. His face was still red, he was breathing heavily and she could see he was trembling.

'What's your name?' she said softly.

'Mind your own business!' he spat out, not looking at her.

'My name is Sarah.'

'That's a stupid name. It's a servant's name. Where's Miss La Touche?' He beat his palms on the table. *'I want Miss La Touche!'*

His father swung on him with such an angry gesture that the boy cowered involuntarily.

'You mustn't shout at your father,' she said gently, taking his hand.

'Don't touch me!' He pulled away violently. 'Who is she? I don't want her – *I want Miss La Touche!'*

'God damn you boy, are you deaf? Miss La Touche has left! Miss Shaw has come to look after you!'

'I don't want her! I won't have her!'

Sarah turned towards the father and whispered, 'Take him in your arms, Mr Mc-Master. Comfort him.'

He looked at her as if she was mad. 'He's a boy, not a milksop,' he muttered angrily.

'He's a boy who needs to be comforted.'

But McMaster flicked her away with his hand, turned on his heel and strode out of the room. Sarah glanced questioningly at Mrs Hudson, who had been clearing up the spilt food.

'I'll get him some warm milk and bread and butter,' she said uncertainly and went out.

Extraordinarily, Sarah now found herself alone with the boy. He was glaring at her and for a moment her mind was blank; when she did speak she said very much the first thing that came into her mind.

'I expect you're hungry,' she said in a matter-of-fact tone, sitting at the table opposite him. 'I know I am. It's this cold weather, it gives one such an appetite. We'll have our breakfast, then we can think of what we want to do today.'

He laughed at her. 'You can have your breakfast. I don't want any.'

'Don't want any?' She affected surprise. 'How do you expect to grow up big and strong?'

'I'm never going to grow up big and strong. How can I?'

'How can you?' she echoed coaxingly, humouring him. 'All little boys grow up big and strong – if they eat their breakfast,' she added with an attempt at a smile.

'You're a fool, then, for you can't see what's staring you in the face.'

'What on earth do you mean?'

'*What on earth do you mean?*' he mimicked. 'Can't you see?'

She was genuinely mystified, though inwardly relieved that he was talking to her in a reasonable tone and had stopped screaming.

'What do you think that is?' He pointed behind her, and turning she saw a child's invalid chair. She was taken by surprise and her mind raced as she studied it.

'Have you been unwell?' she said lightly, turning to him again.

'*Unwell?* I can't walk, that's all,' he said scathingly.

'That's all?' she echoed lightly. 'Well, whether you can or you can't doesn't make any difference. You've still got to grow up – and that means you've still got to eat your breakfast.'

'Don't want any.'

'Look, here's Mrs Hudson. Surely you're not going to disappoint her after all the trouble she's gone to for you?'

'What trouble? It's only bread and butter.'

'Well, no matter.' Sarah adjusted her line of attack. She smiled up at the housekeeper. 'Just in time, Mrs Hudson, I was absolutely dropping.'

Mrs Hudson set a tray on the table.

'I've brought him a cup of cocoa. Were you wanting—'

'Mrs Hudson, it's bitterly cold outside, and I have just had a *very* gruelling interview with

Mr McMaster. A cup of cocoa is the very thing. How clever of you.'

Sarah took the cup from her hands as she was lifting it off the tray, and sipped it. 'And perhaps a boiled egg?'

The housekeeper watched her mystified as she took the plate of bread and butter. 'Very well, miss.'

'Thank you. In the meantime I'll make a start on the bread and butter.'

Apparently taking no notice of the boy she sipped the cocoa again.

In a choked and baffled voice, he spoke at last. 'That – that was *my* bread and butter.'

'Have some,' Sarah said, her mouth full, as she passed the plate across the table.

'And cocoa.'

Sarah nodded towards the door. 'Mrs Hudson is bringing you some.'

Tears welled up in his eyes. 'But that was *mine*.'

She shrugged and pushed the cup and saucer across.

She had not yet worked out exactly what was going on here. She appeared to have landed the job – if she wanted it. McMaster had disappeared leaving her to cope with his son – supposing he was his son – without even introducing him. Thinking this, she said, 'By the way, you haven't told me your name yet.'

'There isn't anyone to introduce us,' the boy said stiffly, munching on bread and butter.

'Well, I call that unfair. I've told you my

name.'

'Yes, well, you had to.'

'What do you mean?'

'You're a servant.'

'I am not a servant! How dare you! Anyway, servants don't sit at the same table as their masters to eat their breakfast.'

There was a pause as he thought this out. 'But my father pays your wages,' he said triumphantly at last.

'Your father does remunerate me, it is true,' she said with all the dignity she could muster, 'and who knows – perhaps someone does the same to him – but that doesn't make him their servant.'

'They pay him fees, if you want to know.'

'Same thing.'

'It isn't.'

'He carried out a service – or whatever he does – and they reward him. What's the difference?'

'But they ask him to act for them – they're very grateful if he agrees – whereas you came here asking for the place.'

'I asked to work for him? How do you know he didn't ask me?'

This really did stop the boy and he could be seen thinking furiously.

While he was thinking, Sarah had leisure to wonder why they should be sitting down to breakfast at half-past eleven – for it must be that at least by now.

Mrs Hudson reappeared with a tray and Sarah set to work on her boiled egg. The boy

65

watched her, interested in spite of himself.

'Oh, by the way, Mrs Hudson, would you be so kind as to introduce us? I am afraid I don't know this young gentleman's name.'

'Master Robin!' The housekeeper turned on the boy. 'Shame on thee! Not tell her thee name? What's the poor lady to think?'

He laughed.

'His name's Robert, miss,' she went on, 'but we call him Robin.'

She went out and Sarah finished her boiled egg.

'What did you use to do with Miss La Touche after breakfast, Robin?' she asked casually, wiping her lips on her napkin.

'We played cards.'

'Who won?'

'Sometimes she did, sometimes I did. I won the most.'

'Do you want to play cards now? I can't guarantee you'll win, though. I'm a demon.'

He sounded curious, though apprehensive. 'So am I,' he said at last.

Sarah grinned. 'Where are the cards?'

He gestured to a sideboard, and she found an old worn pack in a drawer.

'So. What do you want to play?'

'Old Maid.'

'*Old Maid?* Don't you know anything better than that?'

He bridled. 'I like Old Maid.'

She shrugged. 'Well, just for now. But soon I'm going to teach you something *much* more interesting.'

She dealt the cards and for the next half an hour silence reigned, broken only by the impatient and sometimes violent slapping down of cards and furious shouts of victory from the boy. Sarah made sure he won every game.

When Mrs Hudson reappeared and announced it was time for his rest, she was followed by the big servant, who took the boy in his arms and carried him out. As they were leaving the room, the boy glanced over his shoulder and called, 'You will come and see me when I wake up, won't you?'

'Yes,' she called, but as soon as the boy was gone, she caught Mrs Hudson by the arm. 'Mrs Hudson, I must speak to Mr McMaster again. Is he still in the house?'

'He were downstairs a few moments ago, miss.'

'Thank you.'

Sarah went out onto the landing and stood looking down into the gloomy well of the hall; dim old paintings in dark gold frames hung on a crimson wall beside the stairs, lit by a glass skylight overhead. Her eyes strayed over them as she tried to clarify her thoughts. She was unsure of what she wanted to say, how to say it and what he wanted. On what terms was she in this house? He had taken her completely for granted.

Clenching her teeth at last, she went down the stairs, but stopped again at his study door, still uncertain, in the silent hall. She knocked gently; after a moment she heard his voice, and pushed the door open slightly. McMaster was at his desk.

'He seems to have quietened down. He has been put to bed,' she began awkwardly.

Mr McMaster hummed for a moment in thought and rearranged a few papers as if slightly embarrassed, then turned to her with an artificially bright tone. 'Well, you've had a rather abrupt introduction, Miss Shaw, but none the worse for that. You'll find him a quiet enough boy most of the time.'

'Yes. Mr McMaster—'

'Ah, you're wondering about the terms?'

'No. I was wondering whether there was anything else you wished to ask me before proceeding?'

'Proceeding? What do you mean? Don't you want the post?'

'Well—' She was confused. 'Yes, I would be very happy – I fear you have taken me by surprise—'

'Don't worry about that. It's my profession to take people by surprise. When can you start?'

She shook her head in bewilderment. 'Immediately.'

'Good. Where are your things?'

'At a hotel in Whitby.'

'Josiah will take you.'

'Thank you.' She was about to go when something prompted her to turn again; there was something more she wanted to say.

'Mr McMaster, why did you go out like that? Your son needed you.'

He looked up sharply.

'And it was wrong to shout at him.' She took another step towards him. 'He's only a little boy.'

She could read astonishment all over his face and she realized she had made a mistake. His demeanour changed, he stood up and eyed her coldly. 'You have no child of your own – have you?'

'No,' she said uncertainly.

'No,' he repeated emphatically, looming over her.

She was silenced for a moment by his certainty. 'What do you mean?' she asked at last.

'Mean?' He crossed his arms, looking down at her, and spoke forcibly. 'I *mean* that you can have no idea of how much a parent invests in his child; no idea of the hopes and aspirations of a father, of his visions of the future. In this mortal world, Miss Shaw, what do we have but our children? I have been cursed with a feeble runt, half a child, a broken thing, laughable! That I, of all men, should father such a thing!'

She felt a hot flush through her, her face red with shock, and could not help crying out, 'You must *never* say such things! It is impious, unchristian! How could you! How *could* you – to curse your own son!'

'As you say, you have no child of your own,' he said coldly. 'One day perhaps you will understand what I am talking about. I pray you will never know the shame of a deformed son.'

'If...' She hesitated, trying to control her voice. She could feel herself trembling violently. 'If I am ever so fortunate as to be blessed with a child, I should love it, *whatever* it was. I could never curse my own child – and neither should you!'

For a moment he stared at her; she felt her heart racing as she looked him in the face; then at last he broke away to the window. There was a long silence, until she heard him, almost in a mutter, 'Well, get along and collect your things.'

Seven

Ten minutes later she found herself seated beside the manservant as the horse picked its way along the snowy cliff top. In the haze the sea disappeared into the sky, and it was as if they were travelling in a white world. Sarah, trying to digest the extraordinary conversation she had just had, was deeply uncertain. There was something malignant, almost evil about McMaster. How any man could curse his own child – it was beyond her own experience, but she felt chilled to her marrow, as if the cold raw day were replicated inside the house too. But it was that very lovelessness that made it impossible for her to leave. She had not intended it, had not anticipated it, but having found herself there, she did not see she had any option but to stay – even if she were to be only the buffer between father and son.

The trap swayed over the uneven ground and she swayed with it until at last she dragged her thoughts back to the servant hunched beside her.

'Tell me about Mr McMaster, Josiah. Have you been with him long?'

'Nay. Six or seven year – syne he come to t'house. He's not fra around these parts.'

'Oh – where is he from?'

'Liverpool.'

'Why did he come, then – do you know?'

'He said it were for t'boy's sake – for his health – him being sickly, as tha knows.'

'His health?' Sarah glanced about her. 'Here? This weather would kill anybody.'

'Oh aye.' He laughed grimly. 'Mebbe that were his thought – kill or cure.'

She huddled into her cloak and they rocked side by side in silence for some moments.

'And Mr McMaster – what – what does he do?'

He turned to her in surprise. 'Dost not knaw?'

She shook her head.

'Hast never heard of Johnston McMaster QC?'

She shook her head again and he gave a grim laugh. 'The Terror of the Northern Circuit, they call him.'

71

'You mean—'

'Oh aye – a barrister – and a silk. The best in t'north, by a long chalk. You'll be saying your prayers if ever you come up against him. He'll eat you. Eat you, eat the judge, eat the jury, an 'all. Tear you apart.'

Somehow she was not surprised to hear this.

'He's afraid of nobody nor nuthin'. I seen him tellin' off t'judge! Seen him, aye, browbeat t'judge till the old feller were huffin' and puffin', were that worrited he didn't know what day of t'week it were neither. He's a bully.' Josiah had got into his stride. 'But he's cunnin' too; he knaws when to bide his time. He'll wait, he'll lure thee on, all soft and gentle like, waitin' till tha goes that one step too far – and then he's on to thee like a stoat, worrying thee, shoutin' at thee, mekkin' thee look a fool, till th'art quiverin' and weepin' – oh, I've seen it – grown men mind, big men, miners, navvies, I've seen 'em in tears, beggin' 'im to stop. But he won't. He'll wear 'em down, till he has 'em where he wants 'em – has 'em at his mercy.' He paused again, shaking his head. 'Oh, tha wouldn't want to be up against Johnston McMaster.'

Sarah was given a room on the first floor next to Robin's. Apart from her bed, there were two comfortable chairs in front of the fire, and a table and chair at the window where she could write letters or sew. There were several pictures – sea views – on the wall, which was papered in a pretty pink pattern. It was altogether a charming room, larger probably than most governesses enjoyed, and flooded with light from the long window.

When by mid-afternoon she had finished arranging things to her satisfaction a wave of tiredness suddenly swept over her and, telling herself she would just put her feet up for ten minutes, she lay down on her bed and was immediately asleep.

The next thing she knew was that she was being shaken awake and Jenny – a maidservant she had met, a merry, stocky girl – was telling her that Master Robin was ready to go to bed.

Robin had a very large bed indeed, with a canopy and voluminous hangings, and he seemed a curious little thing quite over-whelmed in the midst of quilts and coverings and pillows, propped up like a sultan with books and toys scattered about him on the quilt.

'Well,' she said brightly as she came in, 'what shall we read tonight?'

'We don't read,' he said, in a matter-of-fact tone. 'You tell me a story. Miss La Touche always told me a story.'

'Oh. Very well. Now, first of all, are you comfortable?'

'Nearly. I'm never quite comfortable. But I'm nearly so. That's why I don't sleep very well, I suppose. Every so often I wake up, be-cause I can't get comfortable.'

'Well, we'll try and make you as comfortable as we can.' She fluttered vaguely about the bed, straightening the covers somewhat. 'Is there anything you want before I begin?'

He shook his head. 'Start now. And make it different from Miss La Touche's.'

'What were hers like?'

'Ghoulish. About giants and dragons and ghosts.'

'Ghosts? Did you like those?'

'Sometimes.'

'Did they keep you awake?'

'I don't need ghosts to keep me awake. Only, Miss La Touche would never come if I called in the night. She said she needed her sleep, and it wasn't fair to keep waking her up. Josiah comes, and he curses me for waking him up. But now you're here, you can come.'

'I see.' She drew a breath. 'Well, there won't be any ghosts in my stories.'

'Very well. Start.'

She drew up a chair, made herself comfortable, and glanced once more about the room as if in search of inspiration. Finally she drew another, deeper breath.

'Once upon a time there were three brothers, and their names were Algernon, Marmaduke and Jack. Jack was the youngest. He was much smaller than the others, and they bullied him – but he would never stand for it and always fought back when they hit him...'

A few minutes later he was asleep. She stood looking down at him for some time in the dim candlelight, at his fine, slender features, and his curly hair, and found she could not drag herself away from the bedside. When Josiah had lifted him into bed she had seen the thin useless legs dangling from his nightshirt and it had turned her heart over. She had no child of her own, had no experience of children, apart from visits to her sisters – and their children seemed noisy, spoiled brats – but this evening she had been drawn quite naturally to this boy.

As she was standing at the bedside she heard Jenny's voice at the door in a whisper. 'It's t'mester, Miss Shaw, asks wilt tha dine wi' him?'

Eight

She turned, staring. She had no idea of the etiquette of governesses, but he was paying her wages so presumably he had a right to her services whenever he felt like it. She appeared to have no rights here and besides, only this morning she had been desperate for a job, any kind of a job, to get her out of the White Horse. She couldn't start laying down conditions, especially not on the first evening. But what was she to wear? She had had no notice. Then she remembered her last conversation with him and all these thoughts were cancelled in a second.

'Thank you, Jenny. My compliments to Mr McMaster and please say that I have a headache. I am going to bed and beg to be excused this evening.'

'Very well, miss.'

Sarah turned again to where Robin lay asleep. 'Will someone be here...' She gestured.

'He has his bell, miss; he will ring if he wants anything.'

Sarah was staring idly into her glass, and was about to let her hair down, when there was a diminutive rap at the door, and a moment later Jenny was there again.

'Mr McMaster's compliments, Miss, and he is sorry to hear th'ast a headache, but he says tha'st probably not eaten all day and that best cure for a headache is a hearty meal. He hopes th'alt have second thoughts and join him.'

So that was it: she was a servant, to be ordered about. How dare she have a headache? Servants did not have headaches. When the master commands—

'Thank you, Jenny. Tell your master I shall be down directly.'

The dining room lay behind the drawing room and the door was open as she looked in. Thick curtains shut out the winter night, and a big fire was heaped up. The only other light in the room came from two candles at one end of the polished dining table, where two places had been set. McMaster was standing, his arms folded, staring into the fire, and did not hear her. She watched him for a moment, a strange, brooding figure silhouetted against the firelight with his dog curled up at his feet. As she entered, he heard her footstep and turned; unlike her, he had changed for dinner and was in formal black.

'I should have given you more time to change your gown,' he murmured.

'My gowns were stained by sea water. I have not yet had time to have them cleaned.'

He raised an eyebrow. 'Ah yes – sea water.'

Before she could think of a reply he motioned her to a seat and rang a small bell on the table as he sat opposite her. In the circle of light he loomed before her, an imposing presence which embarrassed her and put her out of countenance. She found it difficult to meet his eye and they waited in silence until Josiah appeared at the door.

'You may serve dinner.'

The servant muttered and went out; shortly afterwards a large bowl of soup was set in front of her. Its aroma reminded her that McMaster was right; she had eaten nothing but a boiled egg since the morning.

'How do you find my son?' McMaster looked up from his soup.

'Very well. I like him exceedingly.'

'Good. The last girl was useless. I had to sack her.'

'Why?'

'She indulged the boy – taught him nothing – spent the whole time playing cards, as far as I could guess. It will be better when he is older and I can engage a tutor. If he lives long enough.'

He said this in such an off-hand way that she felt compelled to come to Robin's defence. 'What does his physician say?'

'Physician?' He gave a small dismissive grunt. 'You should rather use the plural: he has had every man I can find between Edinburgh and Paris. There is nothing any of them can do. It is some failure of the nervous system, so far as can be ascertained.'

'Nervous system?'

'There does not appear to be anything physically wrong with his legs. Some nervous failure – or perhaps some damage to his brain at birth.'

A cold tremor passed through her. 'Did he have a difficult birth?' she asked tentatively.

A long pause and McMaster looked down. 'He did.'

She did not feel adequate to pursuing this line of talk. It was clearly dangerous ground. However she could think of nothing else to say and a silence began to open up between them. She felt more and more awkward.

'You appear to be a woman of some independence of mind,' he said after several minutes of silence.

She said nothing.

'That's good, because I am obliged by my work to be away from home for long periods.'

There was not much to say to this either and there was another lengthy silence.

'I mention this,' he went on finally, 'because I shall be entrusting the care of my son to you in my absence.'

Sarah was grateful. 'Thank you for your confidence,' she said warmly, and smiled mischievously as she felt herself relaxing. 'Especially as you only met me this morning.'

'This morning?'

'Well – ' she stumbled – 'apart from—'

'Quite.' He did not smile. 'But you see, Miss Shaw, in my profession, I am used to summing up a character quickly, to penetrate the essence of a man – or woman.'

'And you have – penetrated my essence?' she asked quietly.

'I should say so. There are a number of unanswered questions, but I believe I understand the essentials.'

'You are not very flattering, Mr McMaster.' She attempted to be arch. 'A woman relies on mystery, you know. It is part of her charm.'

'No woman is a mystery to me.'

'I feel sorry for you, then,' she replied before she could think, feeling a flush of anger.

He looked up. 'May I ask why?'

'Much of the charm of life is lost to you.'

He thought for a second, then nodded gravely. 'You are right. Life does not hold much charm for me.'

She struggled to find an answer to this remark. She was out of her depth but could not see any means of recovering herself. She must have long since forfeited his respect and inwardly cursing herself she floundered on. 'I think perhaps you have given up too easily.'

'Given up?'

'You have many years ahead of you. You cannot assume that your life is over yet. You do not have that right.'

'*Right?* What on earth do you mean?'

He seemed angry now. She was trembling inwardly, but still felt obliged to go on. 'God does not mean us to give up, Mr McMaster. We must struggle on.'

'And you think I have not struggled?'

Her head was whirling. She did not understand how the conversation had got into this channel. 'I am sorry. I have spoken out of turn. Forgive me if I have said more than I should have.'

But he had risen abruptly, thrusting his chair back, and crossed to the fireplace. He stood, one hand on the mantelpiece, staring down into the fire as she sat watching him, trembling all through her limbs. She did not understand what was happening but was only conscious of an enormous force, or cluster of forces pulling in different directions, and only being prevented from exploding by the fierce act of his will.

At last he spoke quietly, as he appeared to master his feelings. 'You may trust me when I say that I have struggled and perhaps life will one day regain its charm for me. Unfortunately it has not done so yet.'

She watched him silently. At last, very slowly, he turned to look at her. He appeared calmer, and his voice was different. 'I have said things I should not—'

'No! It is I who—'

'No! Believe me.' He clenched his jaw. 'I had no right to inflict this on you.' He drew a breath. 'Do not be afraid, Miss Shaw. It will not happen again.'

She smiled, partly through relief, but he did not smile as he sat opposite her. He rang the bell.

The conversation throughout the rest of dinner was muted, distant, concerned with generalities, and she relaxed slowly and thought that probably in the future she would be able to endure his presence; that they would be able to establish some modus vivendi, and that certain topics would by mutual agreement be left unspoken.

As she was rising to wish him goodnight he stopped her.

'Miss Shaw, I wonder ... Would you be so good as to play for me again?'

She was surprised. 'Of course,' she stuttered. 'It would be a pleasure.'

He turned to Josiah. 'We shall take coffee in the drawing room.'

Clearly this was not the moment for Beethoven in his controversial mode, but perhaps she might try the second movement of the Opus 111. It was very personal to her; something she had slaved over for years. At first she was uncertain: it was so long, so strange, and besides she only imperfectly remembered it. Nevertheless, having seated herself, and studied the keyboard in silence, on an impulse she began to play, her fingers trembling softly over the keys as she introduced the delicate fragment of melody which first breaks the silence.

He sat, she was aware, perfectly still, one hand on the dog's back, the coffee cup untouched in his other, as she struggled her way through it. There was a very long silence as she drew at last to the close.

She waited at the keyboard looking down at the keys.

'Thank you,' he said at last, very soft, very low; it was almost a sigh, a breath of heartfelt relief, or gratitude. She could not really make out his face in the dim light but she was conscious of him watching her closely. 'I shall ask you to play again sometime.'

As she was preparing for bed, her mind was still filled with the extraordinary conversation which had passed between them. And lying in the darkness it was a long time before she fell asleep.

She did sleep, however, and slept well, after that day of such excitements. As she opened her eyes Jenny was drawing back the curtains. It was another day of dull grey clouds. 'What time is it?'

'Half-past eight, miss. Master Robin is still asleep. We never wake him early. But Mr

McMaster is already at his breakfast.'

'Oh. Jenny, would you be so very kind – my compliments to Mr McMaster and tell him I think I should take my breakfast with Master Robin when he wakes.'

'Very well, miss. I've left thee water on t'washstand.'

'Thank you.'

When she went in to Robin's bedroom she found him still asleep, and she was uncertain what to do. However, as she stood looking down at him, his eyes opened.

'I was waiting for Jenny.'

'Does Jenny get you up in the morning?'

'Yes. And then Josiah comes and carries me to the table.'

'We'll have breakfast together, shall we?'

'If you like. I heard the piano last night, Miss Shaw.'

'Oh, for goodness' sake, don't call me Miss Shaw. My name is Sarah.'

'Was that you playing?'

'Yes. You shouldn't have been awake.'

'You played very beautifully.'

'I did not. I don't practise enough. I only play to please myself really.'

As Sarah watched Jenny washing and dressing him, she schooled herself not to feel anything. His withered legs hanging uselessly over the edge of the bed shocked her, it was useless to deny it, but she hoped she would grow used to them.

She hoped too that they might be able to go out later but during the morning a fog drifted in from the sea until it lay impenetrable, pressing against the windowpanes.

After lunch Josiah came again to carry Robin to his bed for his afternoon rest.

Sarah tackled him about this after Robin was settled. 'Josiah – he seems to spend his whole life in bed. Would it not be better to take him out for some fresh air?'

'Tek 'im aht? Hast looked aht o' winder? Tha canna see hand before face wi' t'roak.'

'I beg your pardon?'

'Look for theesen, missy. Roak has set in for t'day.'

'I don't understand. You mean the fog?'

'Aye, I do. Only hereabouts folk call it roak – or sea-fret. If th'art thinkin' o' staying, tha'd best learn it an' all.'

The fog had set in, and the whole of the following day it persisted, so that the house seemed marooned, cocooned in its mantle. Sarah hadn't been out of doors for three days, and was desperate for some exercise. And as for Robin – surely it was not good for his health to be forever shut up indoors?

Nine

On Sunday morning after breakfast she saw Mrs Hudson and Josiah leaving the house, dressed in solemn black, she looking very stiff and forbidding in bonnet, gloves and cloak, and he, wooden with dignity in a suit which clearly came out only on Sundays. Each carried a Bible and a hymn book.

Sarah happened to run into Mr McMaster as they left and was able to ask him about them. McMaster was not exactly sarcastic, though not far off it, as he explained, 'They're off to their chapel – very popular in Whitby, and well attended. Some low Church or sect, Baptists, I dare say. The preacher is a very prominent man in the town: the Reverend Mr Hayes. You'll run into him before long if you stay. He has a thriving congregation; half the town is under his influence. "The Reverend Hayes hath them in thrall",' he added witheringly, and was turning away when she stopped him.

'Do you go to church, Mr McMaster?'

'No.'

'I see. And you are content that Robin should not go either?'

'I have no time for organized religion, Miss Shaw.'

It was always an uphill struggle conversing with him but she battled on. 'You see,' she swallowed, 'I was brought up to go to church and though I would not describe myself as very religious, I have always been grateful to my parents for taking me. One should at least know about the religion of one's country, don't you think, whatever private opinions one may have?'

'What is this? I do not wish my son to go to church, that is all.'

'And if I were to read some Bible stories with him – would you have any objection to that?'

'Yes, I would. I do not want his head filled with superstitious nonsense.'

There was a moment as they stared at each other before she muttered a 'Very well,' and turned away upstairs.

'Miss Shaw.' He stopped her as her foot was on the step. She turned. 'If you wish to go to church I have no objection. I would not wish there to be any conflict of conscience between your duties here and your duties to God.'

He said this in such a sardonic tone that she reacted. 'Well, as a matter of fact, Mr Mc-Master, I should like to go. Thank you.' She turned away up the stairs.

It was a relief to escape from the house. As she set off along the cliff, with a clear sky above and the sea lapping lazily beneath her, she felt she had been let out of prison. To stretch her legs, to pace out along the packed snow of the track, to breathe deeply – she felt she had not been out of doors in a year and her spirits rose.

The church, set near the edge of the cliff, looked very old: ancient weathered stones sunk amid the gravestones set about it, as if huddling down against the wind. Inside it was quite different: all white and light from large square windows, and divided up into boxed pews. She was shown by the churchwarden into one of these, close under the pulpit, marked for 'Strangers'.

The pulpit was perched high above the pews and reminded her of a crow's nest at the top of a mast, most appropriate for a sea-faring community. Behind it were fixed two large boards on which were inscribed the Ten Commandments, and as she settled herself on her bench, her eyes wandered idly over them. 'Thou shalt have no other God but me...' Sarah stared up at these injunctions, stern, inflexible, unforgiving ... and thought of the lifeboatmen, drowned at sea and commemorated on a stone outside.

Afterwards, walking back to West Cliff House, she felt lighter and was glad she had decided to go.

It was only a few days later that the opportunity occurred at last to write to her parents. A courier arrived from Liverpool with documents for Mr McMaster – she chanced to be at the top of the stairs as she heard him talking to Josiah; instantly she flew down, took him aside and pressed half a guinea in his hand.

'Post a letter for me in Liverpool,' she whispered, 'and I will be forever in your debt,' and while he was in the kitchen eating his dinner she wrote as fast as she could.

Dearest Mamma and Papa,

I have given no address and, in case you notice that this letter is franked in Liverpool, I assure you categorically that I am not in Liverpool, nor anywhere near it. Please forgive me and understand me when I say that I had absolutely no choice in this. However much you love me, I am afraid that had I told you of my whereabouts, you might, even unwittingly, have communicated it to George. Under no circumstances can I let him know where I am. Please understand that I have only delayed so long in writing because I could find no way of doing so without discovering my whereabouts. This I cannot do. Oh, Mamma dear, I do miss you and Papa so very much; please, please believe me that I would never have run away unless there had been absolutely no choice for me. This will sound melodramatic perhaps, but you have my solemn promise that had I not escaped when I did there was a real chance that George would have killed me. I know you warned me against him before my marriage. I know it, and how I wish I had heeded your wise words. But what's done is done, and there is no going back. Now I know what he is really like I have had leisure to digest my own folly and can only thank God I have got clear away from him, for the moment. I am safe and well, have employment and a roof over my head. It is better that I do not tell you too much but rest assured that, apart from being separated from you, for the moment I have nothing to wish for. Dearest Mamma and Papa, I do miss you both so very much; I hope that you have not been too worried by my disappearance. I will write again as soon as I can find a way of getting the letter to you, as I said, without betraying my whereabouts – which I do most unwillingly.

Your loving daughter,
Sarah

She was awoken abruptly by screams. In a second she knew it was Robin and almost fell out of bed, floundering for a shawl to throw round her shoulders and tripping over the unfamiliar furniture in the dark as she felt for a lucifer to light the candle.

As she ran at last into Robin's room, she saw McMaster in his nightshirt at Robin's bedside, cradling the boy in his arms. He glanced up angrily.

'Where the devil were you? You should have

been here.'

'I came as quickly as I could. How is he?'

'There's nothing the matter with him,' he said brusquely. 'A nightmare. Here, take over. He will speak to you more easily.'

She came quickly to the bedside and took the boy in her arms, sitting on the bed beside him. She glanced up at McMaster, who was watching her; after a moment he turned awkwardly and left the room.

'Hush,' she whispered into the thick curls as she clasped him to her, his body still shaking. 'Now tell me, what was it all about?'

'The Hob-o'-the-moor was chasing me,' he stuttered.

She climbed onto the bed. 'Look, I'll tell you what I'll do. It's cold so I think we'll snuggle up together. Then you can tell me exactly what happened.'

She arranged them both in the enormous bed, well propped up on pillows, her arm round his shoulders. 'Now, start again.'

'The Hob-o'-the-moor was chasing me.'

'And who – or what – is he?'

'He's a horrible monster with big glaring eyes that glower at you, and he's ever so tall and has ever such big teeth and terrible claws and he was chasing me and I was running—'

'You were running?'

'Yes! I was running and running but he was getting closer and closer all the time and I couldn't escape and then I tripped up and he was about to tear out my tummy – because that's what he does – he tears out your

90

tummy even while you're still alive and he eats your tummy and guts even while you're watching—'

Robin stopped, his breath quick and feverish. She squeezed him to her, and waited for a moment before speaking in a low soothing voice. 'Have you ever seen the Hob-o'-the-moor in the daytime?'

'He doesn't come out in the day! He hides in t'Awd Abba Well.'

'What's that?'

'It's so deep that no one has ever reached the bottom – that's why they never see him.'

'Have you ever seen this well?'

'No.'

'Is it far from here?'

He was uncertain. 'I don't know.'

'Well, I'll ask. I think we should go and see it. Who told you about the Hob-o'-the-moor?'

'Miss La Touche. And it doesn't matter if you're indoors, it doesn't even matter if you're in bed, because he can still come and get you and no one can help, it doesn't matter how hard you shout because no one can hear you. They can hear everyone else but they can't hear you.'

Sarah, who was inwardly cursing Miss La Touche, gave him another gentle squeeze. 'We'll go and see the well. You see, Robin, I don't believe in the Hob-o'-the-moor.'

He looked up sharply.

'No, I think Miss La Touche made it up.'

'What do you mean?'

'She invented it. It's just a story.'

'But everybody's heard of the Hob-o'-the-moor.'

'Have they?'

'Oh yes. Mrs Hudson and Josiah, so he—'

'Just because everybody's heard of him, it still doesn't mean he's true. There's no such thing, Robin, I promise you.'

'But if he isn't really there, why do they talk about him?'

'They're very naughty to talk about such things. And Miss La Touche was especially naughty to tell you such fibs.' She yawned. 'And I think we should just go to sleep now, because I've had a very long day...'

Strangely, there was no mention of the Hob-o'-the-moor during their breakfast and she wondered whether he had forgotten it. Later that morning, when she happened to go into the kitchen, she took the opportunity to ask the housekeeper, 'Have you ever heard of t'Awd Abba Well, Mrs Hudson?'

Sarah found Mrs Hudson more than a little intimidating. She spoke briefly and did not smile; when she did speak, it was decisively and to the point. She was making pastry, her hands white with flour, and did not look up from her work. 'Aye. It's o'er past High Hawsker.'

'And what is that?'

'A village.'

'And this well?'

The housekeeper took the ball of dough out

92

of the bowl and thumped it down onto the table. 'Nowt to see, miss. Just a well.'

'How long would it take to get there?'

Mrs Hudson straightened, turned and looked Sarah up and down. 'I should say a gamesome lass like thee could do it in an hour.'

'I wasn't proposing to walk, Mrs Hudson. I am taking Robin.'

'Mester Robin?'

'We can wrap him up.'

'He don't go out, miss.' Mrs Hudson was shaking her head. 'Only mebbe in t'garden on a summer's day – for 'alf an 'our.'

Sarah turned to the window where after days of sea fog and grey skies a bright sun glittered on the snow. 'In the trap it might take half an hour, perhaps?'

'Mebbe – if weather holds. But doctor's orders were clear. He's to be kept in t'warm.'

'But surely, while the sun is shining,' Sarah couldn't help going on, 'it can't be good for him to be always indoors; I'm sure the air would be good for him – and if it's only half an hour...'

There was a moment's pause as they looked at each other. Mrs Hudson was frowning. 'Tha'lt have to ask t'mester,' she said at last.

Sarah was stopped. She had hoped to get out of the house without meeting Mr Mc-Master; but she made up her mind. 'Very well. I will speak to him.'

She went across to the door of his study and knocked. After an indistinct bark from within, she opened the door a few inches. He was at his desk, pen in hand, and looked up at her with a scowl. 'Yes?'

'Mr McMaster, I'm sorry to disturb you. It's such a fine day, I should like to take Robin out for a short ride in the trap. Would that be—'

McMaster sat back and looked out at the sky. 'Very well. He shouldn't be kept in all the time. It would do him good.'

'It was just that the doctors—'

He snorted. 'Doctors don't know everything.'

'Yes.' She paused. 'Mr McMaster,' she added on an impulse, 'perhaps you'd care to come too?'

He frowned and turned back to his papers. 'Can't you see I'm busy?'

She closed the door carefully and turned to Mrs Hudson, who was standing at the kitchen door wiping her hands on a cloth. Neither spoke.

After lunch the three of them were in the trap, Josiah, herself and Robin. The boy was wedged tightly between them in a nest of coats and rugs, scarves, gloves and a hat pulled down over his brow. She laughed when she first saw him. 'I can hardly recognize you.' Then she glanced down at Mrs Hudson's face, wooden, severe.

'Don't worry, Mrs Hudson, we won't be long. Will we, Josiah?'

He hunched his shoulders and gave a flick of the reins. The old mare started into life, and in a moment they were on their way along the cliff track. Everywhere about them the sun glittered on the snow so that it almost hurt the eye. Robin constantly pointed things out – sheep in a field, huddling together in the snow, and then out to sea; the view was clear to the horizon. They pointed out a ship to one another. She was continually amazed that it was all so new to him and at one point she caught Josiah's eye over Robin's head. He raised his eyebrows slightly as if he too understood.

The track brought them to the little village of High Hawsker, low stone and slate farm buildings huddling together as if for warmth, and after half an hour, Josiah stopped the trap. 'It's hereabouts, so far as I knaws.'

'Go and ask at that farm, Josiah.'

He trudged away through the snow to a cluster of farm buildings nearby, and returned soon after. 'Aye, it's in a field. Yer tek this track, he said.' He gestured, and getting up on the trap again they made their way for a few hundred yards down the uneven track. 'Look – yonder.'

Not far away in the field, it stood; looking much as wells do, a low stone balustrade, with a timber frame hanging over it.

'Come on, Robin, this is it,' she said decisively.

'What is it?' he asked apprehensively.

'T'Awd Abba Well, I think.'

He stared at it, then glanced up to her. 'You're not—'

'We're going to have a look.'

'No! He might come out!'

'There are three of us. He can't eat us all together. Besides, it's daytime, and you said he only comes out at night.'

'I don't want to.'

She took his hands. 'Look, Josiah is going to carry you.' The big man nodded. 'It's only a few yards. Even if he did come out he'd have to eat Josiah first. And Josiah isn't afraid, are you, Josiah?'

'Me? I'm too tough for goblins.'

'There you are.'

Josiah descended from the trap and took the boy on his back, and together they tramped across the field to the well. Robin was still apprehensive. 'Don't look in!'

Sarah leaned over the parapet. The well was very deep and simply descended into darkness.

'Anyone there?'

Her voice echoed in the depth.

'Hullo!' And her voice came back, 'Hullo!' She looked up at Robin. 'He doesn't seem to be in. Do you want to have a go?'

Robin, still clinging to Josiah's back, was watching her carefully. He shook his head.

'Robin, we have brought you all the way here. The least you can do is to look in. It's only a well.'

'He might be asleep! You might wake him!'

Sarah leaned in again. 'Mr Hob! Are you there? Mr Hob!'

'No!' Robin called anxiously. 'Don't shout!'

'Mr Hob! I'm waiting! Are you coming out

or not? We've come a long way to see you! It's not very polite!' She paused. 'We're still waiting!'

At last she turned again to Robin, and shook her head. 'No reply. You have a try.'

This time Josiah, without waiting to be asked, stepped forward to the parapet. 'I can't see nowt, an' all.'

At last Robin, clinging tightly on Josiah's back, glanced timidly down into the well. 'It's dark. He might be hiding.'

'Are you hiding?' Sarah called. She looked up. 'Where do you think he's hiding? It's only a well. There's nothing down there but water.'

'There might be...' Robin was confused. He glanced carefully down again, still clinging on to Josiah. 'You can't see anything.'

'All right, listen.' She glanced about, picked up a stone in the field, and dropped it into the well. After a few moments they heard a distant 'plop'.

She raised her eyebrows. 'Deep. That was the water. If there was anybody down there the stone would have hit him, wouldn't it?'

Robin seemed reassured at last. Josiah set him down, supporting him under the arms, and Robin leaned over the parapet. 'Hullo!' he called. 'Mr Hob, are you there?' He laughed. 'Mr Hob! Come out please and say how do you do!' He laughed again. 'Mr Hob! It's very rude to keep us waiting!'

As they set off back to the house he could not help going over and over it: 'If he had been there he would have heard us, wouldn't he, Sarah! He must have! That proves he doesn't exist!' He laughed and wriggled with excitement.

Ten

Their way back was into the wind, which had shifted and now came from the north over the moors. The sun, low in the winter sky, glinted in long crimson streaks across the snow. She had her arm round Robin's little body and felt him shiver. Wrapped up though he was, his thin body felt the cold; she put her own cloak round him, huddling the two of them together as the wind grew steadily keener and the first flurries of snow flicked over them. She glanced apprehensively into the sky and then over Robin's head to Josiah. 'How long?' she whispered.

He shook his head. 'Not much short of an hour if snaw gets up. 'Twill mek way deeper, see.'

The snow came down more heavily and the poor horse bent her head into the biting wind. The landmarks were disappearing until only the track remained before them, becoming obscured as the snow overlay everything. Only the occasional glimpse of a gate or hedge, and once a signpost, showed they were on the right path. In the end she buried

Robin's head completely beneath her cloak, clutching him to her, eaten with anxiety.

They were lost in a world of snow and it was impossible to have any idea where they were or how far they were from home, so it was a miracle when the first houses of Whitby appeared. As they made their way through the streets Sarah was buoyed up but out on the cliffs the track had disappeared and it seemed an eternity before the house appeared faintly through the snow. At last Josiah pulled up at the gate, the door opened and Mrs Hudson hurried down the path.

'Where is he? Bring him in, Josiah!'

The servant, crusted like a snowman, lowered himself from the trap. Sarah unfolded her cloak, and Josiah took Robin.

'Oh, the poor mite, bring him in. Jenny! Bring two hot-water bottles – as quick as tha can!'

Josiah carried the stiff little body into the house and up into his bedroom where Mrs Hudson fussed over him, unwrapping the layers of coats and waistcoats, the scarves, mufflers and gloves, the boots on his little feet, peeled off his socks and underclothes and shuffled him into his bed. Robin, white-faced and stiff, was shivering uncontrollably. Jenny brought in the stone hot-water bottles and together they worked round the bed, slipping in the bottles, arranging the bedding.

'Josiah – mek up t'fire! Jenny, warm some gruel, and mek a cup of beef tea! And quick now!'

Throughout this flurry of activity, Sarah was temporarily sidelined. Watching the shrimp of a child in the housekeeper's hands, seeing him shivering, she could have torn her hair out. Who could have known the weather would change so quickly?

Jenny reappeared shortly with a tray and a bowl of gruel, Mrs Hudson perched herself on the bedside and spooned it between Robin's chattering teeth as he lay with the blankets up to his chin.

'Get this into thee now and lie still. Tha'lt be all right. Josiah's made up a nice fire for thee.'

Sarah looked at Josiah. 'We'd best send for the doctor.'

Mrs Hudson, hearing this, glanced a scowl at her before turning back to Robin.

McMaster appeared in the room at this moment. Sarah went to him. 'Mr McMaster, this is entirely my fault! I don't know how you'll ever forgive me. But the weather changed so suddenly. Perhaps we should send for the doctor?'

He passed, without seeming to hear her, and bent over his son. There was a whispered conversation between him and Mrs Hudson, as she spooned gruel into Robin. He nodded and, straightening, turned at last to Sarah. He was looking very serious. Before she could speak, however, he said, in that voice which brooked no contradiction, 'You should not reproach yourself. It was my fault.'

She was silenced. She could see he was

troubled, clenching his jaws, frowning, and at last passing a hand over his forehead. 'It was my fault. You asked my permission. It was my folly to think it might be safe for him to go. But he is too weak. Too weak.' Shaking his head again he turned away from her and left the room.

This did nothing to ease Sarah's fears, and she returned to the bedside. Mrs Hudson had finished the gruel.

'Just try to drink this, Master Robin, and then tha can sleep.'

Robin was shaking and it was difficult to get him to drink. His teeth chattered against the rim of the cup but he managed at least some of it. Mrs Hudson made him slide down in the bed and tucked him in firmly.

'Doctor's comin' soon to see thee.' As Mrs Hudson was setting the cup and bowl on the tray Sarah approached the bed. Robin did not appear to see her, staring straight up.

'I'll watch with him, Mrs Hudson.'

The other shot her a look and whispered harshly, 'Tha'st done thee best this day. Is this what tha wanted?'

'What? How—'

'Of all the witless things – to tek 'im aht on a freezin' day in winter – wi' t'promise of snaw an 'all, as any fool could see, against doctor's advice—'

'But it was Mr McMaster's wish—'

'Tha'lt not excuse theeself by blamin' t'mester, young lady!' Mrs Hudson thrust her face into Sarah's. 'Mr McMester would never have counselled such a fool's errand!'

'What? But—' Before she could go on, the housekeeper thrust past her and out of the room. For a stunned moment Sarah stared after her.

Then she wiped her eyes brusquely, drew a long breath, and at last, turning to where Robin lay, she pulled a chair to the bedside. What was going on? Mrs Hudson had heard McMaster give her his permission – she had been standing in the hall.

She wrenched her mind back to Robin, who seemed unaware of her. He muttered something, and she darted forward. But he simply shivered, staring upwards.

The doctor arrived, followed by Mrs Hudson. He was rubbing his hands together as he came into the room, and stopped briefly to warm them at the fire.

Sarah told him what had happened as he bent over Robin; he listened but made no comment. He took the boy's temperature and his pulse and turned to Mrs Hudson. 'There's nothing you can do for the moment except to keep him well wrapped up and warm. He's caught a chill, and there are some symptoms of fever. It might set in, or not; I cannot say at this stage. He is a very frail child, so he must be watched carefully.' He took a bottle with a glass stopper out of his bag. 'I have made up a mixture of acetate of ammonia and spirits of nitrous ether.' He turned to Sarah. 'You will be nursing him?' She nodded. 'Very well. This should be administered every three hours, a teaspoon in a glass of warm water. Send for me again if he gets worse.'

'Yes, Doctor.' She followed him to the door. Soon afterwards Mrs Hudson reappeared with a long glass with a spoon in it, and a kettle. 'You heard doctor's orders. There's warm water in t'kettle.' She placed it on the hob beside the fire.

After Mrs Hudson had gone, she settled herself on the bedside chair, stiff, upright and hard. Robin was dozing lightly and occasionally jerked suddenly and altered his position.

There was a sound at the door, and Jenny appeared with a tray. 'Mr McMaster's compliments and he says you'll probably be glad of this.'

It must have been much later when Mr McMaster entered. He crossed at first to look at Robin and seemed for some time to be in thought then straightened at last and looked about as if seeing her for the first time.

'What are you doing on that hard chair? Take the armchair.'

'I did for a while, but found myself falling asleep, sir.'

'Well, take it now for a few minutes; I will watch with you.'

Without speaking she did as he ordered, he carried over her little chair, and they both settled to staring at the fire.

'Mr McMaster,' she began awkwardly, 'I feel, after what has happened today, that you may perhaps no longer have confidence in me; if that is the case, I should wish to leave. If anything should happen to Robin I shall never forgive myself.'

He grunted. 'Rest assured, you did me a favour in coming here. When we met on the ship I was returning from a fruitless errand in London. I went to interview women but could find none that was not either an ignoramus or a fool. In any case I am leaving in a couple of days; I have no time to find a replacement.'

This did not exactly assure her, but he changed the subject almost immediately. 'Why were you so keen to take him out today?'

She told him about Robin's nightmare, about the Hob-o'-the-moor, and t'Awd Abba Well.

'It was that fool of a woman filling his head with stories of ghosts and witches,' he muttered.

'Miss La Touche?'

He nodded.

'I seem to have heard of nothing but Miss La Touche since I arrived.'

'Well, she's gone now, thank God.'

'And you have me instead. I seem to have made a very poor start; I don't know what you must think.'

'The boy seldom goes out. In this weather it is very difficult. And you were right, it did seem a fine day. You were not to know it would turn against you. It is not your fault,

Miss Shaw. You asked my permission, which was entirely correct of you.'

All this would have come as a consolation to Sarah if he had not uttered it in such an off-hand way. There was a long silence as she waited for him to continue.

'Miss La Touche was recommended by a colleague whose judgement I thought I could rely on. A relation they were anxious to dispose of, I imagine. I had only myself to blame if I took her on trust.'

He rose and stood looking down at Robin, who seemed to be sleeping peacefully for the moment.

After a little she faltered, 'You seem to have taken me on trust, Mr McMaster.'

He glanced back to her.

'I mean – ' she hesitated – 'you know nothing about me.'

'A woman of mystery, eh? You never did explain what you were doing on that ship.'

'I am not at liberty to say. But I promise the moment I am free to do so, I shall.'

'So long as you don't go dashing off again. I haven't time to hunt for another woman for the time being. Besides, as I said before, I know more about you perhaps than you realize.'

She was alarmed. 'Do you?'

He noticed this and smiled grimly. 'You give yourself away, Miss Shaw, with every word you utter, every step you take.'

'What do you mean?'

He came back and stood before her, his

hands in his pockets. 'I have cross-questioned men and women in every kind of sordid extremity. There is no human folly, no despair, violence or cruelty I have not peered into; I have spoken with men and women whose lives have been destroyed, who have lost everything; interviewed people who have committed unspeakable acts and are in fear for their very lives – who face the gallows. For twenty years I have done this; do you think I have learned nothing of human nature?' She waited. 'Oh no, Miss Shaw, not much escapes me.'

He turned away to the door, then looked back. 'Who is relieving you?'

'No one. It is all right, Mr McMaster, I will watch Robin. I am young, I can easily do it. Goodnight.'

As he held the doorknob in his hand he turned again. 'I hope you will play for me again before I go.'

'Of course, if you wish it.'

'I do.'

'Goodnight.'

Eleven

During the night she made up the fire. Robin was asleep and, unable to stay awake any longer, she climbed onto his bed and pulled one end of the bedspread over her.

She was woken by Jenny as a grey cold dawn was breaking. 'I think he's worse, miss.'

Sarah sprang off the bed and leaned over Robin. He was awake and turning his head back and forth feverishly on the pillow. His breath was short, and she could make out a dry, crackling noise in his throat. His face was flushed and his forehead was hot.

'What time is the doctor coming?' She looked round uncertainly, saw the bottle on the little table, and snatched it up. 'Let me see – it was a teaspoonful in a glass of warm water.'

'I brought a jug, miss.'

Sarah poured a glass and measured out a teaspoonful of the ether and ammonia mixture. 'Call the master, Jenny.'

She lifted Robin's head and tried to get him to drink. With some difficulty and a lot of spilling, she managed to help him to sip some at least.

As she settled him back on the pillow she

glanced round; the room was cold. She threw herself onto her knees and riddled out the fire. The fire was barely alight, but she coaxed it and with some care managed to bring it back to life. She was sweeping out the old ashes when McMaster came in. He went straight to the bed.

She looked up at him from the fireplace. 'I'm afraid he's running a temperature, sir.'

McMaster placed his hand on Robin's forehead.

'I gave him a drink,' she added uselessly.

McMaster seemed awkward, she thought. 'Robinson should be here soon,' he muttered.

The doctor arrived an hour later. He took Robin's temperature and felt his pulse. 'Help me turn him over, Mrs Hudson, and lift up his nightshirt.'

Between them they turned Robin on his face. She pulled the nightshirt up, revealing his thin little body. Sarah was watching all the time. The doctor placed one hand across the back and tapped on one of the fingers with his other hand. He repeated this several times. He pulled down the nightshirt and they turned Robin over again.

He stepped away from the bed and said softly, 'He won't want much to eat for the time being, thin light foods, but give him plenty to drink; he's going to sweat a lot. Try to keep him comfortable and make sure the room is aired.'

As he was leaving, Sarah approached him uncertainly. 'What do you think—'

108

'It's pneumonia. He's going to need all the care and attention you can give him.'

'Pneumonia?'

'It'll get worse before it gets better. There will be periods of delirium and he may suffer convulsions. Send for me at any time.'

After he left, Sarah was fussing uselessly about the bed. Jenny came over to her. 'Th'ast not had owt to eat this morning, miss. I'll watch wi' Master Robin while tha gets thee breakfast.'

'It's all right, Jenny – if you could just bring me something here. Just let me go next door and wash first.'

Having been in her clothes all night – and slept no more than a few hours – Sarah was dizzy with lack of sleep and beginning to feel very uncomfortable. In her own room she hurriedly undressed, washed and put on another frock. Running a comb through her hair and hastily putting it up, she returned to the sick room, where Jenny had set down a tray.

'I've brought thee a plate of porridge for now, and I'll fetch thee an egg in a moment.'

As Sarah was eating her porridge she heard Robin.

'Open the window, Miss La Touche,' he murmured.

Sarah leapt to the bedside. Robin's eyes were closed and his head was turning on the pillow. 'It's my turn to play.' She watched helplessly. He drifted back into sleep and she returned to her breakfast. As she was

109

finishing, she heard him whisper, 'We went to t'Awd Abba Well, didn't we, Sarah?' He was watching her. His voice was barely a croak. 'There's no such thing as the Hob-o'-the-moor, is there?'

'No,' she smiled encouragingly. 'We proved it.'

'Yes. It was worth it to go, wasn't it?'

'So long as you get better, Robin.' She was at a loss for a moment, then, 'Now let's see. We'd better get on with Jack's adventures, hadn't we?'

He nodded again and Sarah cast round rapidly for a new idea. They had long ago left Zanzibar behind them, and Jack had last been heard of in the Rocky Mountains.

But she had not been speaking long when she glanced across and saw that he had fallen into a light doze again. She studied his face, flushed, feverish, listened to his laboured breathing. The dry crackling had been replaced by a dull rasping from the congested lungs. It was almost more than she could bear having to sit and listen to this; the poor boy had to pull every breath in with all his little strength.

Later the doctor came again, and she pressed him. 'He will recover, won't he?'

The doctor looked her straight in the face and said, 'It is too early to say.' After he had gone she stared down at Robin, and saw the truth in his thin face.

This lovely little boy whom she loved as she never loved any one, even in the few weeks she had known him: the idea forced itself upon her that he might actually die – and that it was entirely her own fault. No one had compelled her, no one had even suggested it. Mrs Hudson had advised against it. Entirely of her own will, she had taken this frail child out on a winter's day into a snowstorm. How could she ever look anyone in the face again? A lovely boy, a beautiful boy, a boy whom she had care over, for whom she had taken responsibility; she killed him. She stalked about the room in an agony of indecision, restlessly turning this way and that, and all the time Robin lay among the hangings of his bed dragging in his breath with that horrible dry cough. The day wore on and he drifted in and out of consciousness. She gave him a drink. She made up the fire; she splashed some cold water on her face to refresh herself a little; stood at the window staring out at the day as the short afternoon began to close in, idly staring, unable to think or concentrate on anything, then turned again through the room, back and forth, stopping to check his condition, hearing all the time his laboured breathing.

Night fell. The doctor called at six and after an examination said he thought the crisis might pass within the next two days. It was still too soon to say for certain.

Robin could take very little to eat; Mrs Hudson brought up cups of beef tea and Sarah managed to spoon into him a bowl of thin gruel. And the evening came on. She was past tiredness by this time. She went into her own room again to splash a little water on her face, and run a comb through her hair; she and Jenny made up a sort of cot for her in Robin's room but she no longer knew whether she was tired or hungry or anything else; it was impossible for her to know anything or think of anything until she knew Robin was safe.

At about ten, as she was sitting by the fire, McMaster came in. He inspected Robin, who was asleep, then crossed to her.

'It's still too early to say,' she began. 'The doctor said—'

'I spoke to him,' McMaster said briefly, and then in a businesslike tone, 'I have to return to Liverpool tomorrow.'

She nodded, and after a moment he turned back to the bed and stood looking down at Robin for a long time. At last she asked tentatively, 'What is it? Is he sleeping quietly?'

He nodded and went on, still looking down, and speaking almost to himself, 'It is probably wrong of me to come here at all. It would be better for both of us to see nothing of the other. The sight of him summons too many painful thoughts in me.'

'What do you mean?' she asked, alarmed.

But he did not seem to hear her and went on, 'Why could I not have had a son such as other men do? A healthy boy to run and play, a boy I could have watched grow into a sturdy man, someone I could one day be proud of? Look at him! Condemned to be a burden on others all his life! In all conscience, would it not be better for him to die tonight?' He snatched up one of the pillows and held it with both hands over Robin's head. 'Would it not be better?'

She watched appalled. 'Don't say that! Never think it! *Never!*' Starting up, she set her own hands on the pillow, ready to wrestle him for it.

He shook her aside effortlessly; she staggered and tripped in her skirts, sprawling across the carpet in front of the fire.

'Let's make an end of it.'

She scrambled to her feet. 'Mr McMaster! Stop!' She threw herself against him again as he stood at the bedside and cried in an urgent whisper, still frightened of waking Robin, 'You shall not!' Exerting all her strength, she clung to the pillow as they swayed for a moment. 'Never!' she repeated more gently, looking up into his haggard face. 'You have a gentle, loving son. Love him in return, Mr McMaster, do.'

'I *cannot.* Oh—' Abruptly he swept her aside. 'Do you think I haven't tried? God knows I have tried! But every time I see his helplessness a rage starts in me; his weakness, his defencelessness – it goads me more than I can say. And then I remember—'

He swept a hand over his face, staring up for a second. Without looking at her, he spoke again, his tone muffled. 'God knows I have tried,' he repeated. 'When I think – that it should have come to this. My hopes, once so fair, when I felt I could do anything, and was the luckiest man in the world, when I had everything to live for...' He drew a shattering sigh. 'And now to come to this – ' He gestured, still unable to look at her, as she watched appalled at his vehemence. 'All lost.'

He sighed again, and dropped his hands, and stood as if deflated; scarcely glancing at her, he went to the door. Just as he was leaving he half-turned, and flapped a hand. 'Do what you can.' And went out, leaving her still staring in amazement, her heart hammering in her chest.

Twelve

For some minutes she stared at the door. Then as the silence lengthened she became aware of herself again and of the room about her; heard the wind outside, the fire in the grate. Slowly, as if coming out of a trance, she turned to the bed, where Robin still lay in a deep sleep. What if she hadn't been there? Was it possible that he would really have murdered his own son?

As these thoughts ran through her mind, she glanced about the room, noticed the fire and knelt to make it up. Undoing the back of her gown, she let it fall to the floor, and pouring some cold water into the bowl splashed her face and arms with it. By these little actions she tried to instil in herself some sense of normality.

But suppose he came back while she was asleep? She dragged her little cot across the room. If he did he would have to climb over her first.

She couldn't sleep. The moment she laid her head on her pillow, the whole grotesque scene ran through her mind again. She stared at the ceiling as the light from the fire flickered over it, hearing his strong hard voice, that almost manic insistence—

Jenny was shaking her. She started up. 'It's all right, miss, he's still asleep.'

'Don't disturb him, Jenny. We'll let him sleep as long as he can. Is Mr McMaster up yet?'

'Mester went at first light, miss.'

Sarah pulled herself up and crossing to the window drew back the curtains. Another low grey sky, a dull muffled light. Jenny was on her knees making up the fire.

'I put a jug of water in thee room, miss.'

Sarah went through into her bedroom, threw off her nightgown, and hastily washed herself. As she was returning from her own room and thrusting a few pins into her hair, Jenny was finishing at the fireplace, where a new fire was burning briskly. She stood up, dusting the ashes from her hands.

'Doctor'll be here in a little.' She leant over

Robin. 'Do you think he looks any better?'

They both examined him. His face was white, his breathing was shallow and difficult. Sarah looked up at Jenny. 'How can you tell?'

Robinson arrived soon after she had finished giving Robin a bowl of gruel. After his examination, he confided that he thought the patient might turn the corner in a day or two. 'So long as nothing happens to inflame the situation. If we can keep him quiet and warm, he may pull through.'

As she was arranging his bedding, she told Robin, 'Your papa has gone to Liverpool, Robin.'

Although Robin said nothing, she knew he was relieved. And while she was fussing about the room, he said unexpectedly, 'Papa hates me because I'm a cripple.'

He seemed curiously calm as he said it, and she was at a loss how to respond. Before she could frame a reply, he went on, still in this matter-of-fact tone, 'You hate me too, I expect. You'll leave me – like all the others.'

'What others?'

'All the other governesses. They never stay. They're afraid of Papa. Because he shouts at them. He always seems angry. It's because Mamma is dead, I think.'

'Did you ever see your mamma?'

'She died when I was little.'

There was no reply to this, but after a moment Sarah said hesitantly, 'He never shouts at me.'

'He hasn't shouted at you yet – but you wait

till he's in one of his rages.'

Sarah sat on the side of the bed and took his hand. 'First of all I don't hate you. Why should I? We get on very well.'

'Yes, but Papa pays your wages. You're bound to obey him. And I know he hates me – so you must hate me too.'

'If he hated you why would he want me to look after you? Everyone here wants to look after you and help you to get better.'

'I don't think Papa wants me to get better.'

'Of course he does.'

'No, he doesn't. I'm just a nuisance to him.'

'But, Robin, your papa came to Whitby especially for your sake – for your health. To make you grow into a big strong boy.'

'That's all tosh! How can I ever grow into a big strong boy?'

Nothing Sarah could say seemed to make any difference. Robin was convinced that he was right. She could only reiterate that his father really did love him – only he wasn't very good at showing it. Eventually, when it was time for his lunch, she was relieved to change the subject.

Later that afternoon, while he slept, she went down to the drawing room and opened the piano. Now that McMaster had gone she felt as if a weight had been lifted from her shoulders. She was free to sit at the keyboard and amuse herself for half an hour without his presence looming in the doorway.

She sat with Robin as he had his tea. She

was relieved to see that his hostile mood of the morning had passed, for he said suddenly, 'I heard you playing this afternoon.'

'I thought you were asleep.'

'I was – but as I was waking up I could hear you. At first I thought it was a dream.'

'What were you dreaming about?'

'My mamma.'

'What is she like?'

He was thoughtful. 'I can't exactly see her face. But I know she is very kind and I can go to her and she will hold me. All warm and snug.'

'Do you often dream of her?'

'Yes. And I know she's there somewhere, watching over me all the time. And I know she loves me, and would be with me if she could.'

Sarah found this conversation very upsetting. It ran through and through her mind; there was something so unjust about it. Why should he be cut off from all normal activities? Who had decreed he must be confined to a chair, never to enjoy all the adventures and activities that other boys knew?

A few days later, Robin had turned the corner. Sarah moved back into her own bedroom.

One afternoon she went into the kitchen to speak to Mrs Hudson. Was this despite – or because of – the hostility she had felt since the disastrous expedition to t'Awd Abba Well? She couldn't be sure.

118

She found Mrs Hudson chopping vegetables at the table. After a brief discussion of
menus – her excuse for being there – she
began, in as off-hand a manner as she could
contrive, 'Do you know when the master will
be back, Mrs Hudson?'

'Easter vacation, as like as not.' Mrs Hudson did not look up and did not slow in her
chopping, which was quick and accurate. She
brought the knife down sharply through the
parsnips. 'He doesn't usually say till last
minute.'

'A busy man, I suppose?'

'You can suppose so if you like.'

Mrs Hudson lifted the chopping board,
emptied the vegetables into a saucepan and
carried it to the range. Despite her brusque
manner Sarah felt impelled to drive on.

'Have you known him long, Mrs Hudson?'

'Seven year.'

'Oh – since the birth of his son?'

'Nay. His son were born before he come
here.'

'Did you ever know Mrs McMaster?'

'No.'

Mrs Hudson opened the back door and
went out. Sarah waited, unsure whether to
stay or go. But a moment later the other
woman reappeared holding a live chicken
upside down by its claws, its wings splayed,
and looking about it, clearly confused by this
abrupt occurrence. Mrs Hudson, without
pausing, holding the claws in one hand, now
took the head in the other and gave an

almighty wrench. There was a brief flurry, a twitch, and the bird was dead in her hands.

Sarah stood, petrified by the sudden violence of the act, and it was only after some time that she was able to regain control of herself and the thread of the conversation. She swallowed and, with some difficulty, withdrew her eyes from the bird on the table.

'I, that is, I meant to say – he's rather a strange man, isn't he?'

Mrs Hudson rested her knuckles on the table. 'Is he?' she asked with a very direct stare.

'Don't you think so?' she faltered.

'I think folk should keep fra pokin' their noses into other people's business.' Sarah was demolished. Mrs Hudson began to pluck feathers from the carcass but she looked up again abruptly as a kind of afterthought. 'But I'll tell thee this, young lady, tha'lt go a long mile before tha'lt find another man as kind and generous as Mr McMaster. And *I* know.'

She was clearly going to say no more so, after a brief word, Sarah withdrew and made her way slowly upstairs in a very thoughtful mood.

As she was about to sit at the piano a few days later she found that the lid of the stool opened and that it contained a pile of sheet music. She eagerly leafed through it, though she cooled as she found it was mostly extremely easy parlour pieces and fashionable dance music of ten or fifteen years earlier. Even so,

120

it gave her a lot of pleasure to set up one of these galops or valses and finger their simple chords and one-note melodies.

When she was with Robin he remarked, 'I love to hear you play, Sarah.'

'They were some old pieces I found in the piano stool. It must belong to the people who own the house. I wonder where they are now?'

Robin had no idea.

'I'll ask Mrs Hudson. I expect she'll know.'

'Mrs Hudson knows everything,' Robin said slowly.

'She does, doesn't she?' Sarah repeated absent-mindedly.

And then it came to her, so obviously that she couldn't understand why she hadn't thought of it before.

'Would you like to play, Robin?'

'I'd *love* to!'

'We'll start tomorrow!'

Robin was strong enough by now to be out of bed during the day and the following after-noon Josiah carried him down to the drawing room. They were not immediately sure how to sit him at the piano – he was unable to balance himself on the stool – but in the end they wedged him into a chair with cushions, so that he was at the right height.

As they sat side by side, she placed his hands over the keyboard directing his fingers. She could see the excitement in his face as he sounded the keys for the first time. His hands were not yet large enough to span the octave. 'Never mind,' she said, 'that'll come in a year or two.'

She showed him middle C and how to play a scale with each hand. She set up the sheet music of one of the parlour ballads, showed him how the chords were fingered by the left hand, and explained a bit about time signatures and the difference between common time and waltz time. Robin took it all in without effort.

'That's enough for today,' she said when she noticed an hour had passed, and Mrs Hudson had looked in to tell her it was his teatime. 'We'll do a bit every day. You don't want to do too much at a time or you'll get indigestion.'

However she felt frustrated that she had no music really suitable for a beginner, and the following morning walked into Whitby to find the music shop that Hardcastle had mentioned.

Although it was now the end of January the snow was still thick on the ground, and might remain till the middle of March, she had been told. There had been nothing like this in London, and she felt the cold keenly as she strode along the cliff path into town. It was weeks since she had been into Whitby and it was a relief to feel the press of crowds around her and to know that normal life was still going on despite the dramas in West Cliff House.

She found the music shop and bought some

simple pieces for beginners and a book of blank staves for exercises. She was about to leave when the bell sounded, the door opened, and she was face to face with Marmaduke Hardcastle. She would have pushed on but he spoke.

'Well! So th'art still here, then?'

She hesitated, holding his look. 'So it seems.'

'Th'aren't a ghost, any road. Go on – tha'st found somebody to tek thee in?'

'I have obtained a post, if that is what you mean,' she replied with all the dignity she could command.

'Oh aye? Wheer?'

'I am working for Mr McMaster – up in West Cliff House.'

'Oh, I know Mr McMaster.' He leered at her and crossed his arms comfortably. She wondered why she was putting up with this impertinence. But there was some foolish residual sense of guilt lurking in her whenever Hardcastle was around.

'I am his son's governess, if you want to know,' she said primly.

He chuckled. 'Payin' thee well, is he?'

'What are you suggesting?'

'Nothin',' he shrugged, but keeping a mysterious smile. 'Only – folk round here know about Mr McMaster.'

'Know – what?'

'Oh...' He tilted his head to one side and raised one eyebrow. 'You just ask folk in town what they know about Mr McMaster – and his wife.'

'His wife?' she said abruptly, puzzled by his mysterious tone.

He held open the door for her, still with that knowing leer, and as she passed him, added, 'Aye. Ask him about that – ask him about his wife. If tha durst.'

The door closed behind her and she looked back through the glass panel, but he had his back to her already and was talking to the proprietor. She turned and made her way thoughtfully through the town and up onto the cliff path.

She didn't attach much importance to anything that Marmaduke Hardcastle might say and she would have dismissed the thought immediately, except for what she had seen that night in Robin's bedroom. Everything she had seen and heard had revealed a man almost unhinged, driven by intense passions. A man who was ready to kill his own son – what did that tell her about his wife? Surely Hardcastle hadn't meant that Mr McMaster had murdered her?

Another thought struck her. McMaster had scoffed at religion; he refused to allow his son to be taken to church or learn about the Bible. By itself she might not have attached much importance to this – she wasn't very religious herself – but taken with the other things, it seemed to point to a man adrift from the rules of civilized behaviour.

What was worse was that she couldn't check what Hardcastle had said. Mrs Hudson was the only person she had discussed him with and she had been strangely loyal; that might mean nothing even so – after all, he was paying her wages. She didn't know what to think.

Thirteen

Over the following weeks she concentrated on Robin's piano lessons. To her great joy he was an eager pupil and took things in without effort. If anything, she had to restrain his impetuosity; he strained to learn – he had a hunger for it, and she realized that he had at last found a way out of the intense frustration of his chair and his bed. So long confined, while he sat at the keyboard he could now be free. This was something he could do, he knew it from the first day and he could not wait to forge on.

It was the middle of March when at last there came days of mild brightness and a softening in the breeze. The snow disappeared, colour returned to the landscape and they were at liberty to go out for a walk. Josiah pulled the little chair with Robin muffled within it as they bumped their way along the cliff path. It was not exactly a cliff, she now noticed, rather a very steep slope down to the beach, covered with gorse and bracken. The eternal sea mist had lifted, the horizon was clear and ships could be made out. Gulls screamed and swooped over them and her heart lifted as winter drew to a close.

It was on one of these walks that she asked Josiah about Mrs Hudson and her loyalty to the master. Robin had temporarily nodded off in his chair and this seemed to be the only safe way into the subject of their employer. She still knew very little about him and she remembered Hardcastle's insinuations word for word.

'Have you been with the master long, Josiah?'

'Syne he come – seven year ago.'

'And Mrs Hudson the same?'

'Theerabouts – I canna remember exactly.'

'Has he been a good master to you?' she went on as casually as she could.

'Oh aye.' He was looking away out to sea.

'I hope you don't mind my asking this. Only I want to know as much about him as I can. Mrs Hudson told me what a kind and generous man he is.'

He grunted and shifted his position. 'Aye – she would,' he remarked after a moment.

Sarah was alert and after another moment, without looking at him, she said, in as off-hand a manner as she could, 'Does she – have some especial cause to be grateful to Mr McMaster?'

He turned to her. 'Tha could say that.' He paused. 'If I tell thee summat, tha'lt not repeat it? She don't want it generally known.'

Sarah was very alert. 'You have my word.'

He coughed. 'Fact is ... Emily – Mrs Hudson – she killed her husband.' He paused again then added inconsequentially, 'If he were her husband, that is. At trial, there weren't any proof ever brought. But she said he were, any road.'

'*She killed her husband?*' Sarah repeated slightly out of breath, glancing down to check that Robin was still asleep.

'Aye.'

'But—'

'So what's she doin' here, then? Eh? Oh, she's a cool one. She went to t'police, told 'em she'd killed 'im. Told 'em straight. So she were arrested and charged wi' murder and sent for trial at York Assizes. And t'mester takes t'case. It looked bad. There were Perce – that were her husband, so called – dead – and she'd confessed. Emily told t'mester she didn't care what happened – said she'd do it again.' He turned to Sarah. 'And that's what's strange. See, it were *t'mester* insisted it were self-defence. It were t'mester made her want to live. She said she didn't care what become of her but he said, "You're innocent and you're goin' to walk free." And he got the whole story out of her. At first she wouldn't talk about it, but in the end it all come out. She had a daughter, fifteen, and Perce had – well – I don't rightly know how

127

to tell thee—'

'You mean – molested his daughter?'

'Molested? Tha might call it that, I suppose. He raped her, missie. And t'girl had told her mother.'

They were staring into each other's eyes. After a moment Sarah gasped breathlessly, 'I see.'

'They were livin' up on t'moors in a farm. There weren't no one else around – no witnesses, no one.' He paused, while Sarah waited almost painfully holding her breath. 'Any road, t'mester underteks defence – he allus teks defence, tha knaws. Prosecution case were straightforward: Emily had confessed therefore she were guilty.'

'What happened?'

'T'mester brought witnesses to Perce's character – that he were a violent man, he'd attacked Emily and the child before. Emily had to show her scars—'

'Scars?'

'Burns, where he'd thrown hot fat over her.'

'Good Lord.'

'In t'end he convinced jury that she had acted in self-defence. Solicitor wanted her to enter a plea of manslaughter but t'mester were adamant she were innocent. And he got her off. She walked free.'

There was a silence as Sarah struggled to digest all this. 'I see,' she said at last. 'And is that why she's here?'

'Ah, that's it. She worshipped t'mester. After what he done there weren't nowt she wouldn't do for 'im. Like a dog she were, fawned on him, offered to work for nowt.' He looked seriously at Sarah and went on heavily, 'God help thee if tha ever crosses t'mester – Emily'd kill thee.'

There was another long pause; Sarah could now make sense of Mrs Hudson's apparently contradictory behaviour. It reminded her too of something McMaster had said to her. This must be one of those 'sordid extremities' he had peered into.

'And what happened to the daughter?'

'Married, Emily says, and gone to Canada. Can't say I blame 'er. After what had happened she wanted to get as far from Yorkshire as she could.'

After this there seemed nothing more to say and they continued in silence as Sarah thought of Mrs Hudson and her dead husband.

As they were walking back, she noticed a group of children on the beach below them, calling to each other and larking about. She did not take much notice, but during the weeks that followed, she saw them several times, and wondered who they might be.

Morning followed morning at the piano. She had long since ceased to sit by him; she stood at the other side of the room, listening as he played. She listened to everything, even his scales, always encouraging him to achieve smoothness. 'It must just flow. You have to make it sound as if it is playing itself.' And then there came the day – a bright day of spring sunshine, a cheering sort of day – when they played a duet. It was the simplest thing: he played the melody and she fitted a few chords beneath it. Simple though it was, there was such excitement in this, such screams of laughter from him and such intense pleasure for her. Suddenly, as they finished, he looked up at her and said, out of nowhere, 'I love you, Sarah.' And before she knew it, there were tears in her eyes, she clasped him to her and whispered into his hair, 'And I love you too, Robin.'

After this there was an awkward minute as she wiped her eyes, and he looked at her in surprise. 'Why are you crying?'

'It's nothing,' she gasped, and laughed a sort of muffled laugh, pulling her handkerchief from her sleeve and blowing her nose. 'Nothing. Something in my eye, I expect.' She drew a sigh, pulled herself up straight, pushed a wisp of hair behind her ear and said, 'Now where were we?'

Afterwards she became quite excited, quite warm, as she thought through the consequences of what they were doing. It occurred to her that though they never discussed his father, Robin's enthusiasm for the piano could be an attempt to win his approval; at last one thing had appeared in his life at which he had the chance to excel. Mr McMaster loved piano music and had often asked Sarah to play for him; if he heard Robin's remarkable progress, he was bound to be impressed. This surely was the way to bring them together. The prize was so great it was worth all her efforts to bring about.

At the same time, she knew now that whatever the outcome she would defend Robin against his father to the utmost of her strength. The piano had become more important to Robin than even she could have guessed.

It would be more difficult than she had realized, however. How difficult was made clear to her one afternoon as they sat at the piano together. Relaxed and without thinking she said merrily, 'Think what your father is going to say when he hears you—'

'*No!*' Robin almost shot out of his chair. 'No! I don't want him to hear! He mustn't hear!' He shrivelled into himself and wriggled in agony beside her.

Taken by surprise she tried to clasp him but he twisted in her arms. 'No! If he hears me he will laugh at me. I know he will! I know it!'

'Robin!' She tried to calm him, tried to hold his squirming body to her. 'He will be so proud!'

'That's stupid! He won't be proud! How can he be! He hates me. He despises me! He mustn't!' He burst into long hysterical sobs and a moment later slammed down the piano lid, narrowly missing her fingers.

There was nothing she could say and in the end, when Mrs Hudson came to find out what was happening, Sarah whispered over Robin's head, 'Can you fetch Josiah?'

Josiah appeared shortly afterwards and took up the little body, which was still racked with sobs, trembling and shivering. There were long silent looks between the three of them as he carried the little boy out of the room and upstairs.

'He's ready for his sleep, I expect,' was all Mrs Hudson said and Sarah followed them both up into Robin's room. They put Robin into bed, and after Mrs Hudson had gone out and he seemed more relaxed, she tried to reason with him.

'Your father loves music, Robin.'

He lay with his head turned away.

'He loves to hear me play,' she went on gently. 'Think how proud he will be one day to hear you play.'

Without speaking or looking at her he shook his head on the pillow.

'He's bound to hear you sooner or later,' she tried again.

He was silent. Then, still as soft and gently as she could be, and leaning over him, 'Why don't you want him to hear you?'

'Why do you think?' he muttered.

'I don't know.'

'Then you're stupid! He hates me, and you know it! He would only laugh if he heard me. He's never going to hear me!'

She waited but he said no more so at last, hunting for the right approach, she replied, 'But suppose – suppose, after you practised for a long time and became very good – and then he heard you – he would be pleased, wouldn't he? He would be proud of you.'

There was a silence, and at last he muttered, 'He'll never be proud of me. It was a stupid idea and I wish I'd never started.'

She forced herself to wait and at last continued, as gently as she could, 'Whatever you say, it wasn't a stupid idea. It was a very good idea; you have made tremendous progress since January. You have a lovely feel for the piano and it would be a real shame to give it up. You must go on.'

After another pause, during which he was clearly thinking very hard, he muttered, 'I'll only play when he isn't here.'

Soon after, fortunately, he fell asleep. Watching him she was relieved to see his face relaxed in sleep after the horrible contortions earlier. The following day nothing was said and the piano remained closed. They went out for a walk, and still she had no idea how she was going to bring him back to the keyboard, if she ever was. She did not dare to raise the subject for fear of another outburst. The piano remained closed.

One warm afternoon in April when they were on the cliffs she spied again, below them among the rock pools of the foreshore, the group of children. There was a teacher with them, giving a lesson. She felt a pang of jealousy as she heard their obvious excitement and enjoyment: lucky children to have a teacher who could inspire such enthusiasm for jellyfish or fossils. And lucky teacher who had charge of such a happy cluster of children.

She glanced down at Robin, who was also watching. The poor boy never saw another child of his own age; what pleasure he would take in such a group.

'Is there some way we could get down to the beach?' she asked Josiah.

'There's a path.'

'Oh.' She hesitated. 'But we could never get Robin's chair down, could we?'

'I dessay I could carry him.'

He took Robin onto his back and together they scrambled down a steep narrow gully to the beach. This was the first time she had been down onto the sand and the first time for Robin too, it seemed. He was immediately interested and pointed things out as they picked their way among the rock pools and over the long low rounded shapes of butter-coloured rock worn smooth by the movement of the waves. The air was filled with the smell of salt water and seaweed.

It took some time to make their way carefully to the group of children, who were clustered again about their teacher. As they approached, Sarah could see that he was a middle-aged man of medium height in a black frock coat and stove-pipe hat, with a full beard.

As they came at last up to them, some of the children looked back to her, and the teacher paused.

'Good afternoon—'

Before she could say another word she recognized one of the children, who was seated a little apart from the others on a stool with a sketch pad on her knees. She turned at the sound of Sarah's voice and Sarah saw that she was an extremely pretty girl of seventeen or so. It was Chrissie, the girl she had spoken to that afternoon in the White Horse. Chrissie had recognized her and seemed frozen with dismay.

'Good afternoon.' Sarah dragged her attention back to the teacher. 'Do forgive me for intruding on your class. We have been watching you from the cliff top, and my pupil and I would be most grateful if we might be permitted to join you.'

She glanced again at Chrissie, who was watching her with frightened attention.

The gentleman stood up from his little camp stool and raised his hat courteously. 'I assure you we should be delighted.'

Sarah turned to introduce Robin. 'This young man is Robin McMaster. He – has difficulty walking so we are carrying him, as you see.'

Immediately, the teacher turned to indicate his stool. 'By all means do come and sit down – and give your giant a rest.' He smiled as Josiah set Robin on the stool.

'Please go on with your lesson,' Sarah insisted, conscious of the other children standing about watching her. There were seven in all, of differing ages; Chrissie seemed the eldest.

135

'This is my governess,' Robin interrupted. 'Her name is Miss Shaw and she plays the piano very well. She is teaching me to play.'

'How do you do?' The teacher shook her hand. 'These young ladies and gentlemen are the Barrington family.'

'Oh, you are all one family? How pleasant to take your lessons together with the same master.'

They burst into laughter and Sarah glanced round puzzled.

'Do you hear that, Papa?' And the laughter continued until a girl of maybe twelve told her sternly, 'That is not our master. That is our pa!'

'I beg your pardon!' Sarah stopped, embarrassed.

'Effie,' her father remonstrated mildly, 'how was Miss Shaw to know?'

'Well, she knows now.' The child seemed remarkably free in her manners; she turned again to Sarah. 'Pa's a marine biologist—'

'Among *many* other things,' added another even smaller girl, 'he knows everything, he can speak Latin and Greek, he knows all of Shakespeare off by heart, he does chemistry experiments, he has been to the West Indies and brought back specimens, and he has a *huge* collection of fossils—'

'He teaches us,' Effie continued. 'We don't go to school but we learn everything: arithmetic, geometry, French, chemistry—'

Their father cut short this effusion in a relaxed and kindly way. He seemed to enjoy

136

their free and easy ways. He turned to Sarah and Robin. 'We have been collecting specimens from the rock pools and shall take home some for dissecting. These are the various species of the genus—' He uttered some obscure Latin terms as he indicated pale, transparent shrimps in a jar. 'We have found no fewer than thirteen in the pools. Which may be one more than Mr Gosse has recorded in his *Native Fauna of the British Coast-line*. I have written to him about it. If I am correct and if the Royal Society approve, my son Dan here may have a shrimp named after him.'

The ten-year-old giggled and the older boy aimed a friendly hand at her ear.

But the father was not to be interrupted. 'The native British shrimp was already known to the Romans as a delicacy—'

'And still is – to some!' interrupted the boy. 'The great advantage of dissecting shrimps, Miss Shaw, is that you can eat the evidence afterwards.'

'Which alas is not the case with the jellyfish. A distinctly nasty fellow – of which we have to take great care.' Mr Barrington was holding up another glass jar, and Robin was able to take a long look.

Sarah was impressed with his unstoppable enthusiasm, which seemed quite oblivious of the high-spirited children who were sometimes listening and interested, and sometimes larking and fooling among themselves. All, that is, except the tall, silent beauty, who still seemed awkward and glanced towards her every so often.

Mr Barrington could see Robin's fascination with every specimen he presented for his inspection, so as they were turning together towards the path up to the cliffs he invited him to visit them one afternoon and see his collection of fossils.

'One of the best in the country – the man from the Royal Society said so,' Dan told him.

As they took their leave Sarah found the tall girl beside her. 'I beg you,' she whispered, 'you won't say anything about...?'

Sarah shook her head slightly. 'And you?'

'I promise,' the girl went on. 'May I write to you?'

'I hoped you would. You know West Cliff House?'

The girl nodded. 'Thank you,' she whispered.

Fourteen

Dear Miss Shaw

(Forgive me if this is not your real name – but I think that is what you called yourself when we met again on the beach.)

You cannot imagine the flutter you put me into when I saw you again. Thank you from the bottom of my heart for saying nothing to Papa. Of course I will say nothing of what you told *me*. And of course I understand perfectly after what you told me that it is necessary for you temporarily to change your name.

I will never be able to thank you as long as I live for what you said to me the day we met in the White Horse. Of course running away to get married was a foolish idea – though I do not blame Frederick in any way – he was inspired only by the highest motives, and is absolutely devoted to me – as I am to him, it goes without saying.

Even so, what you told me on that day did save us both from a very great mistake and I can never thank you enough.

Fortunately all is now well. I have introduced Frederick to Papa and Frederick has asked for my hand, which Papa was delighted to grant! Only he said Frederick had to complete his studies first – which is entirely right and proper! So we are now engaged – only it is to remain a secret until I come out. You cannot conceive my joy when Papa and Frederick shook hands and, as they did so, I thought immediately of you, and of your very wise words. Little did I think we should ever meet again.

I have often thought of the story you told me and of the terrible trials you have had to endure. I do hope that everything will eventually turn out right for you and I beg you to let me share your troubles in any way I can.

In the hope that we may meet again in the not too distant future,

I remain,

With very best wishes,

Christina Barrington

Sarah smiled to herself as she folded up this youthful effusion. How well she remembered the feelings that Chrissie expressed; remembered that blind, unquestioning devotion, that boundless hope and trust in her future together with Frederick. She drew a long breath and stared sightlessly out of the window as a medley of thoughts and memories ran through her mind.

Eventually she stuffed the letter into a pocket and went downstairs. The piano remained closed and she was really upset about this. Robin had been making progress; there was already one little sonata by Beethoven she had started him on – something the great man had composed for a child. Sometimes, too, they had amused themselves with the dances in the piano stool and she had coached him through a polka or schottische. All of this had come to a stop and she had no idea when they might resume their lessons – if they ever would.

The Barrington family lived in a house set in a large garden outside the town. A circular carriage sweep of raked gravel lay outside the front door, and as Josiah brought the trap to a halt, the door was opened by Effie, the twelve-year-old, who appeared to have as much energy as the other six put together – or if not energy, certainly organizing ability.

'Come in. Dan can carry Robin.' Then to Josiah, as he lifted Robin down, 'You can take the trap to the stables.' She pointed to one side of the house. 'Samson will look after your horse and if you go into the kitchen Cook will give you a cup of tea. If you would like to come this way, Miss Shaw, Pa is waiting.' All this was rattled off without a pause for breath.

Dan followed with Robin on his back; they had been joined by a boy of Robin's age who introduced himself as Alfred.

'I expect you'd like to meet Mamma first,' Effie went on. 'This way, please,' leading them through polished mahogany double

141

doors into an oval drawing room, elegantly and lightly furnished, with white walls covered with paintings. Dan, who was beside Sarah, remarked drily, 'Effie has everything arranged. I don't know what we'd do without her.' He turned now to introduce his mother, who was swathed in Indian shawls, propped up on a chaise longue and, to Sarah's astonishment, nursing a baby.

'Do forgive me for not getting up,' she smiled.

'What a lovely baby.' Sarah couldn't help coming forward.

'Do you like him? He's only a month old.' She took him from her breast. 'I think he's had enough; he's falling asleep.'

Mrs Barrington rearranged the baby in its shawl, and covered her breast.

'May I?'

'Of course.' She offered him up to Sarah, who took him in her arms. He was a heavy boy and squirmed lazily.

'Be careful, he's full of milk.'

'I don't mind.' In fact the baby did return a mouthful of milk over his shawl as she held him. He smelt of milk and baby; there was something so adorable, so bewitching, about this morsel of humanity, everything about him, his little mouth still wet with milk, his eyes shut, the fine clarity of his skin, his plump little hands – something so alive, so precious, as he gurgled and turned in her arms, that she felt quite drunk with it.

'He's lovely,' she managed to gasp at last as
142

she returned him to his mother's arms.

'He's called Octavius,' said Effie, who was watching. 'The Eighth.'

'Eight children.' Sarah couldn't help smiling, and had to draw a long breath; she was feeling a little overcome. 'A houseful,' she went on awkwardly.

The general chaos and activity of her children went on round their mother without making much of an impact on the lady herself who, whenever Sarah was there – she was to come many times more – would usually be found on her chaise longue with her shawls, long pearl necklaces and Indian bangles clattering round her wrists, with the baby on her lap and a book on a side table.

Later, Dan took up Robin on his back and Effie led the way to her father's laboratory. They found Mr Barrington in a room at the back of the house, which gave out a strong chemical smell as Effie opened the door. It was a large room, well lit from high windows looking out towards the stables; in the middle stood a square table covered with glass dishes and bottles. Sarah made out a number of sea creatures inside. On another table under the window was a clutter of bottles, dishes, books and papers, and it was here that Mr Barrington had been working. He was in his waistcoat and shirtsleeves, and was rising from a high stool as they came in.

'Pa, you never ate your lunch,' Effie said sternly as she led the way.

He frowned. 'You know, now that I think of

it, I do feel rather peckish.'

'Well, tea is being served, so you had better come and have something now. Miss Shaw and Robin have come to see you.'

He was hastily rolling his sleeves down, and held out a hand to welcome them.

'I don't have to tell you, Miss Shaw, that Pa is inclined to be forgetful when he starts cutting up jellyfish.'

As they sat round the drawing room sipping tea and eating teacakes Chrissie appeared and Sarah was able to whisper that she had received her letter.

Alfred had been keeping Robin occupied, and during tea the two continued their conversation. After tea the boys insisted on taking Robin out to see their horses and Sarah found herself alone with Mrs Barrington. Silence descended.

'I love babies,' Mrs Barrington said after a moment in a dreamy voice as she dandled Octavius in her lap, teasing him and smiling into his face as the baby, looking about him with still unfocused eyes, gurgled and stretched in her arms. She sighed. 'I just go on having them,' and she rubbed noses with Octavius.

'You are lucky to have such children,' Sarah said softly after a moment.

'I am, aren't I?' Mrs Barrington agreed complacently.

For a moment they both admired Octavius, then out of nowhere Mrs Barrington said absently, 'And how do you get on with Mr

144

McMaster?'

Sarah looked up. 'Oh do you know him?'

'I know *of* him, of course. He is quite a celebrity in the town, you know. Besides, my brother is in the law and they meet sometimes. But the ladies have a grudge against him,' she said airily. 'He seems such an enemy of the fair sex – do you find?' She glanced innocently at Sarah.

Sarah did not know how to answer this.

'I know there are several girls in the town who have set their caps at him, but he seems quite impervious.' She glanced slyly again at Sarah, and raised her eyebrows. 'We're all quite curious about him. Have you ever seen...'

The question hung in the air.

'Seen?' Sarah was mystified.

The two women were looking at each other. It was clear that Sarah was not taking the hint so Mrs Barrington altered tack.

'Does he never have visitors?'

'Never.'

'And no sign of a – excuse me, but there are several women of my acquaintance who would be interested to know – no sign of—'

Sarah finally rose to the bait. 'Does he intend to marry, you mean?' she said prosaically. 'I have no idea. He never confides in me. Besides he spends more time in Liverpool than here.'

Mrs Barrington nodded. 'Ah, to be sure. Still, it is strange.' She looked away, speaking in a dreamy, speculative voice. 'One would have thought – after all, he is a very handsome man – don't you find?'

Again she gave Sarah a shrewd look.

'I suppose he is. To tell the truth I've never noticed.'

'Never noticed?'

Sarah felt herself tightening. 'To be honest with you, Mrs Barrington, I have not had time to think of such things.'

Mrs Barrington looked at her from beneath her eyelids with something between suspicion and understanding. 'Of course – you have your duties. Robin must occupy all your time. What a charming boy he is. And such a pity about his legs. He must feel it keenly.'

'He is very brave,' Sarah said quietly. 'He never complains.'

Sarah was rescued by the children, who erupted into the room and demanded that she come and inspect the fossil collection. She and Robin were led up into an attic, a long room, which had the appearance of a museum. Dan carried Robin.

'It *is* a museum,' Effie whispered to Sarah, reading her thoughts. Tables were set out with hundreds of specimens, many unrecognizable – fragments of grey or black rock. However when Mr Barrington offered her one or two to inspect she could distantly make out some evidence of life, a snail-like whorl — 'An ammonite,' he informed her enthusiastically. 'Frequently found in shales of the Lower Jurassic – plentiful down at Robin Hood's Bay and Ravenscar. We've had many a profitable afternoon down there, haven't we?' He glanced at Effie and Dan.

On one wall there was fixed up what looked like a crocodile. 'I'm rather proud of this one,' Mr Barrington confided in a low voice. 'A fossilized ichthyosaurus – a bit of a rarity,' he added modestly. He saw the puzzled look on Sarah's face and went on, 'A sea-water reptile.'

Robin, who was beside her, asked, 'A water dinosaur?'

Barrington beamed down warmly. 'Precisely!'

They stared up at this stone skeleton, which must have been nine or ten feet long. 'The alum miners found it down at Ravenscar. I bought it from them. They've found me a lot of specimens over the years.'

'Pa pays them well,' Effie commented drily.

'Look at his jaws!' Robin breathed.

'Shouldn't like to have met him, if you were out for a swim – eh?'

'I can't swim.'

Barrington did not hesitate and went on immediately, 'And neither can I! We'd both of us be in a pickle, wouldn't we?' He managed to tease a chuckle out of Robin and the moment was forgotten. But much later Sarah was to ask herself whether in fact Robin might be able to swim.

As they were coming downstairs again, Barrington announced, 'And this is the music room.' Sarah's head swung at this, and the door was opened. The room contained a

147

grand piano as well as a concert harp and also a small organ. 'Not much more than a harmonium, actually,' Barrington said apologetically. 'Though you don't have to pedal.'

'No,' Dan said, with a sigh.

Barrington laughed and ran his hand over Dan's head in a gesture that Sarah found very appealing. 'My son is usually so obliging as to pump for me.' He saw the interest with which Sarah had approached the instrument. 'Do you play?'

'A little.' She nodded.

'Would you care to—'

Sarah needed no second invitation. As she sat before the double keyboard she saw the volume of Bach voluntaries on the stand. She looked round at the row upon row of stops. Barrington obligingly leaned over and adjusted a few. Dan had started working the long wooden oar which projected at the back and as she laid her fingers on the keys, a chord sounded. She couldn't help smiling. Barrington was watching her.

'Rather splendid, isn't it – though inclined to give one delusions of grandeur!' He laughed.

The piece in front of her was not particularly difficult and ignoring the foot pedals she began to play. After a very few bars, the majesty of Bach began to work and she played on, forgetting the others.

As she finished she was slightly surprised to hear a small burst of applause. 'Bravo, Miss Shaw – you are too modest. At sight too!'

In the hall, he spoke quietly. 'This summer we are giving my daughter her coming-out ball. I wonder whether you would like to play for us?'

She nodded, almost embarrassed. 'If you think...'

As they were making their way home, swaying together in the little trap, Sarah ran that conversation with Mrs Barrington through her mind. There was something of the Queen Bee about her. Clearly she liked to keep her finger on the pulse of local gossip, but that she could consider Mr McMaster handsome – she was dumbfounded. The idea of women attempting to interest him: I must be very naive indeed, she thought, for the question has never crossed my mind. Thinking about it now, however, she realized that most women would find him good looking. There was a decided manly quality about him, for sure. He had a commanding presence, an incisive manner and a handsome figure. If a woman had known him only at a distance she might well consider him attractive.

She was full of conflicting feelings. There was something so rich, so full, about the life in that house, as if they were privileged beings to whom 'the earth and the fullness thereof' had been given. She felt her own life to be thin by comparison, only problems and mistakes. And to have so many brothers and sisters: it was hard to have to take Robin back to his cold, empty house.

Fifteen

Sarah had to go into town the following morning and on her return, to her surprise, she heard the piano. She listened in the hallway, loath to disturb him, and as she allowed herself gradually to appear at the door Robin glanced up and saw her.

'It has to sound as if it's playing itself,' he said seriously.

She relaxed and came forward. 'If it doesn't sound easy, you're not working hard enough. That was the first thing my teacher told me,' she said. They laughed, and she felt the tension ease.

For a moment they looked at each other again questioningly, then he went on, 'I watched you yesterday when you played that organ. And I wanted to play again. Do you think, one day, Mr Barrington might let me play it?'

'Of course,' she said casually and sat beside him. 'By the way, I had a letter from your father this morning. He's coming home tomorrow.'

Robin whispered to her fiercely, 'You're to say nothing! Promise!' His body was tensing, his knuckles tightening on the edge of the keyboard.

'It's all right, Robin,' she said soothingly.

'Promise!' His face was blazing up at her.

'I promise,' she said at last.

Mr McMaster arrived on a breezy April after-noon. The clouds were high in the sky and the windows stood open. Mrs Hudson had been spring cleaning against his return and there was a feeling of freshness and renewal in the house.

Sarah had thought it might be a good idea to have Robin brought down to the drawing room instead of leaving him isolated in his nursery, so as McMaster came into the room, he was waiting, seated in an armchair.

'Robin!' He stopped, embarrassed for a second. The boy looked up at him, timid, expectant, his large eyes seeming to fill his thin little face. Sarah could sense his trembling expectation. 'Well! I haven't forgotten you.' He glanced round. 'Josiah! Those things in the trap – bring them in!'

Josiah appeared with several packages and the boy found himself suddenly with his lap filled. The three adults stood round him, dwarfed in the big old wing-backed armchair.

'But it's not my birthday,' he faltered, look-ing up again at his father.

'Never mind!' There was something a little forced about McMaster's laugh, thought Sarah, as she watched them with painful concentration.

Robin opened the first package, which contained three new books, with their covers

151

fresh in gold leaf. He turned one over and made out the title. *'The Swiss Family Robinson.'*

'That was a favourite of mine when I was your age.'

Robin glanced timidly up, then turned over the next. *'The Coral Island.* And *Masterman Ready.* Thank you, Papa.'

There was an embarrassed hiatus, which Sarah hastened to fill. 'We'll read them together. We can start tonight! What lovely books!'

'And – ' McMaster, who was in an uncharacteristically expansive mood, swept his arm – 'what have we here?' He took up another package. 'I wonder what you'll make of this?'

Robin tore open the wrapping paper. Inside he found a ship in a bottle. His jaw actually dropped as he examined this miracle of ingenuity, and he took some time to turn it over in his hands, examining the marvellous intricacy of the masts and rigging, the sails fully spread. 'But how—'

McMaster chuckled. 'That's a secret!'

Robin unwrapped a jigsaw puzzle, and a model yacht, completely rigged. He seemed quite overcome, and could only gasp, 'Thank you, Papa.'

McMaster, who had not actually touched his son throughout this scene, only nodded and smiled, and muttered, 'You're a good boy, I know.'

After Robin had returned to his nursery, his

new things carried up with him, Sarah tried to fathom what had happened. Not much, was her verdict. She had never seen a lamer scene between a father and his son; the proceedings had been forced and unnatural. McMaster was trying to make a gesture of sorts, that was clear, and Robin for his part was waiting for a gesture from his father. But the signals had been all wrong. Obviously he had been feeling guilty after the terrible night in January when he was on the verge of murder.

Later he questioned her about Robin and she gave him a report on his progress in reading and writing. A little arithmetic had been attempted and a few words of French. No mention was made of the piano. Robin was fully recovered from his pneumonia and she had been able to take him out often for walks along the cliff. She also mentioned the Barrington family and their lessons on the foreshore. McMaster knew the name.

'Ah yes, the marine biologist. I believe he has been proposed for the Royal Society. A brilliant man. A pity he has not done more with his life.'

She was taken aback by this. 'Done more?'

'A man with his gifts has no right to shut himself away.'

'Mr McMaster,' she stuttered, astonished by his words, 'Mr Barrington, apart from his studies, has been educating his children. Surely—'

He nodded and gave her one of his sardonic smiles. 'I should expect a woman to come to his defence.'

Sarah stiffened. 'He has no need of my defence, Mr McMaster. I think what he is doing is splendid. I cannot imagine anything a man might be more proud of than to educate his children. He has eight children, and from what I can make out they are all a credit to him—'

She stopped abruptly, conscious of what she was saying and for a moment they stared one another in the face. At last McMaster, looking grave, turned away. 'As you say – a credit to him.'

'Mr McMaster – last week Mr Barrington invited Robin and me to see his fossil collection. Have you any objection to such a visit?'

Without turning back, he waved his hand. 'Do as you like,' and he disappeared into his study. Her heart beating, Sarah went into the drawing room and walked back and forth for several minutes, biting her lip as she tried to arrange her thoughts. Of all the tactless things to say; but then, he had provoked it by his supercilious dismissal of Mr Barrington's achievements. Obviously Mr McMaster was used to going out into the world and doing battle with judges and criminals; a gentle scholarly man like Mr Barrington must seem very tame. But at least Mr Barrington did not neglect and ignore his own son. And as she grew angry the phrase returned to her – 'a credit to him'. Why shouldn't Robin be a credit to his father? He *would* be a credit – she would make him a credit – she would force

McMaster to acknowledge the excellence of his own son.

Under the impetus of this thought she was taking the stairs two at a time, but as she reached the landing, she cooled a little. It would take cunning. McMaster was clever; she had to be clever too.

Later a message from Jenny informed her that Mr McMaster expected her to dine with him that evening. As she was arranging her hair at the mirror, she pondered on this brusque command and suddenly smiled as a thought crossed her mind: If only Mrs Barrington could see. Sarah couldn't help smiling again at the thought of that lady agog for gossip and shook her head as she thought of the two of them: If only you knew. The 'handsome Mr McMaster'! A more appropriate phrase might be 'ungracious boor'. A man who could not even take the trouble to come in person to invite a lady to dine but sent a message by his servant.

She opened her wardrobe and surveyed her meagre array of dresses. Well, at least she did have one new gown, and it was the first opportunity she had had of wearing it. She pulled it out and laid it on the bed. She had had it made up by a dressmaker in Whitby: a figured silk in a rich deep blue, which complemented her pale complexion and red hair – she hoped. She had also indulged herself with an Indian shawl. After her visit to the Barringtons' a small voice within her had protested, 'Why shouldn't I have one too?' and on her next walk into town she had bought herself one. Among its rich tones was a blue which she hoped would match the blue of her dress. She had also bought a pair of evening slippers – though ordinarily she was reluctant to spend money on such things, partly because she calculated that uncertain as her future was it would be prudent to save all the money she could, and partly because buying things seemed a sort of pledge, as if she were planning to settle down in West Cliff House, whereas who knew but next week Mr McMaster might take it into his head to employ a tutor for his son and she would find herself in the road with a case full of clothes.

For all her preparations in front of the mirror, she might have saved herself the trouble; McMaster did not appear to notice her dress at all. Having digested this as she settled into her chair, she adjusted the shawl behind her and was free to study him at leisure. He was firing questions at her – about Robin, his progress, his health, his education – which she parried inconsequentially; her mind was elsewhere.

Was he handsome? She supposed he was; seen from a distance, as it were. He needs to smile more, she thought, he needs to laugh. If he could unbend a little, it was true, he might be quite attractive. So, apropos of nothing, she said coolly, 'This will never do, you know.'

He was brought up sharply and frowned.

'What do you mean?' he asked uncertainly.

'I mean, Mr McMaster, that since I walked into the room, you have been firing questions at me and have entirely failed to notice my new dress.'

She smiled, and then laughed outright at the look of amazement on his face. But her laughter died as she now saw his utter mortification. He was awkward in the extreme.

'I beg your pardon,' he stuttered. 'My mind was preoccupied. But now you draw my attention to it – stand up, Miss Shaw, let me look at you.'

She did as he commanded and turned for him in the middle of the room, allowing the fullness of the skirt to bloom. She stopped, smiling at him, willing him to relax. He could not and she still perceived his embarrassment. 'Very elegant – most becoming,' was all he could manage at last.

There was a long silence as she took her seat again and rearranged her shawl. The experiment had been a failure. Well, Mrs Barrington and her friends were welcome to him, but they would have an uphill task. 'An enemy of the fair sex' – it seemed a reasonable assessment. And for the first time since she had known him, she felt a shadow of vexation. She had tried to provoke him, to coquette with him – and it had been a failure; in spite of herself, her vanity was piqued.

After dinner, as she had expected, he asked her to play. She was feeling in no very gracious mood, but did as she was commanded and opened the book that stood on the music stand. It was a collection of Chopin's *Nocturnes*, which she had recently bought. They're restful, she thought cynically; after his dinner, they'll probably lull him to sleep. Without consulting him, or even looking in his direction, she turned the pages to the one she had been practising and, settling the book straight, began to play.

Even so, for all her irritation with herself and him, she was soon caught up by the sheer lyrical beauty of the music. The poignancy, the pathos, the feeling of loss which Chopin expressed so intensely moved her in spite of herself and she was completely unconscious of McMaster, unconscious of the room, unconscious of everything except the touch of her fingers on the keys. What was it about Chopin? she wondered at last as she finished playing. Filled with a sense of achievement and at rest, she stared down at her hands on the keys.

At last she glanced up at McMaster and was jolted back to where she was. He had been seated by the fire with his coffee cup when she began, the dog at his feet. Now he was leaning forward, one elbow on his knee, his head turned away from her with his other hand across his face. Sam had half risen and was looking up at him.

She watched him across the room, unable to move, as if the breath had been knocked out of her body.

He was silent, but she was suddenly aware

of a shudder across his shoulders and he appeared to wipe his hand across his eyes and moved slightly, though still not looking in her direction. There was a long silence, in which neither moved.

At last she managed to whisper, 'Are you all right?'

Without looking up he nodded briefly, then a moment later raised his head and drew a shattering sigh.

'Forgive me – it was that melody. I hadn't heard it since—' He gestured with his other hand and said no more. A moment later he spoke again. 'Stupid of me.' His voice was low, unsteady. 'I should be stronger – after all this time—'

Instinctively she rose and made a step towards him. 'What is the matter?' she began hesitantly. 'Can you not tell me?'

He shook his head, still with his back to her, and drew another sigh. 'It is not your fault. Thank you, you played beautifully. But you can have no idea.' He stood up, made for the door, and a moment later was gone.

For minutes it seemed she continued to stare sightlessly after him. It was a grief she had never encountered before, an intensity with which she was wholly unacquainted.

The worst part was that he was so remote, so alone; it had been almost impossible for her to approach him or to offer any consolation. Poor man! She looked up, as if searching for him through the house – he seemed utterly destroyed.

Sixteen

It was long before she slept – and poor man, she wondered as she lay in the darkness, was he sleeping at all?

In the morning she dragged herself out of bed, dressed as best she could and went in to see to Robin. As they ate their breakfast, she wondered – was it connected with him? Some disappointment connected with his birth? And what about his mother? Had they been married – or was Robin a by-blow, the product of an illicit union? And where was the mother now? Was she still alive? Was she prevented from seeing her son? For all she knew there was a woman living somewhere in the country – or abroad perhaps – pining for him. Or was it the other way round? Had the mother disowned her crippled son – some frivolous beauty, an actress perhaps? Or a titled lady, terrified of the shame? Was the mother even still alive? What if McMaster had been responsible for her death? Perhaps the music had triggered a guilty memory?

Fortunately she had little time for these improbable speculations since Robin demanded all her attention, and she was ashamed of herself for entertaining them – until she remembered the night when she had struggled with McMaster over Robin's bed. A man capable of smothering his own son...

She remained upstairs with Robin throughout the morning, and fortunately Mr McMaster seemed to be occupied elsewhere – she did not enquire. He was very unlikely to want to see her.

That afternoon, however, as she was going downstairs he came out of his study. He stopped. His back was to the light and she could not make out his face very well.

'Miss Shaw,' he said gravely, 'I fear I owe you an apology.'

She waited; he was clearly ill at ease. 'Last night – I should be grateful if you would forget – attempt to forget – what you saw. It was something I – that is – something which took me by surprise.' He rallied himself. 'Something I had hoped to forget. But I had no right to inflict it on you. I apologize,' he repeated.

She was not to be fobbed off by this.

'First of all, sir, there is nothing for you to apologize for or feel ashamed of in any way. I am only sorry that I was unable to be of any comfort.'

They stared at each other. He frowned; it was as if she was rebuking him for not explaining himself. 'Comfort?'

'I could not bear to see you so alone,' she said simply.

'Ah,' he said shortly, and then after another moment, as if he was now anxious to escape,

'I can rely on your discretion to say nothing of this, to anyone?'

'Of course, if you wish.'

'I do.' He was firmer now, as if regaining his usual commanding position. 'Thank you,' he said briefly, and turned into his room.

Annoyed with herself, she went into the drawing room and stood a long time staring out of the window. For one moment he had been exposed and there had been the chance to get him to speak, to explain what it was that had upset him so badly. But it had slipped past and she had allowed him to retreat again into his shell.

A week later he went away again, she was left with Robin, and life went on as before. Lessons continued, piano practice, and another visit was made to the 'Casa Barrington'. This name puzzled her at first, but its significance was made clear at the *conversazione* (another word whose meaning was not clear) to which she and Robin were invited some weeks later and which turned out to be a garden party. It was early June and the Barringtons' garden was in rich, full leaf. Sarah was not sure whether she was there in her own right, or as Robin's governess; in the event, Robin was carried off immediately by Dan and the other children and Mrs Barrington – who had for this occasion risen from her chaise longue – took her arm, secured it snugly beneath her own and conducted her into the drawing room to show off her collection of paintings. At first Sarah feared she was in for another cross-questioning on the subject of her employer, but for the moment she was safe.

It turned out that Mrs Barrington fancied herself an Italophile; she spoke the language, and the previous summer there had been a trip to Florence. The trip accounted for the many small paintings Sarah had noticed on the wall.

'The *quattrocento*,' Mrs Barrington enunciated as she gave Sarah a tour of the collection: 'The Golden Age of Italian art! This one is a Filippo Lippi – charming, don't you think? And that one a Benozzo Gozzoli – an Annunciation. You haven't had the chance to visit Italy? *Poverina!*' She tinkled a laugh then drew an aesthete's sigh, squeezing Sarah's arm. 'One has to see Florence to appreciate them. One has to *know* Florence. *Firenze!* We were the guests of the Count Ladispoli – between ourselves, my dear, he hadn't two pennies to rub together and was only too glad to lease the palazzo; it was a revelation! Not a *stick* of furniture had been moved since the Renaissance – one fancied oneself in the world of Lorenzo dei Medici, of Leonardo, of Michelangelo – every *stone* had a tale to tell. And the countryside! We took excursions everywhere – through the hills, past old castles, through olive groves and vineyards; ah, the smell of the hot grass in the summer sun, the sound of the cicadas, the glimpses of Florence from the hilltops – that incomparable city! Here, alas,' she sighed as she glanced round at her collection and shook her head sadly, 'in our foggy climate they seem a little lost.'

'Did you take your children to Italy?' Sarah asked innocently.

'Of course! Do you think I could leave my pretty lambs behind? Never! We all went – though this was before the birth of Octavius.' She leaned in to Sarah and smiled confidentially. 'In fact, I'll let you into a secret, my dear – Octavius was *conceived* in Italy. He's my Italian baby!'

Soon afterwards other guests demanded her attention and Sarah found herself free to wander through the garden, nodding politely to complete strangers, whom she took to be the cream of Whitby society, until eventually she found herself before a goldfish pond, where she glimpsed Chrissie in earnest conversation with a slim young man. She was about to turn away when Chrissie noticed her and moved immediately in her direction.

'Miss Shaw – don't go. We didn't have a chance to talk the last time you were here – Mamma collared you. But I – ' she coughed – 'I should like you to meet Mr James.' She nodded in a knowing way as Sarah performed a curtsy and he bowed. 'We don't like to be seen too much together – as I told you,' Chrissie went on in a low voice, 'because it's still secret, but I did so much want you to meet.'

'Delighted,' Sarah smiled. 'Your secret is

164

safe with me.'

The young man was little more than a boy, she thought, as she watched him smooth down his wispy moustaches, pat his hair into place and smirk at her. Looking him over, she remembered: this is the man who very nearly ruined Chrissie. Why should I be nice to him? The girl was ready to give him *everything* – and he was ready to take it. It was the purest luck that she had been able to warn her in time. She listened for a while as he prattled – for he was very ready to talk and seemed full of himself – dismissing the little misunderstanding at Christmas almost as if it had happened to someone else and it hadn't been him at all who had been on the brink of seducing Chrissie.

But after a moment Chrissie, who had been hovering in the conversation all the time glancing about her nervously, whispered to the boy and with a bow he took himself off. As soon as he was gone she closed in on Sarah.

'What do you think?' Her face was screwed up in anxiety as she examined Sarah's for a verdict.

'He seems a gentleman,' was all Sarah could think of for the moment.

'Oh he is! He is! The most perfect gentleman. We don't like to be seen too much together in public, you understand, because it's still secret—'

'I understand.' Sarah wanted to get off this subject, which was becoming tedious. 'Your mother has been telling me about your visit to Italy. How did you like it?'

'Oh, I adored it! Florence was so beautiful! So old, as if every stone had been there for ever. Mamma was very tiresome, though, I don't have to tell you. She would insist on trying to speak Italian and she can't. It was very embarrassing; and she made up to all these old Italian counts and princes; I think they laughed at her behind her back – and they sold her all those pictures. Told her they were priceless old masters.'

'Aren't they?'

Chrissie shrugged and made a face.

'Did your father enjoy it?'

'Not sure. To be honest—' She took Sarah's arm and turned her away from the crowd of other guests who moved about them so that they were strolling beside the pond. 'To be honest, I don't think he liked the way Mamma was so intimate with Count Ladispoli. It was perfectly scandalous the way she flirted with him.'

'You astonish me.'

'It was very embarrassing. She would send Papa and us out to inspect churches while she went off with the count for a drive in our carriage. She would make up some excuse that the count had a new picture to show her. But you know Papa. He always makes the best of things and he so wanted us to enjoy the trip. He made up for it – to us, I mean.'

'Your father is a lovely man. I sometimes wish ... I shouldn't say this, perhaps. I sometimes wish Robin could have had such a kind father.'

'Oh – you mean...'

'It's hard for him. It's the one thing he desires in all the world.' She burst out, 'He only wants his father to love him!' Chrissie did not reply, and Sarah went on, 'I know I shouldn't be talking like this and you may not be able to understand what I am trying to say. But you are the only woman in the world at the moment to whom I can say it.'

Chrissie squeezed her arm and a moment later she continued, 'I can't explain it very well; I know he has feelings, and I think he wants to love his son – but for some reason, he isn't able to express it. His feelings are all locked up,' she finished helplessly.

Throughout the afternoon Robin had been with the children. As he was being stowed in the trap for the journey home, however, he exclaimed, 'Mr Barrington is going to give a lecture!'

Effie explained, 'Pa's giving a talk to the Literary and Philosophical Society.'

'About his fossils. It's the twenty-seventh of next month,' Dan added drily, leaning on the edge of the trap. 'In the Angel. I think he'd appreciate your support. He gets very nervous in front of an audience.'

'I don't know whether Mr McMaster will be home by then,' Sarah said doubtfully. 'Though I'm sure he would be interested,'

'Don't be such a dunce. It's you who are

invited!' Effie exploded. 'Didn't you hear what Dan said? Pa needs all the support he can get!'

'I don't understand.'

'Father's not very popular in certain quarters.'

'He wrote an article in the newspaper about his fossils,' Effie burst in, 'and was attacked for it.'

'*Really?* Your father? What did he say?'

'Oh, I don't know,' Dan went on, 'but Mr Hayes wrote a letter in reply and called him ungodly and impious and all sorts of things.'

'*Fossils?*' The two children nodded vigorously. 'But how—'

'Anyway, you've got to come and give him moral support.'

'If I can get away I certainly will come,' Sarah was still puzzled by this little explosion. 'And I will tell Mr McMaster.'

There was an unexpected sequel to this outing. One afternoon a few days later, while Robin was taking his nap, Sarah walked into town with Josiah. He had been sent on an errand by Mrs Hudson, and Sarah had one or two of her own to perform. Josiah was a big man, but gentle too; he spoke little and probably was easily led, she thought. In a word, he was relaxing to be with, and it was a pleasure to stroll along the quay with him among the busy life of the fishing port. It was a summer afternoon, the sun was bright, and she had on her one and only summer muslin frock, and a pretty straw hat she had recently allowed herself. They crossed the bridge and were turning into Church Street towards the fish market, when they were accosted by a small man stumping along energetically on a wooden leg.

He was dressed in black and wore a low crowned broad brimmed hat such as clergy sometimes wore. His beard, cut in a spade shape without moustaches, jutted forward and added to his terrier-like, pugnacious manner.

'Brother Barnby!'

It took Sarah a moment to realize that it was Josiah he was addressing; she had never before heard his surname. She looked down at the little man in front of her and for a moment was slightly amused. She quickly noticed though that Josiah was more respectful.

'Brother Hayes,' he faltered.

'Brother Barnby, tha' wert looked for.' The other fixed him with a bright eye.

Josiah was clutching his hands together. Josiah was a big man: strong, broad shouldered, and brave too as she had noticed on a couple of occasions. At this moment he was visibly in awe of the minister.

'Tha'st not been as zealous in t'Lord's service as tha might be, Brother. Tha wert missed a' Sunday; tha wert prayed for – that thee *back-slidin'* might amend.'

Josiah was stricken. 'I explained to Mrs Hudson – there were a reason, Brother—'

169

'A *reason?*' Mr Hayes snorted with contempt. 'A reason for not observin' Lord's Day?'

Josiah was clutching and unclutching his hat which he had unconsciously taken off and was moulding in his hands. 'I explained to Mrs Hudson,' he repeated.

'I suspect there may be other temptations, brother.' The Reverend Hayes, who was perpetually wound up for battle, posturing like a prize fighter, cast a ferocious eye on Sarah. 'I suspect tha'st felt temptations of t'flesh – that tha'st been led astray from true path into ways of dalliance.'

'I assure thee, Brother—' Josiah was more distressed than ever. But Mr Hayes now cast his eye on Sarah.

'Led astray b'the lightness of women, p'rhaps—' he flashed his bright little eyes on her.

At this moment Sarah understood what had happened.

'As a matter of fact, the fault is mine. Or to be precise—'

'The fault is thine?' He glared sharply at her.

'Yes,' she went on calmly, 'my master's son was invited to a garden party on Sunday and I asked Josiah to drive us. I am afraid I completely forgot—'

'A *garden party?* On t'Lord's day? Brother Barnby, can I believe my ears?'

Sarah ignored him and turned to Josiah in his distress. 'Josiah, I am most deeply sorry to have caused you this trouble. I cannot think how I could have forgotten.' She turned again to the minister. 'You have my assurance, sir, Mr Barnby is blameless in this matter. I shall take better care in future. Good afternoon,' she finished loudly and made to set forward.

The minister was not going to let them get away so lightly. 'Next Sunday, Brother. There is a heavy load of sin on thee conscience. T'congregation will pray for thee.'

'I'll not fail, Brother Hayes, I'll be there,' Josiah hastily assured him as he turned away.

There was a moment as they both drew a sigh of relief, then Sarah turned to Josiah again. 'Why on earth did you not remind me of your meeting?'

Josiah looked uncomfortable. 'It's not my place, Miss Shaw. Master Robin were invited to Mr Barrington's—'

'But you always go to your meeting on Sunday. You could have mentioned it. You know Mr McMaster lets you go. Didn't Mrs Hudson remind you?'

'Mrs Hudson did remind me, and I give her a message to carry t'meeting. I knaw Mr McMaster would have excused me – but you see, knawin' Master Robin were that set on goin' t'Barringtons', I didn't like to say anythin'.'

She was silent for a moment, as they made their way along the narrow cobbled street, then she turned again. 'Well, I think it was very kind of you – and I'm only sorry you have got into trouble with Mr Hayes.'

They were silent for a moment, then she changed the subject. 'How did he come by his wooden leg?'

'Oh, he often talks of it. In his younger days he were a seaman, a whaler, and made many a voyage in Greenland waters. Well, one day he were on this ice floe and somehow slipped, and his leg were crushed as the floes drove into each other.' He walked on for a moment. 'Brother Hayes took it for a sign of God's displeasure; and from that time forth his sinful life of cussin' and drinkin' begun to weigh on his soul. And when he come ashore he thanked God that He had vouchsafed him a sign to amend his sinful ways; that He had called him to a life of repentance. And so he took up his holy callin'. I never knew of him meself till Mrs Hudson called me to join his holy band. And ever syne I've striven to make meself worthy.'

Seventeen

In July, Mr McMaster returned for the long summer vacation. Sarah foolishly imagined that this meant a holiday; it was soon clear, however, from the bags and bags of papers, the boxes and the bundles of documents bound in red tape she glimpsed on his desk that this was far from the case.

He questioned her about Robin as usual in his barrister's way, then dismissed the subject and returned to his work. They saw little of each other from day to day; he still asked her to play for him but there was no repetition of the scene she had witnessed after the Chopin. Even so she found herself thinking of him much more. She would often find herself running scenes through her mind, searching for some clue to his behaviour.

One day she woke when the house was still silent, before even Mrs Hudson was stirring. She drew back the curtains; it was a glorious early morning, the garden was fresh with dew and the sun was already bright in preparation for a hot day. Feeling energetic, she dressed hurriedly and went for a walk along the cliffs. She called Sam, but he was not to be found. This puzzled her; Josiah had risen even earlier than she had, perhaps, and had taken the dog out already.

She set off westwards away from the town and was content simply to breathe the clean fresh air, with its salty tang, and to feel the breeze on her cheek. She had not even put on her bonnet and she released the ribbon from her hair so that it blew freely about her head. It was wonderful to be alone, to enjoy the peace of the early morning, to hear the gulls, and to watch in the distance a fleet of red-sailed fishing boats on their way into harbour after their night's work. The gorse on the steep slope down to the beach was now brilliant with yellow bloom, and rabbits scuttled suddenly between the clumps.

She had turned back towards the house when she heard Sam's bark and glancing down saw him on the sand, prancing about and dashing up and down in an ecstasy of enjoyment as the long rollers crashed on the beach. As she watched, she saw Mr Mc-Master emerge from the sea, fighting his way clear of the breakers and making for a pile of clothes on a rock. He was naked. She would have turned away but for one frozen moment found she couldn't. It wasn't simply that she was taken by surprise; the sight of him triggered something in her which she understood only too well and she found herself staring at him in a way which, when she did regain control of herself, made her blush.

She wrenched her eyes away and after a moment, as she attempted to recover her

174

breath, tried to laugh it off, or, since she couldn't do that – she had never felt less like laughing in her life – tried at least to get her thoughts in order. 'No wonder the women gossip about him. I wonder half the female population of the town isn't up here...'

What was worse was that he had seen her and must have seen how she had remained frozen to the spot. What must he have thought? It was too far to make out his expression but she could imagine his sardonic smile only too easily.

Long after she had returned to the house, the sight remained imprinted on her retina so that she seemed to see him everywhere she looked. She tried to rationalize it away; she had seen other naked men – she had seen George in his bath – but for the rest of the day she could not escape the memory, which would insist on popping most inappropriately into her thoughts.

She found that evening that although she was making strenuous attempts to forget what she had seen, he was equally determined not to let her. He was in a strange mood as they sat down to dinner; this was itself out of the ordinary but she did not at first make the connection, which dawned on her only gradually as they talked.

'You were not wearing your bonnet this morning,' he remarked casually as he took up the bread roll on his side plate and broke it.

'No,' she said innocently. 'It was such a

glorious morning, and the path was quite deserted. I thought I might be forgiven for once. I hope you do not think I was acting improperly,' she added with a hint of sarcasm.

'Ah, but I do,' he went on, spreading a little butter on his roll. 'You should take more care of your health. To be sure, there was no one about; that is not the point. To go out with your head uncovered could be dangerous. You were exposing yourself to a chill morning breeze. Who knows what might have come of it?'

She thought he was making rather heavy weather of this and was embarrassed that he was referring so casually to their meeting, so she replied more severely than she might otherwise have done. 'First of all, the breeze was very light and by no means chilly. And secondly, I promise you, my health is more robust than you think.'

'Nevertheless,' he continued in this serious tone, 'I don't like to think of you exposing yourself like that. You should not go out with any part of yourself uncovered. The human body is not meant to be uncovered; Man has been wearing clothes since the earliest times. For example,' he went on, warming to his theme, 'suppose it had come on to rain? You would have got your head wet. And in such a flimsy frock, too. You might have caught a chill. If you get your body wet and are exposed to a sea breeze, the consequences can be severe.'

She stared into his face. Unless she was dreaming, Mr McMaster was teasing her. He bit unconcernedly into his roll, while she could feel a warmth in her cheek as she tried to stand up for herself. 'There was not the slightest possibility of my getting wet,' she said as severely as she could.

'Ah, but that was because you were up on the cliff.' He gestured with the roll. He was making very great play with this innocent piece of bread. 'But what if you had come down to the water's edge? Suppose you had taken your morning stroll along the seashore instead of on top of the cliffs – what then? You might have got wet. And think of the consequences. If you had been down by the sea this morning who knows what might have developed?'

She held his look hard and could feel her heart thudding. She ran her tongue over her lips. 'It was lucky for me, then, that I was up on the cliffs,' she croaked at last, and was rescued at that moment by the soup.

She seemed unable to escape him; everywhere she turned he was there, looming before her, larger than her, shutting out the light. She could no longer turn away from him and if she did so, he was there again. She closed her eyes to shut him out; she opened them, and he was there. She went to bed with him at night; she woke up with him in the morning. She thought, I am drowning. If I don't do something soon, I shall fall in love

177

with him.

That night she dreamed of him, a dream that when she remembered it in the morning – and she remembered it exactly – made her blush. How could she have such thoughts? She had been walking along the shore, just as he had hinted, as the waves rolled in, in their long lazy way, to crash onto the sand. She was wearing only her summer frock, which in the dream was very flimsy, when she saw him before her on the shore, the waves breaking at his feet. He was naked. They were moving towards each other, floating effortlessly in a dreamlike way, and she was conscious of his nakedness, taking it in, absorbing the sense of his physical presence, as if she had never really looked at him before, never been aware of him before. She was conscious of him now a thousand times more intensely than when she had seen him in the morning. They moved towards each other until they were facing one another; she could scarcely bear it, she was trembling, it was insupportable, her body heavy with desire, as he took her in his arms. Her dress simply dissolved about her, so that they were naked together and he was carrying her into the sea. In her dream she had no fear of drowning; they were somehow dissolving, swirling together in the heavy weight and thrust of the long rollers, lifting and washing together as the water foamed and thrashed about her and she herself was dissolving and could feel herself being swallowed up, annihilated in his greater being.

When she awoke suddenly she was hot and sweating, her body suffused with desire, her breathing quick. She threw herself back on the pillow as the intensity of the dream still surged through her.

What is the matter with me? she asked herself at last as the feeling subsided. This is madness.

Later, as she managed to drag herself heavily out of bed and wash herself, she tried to introduce some order into her thoughts.

I shall have to leave this house – she had long since got over her early panic, the terror in which she had fled her home – I must return; somehow I must go back to confront George and sort out my future.

At last she attempted to take her mind off herself. I am losing sight of the important thing, which is Robin. I am not important. The question is: what to do about Robin? So long as Mr McMaster is in the house, Robin will not open the piano. This cannot continue – he is too good a player to lose so much time. His father is going to be in the house for months to come; I have to find a way to break down his fear.

Fortunately McMaster always went out during the afternoon, for a walk, into town or on some other business. She decided to persuade Robin to resume his practice during these hours.

He needed a lot of persuading. At first he flatly refused. 'But he might come in. I'm not

179

ready!'

This was an important admission, she noticed immediately. It seemed Robin could at least imagine a time when he might play before his father.

'Well, I simply can't let you stop practising for three solid months. Your father won't be going away again till October; it's too long. You have been making such good progress; it's essential to practise regularly. Little and often is the golden rule.'

Robin looked worried. 'Only so long as you're sure.'

'Don't worry. In fact now I think about it, he told me he was going to London to see a client next week. He'll be away for days. Look, he's out now: let's take a look at this. I wonder whether you'd be up to it?'

She called Josiah, who carried Robin down to the drawing room. Opening the book, a Beethoven sonatina, she set it up on the music stand. Robin studied the first few bars, and before he knew it was trying out the chords in the left hand.

Every afternoon that week he worked while McMaster was out; then the following week, after his father had departed for London, they worked together for hours at a time until he began to feel confident in the piece.

She never knew afterwards whether it had been by accident or design, but as they were seated side by side at the keyboard one afternoon she glimpsed far off along the cliff path Josiah in the trap and a figure with him.

180

McMaster was returning early.

'Start again from the top,' she remarked casually. 'I'm just going upstairs for a hand-kerchief.' But instead of going upstairs she waited by the door and a moment later Mc-Master himself appeared. She held her finger to her lips, and beckoned to him.

By pure chance Robin had hesitated for a moment as he studied the notes, but a moment later, as McMaster was looking at Sarah with a puzzled expression and was about to speak, she darted forward, put her hand on his arm and motioned him to silence again.

At that moment Robin began the sonatina again from the beginning. McMaster's head shot round and he was about to speak, but she placed her hand quickly over his mouth. 'Listen!' she whispered.

Overawed by her insistence, he stood there silent as the music continued. Robin played through to the end of the piece and a moment later she heard him call, 'Sarah!'

She had never seen McMaster so stunned; after a moment, he gestured faintly – 'Who was that?'

She motioned him again to silence. 'Wait here. And listen.'

She went back into the drawing room, stuffing a little handkerchief into her sleeve, and took her place beside Robin.

'That was much better. Now let's see. Take it again from here; and remember it is a waltz. Let it lilt...'

As he began to play she saw McMaster

appear in the doorway, watching silently, rigid with concentration.

And after a moment as Robin paused again, she said lightly, 'You are really coming on. I think you'll soon be ready to let your father hear you.'

'No!' Robin jerked round. 'No, Sarah, not yet! I know what he'll say, I know it.'

'He'll be proud of you. Really!'

'He won't! Don't say that! It's a lie; I don't want him to hear me!'

'But why?'

'You know very well why. He's ashamed of me! He'll only laugh or say something rude!'

McMaster stood in the doorway. She gestured him back.

'Anyway, that's enough for today,' she said briskly.

'Ashamed of him?' McMaster whispered. They were in the drawing room after Josiah had carried Robin upstairs. He seemed haunted by what he had seen. 'He thinks I'm ashamed of him?'

Sarah was silent as he groped for words. 'How long – how long have you been teaching him?'

'Since January. After you went away.'

'Since January?' he echoed. 'Six months? He has made astonishing progress. Why did you not tell me before?'

'It was by Robin's wish.'

McMaster was silent, his whole body rigid with thought. He looked up at her again,

182

searching her face. 'Because he thought I would be ashamed of him?'

She did not reply and he turned away across the room and stood for a long moment in silence staring out of the window. At last he turned back, a haunted look in his eyes.

'What must you think of me, Miss Shaw? My own son, afraid of his father?' He raised his hands only to let them drop again. She still could find nothing to say. 'Yet,' he went on in a faraway voice, 'he played beautifully, quite beautifully. And in six months.' He turned again, still full of conflicting thoughts.

'Mr McMaster – if you speak to him,' she hesitated, 'you will be careful, won't you? You heard what he said.'

Looking at him, she had the impression that he did not know what to do. She had never seen a man so helpless.

'Be careful?'

'Don't mention the piano – yet.'

He nodded, taking his cue from her. There was another awkward hiatus.

'Perhaps if you were to go up now – he's having his tea.'

He seized on this idea; she followed him up. Robin jerked his head up as his father entered the room and Sarah saw the apprehension in his eyes; she saw too that McMaster had seen it.

'Papa?'

McMaster sat at the table with him. 'Jenny – won't you bring another cup? And bring one for Miss Shaw too.'

'Are you having tea with me, Papa?'

McMaster smiled awkwardly and ran his hand over his son's head. 'Why not? Let's have tea, all three of us together, eh? Would you like that?'

'Oh yes, Papa!'

After Robin had been put to bed his father reappeared in the room. 'Now let's see. We must have a bedtime story, mustn't we?'

'Sarah always tells me a story.'

'Does she?' He glanced at her.

'But I'd much rather you read to me!' He turned over several books that lay scattered on the counterpane, and Sarah let herself out quietly.

She waited for him in the dining room. She waited a long time and then, going to the door and looking up the stairs, she heard McMaster's voice and then Robin's bursting into a peal of childish laughter. She turned into the dining room again and looked out over the lawn as the evening shadows slowly lengthened. She was full of thoughts.

McMaster appeared at the door. He was full of energy.

'I'm sorry to have kept you so long. You must be famished.' He rang the little bell which stood on the table. 'Sit, Miss Shaw, sit.' He gestured to her chair and looked across to her as he shook out his napkin. 'You are a sly one,' he murmured.

She looked up.

'Yes. To think, all these months you have been coaching him. Yet you never said a word to me.'

She was uncomfortable. 'As I said, sir, it was by his wish. I was going to tell you eventually, of course. When I thought he had gained sufficient confidence. You yourself are so naturally confident, you perhaps cannot understand...' She let the sentence hang in the air.

He was silent and at last looked up at her from beneath his brows. 'Naturally confident? You mean, you consider me an overbearing bully?'

'No!'

He chuckled. 'But you are right.' He paused. 'It comes of being an only son, you know.' He became serious. 'But it is a lesson that I must learn, I see now.'

He reached into an inside pocket, took out a folded paper and passed it across to her. She opened it and saw that it was a cheque. A generous one.

'Not so long ago, you reprimanded me for my blindness,' he said before she had a chance to speak.

'What do you mean?'

'Oh –' he adopted an airy tone, looking away as he strove to recall the words – 'I remember a particularly embarrassing moment a few months ago, when I completely failed – I believe that was the phrase you used – I "completely failed to notice" your new frock. These words preyed on my mind. It was a warning to me. I could see how far I had – in short, I could see that I was in danger of becoming a bad-tempered bear. I had blundered, Miss Shaw. Blundered grievously, I fear. I promise I won't be so unobservant next time.'

'This is very generous—'

He shook his head impatiently. 'You have achieved far more with him than I could have hoped. You understand, money cannot express my gratitude. Nevertheless, I hope you won't feel insulted?'

'Of course not.'

Eighteen

That night she took out the cheque again and stared at it. What was it that nagged at her? He was a generous man, no doubt, and the cheque was a large one. Why not take the money and be grateful? She sighed, and stared across the room. How to explain it? It was quite unconscious on his part no doubt, but in writing the cheque he was rebuking her: 'Remember that you are a servant. You are a stranger in my house, hired to educate my son.'

She lay on her bed and tried to take a sober view of her situation. To think that she had been on the point of falling in love with him! She remembered her erotic fantasy and writhed for a moment in embarrassment. Well, the cheque had served very efficiently to put her in her place. The fact was, she had been a great fool to allow it to come to this. If he had known she had been dreaming about him—

She stared at the cheque again, and yet for all her efforts to take a rational view of his gift, couldn't help feeling a lump in her throat and a foolish, illogical, feeling of disappointment.

The following morning she had no choice but to be herself again. Governesses do not have headaches, do not have moods, are not out of sorts. Governesses are alert, bright, efficient. Sarah was all of these things. Whether or not she had slept the previous night was beside the point, and in any case her business only. In the event she appeared, neatly dressed, her hair combed, and ready for breakfast with Robin.

Things had changed. 'From now on, we shall eat together,' Mr McMaster announced, 'as a family.'

'Yes, as a family,' echoed Robin.

It was McMaster himself who carried his son downstairs, installed him at the breakfast table and throughout breakfast was forever solicitous, helping him, talking to him, correcting his grammar at one point. Robin glanced at Sarah and grinned, and of course she smiled back. Things had worked out better than she could have dreamed. Father and son united; it had been her wish for so long. What was it, then, that nagged at her oddly? Could it be, she asked herself at length, that she resented the way McMaster was taking over? Intruding between herself and Robin?

This unworthy thought soon passed as he disappeared to his study and she and Robin were installed once more upstairs for some arithmetic and French.

She adjusted herself to the new state of affairs. It was her job after all, and her little fantasy about McMaster would pass – like all things, she thought wryly. No more dreams of running naked on the beach.

A few days later she saw the announcement in the newspaper of Mr Barrington's forthcoming lecture to the Literary and Philosophical Society, which she had forgotten. She mentioned it to McMaster.

'Would you have any objection if I were to be out next Thursday evening?' she asked. 'I promised to go to a meeting.'

He looked up from his desk. 'What meeting?'

She showed him the advertisement and mentioned the garden party. 'They invited me to go.'

McMaster brightened. 'Of course you may go.' He glanced at the newspaper again and thought for a moment. 'And I shall have the pleasure of escorting you, Miss Shaw! Barrington is a clever man. No doubt he will have much of interest to impart.'

She wondered about as this as she read through the advertisement again: "The Lesson of the Rocks" – it sounded pretty dry stuff.

On the Thursday, since it was a fine clear evening, they walked into town. The meeting was to be held in a room in the Angel, the largest and most important hotel in the town, and as they arrived they found that it was well attended. They barely managed to cram into the room. The air was filled with lively chatter, with calls and cries of recognition. Towards the front Sarah spied Effie, who waved, and managed to worm her way through the crowd.

'I say, thanks awfully for coming. Pa's ever so nervous. I told him all his friends would be here, but you know what he's like. I made him write it all out, so he only has to read it aloud. He wanted to get someone else to read it for him! Keep your fingers crossed.' She disappeared through the crowd again.

At last everyone seemed to have found a seat – extra chairs had by this time been brought into the hall – and attention gradually focused on the platform, where several gentlemen now appeared and took their seats. Among them was Mr Barrington.

A sober-looking elderly man rose to address the meeting, announced other events and meetings of the Society, a note or two concerning the finances and other matters and then, turning to Barrington, introduced him, mentioning his many accomplishments, his wide learning, the papers he had submitted to learned societies, the previous paper he had read to this society and which had been so well received, finishing by expressing the conviction that they would enjoy and profit by the paper he was to read to them that evening and to which they all looked forward with such anticipation.

Throughout this she had been studying Mr Barrington carefully. He was staring at the floor, so it was difficult to make out his feelings.

He rose and moved to the lectern, picked up a sheaf of papers and immediately let them fall to the floor. He glanced across the audience with a sort of terrified helplessness but a colleague darted forward, gathered them up and replaced them.

This was not an auspicious start. Nevertheless, with a cough and another nervous glance across the audience he began to read.

Ours, he told them, was an age of geology. Over the last thirty years colossal strides had been made in the examination and interpretation of the earth on which we lived. Our grandfathers could have had no inkling of the discoveries which had been made and, he added, in no other part of these islands more significantly than in their own county. The Yorkshire coastline had yielded the most astonishing insights into the origin and composition of the earth. It was now apparent that the process of the creation of the earth, of its long gestation and transformation, had forced us to rethink all our previously held opinions and in many cases to jettison them completely.

His reading manner was not lively, not calculated to grip an audience. He held the papers to his nose and read in a low soft monotone. So far, however, the audience was giving him the benefit of the doubt.

To think, he went on, laying down a page, that barely two hundred years ago, the age of the earth had been computed at less than six thousand years! It was incredible. We now knew for a certainty that it must be calculated in many millions of years, many, many millions. Years of the incredibly slow rise and fall of continents, of the uplifting of strata, of their gradual erosion and denudation. Where now the cold north wind chilled the hardy sheep as they cropped the tough moorland grass, there had once been a tropical forest, home to the most fantastic of reptiles! This had forced to us to make a painful reappraisal of some of our most deeply held beliefs. This fossil – and here he held up a piece of black rock on which nothing was visible at a distance – this fossil from the Lower Jurassic was once the shell of a creature living beneath the sea, yet it had been found in a rock at least a hundred feet above sea level! 'What are we to make of this?' he asked and at last looked round at his audience.

'*What are we to make of it?*' thundered a voice from the audience. 'I'll tell thee what we are to make of it, my friend!'

Mr Barrington looked as if he had been shot and heads turned. Sarah looked round too, and saw a man dressed in black with a spade-shape beard. 'Flat blasphemy is what we are to make of it! There are women here tonight! There are children here tonight!' he roared. 'The sanctity of the home is undermined. What is the mother to tell her child lisping its prayers at her knee—'

The audience was now beginning to react. Voices cried, 'Sit down!' But other voices she noticed, cried, 'Hear, hear, Reverend Hayes! Speak!'

On the platform Barrington was looking imploringly at the chairman. He was on his feet and was holding out his arms in an attempt to restore order. But the Reverend Hayes, who had a voice of bronze, was not easily to be stopped.

'Oh, tha cower'st under a cloak of respectability!' he sneered. 'But tha betray'st t'position in which God has placed thee! He set the rich and poor each in His estate. The privileged, educated classes were set over the poor and ignorant that they might guide them in wisdom and prudence. Tha'st betrayed that trust! The Lord God has given us a complete description of t'creation of the earth which has sufficed untold generations. Men have been born, grown to manhood and gone to their graves, secure in the knowledge of t'Lord's work. It sufficed for them. But it does not suffice thee! Tha must rise – tha Jonah Barrington – tha must rise, arrayed in pride and folly, to mock t'face of t'Lord! Tha'st risen up wi' a sulphurous stench of corruption, to betray wi' lies and deceit all that is most sanctified and holy in our lives, to spread doubt and confusion and to do t'devil's work!'

There was now uproar throughout the hall, as different voices rose either in support or in opposition to Hayes. Barrington was standing paralysed on the platform. As the meeting looked like breaking up, McMaster rose.

'Mr Hayes!' he asked; his voice, strong, clear, focused, cut effortlessly through the hubbub. 'Is God eternal?'

This silenced the room and everyone looked round to see who had interrupted the preacher. The minister turned magisterially on McMaster. 'Eternal, my friend, everlastin', all-wise,' he boomed.

'Quite so. Eternal, all-wise. Mr Hayes, in your opinion, does God ever change His mind?'

The minister uttered a short jerky laugh of disbelief. 'Does God ever change His mind?' he repeated, looking about him, as if to draw the attention of the room to this lunatic, and finally retorted in a voice dripping with sarcasm, 'I rather think not.' This clearly was the last word on that subject and it drew a scattered laugh from the crowd.

Meanwhile McMaster, to Sarah's astonishment, had produced a Bible from somewhere and was leafing casually through it. 'Now this is a book you will be familiar with, Mr Hayes,' he said quietly, 'the Holy Bible.'

'I have had it constantly by me this half-century,' boomed the minister. 'It is t'literal word o' God – a priceless treasure, which this gentleman has seen fit to disparage!'

'I am pleased to hear it,' McMaster went on in the casual and reasonable tone which, Sarah had learned, meant trouble to come. 'You have had the Bible constantly by you over a period of fifty years. Then you will be doubtless familiar with this passage in Leviticus,' and he quoted, 'Chapter 20, Verse 21: "And if a man shall take his brother's wife it is an unclean thing; he hath uncovered his brother's nakedness; they shall be childless." ' He looked up. 'Is that the literal word of God?'

'God hath vouchsafed—'

'Come, come, Mr Hayes,' McMaster interrupted brusquely. 'It is a simple question. Just answer yes or no.'

'Indeed it is,' the minister said stoutly.

'And yet, if we turn to Deuteronomy,' and he quoted again, 'we find, Chapter 25, Verse 5, "If brethren dwell together and one of them die and have no child, the wife of the dead man shall not marry without unto a stranger: her husband's brother shall go in unto her and take her to him to wife and perform the duty of an husband's brother unto her." ' He paused, then repeated with heavy emphasis, '"The duty of an husband's brother". This is also the literal word of God – is that so?'

'There are many here—' Hayes began looking round the room.

'*What?* You won't answer?' McMaster cut across him brutally. 'I asked you a simple question. Is that the literal word of God? Yes or no?'

The minister hesitated, and 'Yes,' came forth a little slower than before.

'Yes, it is the literal word of God?'

'That is so.'

'That is so,' McMaster repeated with powerful finality. *'The literal word of God.* Mr Hayes,' he went on, before the minister could frame a reply, 'I will repeat a question I put to you earlier. Does God ever have second thoughts?'

'Never!' the minister repeated, but with every reply his assurance diminished. He seemed to be shrinking visibly as Sarah watched him.

'Nevertheless, it appears that between writing Leviticus and Deuteronomy He did change his mind – for the two quotations I have given flatly contradict one another. Do they not?' There was an awkward silence. 'Come, Mr Hayes,' McMaster went on in a more conciliatory tone, 'I'll make it easier for you. Is it possible, in your opinion, that in taking down the word of God, or perhaps in copying it, the scribe made some error? After all, to err is human.'

The minister, who was now clearly in difficulties, grasped at this possibility. 'Perhaps the scribe had made an error in transcribing the word of God,' he agreed in a low voice.

'Very good. And a perfectly reasonable assumption too, in my opinion. We all make mistakes sometimes. And why not a Hebrew scribe?' He looked about him at the audience who were all hanging on his words, with an expression of sweet reasonableness. 'For all we know, the Bible was copied by hand many times before it came down to us. After all, it is thousands of years old, and printing had not been invented. And if a scribe made an error in transcribing the Book of Leviticus – or Deuteronomy – it is possible he made an error also in transcribing other books, in transcribing the Book of Genesis, for example. Is that not so?'

'It is possible,' the minister said at length.

'*It is possible!*' McMaster repeated loudly. 'And if the Bible tells us that the earth was created in six days, it is possible that this too was a scribe's error, is it not?'

There was silence, but McMaster was not now to be stopped. 'What? You won't answer?'

'It is possible.' The minister was barely audible.

There was a very long silence, and McMaster looked slowly about the room, and at last back to Hayes, before he finally sat down.

Sarah had never heard anything like it. The minister was demolished and a moment later he pushed angrily along the row, and stumped out of the room.

There were a few moments of excited chatter, then the chairman called the meeting to order and eventually, in a very different atmosphere, Barrington continued with his talk.

Afterwards they were standing in the hallway of the hotel; many people spoke to McMaster and shook him by the hand. Even those who did not speak to him couldn't take their eyes off him. Suddenly Chrissie appeared, pushing through the crowd and hurried up to him, her face burning with enthusiasm.

'Oh, Mr McMaster, I shall never be able to thank you enough for what you did! That horrible, horrible Mr Hayes; I was so afraid for Papa – for he cannot bear an interruption of any kind and I just knew what he must be feeling. And no one was standing up to Mr Hayes and then you stood up and you simply annihilated him!'

In her enthusiasm and admiration for him, Sarah had never seen Chrissie look so lovely; her eyes were bright, her colour heightened, her lips breathlessly parted; she simply glowed with admiration. Sarah noticed that McMaster, with all his customary composure, was blown slightly off course by this gust of worship. A moment later Mr Barrington came through the crowd escorted by Effie and Dan. McMaster would not allow them to praise him – that was not his style – he had done this sort of thing many times before,

Sarah realized – and after a few conventional remarks, they set out for home.

Sarah was full of thoughts. McMaster had simply dominated the hall; everyone had hung on his words, friend and foe alike. As for the demolition of Mr Hayes, she had never seen anything like it. Of course she knew McMaster was a barrister and Josiah had talked about him; tonight she had seen him in action. She found her thoughts hard to put into words, however, especially since everything had already been said by Mr Barrington's family and especially by Chrissie. She thought too he had probably heard enough praise for one night. After they had been walking in silence for some minutes, he spoke.

'That was Barrington's eldest daughter, wasn't it?'

'It was.'

'I didn't recognize her at first. She has grown since we last met.'

'She has become very beautiful,' Sarah agreed. 'Quite a belle.'

He nodded without saying more and remained thoughtful; Chrissie had made an impression on him and some instinct in Sarah reacted. It was time to change the subject.

'Well, Mr McMaster, you took me by surprise this evening.'

'Oh?'

'Yes. I would have never taken you for a biblical scholar. It was very impressive. I fear you have missed your vocation.' He glanced at her but she returned his look coolly. 'And after all the unkind things you said about the Church.'

'What do you mean?'

'I distinctly remember you telling me you did not want your son brought up with all that superstitious nonsense. Curious too that you should have the Bible so handy.'

'Oh,' he said airily, 'I had an idea what was afoot.'

'So you just thought you'd slip your Bible in your pocket in case of trouble?'

'Something like that.'

'But you see, I don't believe you. No,' she went on casually, 'I think there's more to it than that. I think you are a closet believer.'

He stopped and looked at her in mystification. It was late by now, the evening sun had set, but there may have been just enough light left for him to see the smile playing about her lips.

'A man who knows his Deuteronomy; who knows his Leviticus. We can't put it down simply to coincidence – or even the possibility of a joust with the Reverend Hayes. Can we?'

McMaster stared hard into her eyes for a long time, but she would not let him go. At long last he looked away and they continued their walk.

'There was a time when it was otherwise,' he said with difficulty.

'You were a believer – once?' she asked carefully.

He nodded.

'And then you – gave it up?'

He did not reply.

'Something happened?'

He looked down, but did not reply. He seemed to be thinking hard.

'But you prefer not to talk about it?' she said gently.

He nodded.

Nineteen

Over the following days, she tried to put together everything she knew about him. It all seemed to come down to one thing – his wife. Where was she? Was she dead? Had she deserted him for another man? It would make sense; there was something so bitter, so harsh, about his forensic manner; the prisoners in the dock were paying for his humiliation. And the crippled son, too; a humiliation for an athletic father.

Thinking about him, which she did most of her waking hours, she could only feel a great pity. Something was wrong, for certain. But what it was – and how she could ever get him to talk about it – she did not know.

A week later, as she was sitting with Robin at the breakfast table, she glimpsed through the window a horseman galloping along the cliff path towards the house; it was a sunny morning and there was something very impetuous, very dashing about the sight. Especially when he took the garden wall at a jump, crossed the lawn and drew up sharply before the door.

It was Dan Barrington. She ran to the door, and as she opened it, he leapt from the saddle, one hand on the bridle. He was flushed with the sun and exercise, his collar open, his hair flying about his face. In his way he was as beautiful as his sister, she thought.

'Dan! Come in – no, wait, take your horse to the stable. Josiah will take care of her – then come inside.' She rang the bell, and as Jenny appeared, 'It's young Mr Barrington – can you bring him a glass of lemonade?'

She soon found out what had brought him when he presented her with a large envelope which contained an invitation to Chrissie's coming-out ball.

'It's for Mr McMaster – and you. Pa says you're going to play the piano.'

'He did ask me, it is true. But it was a long time ago. I thought he would have forgotten.'

'Well, he hasn't. Oh, you needn't worry,' Dan went on, sipping his lemonade, 'there's a band as well. You'll probably only be wanted to accompany Chrissie when she sings.'

'That's a relief.'

'Oh bosh, Sarah!' Robin cut in. 'You know you'd knock them all for six if you played!'

'Robin is my greatest admirer. I am afraid he has to put up with my meanderings.'

'Meanderings! Dan, she plays...' He paused for thought. 'She plays as if she had just made it up.'

'Well!' she laughed. 'That is the nicest thing anyone has ever said about me!'

'Anyway, you must go, Sarah,' Robin was insistent. 'And you must make Papa go too.'

Sarah looked round. Robin saw the puzzled look in her face, and went on, 'He won't go, you know – unless you persuade him.'

'He won't go?'

'He never goes to balls. He never goes to anything.'

'Well, if he won't go, it would be awkward for me, wouldn't it?'

'Effie is counting on you, Miss Shaw.' Dan looked worried. 'She has drawn up a complete programme for the evening, and you're down to play.'

Sarah was in difficulties.

'I will try to speak to Mr McMaster,' she said at last. 'Perhaps he can be persuaded this once.'

All this time McMaster had been closeted in his study. Generally, he was not to be disturbed during the morning so it was not until after Dan had left that she was able to mention the invitation.

To her surprise he was evasive. They were sitting down to lunch, and Robin was full of their recent conversation. Sarah, ever alert to his father's moods, quickly silenced Robin with a look. 'We'll talk about it later,' she said brightly.

Although Robin pestered her several times during the day to speak to his father, it was not until after dinner that she finally raised the subject.

'Robin is very excited about Miss Barrington's ball,' she began diplomatically.

'I am not going to the ball. I never go to dances.'

Sarah waited, uncertain whether to continue with this subject, until unexpectedly something now clicked into place in her mind. 'Because of your wife?' she asked carefully.

'Yes.' He said it so emphatically that she was afraid to go on. There was another silence until at last she began again.

'Did you ever go to a ball with her?' She waited, trembling inwardly.

'Of course I did! She loved to dance! And I loved to dance with her! I fell in love with her at a dance, watching her in a muslin frock, all white with a sprig of flowers at her breast; watching her feet in dainty slippers – how light she was, gossamer light! She eclipsed them all.'

'Is Robin like her?'

'A little.' Then at last grudgingly, 'Very much. For so long I could not bear to look at him. If I did I would see her. It was too much to bear. You cannot understand.'

'What was her name?'

'Thérèse.' And he began, slowly, to speak about her. Sarah waited, scarcely daring to breathe. He spoke slowly, in a low voice, staring out of the window. 'I was on holiday with my parents in Deauville. I was thirty-two, I'd been called to the bar eight years, I had been successful, too successful, perhaps, too full of myself. I was unmarried. There had been one woman and for a while we were engaged – but she married someone else. Perhaps I was too ambitious, worked too hard, I didn't seem to have time for thoughts of marriage or a home. Well,' he resumed, 'I had taken my parents on holiday. Thérèse was also on holiday. I remember the first time I saw her in the hotel at breakfast. I watched her, admired her for several days.' He paused, thinking, then gave a small laugh. 'It sounds foolish enough telling it to someone else. I had gone for a walk along the sands, and was returning to the hotel when it came on to rain. I had an umbrella – and then I saw her, huddling against the side of a house trying to keep out of the rain. I offered her the use of my umbrella. It was raining hard – she didn't have much choice.' He grunted again slightly, as the thoughts came crowding back into his mind. *'Le parapluie!* As we walked, she took my arm and we crowded beneath the umbrella; I spoke some French – just as well, since she spoke no English – and we were able to converse. And then, well, the ice was broken, she introduced me to her parents, it was all very respectable, I introduced her to my parents. We met again. The days melted away, I seemed to be with Thérèse every day.

I felt indescribably light. As if for years and years I had been struggling under some relentless pressure and suddenly the weight was gone. I was in a dream. I had never seen anyone like her; I was mad, drunk, I wanted to laugh all the time. I thought if I didn't marry her my life would have no meaning. I would do anything, make whatever sacrifice necessary to make her my wife.

'I went to her parents. They were uncertain, unhappy. I was English, a Protestant; it was difficult. I can still hear their voices. But I was not to be stopped. I overrode their objections, promised them anything, and eventually they consented. I went to Thérèse; I asked her to marry me and come with me to England. She was eighteen, still under the protection of her parents. I said she had to come with me; her parents had given their permission. I would tolerate no opposition. I told her if she did not come with me to England, my life would be in vain. If she did not become my wife there was no point in my going on living. We embraced, there were tears, she said she would die for me if I asked her to. I told her I would die for her. It was all madness.

'Well, we were married and she came with me to Liverpool. I had money; there were no problems from that point of view. I was able to set her up in a home worthy of her; I gave her whatever she asked for. She studied English.

'Things were perhaps difficult for her at first, in a strange land, in a big city. She had been brought up in a small country town and she was homesick. But she was a married woman now. Her parents came to visit, they were impressed with her new home. That helped; still, there was much that was strange; it would take time. And gradually she became used to England. I introduced her to my friends. I cannot tell you how proud I was to show her off. At last my life made sense. I felt I had arrived; achieved my proper place in the world, and could stand proudly with her at my side.'

He hesitated, then went on more sombrely. 'She conceived a child. I was delirious with happiness. You cannot know – no woman can know the feelings of a man when he learns he is to be a father. Thérèse and I looked forward to the birth. We prepared the nursery, I bought toys, a cradle, engaged a nurse for our first-born.'

He paused again. 'Thérèse was slim, delicate. But she was in good health; I never for an instant suspected there might be complications.'

Sarah felt a chill, and instinctively moved a step towards him. Hesitantly, she placed a hand on his arm. A tear had appeared and was tracing a path slowly down his cheek. 'I don't – I don't think I shall ever forget that night.' He wiped the tear brusquely away. 'At first I waited in a neighbouring room. I heard Thérèse's cries. It was horrible, but I was prepared for them – I knew it was never easy. But it didn't seem to stop, and after what seemed forever the midwife hurried into the room. "Send for the doctor!" I dispatched a man immediately, and no longer able to help myself I went into where Thérèse was lying. My poor darling was in the utmost agony, her face contorted, the hair matted about her head, her nightdress soaked in sweat. I was never so helpless in my life! What could I do? I had no idea! I knelt by her, I took her hand, I tried to comfort her – but she was scarcely conscious of me. Her screams tore out my heart. At length the surgeon arrived. He was grave. He said it was late, but he would do what he could. He decided there and then on a Caesarean section. The child was wrongly presented, birth had begun, the child some-how – oh I didn't understand exactly what he said – I was at my wits' ends.' He shook his head, the tears flowed fast now. He wiped his eyes. 'There was blood everywhere, Thérèse was in agony, her screams were appalling. But at length a child was born; a tiny thing, twisted, red, covered in blood, but alive. I didn't care about the child. I only wanted to know Thérèse was safe.

"'She has lost a lot of blood," he said. "I am giving her a sedative, then I'll try to stitch her up as best I can. It's been a messy business." He talked like a butcher instead of a surgeon. "A messy business"! My poor darling had been ripped almost in half!'

He covered his face with his hands, and wept uncontrollably.

At length he drew a shattering breath and

wiped his eyes with his handkerchief. After what seemed minutes he began again. 'The following day I knew immediately she was not going to live. She looked unspeakable; her face grey, her eyes sunken. I knelt by her bed, her hand in mine. "Take care of my baby," she whispered. I hated the baby! Hated it! That Thérèse had suffered these unspeakable torments to bring this thing in the world. I never wanted to see it again! "And, John," she said, "see that he is baptised a Catholic."' He paused. 'Never! Her religion had always been a trouble between her parents and me. I hated her religion. What god could allow this?'

He drew another sigh and Sarah waited for him to go on. The silence lengthened, but at last in a low voice he continued. 'Three days later I followed her to the graveyard. I was mad. I didn't eat, I didn't go out. They wanted to show me my son. I never wanted to see it. They told me it had been born deformed. I could have cried aloud. It was a punishment! I had been too happy. And this thing had been sent to punish me – this *thing* had killed my darling.'

Sarah was appalled. Her whole body was rigid and she could feel herself staring at him. He was still looking away from her and now at last sat in a chair, resting his face on his hand.

Without thinking she crossed to him, knelt by his chair, and took his free hand. Pressing it to her face she kissed it. 'My poor, poor darling,' she whispered.

Gradually he lifted his head, looking down at her. She looked up at him and, perhaps conscious of what she had done, she started back. They stared into each other's eyes for a moment. Some realization seemed to dawn in his eyes, and he took her hand again.

'I could have spoken of this to no one else,' he said at last, and there was another long silence as his eyes roamed over her face. His voice was low, drained of emotion. 'I have never spoken of this to a soul. Never. Not since the day she died.'

'Would you like to go outside?' she suggested in a whisper. He stood, unsteadily, with his arm about her shoulder, as if he were a wounded soldier and she his nurse.

'Let's sit here,' she whispered. They sat on a garden seat, his arm about her shoulder still, and again there was silence. The night was warm, and the air was filled with the scent of night-perfumed flowers.

'Thank you,' he said softly after what seemed minutes. He sounded exhausted, deflated, but also tranquil and at rest. 'Thank you. You have been very good.'

He looked up at the stars, twinkling in the clear sky. 'Do you think she can see us?' he whispered. 'Do you think she is looking down?'

'I am sure she is.'

After another long silence he went on in the same dreamy tone, 'How strange.'

'What is?'

'You know, I feel free. Thérèse is still with me – but she is happy now.'

'She is happy because you and Robin are reconciled.'

He seized on this idea. 'You are right! It was what she wanted.'

He turned back to Sarah. She could barely make out his face. 'And it was you – you who helped me.' He took her hands. 'You, Miss Shaw – Sarah – you did it.'

There was nothing for her to say; she waited, her heart thudding, unable to tear her eyes from his face. 'I seem to owe everything to you,' he went on. 'It was you who brought Robin and me together, and now this evening – it is you who helped me to – to speak of these things. You cannot imagine – I have carried the image of that night with me for nine years. Nine years I have suffered with my darling, nine years I have lived and relived that night. And now, this evening, you have freed me.'

'Thérèse would not have wanted you to grieve for ever,' Sarah said at last.

Twenty

When they finally separated and she went to her room she found it impossible to sleep, impossible to efface the extraordinary pictures conjured up as he had recounted the story of his wife's death. It completely eclipsed her own sufferings and had revealed a depth of feeling she had never known before. No wonder he had been so hostile to Robin. However irrational it might have seemed, she could understand that now. And how her heart had gone out to him in that moment of unburdening. What it must have cost him – but what a relief when he had finally been able to speak!

She remembered the moment when she had taken his hand and kissed it. How could she help loving such a man?

'Did you sleep at all? Are you rested?' she asked tentatively. They had met in the hall the following morning.

'I am. And I did sleep well,' he said, a surprised note in his voice. 'And, do you know, this morning, as soon as I woke, although I remembered everything that we said last night, I felt light and I realized – life must go

211

on. Does that sound callous?'

'No!'

'I believe Thérèse would be happy to know that we ... I mean—' He seemed confused. 'She would be happy for me to go on with life. Don't you think so?'

'I do.'

'So ... I have written to Mrs Barrington, and accepted her invitation on your behalf and mine.'

Sarah nodded gravely. 'You have that right.'

He was watching her uncertainly.

'I mean,' she went on, 'the right to happiness.'

Again there was a moment of silence as they stared into each other's eyes.

'Thank you.' He suddenly became lighter. 'And I hope – I hope, Miss Shaw – you will have a new gown made up for the occasion?'

She smiled. 'I shall!'

She concentrated on this. She had his cheque, a large one. Very well, she would have the best. Why not? She had enough self-respect; there would be belles enough at this ball, to be sure; why should she be a wallflower? She had plenty of ideas too; she had spent money enough on clothes in the past. Even so, as the dressmaker measured her she found she was thinner and sobered a little. Not difficult to imagine why. Again her pride asserted itself; no matter for that, she told herself, and concentrated again on the details of the gown. Not white; Chrissie would be in white.

What then – pink? A pale forget-me-not? Cerise? Or something more dramatic – a powerful Regency green-and-white stripe? Yes. Something strong – that was natural to her. And there would be a break in the dancing when Chrissie would be asked to sing and Sarah would be expected to contribute some short piece; she would astonish them with Liszt.

As the days went by and the ball came nearer, as she was fitted for her new gown and was pleased with her choice, when she found herself in town making little purchases – a pair of dancing slippers, some stockings – she became more cheerful and began to look forward to it very much. This was also because McMaster was so enthusiastic. One afternoon he asked her about dance steps. 'Miss Shaw,' he said, 'I have not been into a ballroom for nearly ten years. I am grievously out of practice. You may perhaps think me very silly, but I am anxious not to disgrace myself.'

He seemed as nervous as a boy. If Mrs Barrington could see him now, she thought, as he took her in his arms and they waltzed round the drawing room. As he rediscovered the steps, as he remembered the pleasure of the dance, as the intoxication of movement gripped him and he grew freer and less inhibited, so she too was inevitably carried away. She who loved to dance above all things and had expected never to dance again, now found herself in the arms of this tall handsome man as he held her and guided her through the steps; what more could she wish for? If only they could go on dancing together like this; if she could only go on, lilting round the room in his arms and never stop...

'Well, sir,' she said, slightly breathless, 'I don't think you are going to disgrace yourself,' and then becoming brisk and schoolmasterly, 'We had better try our hand at the polka...'

One afternoon she was returning from town with a few purchases and was just letting herself into the house when she heard Robin at the piano. She stopped immediately, listening. As she hunted in her mind for an explanation the playing stopped and she heard his voice, excited. She was about to go forward into the drawing room when she heard McMaster's voice, then Robin's laugh.

She could just glimpse the two of them sitting side by side at the piano. Robin eagerly snatched down a sheet from the top of the instrument and set it on the stand.

'Listen to this, Papa.'

Sarah retreated silently from the doorway and made her way carefully up to her room.

On the night of the ball it was eight o'clock when she finished her preparations. Jenny inspected her hair and the flowers woven into it; she adjusted her stockings, wriggled into her slippers, smoothed down her dress and straightened the waist, biting her lip as she inspected herself for the last time. She had not a scrap of jewellery, but there was no helping that. She thought of Mr McMaster waiting for her downstairs; in truth what was she going for if not the chance of dancing with him? In a few moments she would be descending the staircase, he would see her; he would inspect her, appraise her...

She went into Robin's room to say good-night. 'Wish me luck,' she whispered.

'Papa looks so smart, Sarah.'

'Doesn't he?'

'All the girls will want to dance with him, won't they?'

'They will.'

As she was going downstairs, she thought, yes, they will. He can take his pick tonight; the most eligible bachelor in Whitby.

She tried not to catch his eye as they met in the hall, passing him quickly into the drawing room to collect her sheet music.

'Not so fast,' he called jovially. 'Let me have a look at you, Miss Shaw. This is the first time I have seen your new gown. And I have not forgotten your words.' He gave her a rueful, considering look, as he glanced over her gown. 'I used to be something of a judge of these things, you know.' He turned her round, adjusted her belt and the chaplet of flowers in her hair, and finally pronounced himself satisfied.

As they installed themselves in the trap, however, his confidence seemed to evaporate and he gave her a worried look. 'Do you think any of the girls will dance with an old man?' he asked half in jest.

'Mr McMaster! *Old man?*' She pretended to look about her in comic disbelief. 'What are you talking about? I cannot see any old man.'

He relaxed a little, and laughed as he jogged the horse into motion.

The front door was open, light blazed from every window. Music could be heard from somewhere within, and figures were visible dashing by in the dance.

They were greeted at the door by Mr and Mrs Barrington with Chrissie, who seemed in a cruel mixture of high spirits and trepidation. Her eyes lit up when she saw Mr McMaster and she hastened to welcome him, taking up in her gloved hands the white muslin and silk skirt which swayed about her. She will thaw out soon, Sarah thought; the girl was quite beautiful tonight, even more than usual, if that were possible. The excitement had brought up her natural colour, her eyes sparkled – but there was no need to itemize Chrissie's perfections; they were all too obvious and the natural bashfulness of her manner, her almost painful eagerness to please only made her the more intoxicating. Sarah could see that McMaster thought so too. There was something pathetically obvious about the way he accosted her, taking her hand to kiss it, whispering something in her ear that made her laugh, and a moment later Sarah saw Chrissie take up her dance card and scribble into it.

She drew a breath and out of curiosity looked about for Mr James, the 'secret betrothed'; she wondered whether the engagement might not be announced tonight? She did see him a moment later, a glass in hand, in energetic conversation with a man and laughing boisterously.

It was only belatedly that Chrissie turned to welcome her. 'Isn't Mr McMaster looking handsome tonight,' she whispered. 'He asked me to dance immediately, you know.'

'Did you have any space left?'

Chrissie blushed. 'I had to kick Freddy off a couple.'

They both glanced round in his direction.

'Do you think he'll mind?' Sarah asked as they watched him empty his glass.

'To tell the truth, Freddy isn't very interested in dancing.' Chrissie was watching anxiously.

'Are you?'

'I adore dancing!' she said in a heartfelt whisper.

At that moment they were interrupted by a young man whom Sarah did not know who reminded Chrissie that the quadrille was about to begin and conducted her off.

And then Dan was at her side, looking very smart and grown-up, with a cravat high under his chin, offering her a white-gloved hand, and enquiring whether she might be free – and before she knew it she was in the dance, and the orchestra had struck up, forming squares, passing back and forth, curtsying, and turning to her new partner...

At the end of the dance she stood for a few minutes with Mrs Barrington, watching Mr McMaster in conversation with a young girl she did not know.

'They've talked of no one else in this house, you know, since Barrington's lecture. Your Mr McMaster is the hero of the hour.'

'It was quite a performance,' Sarah agreed, 'but then you know, it is his profession. He has a reputation for that sort of thing.'

'I've never been able to tempt him before,' the older lady went on as McMaster took the girl by the hand for the next dance. 'In fact I was astonished when I received his note. I wonder, Miss Shaw,' she turned and tapped Sarah on the arm with her fan, 'I wonder whether we should not ascribe this achievement to you? How did you do it? What magic arts did you use to draw him out of his shell? Hmm?' She raised her eyebrows.

Before Sarah had the chance to frame a reply, fortunately, Mr Barrington had appeared on her other side.

'I never took him for a dancing man, but he seems to know his way round a dance floor.'

He does, Sarah thought. He had never looked so dashing; his evening clothes fitted him like a glove, everything about him was shapely and striking. As for his dancing, it seemed as if he did it every day of the week. He was smiling, and said something to make the girl laugh ... and in spite of everything, a

218

sort of lethargy settled on Sarah, a lowness of spirits.

However it was not long after this that he appeared at her side. As they waited for the dance to start, he cast his eye over the dancing couples and murmured, 'I have been comparing your gown with some of the others. The belles of Whitby have spared no expense, have strained every nerve, to appear at their best tonight. That is clear. For the last two months, all over town, needles have been at work. Early and late, delicate hands have been busy, brows have been furrowed, tears shed. But I fear you have the advantage of them all, Miss Shaw. Your gown has a touch of metropolitan sophistication which they have sought in vain.'

He flicked a glance to her.

'Thank you, kind sir.' She bobbed a curtsy. 'You are too flattering. And I am glad to see you have taken my lesson to heart.'

He chuckled. 'But I have not yet asked you to dance. What must you think of me? Would you favour me with the next if you are not already engaged?'

Sarah opened her card. 'I believe I may be able to fit you in,' she said archly.

The music struck up again, and they were together at last in the dance. She wanted nothing more. If he does not ask me again tonight, if he dances with every other girl in the room three times over, it will have been worth it – for these few minutes. And what did he mean, he is out of practice? He moves

219

so effortlessly, he is so perfectly handsome, he is the handsomest man here; the cleverest, the most talented ... A little later she reprimanded herself: Who am I deceiving? I do begrudge the other girls, I am greedy for him, I want him in *my* arms only, dancing with *me* only, talking to *me* only, making only *me* laugh...

The dance was over; the charm was broken. McMaster was talking to a man beside him, introducing her, waving to someone else. He seemed to know so many people. Of course, as Mrs Barrington was saying soon afterwards, he was a well-known figure in the town; everyone was eager to make themselves known. There was a man now introducing a girl to him. Still, in spite of all, as Sarah listened politely, the glow remained in her limbs, the memory of them together. She studied to remember it; did not want to lose it, wanted to cling on to it...

Then he was dancing with Chrissie and it was like a knife through her. They seemed made for each other; the handsomest man and the prettiest girl. And how beautifully they moved, flowing together, everything so effortless, so graceful.

She was joined again by Mrs Barrington, who was watching complacently.

At the end of the dance there was a little polite round of applause; as McMaster led Chrissie from the floor Sarah realized with a jolt that it was for them. Mrs Barrington turned to her as the applause died down.

'They seem almost made for each other,' she said, echoing Sarah's thoughts, and went on wistfully, 'I wonder if we shouldn't, you and I...' She gave Sarah a conspiratorial look.

Sarah was mystified. But the older woman took her arm and led her away a step. 'Christina has such a gentle, pliable nature. It wouldn't take very much ... And McMaster seems ripe for marriage. It would be a sin to let him remain single. I am sure that we could achieve much, my dear. I shall have a word with her – and you, I am sure can easily find a moment with Mr McMaster: a few words judiciously hinted?'

'But I thought—'

Mrs Barrington grew severe as she leant in. 'A passing infatuation. Her father has been far too lenient. The boy is too young, so in any case the marriage couldn't take place for several years. And in the meantime ... Give it some thought...' She left the question hanging and tapped Sarah on the arm with her fan as she turned away.

Before Sarah had time to brood on this, Effie had appeared beside her. 'After the next dance, there'll be an intermission for supper.' She was clutching a paper. 'And then Chrissie's going to sing. You did practise it, didn't you?'

'Of course.' The music had been sent over a couple of weeks earlier. It was a pathetically easy accompaniment for Chrissie's parlour ditties.

'Have you brought something to play yourself?'

Sarah nodded. 'I put it on the piano when I arrived.'

'I think it should work out very nicely. Mr Sanderson is going to sing a comic song with his banjo, then Chrissie will sing two ballads, then you play your piece.'

Dan reappeared soon afterwards to escort her into supper, and they made small talk over the buffet. Sarah couldn't free herself of the sight of McMaster and Chrissie talking together, however, or of Mrs Barrington's scheme. As she watched them, it seemed true; they were made for each other. At that moment Chrissie said something and he leaned across the buffet table to reach her a dish; they were becoming more and more intimate by the minute.

So where was Mr James and why wasn't he by her side? Surely this evening was the opportunity to make their engagement public? Sarah looked about for him but couldn't find him. More and more puzzled she left the room and walked through the hall. There was still no sign of him. Most of the guests were in the supper room, but others were scattered about, some sitting on the stairs as they ate. She looked into the drawing room. The French windows were open to the summer night and on impulse she went out into the garden. A number of couples were out here too and then turning along under the veranda she suddenly came upon the fiancé.

'Mr James.'

He swung slowly about, and looked her over.

'Not eating?' she said lightly.

He gave her another inspection, and came a step closer. There was a slight unsteadiness in his movement which she noticed immediately. 'Not hungry.'

And then, reaching a hand behind her to steady himself against the door frame, he breathed down on her the well-remembered smell of brandy. 'Don't know you. What's your name?'

'Sarah Shaw. Why don't you come in and have something?'

'Got a better idea, Sarah. Why don't you come here?'

His arm was about her waist and she found herself suddenly pressed against his chest.

'Not a good idea, Freddy.' She untangled herself with difficulty and could feel a heat in her face. 'Especially when your fiancée is inside, wondering where you've got to,' she went on with difficulty.

He lurched away slightly.

'That is – if you are still engaged?'

'I am.' She had realized by now that he was drunk.

'Then why don't you save your attentions for her?'

'Secret engagement.'

'That doesn't stop you dancing with her.'

'Mustn't make it too obvious. She told me. Got to be a secret. Secret,' he repeated, 'till

223

it's official.' He lurched against the doorframe again and steadied himself while he marshalled his thoughts. 'Trouble with Chrissie is, she's too perfect. Too good for me. The perfect paragon,' he repeated drunkenly. 'Doesn't understand a chap like me. I'm just an ordinary sort of fellow, Sarah. Chrissie's a goddess; what's she doing with a fellow like me anyway?'

'She loves you. Isn't that enough?'

'S'pose so,' he replied morosely. 'But I mean to say, a fellow wants a bit of fun once in a while, a bit of a frolic, a bit of a laugh and a drink. Can you imagine Chrissie wanting a laugh and a drink?'

Sarah spoke carefully. 'Well, she's very young, for one thing. I expect in time she'll learn about such things, if that's what you want. But don't forget, she'll do anything you ask her.'

'Yes, she will, won't she?' It didn't seem to give him much satisfaction.

Twenty-One

At that moment from distantly inside the house she heard a man's voice raised in song and the unmistakable sound of a banjo. Without saying another word, she turned quickly and hurried into the house. The guests were all crowded into the music room and she had difficulty in forcing her way through the door. An amiable young man, his face flushed with heat and drink, held the floor. One foot on a chair and a banjo on his knee, he was singing a song which had to do with farmyards and involved an imitation of various animals. The guests were rocking with laughter. A second later Effie was beside her.

'Where on earth were you?' she whispered severely. 'I looked everywhere.'

'I went to find Mr James.'

'What? Where is he?'

'In the garden.'

'Well, he'd better get in here soon. Pa wants to announce the engagement after the songs.'

'He can't.'

'What do you mean?'

'Have you seen him? He's – I mean – Effie,' she whispered close into Effie's ear. 'He's *drunk*. It's out of the question.'

'Oh, Lor'. I'd better find Ma. How *could* he?' She disappeared.

The song came to an end and Mr Sanderson took his bow to ecstatic applause. The audience were well warmed up and ready to be entertained. Sarah pushed through the crowd, crossed the small open space and took her seat at the piano as Chrissie came forward. Sarah opened the sheet on the music stand and smiled up at Chrissie. 'You'll be lovely,' she whispered. '"By the Sweet Waters" first, all right?'

Chrissie nodded, swallowed and turned to the audience. Sarah played the soft introduction, with its rippling effect in the bass and the gentle harmonies above, and Chrissie began to sing. Her voice was not big but she had been taking lessons since she was a child and despite her nerves had enough command to get through the song. Even so, Sarah knew she wasn't enjoying it; Chrissie was not a natural performer.

Another sentimental ballad followed and Chrissie received enthusiastic applause. How could they help themselves? Sarah thought. The girl is so pretty it scarcely matters what she does.

Mr McMaster sprang forward from the audience to be the first to offer his congratulations and handed her to a seat. He had been holding her shawl, which he now arranged about her shoulders. They settled themselves side by side directly in front of Sarah as she mechanically opened the sheet music on the

226

stand; suddenly she was confronted by Liszt. Mr Barrington was standing beside her ready to turn the pages. In all the excitements of the evening, Sarah had given no thought to her own performance and suddenly she was forced to concentrate on these massed clusters, these thick handfuls of notes. What idiocy had made her choose this? It was typical of Liszt to compose the piece in seven sharps; she hadn't practised it properly and all she could see, over and over, was Mc-Master arranging the shawl about Chrissie's shoulders.

She launched into this tempestuous piece and almost immediately missed her place; she had to stop, stare at the sheet and concentrate on the notes for a second to remind herself. Glancing up to apologize to the audience for the interruption all she could see was that couple directly before her. What folly made her choose a piece like this? They wanted farmyard songs, they wanted pretty girls singing sentimental ballads. Why on earth was she attacking this violent and dramatic piece?

And it was too long. Oh damn she had lost the place again – she should be in the line above. She was going crazy – she had never played so badly in her life. Now Mr Barrington turned the page too soon – no wonder with Liszt – oh God, please let it be over soon. And had they found Freddy? Were they at this moment holding his head under the pump? Please, please let them announce the engagement tonight then Mr McMaster will stop flirting with Chrissie—

She came to the end. To her astonishment there was enthusiastic applause. They were probably glad she had stopped; it was the worst performance of her life. Mr McMaster had heard her a thousand times – he would recognize the difference. He could tell them she played better than this and it was only the sight of him with Chrissie and Freddy James drunk with his arm round her waist and the forthcoming announcement—

'Ladies and gentlemen, dancing will recommence in five minutes in the library,' came a voice from somewhere at the back as the guests broke into excited chatter and made their way out of the room.

McMaster and Chrissie were approaching her. Sarah concentrated on folding up her score.

'I don't remember to have heard that one before, Miss Shaw.'

She couldn't look at them. 'I am sorry. It was a bad choice. I cannot think what made me...'

At last she looked up at him. He was studying her carefully. 'You weren't at your best, it is true,' he said kindly. 'What is it?'

She shrugged and busied herself with the manuscript. 'A foolish choice, I am afraid,' she said briskly. 'Too ambitious! My own fault. I apologize.'

Before the conversation could go on, Mrs Barrington crossed the nearly empty room and took Chrissie by the elbow.

'Excuse us—' She hurried the girl out of the room.

McMaster noticed nothing, but Sarah felt obliged to remark vaguely, 'It must be such a headache organizing a ball on this scale, don't you think?'

He nodded earnestly. It was obviously something about which he knew nothing. 'Come then, Miss Shaw, since the mistress of the house and her daughter have so much to attend to, perhaps you will favour me again? We mustn't lose any opportunity. I intend to dance every dance tonight. I have a lot to make up for.'

As they danced however it was inevitable that Chrissie's singing should be the theme of their conversation: her taste, her skill, her charm, her perfect musicianship. Sarah, in spite of everything, felt obliged to stop him.

'In all truth, Mr McMaster, it cannot be the *most perfect* singing you have ever heard?'

'It was delightful—'

'No. Your actual words were, the *most perfect*. Miss Barrington sings very charmingly, it is true, and on an evening such as this, one could not ask for more. But she is not the *most perfect* singer you have ever heard. Is she?'

He was puzzled. 'I don't understand you.'

'Don't you? Then you must have a very short memory.'

He did not reply and for a long time they danced in silence; he was clearly full of thoughts.

'Why did you remind me of that?' he asked at last, looking away over her shoulder.

'I don't know.'

'Did I seem too happy?'

She felt mean; angry with herself. There had been no need to bring up the memory of his dead wife, after all. 'Forgive me; it was stupid of me.'

McMaster seemed hurt and anxious to justify himself. 'I don't think Thérèse would be unhappy to know – to know that we admired Miss Barrington's singing, surely? I mean – we discussed it, didn't we – you and I? About Thérèse, I mean.'

'Was it just her singing?'

'She is a most delightful girl, why deny it? I am sure every man in the room, in the town, would agree. I have been very fortunate to be singled out tonight for her attention.'

And as the dance ended he repeated, 'There was no need.'

She excused herself with a word, and went off in search of Chrissie. She wished herself dead; how could she have been so tactless? If only she hadn't been so angry and hurt to see him enjoying himself with the girl.

There was no sign of Chrissie or her mother in the downstairs rooms, so she ventured upstairs. It didn't take her long to find them in Chrissie's bedroom.

The girl was sitting on the edge of the bed in tears, her mother was beside her, her arm round Chrissie's shoulders, and Effie was standing near the door.

'We found Mr James,' Effie whispered as Sarah closed the door behind her. 'Just like you said. It's impossible to say anything to-night – and Chrissie had so looked forward to it.'

'Where is Mr James now?'

'Dan made him go out into the stables; he's trying to get him sobered up.'

Chrissie burst out afresh, 'How could he?' in a muffled sob as she collapsed onto her mother's bosom.

'There there,' her mother patted her shoulder as Chrissie sobbed helplessly.

'We can put the announcement in the papers,' Effie said helpfully.

'Time enough for that,' Mrs Barrington said briskly, and gave Sarah a hard look.

'I must go to him.' Chrissie started up, but was restrained almost immediately.

'Not in this state.' Her mother was firm. 'This is your ball, Christina. What are your guests to think? You'd better stop crying and wash your face; you've got to go down or they'll be wondering where you are. And don't worry; Daniel is keeping Mr James out of harm's way for the moment.'

'Poor dear Freddy – he was so looking forward to it. And now – oh, why did he have to do it?'

She was about to launch into a fresh shower of tears but her mother raised her from the bed. 'That's what men do, my dear,' she said. 'It's something you get used to.'

'But Papa doesn't.'

'Your father is different. Thank God. Now come.' She poured water into the bowl on the washstand. 'Wash your face, then I am sure Miss Shaw will help you with your hair. I must get downstairs. Come, Effie. Thank heaven at least one of my children has a head on her shoulders.'

'Of course.' Sarah closed the door behind them, and turned back to Chrissie. 'As your mother said, they will be wondering where you've got to. Wash your face, dear.'

The poor girl crossed to the washstand, and began splashing cold water on her face. She looked up into the mirror at her red-rimmed eyes.

'Have you any witch hazel?' Sarah felt old enough to be her mother.

'Somewhere,' Chrissie said in a daze.

After she had dried her face, Sarah made her sit in a chair and set about making repairs to her hair. 'You'll laugh about this one day.' She tried to sound cheerful. Chrissie in the mirror looked anything but cheerful.

'Believe me, worse things can happen.'

Again Chrissie caught her eye. There was a pause, then, 'Have you – heard from your husband?'

Sarah shook her head. 'I hope I never shall.'

'Have you any idea what you will do?'

'None. Just let things go on as they are, I think. So long as Mr McMaster wants me.' She was glad in a way that she had managed to drag Chrissie's thoughts away from her fiancé.

'Oh yes, Mr McMaster,' Chrissie said thoughtfully.

Sarah busied herself behind Chrissie's head.

'He's been very kind,' Chrissie went on.

'He certainly seems to think a lot of you. You've been dancing together all evening.'

'What? Oh, I hope you don't think – ' she looked horrified – 'I hope no one thought – oh my goodness, how foolish of me!'

'I don't understand.'

'Sarah, I hope Mr McMaster didn't get the wrong idea!'

'Because of your invisible fiancé?'

Chrissie wrenched round in her chair to look up at Sarah. 'I love Freddy! I know what he did was wrong but – oh, it was all my own fault because I said we had to keep it secret! What a fool I've been! Oh poor dear Freddy! He only drank because he was unhappy. He only wants to marry me, and I've been so unkind! What a wretch I am!'

Sarah placed her hands on Chrissie's shoulders to calm her, and hold her in her seat. 'We'll leave Mr James to Dan for the moment. He won't go away. Don't worry. Tomorrow when your heads are clearer you will be able to talk about it and decide what is the best thing to do.'

Half an hour later Chrissie was sufficiently recovered to reappear among her guests; they had all been enjoying themselves so much that she had been scarcely missed – except by

Mr McMaster, who had been searching for her, and quickly came to claim her for a dance. As Sarah watched she was relieved to see that Chrissie had regained her composure and was able to carry on a trifling conversation.

It was after four o'clock before they were on their way home once more. Dawn was just breaking, and there were long streaks of pink and green in the eastern sky. She shivered slightly in the morning air, and huddled her shawl round her shoulders. She didn't feel tired exactly, but in a slightly unreal state, not thinking of anything, and glad to breathe the crisp air after the stuffy rooms.

For a while there was silence. The horse trotted before them, and McMaster held the reins lightly.

He chuckled slightly, and she glanced towards him.

'What is it?'

'Do you know – I owe it all to you.'

She said nothing.

'It was you, Miss Shaw. Without you, I should never have come tonight.' He chuckled again. 'When I think of the invitations I have turned down. The years when I had not the heart to watch others enjoying themselves. And now tonight – I have been given my freedom back. I have been given my life back,' he added thoughtfully.

'I am glad,' she said softly.

'And it was thanks to you. Wasn't she

beautiful?' he went on immediately.

'Miss Barrington? Very. Mr McMaster, please forgive me for what I said,' she added quickly. 'It was very unkind. I should never—'

He hadn't heard her. 'I don't think I ever saw anyone like her,' he went on, pursuing his own thoughts. 'I never saw – it was a vision, a dream...'

And when they had arrived and were in the hall, he couldn't let the subject go.

'I don't feel at all tired, do you? Thirsty, though.'

'Mrs Hudson made some lemonade. I'll see if I can find it.'

It was now dawn as she returned to the drawing room with two glasses. They sipped the cool drink as the crimson edge of the sun was visible over the rim of the sea. 'Mm. I was thirsty too.'

'Too much champagne!' He laughed. 'I don't think I have a head for drink anymore. Do you know, I can't remember the last time I drank champagne. But tonight – it seemed right. It *was* right. Yes, I was celebrating.'

He soon reverted to Chrissie.

'Do you know, she reminded me of Thérèse? She was just that age when I first met her.' He laughed again. 'It's absurd, but I feel tonight I have regained my youth. I feel like a love-struck boy! What did she think of me, I wonder? She must have seen how much I admired her.' He turned to Sarah, who was standing still, holding her glass, and watching

235

him. 'Sarah, tell me honestly. What would she say to me as a suitor, do you think?'

Sarah looked down, thinking quickly. 'I think any girl would—'

'No, not any girl – Miss Barrington.'

'Mr McMaster, there is something – something you should know about Miss Barrington – which should have been announced this evening. Except there was a misunderstanding, a muddle.'

'What muddle?'

Sarah felt extremely awkward. 'I can only tell you what Miss Barrington told me.'

'Yes?'

'At the moment, she is engaged. It should have been announced tonight, only as I said, there was a muddle, and the announcement has been delayed.'

'*Engaged?*'

'I cannot explain exactly what it was but you have my word, that as far as she is concerned, she is engaged.'

He was silent, and a moment later she went on, 'I don't think you know her fiancé. It's very awkward, because it is supposed to be a secret; it would be best if I did not name him.'

'*Engaged?*'

She waited.

'But that's absurd.' He groped for words. 'We danced together the whole evening; she was charming—'

'I know. Mr McMaster – you mustn't blame her! She is very young; it simply comes naturally to her. She is not a flirt, honestly! She can't help it; she is charming to everybody. Everybody loves her. But she loves only one man. I'm sorry.'

McMaster was silent, and she waited for his reaction. At last he turned away, a thoughtful look in his eyes. He shook his head.

'What a fool I am!' He laughed ruefully. 'Forty-two years old, Sarah, and making eyes at a girl of eighteen! What must she have thought?' She waited. 'It was after I finally unburdened myself to you,' he went on at last. 'I felt so light, I thought I could do anything – and the first pretty girl I meet, I fall head over heels in love. Was it very obvious? Do you think they are laughing at me?'

'Laughing at you?' she burst out at last in the words she had been dying to speak the whole evening. 'Mr McMaster, you were the most handsome man, the most debonair, the wittiest, most stylish man in the room!'

He looked up, surprised at her outburst. For a moment they were staring into each other's eyes, then she looked down. 'It is true,' she muttered, embarrassed. 'Any girl thought herself lucky if you so much as looked at her. When you danced with Miss Barrington every woman in the room was watching you.'

She was suddenly aware that he was looking at her hard, and turned her head away. 'It's true,' she repeated listlessly. 'And Miss Barrington was the only one who couldn't see it.'

She suddenly felt very tired. 'Excuse me, Mr McMaster, I must go to bed.'

Without looking at him, she turned and left the room.

Twenty-Two

What she was to do, she had not the faintest idea. She couldn't leave; she couldn't stay.

In the morning she dragged her head off the pillow. It was all very well to go to bed at five o'clock but Robin was awake at seven. She pulled herself up and went into breakfast.

As Robin fired questions at her about the ball, she sat, her head on one hand, sipping tea. Did they like the Liszt? They were very polite but she hadn't played well; Liszt was too hard for her.

'Oh, rubbish,' Robin cried, 'you can play anything!'

Soon after breakfast they continued with his practice. If I can hang on for a little longer then I can leave; I can hand over to a *real* teacher. He's going to outgrow me soon in any case; he's going to want a tutor, as Mr McMaster always said.

Later in the morning they paused for a cup of coffee; her head was feeling clearer, though she still felt a slight trembling in her limbs.

McMaster came in to join them. She found it difficult to look at him.

'I have been listening,' he said cheerfully. The exertions of the night did not seem to have taxed him. He seemed as vigorous as ever. 'He has made such strides; he should have come to play last night. Don't you agree, Sarah?'

She glanced up at him. Was this a joke at her expense? But he was smiling at her and now reached over and took her hand. 'Forgive me – I know I should have addressed you as Miss Shaw, but I feel we know one another so well, it seems more comfortable, as if you were one of the family. You don't mind?'

She shook her head without speaking at first and at last muttered, 'Of course not.'

Later he returned to his study and the practice continued.

How could he be so tactless? She could never be one of the family. She could – and would – be replaced. A young man, no doubt a graduate of one of the ancient universities, properly educated, a man who knew Latin and mathematics, would take over and Robin would receive the education befitting a gentleman's son. Robin would have to grow up; obviously they could not continue this haphazard, playful game they indulged in, in which they looked into whatever book happened to hand, geography one day, history another, and there was no order or regularity about any of it.

She looked down at his curly head as he

concentrated on the page in front of him. I love him, I don't think I could bear to leave him. He is so pretty, so affectionate, and we are so happy together...

That evening, after Robin had been put to bed and they were together in the drawing room, she could see that McMaster had something on his mind. Eventually, he roused himself to speak.

'I have been thinking over what you said. I wonder whether I shouldn't write to Miss Barrington to apologize?'

'Apologize? What for?'

'You don't think she might have found me too – I don't know – too presumptuous?'

'Mr McMaster, please don't talk such nonsense. Please!'

'But you don't think she might have ... got the wrong idea?'

'What wrong idea? That you found her very attractive? There's nothing very strange about that. So did every man in the room.'

That night she went to bed, if possible even more depressed than the previous night. Even after he had digested the fact of Chrissie's engagement, there must inevitably be other young women. Every time he spoke to a young woman she would be wondering – is this the one? She decided, at some hour of the night, she must leave. She got out of bed – it was a warm summer night – lit a candle, sat at her table, and began a letter.

She began a letter but found it very hard to

finish. She started several times, with convoluted excuses and apologies for abandoning Robin – and each time came to a halt. That was it. Even if only for Robin, she must stay until he was a little older. If she were to leave now it would make him unhappy. He would certainly abandon the piano and all their work together would be wasted. She could not do it – yet. Soon, perhaps, when he was older and could more easily accept it – and when she knew she was handing him over to someone educated and capable.

Then she just sat at the table, her head in her hands, and wept.

The following morning she was not weeping. She was pleasant, she allowed Mr McMaster to call her Sarah, she allowed him to indulge the fiction that they were a family; and she continued with Robin's lessons upstairs.

McMaster disappeared for a few days to London on business; and it was a relief. Life was so much simpler without him. She could concentrate on his son.

He returned, however, and continued to take a close interest in Robin's lessons. He would often appear at the door as they sat at the piano and she would be very conscious of him.

'I have never been so happy,' he told her after the lesson one afternoon. 'Watching you two together and seeing what progress Robin has made, I did not think I could ever be so happy again. I owe you so much.'

She smiled pleasantly and muttered some platitude.

But it was on another of these afternoons that she could suddenly take no more.

It was warm and the French windows stood open so that they could hear the gentle summer rain; it had a healing and beneficial sound. Beyond the window and the veranda, the garden stretched away, thick with vigorous summer growth, and it seemed the flowers were reaching upwards for the life-giving water. Summer had come late to North Yorkshire, but it was here in all its glory, and the wallflowers, the stocks, the roses crowded along the verge of the lawn.

She was standing beside Robin as he sat at the keyboard, looking out at the garden, her mind far away, when McMaster came into the room. As Robin finished the piece, he came towards them.

'It was impossible to concentrate while you were playing. I had to come in to listen.'

'Oh,' she turned, 'I'm sorry! I should have closed the door.'

'No!' he laughed. 'I assure you. I would rather a thousand times be listening. He has made such amazing progress. I feel he has it in him to become a really first-class player. To think, Sarah, in five or ten years' time we may see his name on a poster – we may be sitting at a concert to hear him play!'

At the manifest absurdity of this something in her snapped. All the weight of the last months were too much for her; the thought of being still, in five or ten years' time, his tame governess – it all rushed over her and, without knowing what she did, she dashed out through the French windows and covered her face as she wept hopeless tears.

For minutes she could be aware only of the hot grief flooding through her, but gradually she became aware of the rain beating on her head and shoulders and then that he was standing behind her; became aware of his voice, softened by the sound of the rain.

'Sarah...' It was tentative. And then, 'Are you all right?' Another pause. 'What is the matter?'

She couldn't speak, and only wept help-lessly.

'Sarah – do come inside – you will be soak-ed through.' A pause. 'I'm sorry if it's any-thing I said. Won't you come in?'

'I'm sorry, Mr McMaster,' she hiccupped at last, her voice muffled in her hands, 'I shall have to give notice.'

'Give notice? What on earth do you mean? And do for Heaven's sake come inside. You will be saturated. Sarah – what is the matter? For God's sake, tell me what's wrong.'

'I can't tell you and I must leave.'

'But that's absurd!' He took her by the shoulders and forced her to face him. Her hair was plastered down, her thin summer frock was pressing wet against her. She could not face him; she could not stop crying, she felt helpless, weak, as if she would dissolve completely in the rain.

Now at last some door of understanding opened in his mind; now at last he perceived what had so long been staring him in the face. He pressed her to him and kissed her hard, passionately on the mouth, slipping, sliding his lips against her wet skin, kissing her again on her lips, on her cheek, on her forehead, covering her face with his kisses, while she felt his hands all about her, clasping, pressing her through the flimsy muslin. Inert, passive in his arms, she had surrendered all power over herself into his hands; he must do with her as he would.

'What's the matter? What are you doing?' She heard Robin's voice distantly from the room.

She disentangled herself from him and for a moment they were staring into each other's eyes.

His eyes were filled with a burning concentration. 'I must have been blind,' he whispered. 'It was you. It was always you. Why didn't I see that?'

She shuddered, still unable to think, to order a coherent thought or to frame a word.

'Are you cold? Come inside.'

'No. No, I am all right.' She drew a jagged breath, and her hand reached for her hair. She looked round as if only now understanding where she was or what she was doing. His arms were still round her. She smiled wanly at him. 'I am sorry to have caused so much trouble.'

244

He laughed a low soft laugh. 'My darling, darling Sarah. My good angel.'

She regained a little more strength, and laughed too, looking down, and then looked up shyly again. 'Go in. Robin is wondering what we are doing. I will go round to the kitchen, and then go up and change my dress. I will come down in a few minutes.'

In her room she peeled off her wet clothes. She still felt weak and shivery and her mind was a jumble of incoherent thoughts, but all through her there was a glowing warmth, that at last he had *seen* her, and known that it was her all the time, her that he loved. But as she dressed herself hurriedly in dry things, as this wonderful feeling buoyed her up, so that she felt indescribably light, indescribably happy, she suddenly also felt exhausted, as if the experience – the discovery – and the rain had washed all the energy out of her. She decided to lie down and rest for a second and was immediately asleep.

As soon as she woke, she wondered whether it had not been a dream. And even when she had reassured herself, she asked, had he really meant it? Was it an aberration – because of her tears and the rain? And his happiness about Robin? Something in her, however, told her that he did really mean it. As she arranged her dress and her hair before going downstairs, she trembled again, unsure of how to address him; what he would expect or intend.

And in the meantime she had simply abandoned Robin. With any luck his father would have made some excuse.

Eventually she did descend to dinner. It was immediately clear that McMaster had satisfied Robin's curiosity and as she sat at the table the little boy was sympathetic and hoped her headache was better now.

'Much better, thank you.'

She hardly dared to catch his father's eye and found it easier to talk to Robin; she knew however that his eyes were on her throughout the dinner.

Later there came the inevitable moment when they were alone together. As she came downstairs and into the drawing room, he was waiting for her. He seemed undecided and she paused at the door, so that they were regarding one another silently and it was as if each were waiting for the other to make a move, to reassure them that it had really happened.

He must have seen from the expression in her eyes that he had been right, however, because he moved to her, took her hands and raised them to his lips. Then he took her in his arms, kissed her gently on her lips and held her silently.

After a minute, they parted slightly and he looked down into her face. 'I don't know what to say to you. Either everything – or nothing. As if on the one hand everything were already understood between us, so that we have no need to say anything; or on the

246

other a rushing urge to tell you all the hundred feelings and thoughts, the prayers and memories and wishes, that have been crowding into my brain since this afternoon. Was it really us? Did I really kiss you? Oh yes, I will never forget that moment; you so beautiful, so – I don't know – so vulnerable, so helpless.'

She laughed slightly. 'You mean I was looking like a drowned rat?'

'Don't laugh,' he replied quickly. 'You cannot imagine, you will never know, the thoughts that have rushed through my brain. That you have been here all these months beneath my roof, and I never *saw* you. All the time, Sarah, it was you, *you*, and I could not see it. What a fool I have been! What must you have thought of me?'

She did not reply, and after a moment he went on thoughtfully, not really wanting a reply, 'I think I must have known something, though, ever since the first time I saw you. No – perhaps even on the ship – perhaps then, when you held your face up to the wind and the snow – as if you *welcomed* it—'

'I did welcome it,' she murmured.

'Even then, that first time, I knew there was something about you, something that I could respond to. And then that first time you played the piano, and you were, I don't know, you were *seized* by the music, perfectly responsive to the feeling. I think I knew even then – though I did not know I knew it.'

Still holding her they sat side by side, his arm round her, her head on his shoulder.

After a long time it was she now who began to speak. 'When did I know I loved you? I can't remember. A day just came and I knew it, and I couldn't remember afterwards what it had been like before I loved you. I think I always loved you, even before I knew you, even before I had met you. I was just waiting to meet you, and to discover that it was you that was the one.' She paused. 'I think it was because I was sorry for you. You seemed so desperately unhappy.'

'You could tell?'

'I think so.'

'I was unhappy, though I didn't know it myself. There was a great void in my life, after the death of Thérèse, that I didn't know how to fill.'

He looked down into her face.

'And now it is filled?'

He nodded and kissed her slowly, gently brushing her lips with his, and running them across her forehead and into her hair. And she knew all his lovemaking would be like this, exploring her slowly, tenderly. And there was already within her a melting, yearning, desire as she arched her back, and reached her face to his kiss.

Twenty-Three

By the time they reached the top of the stairs she was convinced of it; there seemed such a massive certainty between them, such a huge necessity, such an irresistible pressure. His arm was about her waist and she looked up into his face in the half light of the dusk, in the silence of the house, and could hear her heart beating until it would burst, could feel the trembling in her limbs. He bent to kiss her again, as they had been kissing the last hour, kissing, touching, brushing their lips together until she thought she would die or melt or dissolve in a bath of yearning need. But now, as they came to her bedroom door, they turned to face one another.

He kissed her again.

'Now that I have found you I shall not let you escape.' His lips brushed her face, his hand ran across her hair, caressed her cheek.

'Oh my darling,' she gasped, choking with desire. She wanted to go on, Why can't we do it now? Please, don't think, don't ask me any questions, just make love to me, or I shall die. Instead, struggling to stay in control, she pulled slightly away. 'But—'

He seemed to understand and relaxed his

hold on her. They looked into each other's eyes, and at last, kissing her on the forehead, he whispered, 'Goodnight, my own true love.'

With a last caress, he turned away along the landing to his own door.

As she shut the door behind her, she could still feel the trembling through her. She was ready to die for him – or to die in his arms. It seemed madness, the two of them sitting in different rooms, when all they wanted was to fly into each other's arms.

She sat on the edge of her bed and tried to cool her head. This was not the way. Throw herself into bed with him and make love furiously all night? Conceive his child? And then? Tomorrow tell him about George? John had never asked about her family. Soon he must; soon she must tell him everything, tell him her real situation. How could she give herself to him before she had explained everything?

And then what would he do? Send her back to her husband?

She did not sleep much that night; and neither, she suspected, did he. As soon as she woke, heavy headed from a shallow sleep filled with dreams, she thought, the best thing would be simply to lie. John would want to marry her, she knew and he was the sort of man who did not hesitate to go after the thing he wanted – he had made that abundantly clear in telling her the story of Thérèse. He would simply push ahead with arrangements for a wedding.

A very simple but very bold idea came to her. If he asked her, why not simply say yes? She had been here this long time and nothing had been heard from London.

It would solve all her problems. The three of them would live here in Whitby; they could go on all their lives together and no one the wiser.

But then, what about her parents? Sooner or later she must speak to them. They had disowned her on her marriage to George, but she had always meant to seek a reconciliation. Especially when she should chance to have a child.

But as things stood at present it would be impossible. 'How do you do, mamma dear? This is John. We are lovers and I am expecting his baby.' Or, 'We are bigamously married – but never mind about that'?

That morning, however, she found it impossible to raise the subject. As soon as they were alone together, his arm snaked about her waist. All day they went on like this, touching, caressing, fondling. She thought everybody must be aware of what had happened: Mrs Hudson, Josiah, Robin. It was so difficult to keep themselves from touching each other.

As the days passed their desire, because it found no physical release, built within them, hotter and hotter. She felt herself consumed, burning within. Sometimes she would just sit and stare at him; the masculine weight of

251

him, the solid body which she had seen on the beach, the nakedness which had triggered such a feverish dream, it was all there, every day in the house with her, passing her, she had only to reach out to touch him. When he took her in his arms, and she put her arms round his neck, and he pressed her to him, she held that heavy man's strength. She wanted it, wanted it in her, wanted them to fuse together, to become one. She was dizzy with desire.

And she had an idea that he was too. One morning as they were embracing, his arms about her, as he kissed her forehead, and ran his hand through her hair, he said, 'I should like to give you a treat. How would you like to go to the theatre?'

'I should love it. But there is no theatre in Whitby.'

'But there is in Scarborough.' He gave her a conspiratorial smile.

'Scarborough?' She felt very stupid, as she grasped for his meaning. 'But isn't that – well, isn't that rather far to go to the theatre?'

He looked at her seriously. 'I thought we could stay at a hotel. For a few days.'

There was a pause, while she stared into his eyes, thinking fast. Surely he wasn't thinking the thought which immediately flashed into her mind? In her experience a man and a woman, if they weren't married, went to a hotel for one thing only.

'Have I offended you?' he asked calmly.

'No, of course not,' she said hurriedly. She

swallowed. 'Will you allow me to think about it?'

He kissed her lovingly. 'Think about it. As long as you like,' he whispered caressingly.

How could she refuse? It was all madness anyway. She had no idea how it was going to turn out. That afternoon, she took his hand. 'I have thought about what – you suggested, my darling. If it is what you want, I should be very happy to...' She swallowed again, and could not meet his eyes.

His hand snaked behind her head, and he kissed her hair. 'My darling,' he breathed.

There was something conspiratorial, illicit, about it that set her pulse racing. It was wrong, but it was what they both wanted.

He insisted on her having fresh clothes, pretty things, a new bonnet trimmed with flowers, new shoes, and on a Saturday morning they set out in the trap, boxes and bags under their feet.

They crossed down through the town, and then, for the first time since the ill-fated trip to 't'Awd Abba Well', she was out on the moors, the landscape spread about them, long stretches of furze and heather now purple. There was a fine blue sky with little puffy clouds, a fresh breeze in her face, and as she took long breaths she could hear larks far above. Sometimes they would catch glimpses of the sea, sparkling in the bright sunshine. The horse trotted contentedly before them.

It was barely an hour and a half before they rolled down into Scarborough and were

253

clattering through the busy streets of what she could see immediately was a large cosmopolitan town filled with summer visitors. They drove to a hotel on the seafront, their bags were taken out by uniformed flunkeys and a groom led the trap round to the stables. As they went up into the hotel the door was opened by a giant of a doorman; inside it was carpeted and managers and staff crossed the spacious lobby dressed smartly in livery or frock coats. An unctuous receptionist passed the large leather-bound volume for him to sign then the pen was passed to her and without thinking she signed Mrs McMaster.

The porter set down their bags and boxes, John tossed him a coin, the door was closed behind him, and John turned to her. Now that they were here she was suddenly very uncertain again and before he could reach her she turned away to the window and threw it up. She had to make up her mind; whatever happened, she must tell him the truth first. But if she did – what then? Would he not send her back to her husband? A man in his situation? She looked out at the panorama spread before them. The air was intoxicating.

He took her gently in his arms and turned her. She couldn't stop herself trembling and he noticed this.

'You're not unhappy about this?' he asked tentatively.

Without saying anything, she swallowed, and shook her head slightly. At last she whispered, 'You have been very good to me.'

'Good to you? I am infernally selfish. I am doing this entirely for my own pleasure.'

He really did think she was a virgin, it was clear.

He kissed her and immediately the chemistry began to work; they collapsed on the bed, kissing hectically, and he was over her, pressing her, his hands everywhere. She thought, if this goes on another fifteen seconds it will be too late. She barely had the strength of will to work herself loose; her head ringing with a throbbing desire, she sat up, slightly dizzy.

'John – please – give me a little time—'

He sat up too and reached for her hand. 'Don't worry my darling,' he brought her hand to his lips, 'I can wait.'

'No – it's not that – I – it's just that—'

'You don't have to explain.' He touched her hair tenderly; almost a fatherly touch, it seemed. Poor man, she thought, I can see the thoughts running through your head: What a brute I am, forcing my lustful attentions on this pure flower, this unspotted maiden – etc, etc. Oh God if only he knew.

An hour later they were strolling up and down the promenade. The beach was filled, bathing machines were ranged at the waterside, donkeys paraded solemnly with little children on their backs. It was very lively and cheering.

Later they returned to the hotel and after tea went to their room to prepare for the theatre visit. In all her other preoccupations,

255

she had given it scarcely a thought. Standing before the looking glass, she adjusted her dress, which was silk with a wide full skirt, set off the shoulder and cut revealingly round the bodice. During her discussions with the dressmaker she had decided to make the dress as attractive, and even as provocative, as she could. She so wanted to give him pleasure.

When they were ready to go out, he surveyed her preparations. He took her hands in his, gloved, and brought them to his lips.

'Don't you look a peach!'

They laughed and she almost blushed. 'Where did you ever hear such a phrase?'

'It was something Robin said about you one day. Took me by surprise too.'

As they arrived at the theatre and were mingling with the audience she found that her London tastes were rather in advance of Yorkshire and she felt distinctly undressed in comparison with many of the women about her. John also was conscious of this and she quickly detected that he was not unhappy about it. Taking her arm under his, he squired her proudly through the crowd to their seats.

The theatre was full and everyone looked so well, she thought, glowing with health and high spirits, red-faced from the sea air. Below her in the pit, people jostled on their benches and in front the orchestra were beginning to assemble and tune up. She couldn't help turning to John, taking his hand and giving it a squeeze. 'Thank you for bringing me,' she whispered and, turning back to look over the audience, drew a long breath of happiness. What a fool she was! She had completely lost sight of the most important thing – that she and John had found each other, and whatever difficulties might lie ahead, they would fight their way through together: she and John and Robin, and soon, with God's will, more children. And for a second she felt a smarting of tears at the corner of her eyes. And she owed it all to him, the dear man. Tonight, she decided, come what might, she would repay him.

The programme was mixed: a ballet to begin with, followed by a ferocious drama, involving a helpless maiden, the heiress to an ancient fortune, her handsome betrothed and his scheming brother. Though she couldn't take it too seriously, she was in a mood to enjoy everything that evening and entered into the spirit of it thoroughly. When justice had been done and the lovers reunited, and the curtain swung down to tumultuous applause, she joined in as readily as any.

It was now the interval and Sarah excused herself briefly. Feeling uplifted and still gripped by the thrills of the play they had seen, she was passing through the jolly crowds in the foyer and the bar in search of the ladies' room when she heard a voice clearly through the hubbub. It ran through her like an electric shock.

'By Jove, that's Sally Bradley!'

Twenty-Four

For a second her body was grasped in a frozen embrace. In another moment, however, without turning, she hurried on – only to be stopped again.

'Sally! Hi! Wait!'

She looked up and about her. There was a circular balcony round the foyer and a man was leaning over it waving at her. She knew him very well – Marcus Collins, one of George's drinking companions.

Without thinking, she took up her skirts and ran into the street.

She heard, 'Sally! Wait!' but she did not stop running. It was still light on the promenade as she pushed blindly through the crowds, dodging across the street and narrowly avoiding a carriage, not watching where she was going or slowing down until she reached the hotel, ran up the steps, stopped breathlessly at the reception to ask for her key and ran up to their room. She slammed the door behind her and sat heavily on the side of the bed.

She was still dragging the breath into her and her heart was thudding in her chest. Her whole body was trembling; she clutched herself in an attempt to control it. She must go;

they must leave. If Marcus saw her again, he would insist she return to George. If he saw her with John, he would tell him everything. Then John would send her back without a doubt...

But how could she ask John to leave? He would demand an explanation. She started to her feet, turned to the window, saw nothing, turned back and sat on the edge of the bed again. Oh God, he must be wondering where she had got to. He might think she had had an accident. But she dared not go out; if Marcus Collins found her he was quite capable of carrying her bodily back to London. And whatever happened she mustn't let Marcus meet John. It was impossible. And now! John had been looking forward to this moment – and so had she – she clutched her head in her hands and burst into tears. Of course it could never work. What a fool she had been even to think it.

She wiped her eyes. This was no good. She had to think up a story. She washed her face and sat down to wait for John.

It must have been two hours later that he came in. It was nearly midnight and the room had grown quite dark. He was intensely relieved when he saw her.

'Sarah – are you there? Oh my darling, thank God you're safe! But why haven't you lit a candle? I've been looking everywhere – I thought there had been an accident! Are you all right?'

She seized this opportunity to busy herself

259

with the candle. As she hunted for the lucifers she muttered, 'I'm sorry I had to leave you like that. Please forgive me. I suddenly felt—'

The candle was lit but she did not turn. He was behind her and took her in his arms, turning her to face him. 'Sarah, my dearest, what *is* the matter?' He studied her face. 'Are you unwell? Shall I call a doctor?'

She shook her head. 'No – I'm better now.'

'But you're shivering. Here.' He reached for her shawl and draped it about her shoulders. He crossed to the window, closed it, and drew the curtains. 'You've been sitting in the draught. What on earth happened?' He sat her on the edge of the bed, his arm round her shoulders.

However, before she could say anything, he went on, 'No, don't say anything. I understand.'

'Do you?'

She looked up into his face and he could see she had been weeping.

'Oh yes.' He drew a sigh. 'I understand all right. I've been immensely stupid. What must you think of me, to take advantage of you like this? What an oaf I am.' He was silent, then went on in a low voice, 'You see, after Thérèse died I never thought I would hold a woman in my arms again. I thought all that was gone for ever. Then, when you were kind to Robin and when I watched you with him, I suddenly had a picture of us all together, as if my life were not over but there could be happiness for me in this world after all and that I could walk down the street or into a room with you on my arm and people would admire you and congratulate me for a lucky dog. That I should have a second chance at happiness...'

There was a long silence as he gradually released his arm from her shoulders and all the time she was thinking, I must tell him, why don't I tell him? What a coward I am; he is so unhappy and it's all my fault.

She could not bring herself to speak and, after a long silence in which they sat side by side, he rose at last.

'You take the bed. I will make myself comfortable on the sofa.' He coughed, evidently embarrassed now. 'I'll go downstairs for ten minutes to give you a chance to prepare yourself for bed.'

Then he was gone. She had never felt less like sleep in her life.

Eventually, however, she forced herself to undress and get into bed. She partially drew the curtains about her and lay waiting for him to return. What was she to say? There was only one thing – one honest thing – to say, but she didn't have the strength to say it. Oh God, what a coward I am! She turned over, staring up into the drapes around the bed.

Why don't I just tell him the truth – and offer to become his mistress? We can go on living together and nobody would be the wiser.

But would he agree? He wants to marry me. And he can't.

She heard the door move and turned away, staring into the dark corner of the room. After a few moments, the candle was extinguished.

The journey home was made in silence. Robin was surprised to see them. Sarah explained that she had been unwell, and thought it better to return. Nothing more was said and lessons were resumed but she knew Robin must notice something. Meals were consumed in silence and eye contact was avoided. Everything was her fault and she did not know how to break out of the situation. It was worse than it had been before. They were supposed to be in love; that meant there should be no secrets between them. Instead there was an enormous secret. McMaster knew that something was wrong. He imagined, however, that it was his fault; that he had blundered, presumed upon her, and thought she must be offended with him.

It was all madness and she knew it couldn't last long; she *must* take the matter into her own hands, tell the truth and trust to providence – she couldn't see what else she could do.

This situation went on for three weeks and still she had not plucked up the resolution to bring it to a head. Then one day she received a note from the White Horse that a parcel had arrived for her. She could not remember having ordered anything by post. Nevertheless, as it was a fine afternoon she walked into town.

She met Mr Empson in the hallway and was told there was a gentleman waiting for her in the parlour. Before she had time to think, she turned into the parlour and found her husband.

She was so surprised that for a moment she could not move. George had been sitting in an armchair but in a moment he was on his feet and moved quickly to close the door behind her. She could not escape.

'Sorry about the little stratagem, but I was afraid you might give me the slip otherwise.'

'What do you want?' she said weakly. She found herself slightly breathless.

'Pretty obvious, I would have thought,' he said casually. He seemed in no great hurry. 'I want my wife back.'

'I'm not coming back.'

She wouldn't look at him. After a moment he went on, quite simply, 'I've missed you, Sally. Really. It's been no fun since you left. Damn miserable, it's a fact.'

'You know why I left.'

He walked round until she could see him. She was about to turn away again, but found she couldn't. As she looked at him, he was just as he had always been: a heavy sort of man; the sort of man who looked a bit lived in, his clothes rumpled, his cravat untidy, a man who took no care of his health, who seemed to live from day to day, who liked his food and drink, and generally was out for fun.

A man not given to introspection and completely without ambition.

'Sally, darling,' he said, his head slightly on one side, 'you know what I'm like. I blow up, and then it's over. You shouldn't take it to heart.'

'Take it to heart? You were ready to kill me.'

'No! On my life!' He came a step nearer. 'How could I? You had it all wrong, honestly. Sally, my dearest, it was a moment – just a moment – I lost my head. I would never hurt you – how could I? You're my little mouse, my ray of sunshine; honestly, you're my – well, my reason for living. You're all I have. Honestly, it's true. All the rest, all those hangers-on, a set of spongers – you know yourself. I'm going to chuck 'em all. Give up the drink – well, cut down anyway—' He flashed that gleaming smile that used to make her heart turn over.

He came another step closer, smiling down at her, and spoke more quietly, caressingly. 'We'll settle down, be a good little husband and wife; have a little George and Sally too. What do you say? Hmm? Come back with me – do.'

He took her hand.

'We were made for each other, you know it. I've not looked at another woman since you left. Just been thinking of you. All the time. Dreaming of you.'

She knew it all, every turn of his head, every intonation of his voice – oh she knew him. Only too well. And for a moment could feel

264

herself sliding back. That body she had held so often, that she knew so well, every gesture, every little movement. The winning way he would tilt his head when he wanted something from her. How many times had he sidled up to her and slid his arm round her waist, nuzzling the side of her neck with his lips. Why was she so wretchedly *weak*?

'How did you find me?' she asked at last.

He shrugged. 'Easy enough. After Collins wired me, I got him to put a notice in the local paper. We soon had an answer, then I came up.'

'Someone knew me in Scarborough?'

'Well, he wasn't a native – a commercial traveller. Very helpful, he was. Told me all I needed to know.'

She had grasped it by now. 'Mr Hardcastle, no doubt,' she said briefly.

'Yes,' George went on casually. 'Very helpful he was.'

'What else did he tell you?'

'Everything. Pretty much.'

'Why didn't you come to the house, then?'

'Well,' he hesitated, 'I thought it might be simpler for us to have a quiet little chat first – without any histrionics. No raised voices. Look, Sally,' he went on more briskly, 'I know the situation. I'm not going to make a fuss. You come home now, like a good little wife, and we'll say no more. Draw a line under it. Forget it ever happened. That's fair.'

'I'm not going home.'

'Go on,' he urged, coming a step nearer.

'Why make a fuss? You've had a nice holiday. We've both learned our lesson. Time to go home.'

'I'm not going home,' she repeated in a low voice. 'And I had no lesson to learn.' She turned into his face. 'Now let me make this clear. I am not coming home, I am never coming to any home with you. I never want to see you again. Not as long as I live. Goodbye.'

She turned to the door, but George went past her and stood with his back to it.

'Sally! You can't do this. You're my wife. I'm not letting anyone take you away from me.'

By this time she had crossed to the fireplace and rung the bell.

There was a moment of silence, and then the door was opened by Mr Empson. George was forced to stand aside. Sarah walked briskly past him.

'Goodbye. We shall not meet again.'

As she was walking out of the door, she noticed Marcus Collins in the doorway opposite. She walked out into the street and headed for the bridge.

A moment later George was beside her.

'Sally! Don't be so hot-headed! What do you think you're going to do with this barrister of yours? You can't marry him.'

She said nothing and went marching briskly on. George attempted to take her arm but she shook him off.

'Have you considered what your parents are going to say when they find out you're living with another man?'

'I'll write to them myself. In any case I am not living with him. I merely lodge in his house – along with the other servants.'

'Who's going to believe you? No one. And what happens when he's tired of you? Have you thought about that? You'll be ruined!'

'I'll worry about that when it happens. In any case he isn't going to. Get off me!'

She shook herself free of him again with a violent gesture and continued. They were crossing the bridge. 'Go back to London, George. I'm not coming with you.'

'By God, we'll see about that.' He stopped at last and let her continue.

She marched quickly all the way back along the cliff-top path, seeing nothing except George's face, and seething with a mixture of anger and indignation, rage and also somewhere deep inside, fear.

When she got back she threw herself into an armchair and sat for some minutes staring out of the window. Nothing would come into focus. She only knew one thing. She must tell him now.

She knocked at his study door and went in. McMaster was at his desk.

'John, there is something I must tell you.'

It was so abrupt that he looked up in surprise. He understood her tone immediately.

'What is it?'

'Please come with me into the drawing room.'

They crossed the hall, went in, and she closed the door behind her.

'John,' she began before he had a chance to speak, 'there is something I have to tell you. Something I should have said months ago. Please sit down.'

He sat without speaking and looked up at her.

She walked to the window and back before going on. 'The fact is, I am married.'

He did not speak and after a moment she sat in the chair opposite him. 'My husband's name is George Bradley. We have been married eighteen months. We have no children. Unfortunately my husband is a very erratic man, capricious. Very unreliable. He can be charming and funny. I was in love with him when we married. I will be honest: I loved him passionately, even though before we married I had begun to know what he was like, I had seen the way his mood could change.' She sighed. 'Strange as it may sound, I found it attractive, as if he were some romantic figure, Byronic, a bit out of the ordinary. But of course once we were married and I got to know his changes of mood better, I became anxious and had to watch him carefully, to try to head them off. The situation was made infinitely worse for many reasons. First of all I had married against my parents' wishes. Then I discovered George had no steady employment or any regular income. He is one of those men who cannot understand why they are not living in comfortable circumstances and never comprehend it is themselves who are at fault. Our financial crises were always someone else's fault. The situation became worse when he began to beat me. The first time it happened I thought I would never stand for this. I would leave him. But I did not leave him. Where could I go? To my parents? They would not have me. To my sister? Her house was far too small. Besides her husband thought I only had myself to blame for marrying George in the first place. So I tolerated it, until one Saturday night last December when he attacked me so violently I thought if I didn't get out, he would kill me.'

As these memories crowded back, she could feel her defences crumbling.

'I'm sorry. I should have told you all this before. But I was always afraid you would send me back.'

McMaster had listened in silence up till now. He looked into her eyes. 'Couldn't you have trusted me?' he said softly.

'Yes! I did know I could trust you. But I was frightened too. When we went to Scarborough, I was ready to give myself to you. I didn't care any longer, I just loved you so madly, I tried to forget everything, and I thought we could just be happy together. Then when we were in the theatre I saw a friend of George's and he recognized me. That's why I fled back to the hotel. I had been so looking forward to us – being together that night.'

She bit her lip, trying desperately to control herself. 'I could see how upset you were. Can you imagine how *I* felt?'

McMaster reached forward and took her in his arms. He held her close for a long minute. At last she separated a little and looked up.

'But, John – now, you see, he's here.'

'In Whitby?'

She nodded. 'I have just seen him – at the White Horse. He asked me to go back with him.'

'What did you say?'

'I would never go back with him.'

He smiled, a grim smile. 'Good girl.'

'But, John – now that you have heard – all this—'

He was still holding her hands. 'We shall institute proceedings for a judicial separation.'

'Oh,' she hesitated, 'so – I shouldn't apply for a divorce?'

'Has he been unfaithful?'

'I don't know. I don't think so.'

'A wife cannot obtain a divorce from her husband without proof of adultery on his part.'

'But he nearly killed me.'

'There is no law against a husband beating his wife, Sarah.'

Twenty-Five

Dear George,

How can I ever forget the night you nearly murdered me? Do you in all seriousness expect me ever to set foot in your house again? I would sooner die. Since I have been here in Whitby I have had the tremendous good fortune to be employed by Mr McMaster as governess to his son. Over these last few months we have come to love one another, all three of us, and I could not dream of deserting him or his son. John McMaster means more to me than life itself. I love him and I will never return to you.

Sarah

She sealed up the letter and began a second, to her parents. The tone was less emphatic. She acknowledged that her father had been right about George and hoped that in time they might be reconciled. It was something she wished for more than anything. In the meantime they were not to worry about her. She was safe and well, she was in employment and had nothing to worry about.

Then she sat down to wait. She hoped that

George would take the hint and leave her alone, but she had an idea that he wouldn't. Everything in his tone spoke of a man who felt he was in the right. He had taken nothing she said seriously, regarding it in the light of the vagaries of women, something that a husband had the right to ignore and trample over. What was worse, she knew that ninety-nine men out of a hundred would agree with him. She was his wife; he had a right to her. Her place was at his side. If he had chosen to make a scene in the street he could easily have got half a dozen men to help him man-handle her into a carriage. In fact, looking back on it, it was a wonder he hadn't.

The reaction was not long in coming.

Late the following morning, towards midday, she was sitting at the table with Robin going over some French when she saw George coming along the cliff path with Marcus Collins. She rang for Josiah immediately, and as he scooped Robin up she said hurriedly, 'There are two men coming to see your papa on business, Robin. Josiah will take you upstairs and Mrs Hudson will bring you your lunch in a moment.'

'Are you coming with me?' Robin said as he was at the doorway on Josiah's back.

'I will in a moment, darling. I'll just wait to see what these men want.'

Josiah had barely disappeared upstairs when there was a tremendous hammering at the door.

'Open up! I know you're in there!'

Another thunderous burst of hammering. John emerged from his study as Josiah was coming down the stairs. McMaster glanced up at him. 'Get Jenny to sit with Robin, Josiah, till I get rid of these two.'

He opened the door and George almost fell on top of him. His face was puffed and flushed, his eyes bloodshot. It was not a pretty sight.

George reared up and thrust his forefinger at McMaster's chest.

'So you're the man! The wife-stealer!'

McMaster took him by the arm and hauled in. George stumbled forward, caught off balance as Marcus Collins followed him and in a moment they were all in the drawing room. McMaster closed the door.

'I'll give you five minutes,' he said calmly.

'You're a villain, sir, a thief. You've stolen another man's wife! Do you know the trouble she's caused? Her parents were mad with anxiety! We didn't know whether she was alive or dead! We scoured the morgues! Dragged the Serpentine! Wired to Paris and Amsterdam! And it could all have been avoided with one wire! Just one wire, sir! Now, I'm taking her home with me and I'd just like to see you stop me. Sally, I've wired your parents and they're coming to see you as soon as we get home. I can't tell you how relieved they were to know you were safe. We're all going to let bygones be bygones. Turn over a new leaf, start afresh. Now pack your bags – ' turning back to McMaster and waving wildly at him – 'and don't you try to interfere – or it'll be the worse for you!'

McMaster wasn't impressed by this drunken bluster. His voice never rose. 'Mrs Bradley isn't leaving this house against her will, you have my word for that. Sarah, are you going with him?'

'Never.'

'In that case, gentlemen,' McMaster came forward in a relaxed manner, 'it is time to come to terms.'

George swung on him, mystified.

'Terms, gentlemen. You understand the word?'

George made a move towards Sarah but McMaster also moved to cut him off. There was something alert, athletic about McMaster's movements; it was clear to all that he could handle the pair of them if they did try anything. There was an embarrassed pause before McMaster continued in his calm voice.

'As I said, terms. It's very simple. I'm prepared to buy your wife off you.'

'*Buy* her?'

'Yes. What's so strange about that? You're always short of money, I'm told. I'll finance your action for divorce. You can cite me as co-respondent, the action will be undefended, and I'll add a decent premium on top. Say, a thousand?'

George stepped back; he appeared scandalized. '*Buy my wife?* What do you take me for?'

'I'll tell you what I take you for,' said

McMaster calmly, 'a scoundrel. I've made you an offer, a very decent offer in my opinion. You won't get a better. Your wife is never coming back to you – why not save yourself a lot of trouble, and make a nice profit into the bargain? Think it over.'

'I'm talking to my solicitors! I want my wife back! She's made me look an utter fool! I'll not stand for it, I tell you straight.' It was as if he had heard nothing McMaster had said. 'Sally, get your things, we're going home.' He thrust out his finger at McMaster. 'And don't you say anything more!'

McMaster glanced at Sarah for a second and could see the determination in her eye.

'All right,' he said calmly. 'You've had your say and you've heard my terms. Good terms they are and you won't get better. Now get out.'

'I'm not leaving without my wife.'

'You're leaving now, if you have to be thrown out.'

'Ah, come to that has it, a threat of violence? A man of the law, too. You heard that Marcus, he threatened me. You're a witness.'

'Get out,' McMaster said in a low final voice.

'Not without my wife.'

'Very well, you leave me no choice.' He crossed to the fireplace and tugged at the bell.

George laughed. 'Calling up reinforcements, are we?'

'It'll be simpler.'

A moment later there was a slight knock

and Josiah came into the room. For all his gentle manners, he towered over George and Marcus.

'These two gentlemen are just leaving, Josiah, show them to the door, will you?'

George took a moment to size up Josiah's broad shoulders. Nevertheless, as he was passing McMaster towards the door, he leered at him.

'Hiding behind the butler!' and laughed.

In a second McMaster had stretched him on the carpet. There was a look of surprise on George's face as he reached for his nose, where a trickle of blood had appeared. He wiped his hand over his nose and examined the blood on his fingers as he tried to make sense of what had happened. At last, as he was struggling to his feet he glanced to his friend. 'You saw that, Marcus. He used violence.'

'Get out.'

'That'll look good in the report, won't it?'

Then they were gone.

As the door was closed behind them, she heard Robin's voice from above.

'Sarah? What's happened?'

She looked up into McMaster's face and he read there the agony she had undergone. He took her in his arms and for a moment they stood locked together in silence. At last she drew away, drew a deep breath.

'I'd better see to Robin.'

As she went into his room he was seated at the table with Jenny.

'What was all the shouting?'

'One of your papa's clients making a fuss. He wasn't satisfied.' She sat at the table beside them, where a lunch was laid out and Robin had been eating bread and butter.

'But why did they come here?'

'I don't know. It was very silly. They should have spoken to the solicitor.'

'Is it something Papa has done?' Robin asked nervously.

'No! Nothing to do with him. It was all a misunderstanding.'

After some more wrangling of this kind she managed to get him off the subject. She tried to pretend nothing had happened, whereas in fact it was with her all the time like a nightmare from which she couldn't awake. And when she met McMaster later they looked at one another in silence as each tried to read the thoughts of the other.

He took her in his arms, and held her a long time without speaking; she was able to relax in his grasp and try to calm herself.

'What do you think he will do?' she asked at last.

'There's nothing he can do,' McMaster said quietly. 'There is something we can do, however. I have written to Furniss – he's a solicitor in the town – instructing him to start an action for judicial separation.'

'Will that take long?'

'It partly depends on your husband's solicitors – and your husband, of course. It could take a while. You're not to worry. You'll stay here. You're quite safe. He's a pest, that's all, and in the end he'll get tired of making a nuisance of himself.'

She sighed. 'I can't tell you how comforting you are. When I saw George yesterday it was like a ghost come back from the dead. I had hoped never to see him again.'

'Ssh.' He stroked her hair as he held her. 'It's over. You won't see him again.'

During the night she was awakened by shouting and the sound of feet on the stairs. In a second she was awake, fumbling to light a candle. Throwing a shawl over her nightgown she went out on the landing in time to hear the front door opening and McMaster's voice outside. Then she heard Sam barking, and Josiah hurried past her pushing his shirt into his trousers as he ran downstairs and towards the door. She was about to run down herself when she heard Robin's voice. Turning into his room, she saw him starting up in bed.

They stared at each in the uncertain light of the candle. Robin was frightened.

'What is it? What's happening?'

'I don't know – I think it was some village boys making mischief, that's all. Your papa has set Sam onto them. That'll soon chase them away.' She even managed to chuckle. They listened for a moment but could hear nothing more. 'Anyway, it's all over and I'm going back to bed. And you had better snuggle down too.'

She sat beside him on the bed, arranging

the covers over him, and at last bent to kiss him.

'Sarah, you're sure it's all right now?'

'Quite sure. Goodnight.'

When she emerged onto the landing, John was waiting.

'They've gone,' he whispered. 'Go back to bed. I'll tell you about it in the morning.'

But it was a long time before she could get to sleep. She racked her memory for what she had heard. Not much. John and Josiah had run out of the front door, there had been some shouting, and Sam was heard barking. Still, it didn't take much imagination to associate George with this.

After breakfast, Robin was carried up to his room, and McMaster took her into the drawing room. As they entered Mrs Hudson was on her knees with a dustpan and brush. In one of the windows the glass hung in long jagged shards.

'I heard the smashing of the glass,' he said. 'I got dressed as quickly as I could, called Sam from the kitchen, took a walking stick and went outside. Your husband was completely drunk, I'm afraid. His friend was with him too, trying to control him – rather ineffectually.'

'What did he say?'

'Bradley? Only the same as yesterday. Shouting that he wanted his wife back, and so forth, calling me an adulterer, he'd have the law. I told him I'd have the law on him for damage to private property! He was demented, crying out your name, he fell on his knees, raving and calling for you. I told him to take himself off or I'd set the dog on him.'

She listened in silence. At last in a low voice, 'I'm so sorry to have brought this on you. I wonder whether I shouldn't go and see him again?'

'Hush.'

Mrs Hudson had finished clearing up the broken glass and was going out, when he stopped her.

'Mrs Hudson, I owe you an explanation. You heard the fuss last night, I imagine? That man – George Bradley – is Sarah's – Miss Shaw's – husband. She fled from her home after he beat her. He came here yesterday afternoon demanding her return – you heard that too, I expect. He's making a confounded nuisance of himself. But he won't get the better of us, you can depend on that.'

'No, sir.'

'If he shows up again while I am not here, you have my leave to send for the police.'

'Yes, sir.'

'And Mrs Hudson, I have told Miss Shaw – or Mrs Bradley – that she is safe here as long as she wishes to remain.'

'Very good, sir.' Mrs Hudson gave Sarah a level, serious look before disappearing.

John turned to the window. 'I'll tell Josiah to get the glazier up to mend that.'

Sarah sank into a chair. 'I have no right to inflict this on you. And Robin.'

'You're too late. It's been done, and there's

280

no going back. Don't worry, Sarah, my darling, we're together, we're going to stay together, and there is no power on earth can stop us.'

She looked up into his face, as he raised her from the chair, and held her.

'Oh, I do love you,' she whispered as she raised her arms about his neck.

Eventually she was sufficiently composed to return to Robin's room and continue with the books. She thought that Robin probably didn't believe the story about the village boys but she stuck to it and tried to appear as cheerful and composed as she could. So they got through the morning and after Robin had been put to bed for his afternoon rest she too went to her room. She felt tired but, as soon as she slipped her shoes off and lay down, as soon as she allowed her thoughts free rein, she sank into a miasma of misery. She couldn't see how they were going to get out of this. Even if George by some miracle did go back to London, even if John were able to get her a separation, the problem remained. They could never be together. They could never walk into a room and be introduced as man and wife. John was a professional man, he was a busy man, he knew hundreds of people, he must be invited out to dinners constantly. He would never be able to take her. They could never go anywhere together. Even if they did live together it would always be in a clandestine, hole-in-the-corner fashion. John had once told her how proud he had been to stand before the world with Thérèse on his arm. But he could never stand before the world with Sarah on his arm. That was forbidden. The best she could hope for was to be kept round the corner in a little cottage, somewhere out of sight. And their children – because she wanted above all things to have his children – their children would carry the stigma of illegitimacy all their lives. As these thoughts ran through her mind, in spite of herself, she felt the tears trickle down her face and had not the strength to brush them away.

However, nothing more was heard from George that day, or that night, or the following day. Hour by hour she was on the lookout for him. But there was a silence.

She and Josiah and Robin walked together along the cliff. It was still glorious summer weather, clear skies with little clouds high up, and far away to the south, beyond the town, beyond the abbey, the green fields running to the cliff edge. It was hard not to feel your spirits lift on such a glorious afternoon and to believe, however briefly, that everything would turn out all right.

The following Thursday, John was reading the Whitby newspaper when he suddenly exploded and thrust the sheet down on his lap. 'Confound him!'

'What is it?' She was frightened at once.

'Damn his impudence! By God, he'll pay

for this.' He stood up abruptly, and was going towards the door.

'John, for Heaven's sake, what is it?'

'Infernal scoundrel!'

'What? Tell me!'

He drew a breath, collected himself, returned and picked up the newspaper, found the place and thrust it before her.

'There!' He pointed at a column. As she gathered her wits, she began to read:

We have it on good authority that a certain respected member of this community may not be all that he seems. It comes to something when a man may live in open concubinage with another man's wife in defiance of every right feeling. This is a warning to us all. If any other poor fellow should find himself in similar circumstances and be so misguided as to ask for his wife back, let him beware lest he too be shown the door with a stick and a dog snapping at his heels. We wonder where it will end when a man 'learned in the law' so far forgets the law as to bring shame on himself, his innocent child, and those upright and honest citizens who have the misfortune to be his neighbours.

John was looking down on her as she finished. His face was black. She had never seen him moved like this. 'By God, I'll thrash him.'

She reached for his hand. 'It won't do any good. You hit him already. We must go by the book.'

He was staring into her eyes, then suddenly relaxed, and even laughed slightly. 'Sarah! I do believe you're right. Telling me my duty. Quite right. But they shall publish a retraction. Upon my soul they shall.'

He went out, and soon afterwards she saw him striding along the cliffs into town.

Twenty-Six

John returned later that afternoon, satisfied with his work. The editor, having been apprised of the true facts, as John put it, and having been reminded of his legal position, had undertaken to publish a retraction the following Thursday. The business appeared to be taken care of.

It wasn't.

The following Sunday afternoon as she was coming out of Robin's room Sarah found Josiah waiting on the landing.

'Mrs Bradley,' he whispered. It sounded odd to hear her name on his lips. He went on in a conspiratorial tone, 'Can I have a word? In private?'

'Let's go out into the garden.'

As soon as they were through the door, he began in a low voice, 'It's only fair to warn thee—'

'Warn me?'

'I were at chapel this morning,' he hurried on. 'Tha'st seen notice in t'paper, I tek it?'

Sarah nodded. Josiah seemed quite out of character. His usual laconic diffidence had vanished and he was looking very serious.

'Aye, well, so has rest of t'town. They're all agog wi' it. So, what happens this mornin'? Reverend Hayes teks it into his head to preach a sermon on t'subject of adultery. Tha knaws him. He don't mince his words. When he gets hold of his text he's like a terrier, he worries it, worries the life out of it. He give to thee and t'mester hot and strong – not by name, mind, he never mentioned no names, but there weren't a soul there, man woman or child, who didn't know who he were talkin' about.'

He paused. 'I just thought I'd warn thee.'

'Thank you. What...' She wasn't sure what this was leading to.

'There's them in t'town who think th'art no better than th' ought to be,' he continued. 'Tha tek me meanin'? Tha'd best mind thy back, that's all – for a day or two. I dessay it'll all blow over eventually. Still...'

He paused, and then turned to Sarah again. 'But I'll tell thee this. Hayes'll never see me inside Sion Chapel again!' He was quite vehement, and suddenly took Sarah by the arm, speaking close up into her face. 'Tha canna imagine what it were like in this house afore tha come. Mr McMester stamped about, he were that gloomy, always shoutin', hectorin', threatenin'. It were a trial. And it made me heart sore to see 'em so far apart, son in t'fear of father, and father shoutin' and terrifyin' his son. The way he shouted it were sickenin' to hear. Then tha come and gradually everythin' changed. I knew summat were in t'air when I heard thee playin' t'piano. It were thee that brought father and son together. Tha'st rescued Mr McMester, anyone can see it. Tha'st brought him back to life – and tha'st given Robin summat he can be proud of. And I bless thee for it, from t'bottom of my heart!'

He took Sarah by the hand and pressed it, then turned away, leaving her staring after him in bewilderment.

There was another unexpected sequel to the newspaper item. Chrissie Barrington came to call. It was a cool overcast day and she was wearing a blue cloak over her dress. As she helped her off with it, Sarah noticed a piece of pretty embroidery Chrissie had done round the collar.

As soon as they were alone together Chrissie came to the point. 'We saw the notice in the newspaper, Sarah. Of course I knew it must be you and Mr McMaster immediately. Papa and Mamma were surprised, as you can imagine. They wondered whether it referred to Mr McMaster – though it was obvious it did – and I wondered whether to tell them I knew. But I thought it best to say so, and from the second that I confirmed it, they were on your side, firmly on your side, I promise you.

286

There was not a moment's hesitation! Of course they would not believe such a slur on your honour...'

There was a pause as Chrissie gradually raised her eyes to meet Sarah's and looked at her enquiringly, as if waiting for confirmation. Sarah had to take a moment to collect her thoughts. She swallowed.

'We are not living in *concubinage*, as they said, Christina. In a house with three servants and Robin that would be very difficult to keep secret. But I cannot disguise from you that I love Mr McMaster and – I believe he loves me. He has told me so.'

She waited painfully for Chrissie's reaction. Chrissie reached for Sarah's hands and said with a gush, 'Oh I'm so glad! He is such a good man, and I knew from the start that you – and he—'

'You knew?'

'I knew – at the ball.'

'Really? How?'

Chrissie smiled. 'From the way you danced together. Anyone watching you together could see you loved him.'

Sarah was silent. This had never occurred to her. She smiled painfully. She was slightly taken aback to find Chrissie more perceptive than she had imagined. 'You know, all that evening I was in agony because I thought he was in love with *you*.' She rose from her chair and crossed to the window. 'But, Chrissie, unfortunately, this is only the beginning of my troubles. My husband has been here twice

– what it said in the newspaper by the way was true – he was chased off with stick and dog. It omitted to mention that he was completely drunk and had thrown a brick through the window. He refuses to give me a divorce. Even though Mr McMaster offered to pay all the expenses. So, at this minute, I have no idea what is to become of us. Mr McMaster lives such a public life. He has already made a huge sacrifice of his reputation in this town for my sake. But even if we went away – he has a house in Liverpool – we can never live together as man and wife. For a man in his position it would be impossible – unless he were to give up his profession. How could I ask that of him? It is his life! And if I were to bear him a child it could never take his name—' She stopped and covered her face with her hands. 'I don't know what we are going to do. There seems no way out.'

Chrissie came to her, and laid her hand round her shoulder as Sarah wept helplessly. 'There is still time. Your husband may change his mind. What has he to gain by denying you your freedom? You will never return to him. Will you?'

Sarah shook her head without speaking.

'Well, then. So long as he is married to you he cannot marry again, either. Surely in time he will see the sense of Mr McMaster's proposal. He must.'

'You don't know him,' Sarah said at last. 'He would hang on just to spite me. I've never known him look at another woman. Oh God, what are we going to do?'

'Come,' Chrissie said coaxingly. 'The sun has come out again. Let's take a walk along the cliff path. It will help to calm you.'

Gently she led Sarah out of the front door and away from the town. For a while they walked silently arm in arm.

'Thank you,' Sarah said eventually. 'That's better.' She drew a handkerchief from her sleeve and dabbed at her eyes. 'It is as if the whole world has come crashing on my head. To think, only two – or is it three? – weeks ago, John and I went to Scarborough – to a hotel—' She glanced at Chrissie, and took a hand in her own, squeezing it as she spoke. 'I'll be honest with you. I loved him so badly I was ready – I wanted to – I wanted us to become lovers. And we would have done too! Except that night I saw one of George's friends in the theatre. I was so terrified I fled back to the hotel. Of course any thoughts of love flew out of the window.'

'So you have never—'

Sarah shook her head and looked up, drawing a deep breath. 'If it is of any comfort, I am as innocent as any blushing virgin.'

She stopped as she thought what she just said, and glanced at Chrissie. There was silence as they walked.

'There is something I wanted to tell you,' Chrissie said quietly at last. She paused. 'I suppose it is something I should have done long ago.' She hesitated. 'I have broken off with Freddy.'

Sarah stopped and swung round to face her. Chrissie nodded.

'He was no good, Sarah. I see it now. I am well rid of him.'

'My dear – but you were so in love – I remember, that day in the White Horse...'

'I know.' Chrissie seemed remarkably calm. 'I know,' she went on in a dreamy voice, looking away. 'And even at my coming-out ball, when he was drunk, I was ready to make excuses for him. I thought it was in some way *my* fault.'

'What made you change your mind?'

'Nothing really. Or little things. He came to tea a few weeks ago. We were sitting together with the others and, as Mamma was speaking, I saw him make a face at her behind his hand while she was looking the other way. Effie saw it too, and she glanced at me in disgust. I suddenly realized: he doesn't care for anybody – or anything. So why should he care for me? Why should I make excuses for him, Sarah?'

Sarah was astonished and needed a few minutes to digest this revelation. Chrissie was growing up fast.

As they approached the house they saw McMaster in the trap about to set off for town. He was pleased to see Chrissie, and Sarah watched his reaction carefully. He hadn't seen her since the night of the ball, when he had been so bewitched by her beauty.

'Miss Barrington! You haven't been put off

by the piece in the newspaper, then?'

'Never! We are all on your side, Mr Mc-Master! Every one of us. We were so furious when we saw that notice.'

McMaster laughed. He seemed quite relaxed about it. 'It's of no account. They're going to print a retraction, you'll see. I'm afraid they got quite the wrong end of the stick. I expect Sarah has explained?'

'Yes – she told me everything.'

'And did she tell you how we met?'

'No.'

'Look, I'm just going into town – can I offer you a lift home? I'll tell you the story as we jog along.'

'Thank you.'

In a moment she was seated beside him in the trap.

'Will you be long?' Sarah called.

'No – just going in for a chat with Furniss – the business we talked of.' He gee'd the mare into motion.

Instead of returning to the house she turned again along the path, and eventually sat at the edge of the steep slope down to the beach, staring out to sea. The breeze whispered among the furze bushes and above her somewhere she could hear a lark.

For a long while she mused on what Chrissie had told her. She remembered the scene in the White Horse. She had heard, in every word Chrissie spoke, the white-hot love she had felt for him then. And now? She had simply grown out of him. Chrissie had

291

certainly taken her by surprise.

Sarah sat a long time staring at the horizon, breathing the salt air, and at last lazily pulled the ribbon from her hair, shook it free and let the breeze ruffle it about her shoulders. Gradually she felt herself calming.

A few days later she was walking into town along the quay. It was a sunny morning and the fishing boats had returned from a night's work. The harbour was filled with their red sails, and the men were everywhere about them, coiling ropes, piling wicker baskets and making all neat. Along the quay primitive stalls were set up – boards lying across barrels – and the air was filled with fishy smells and the voices of the fishwives calling their wares. They were a hardy breed, ruddy-faced, strong-armed with their sleeves rolled, wrapped in sacking aprons and wearing thick boots.

Sarah glanced over the soles, the silvery herring, flounders, the long cod, and couldn't help noticing some of the rarer ones on display, some she had barely seen before – skate, and a ray – and others she had no knowledge of. For a moment she became quite engrossed and stood studying some of the more exotic species.

At that moment she felt a blow on her back. She turned; several of the women were staring at her. None was near, none of them spoke. Sarah was so taken by surprise that she didn't know what to make of it.

'What was that?' she asked uncertainly, of no one in particular.

A fish lay on the ground at her feet. She looked up completely perplexed. She turned to the woman standing nearest. 'Did you see what happened?'

The woman raised her eyebrows in a comical expression and shrugged but said nothing.

At last Sarah turned on her way. But only a moment later something struck the back of her head and she heard a burst of raucous laughter. In a mixture of apprehension and anger she whirled sharply about.

'Who did that?'

'What's the matter?' called one of the fish-wives. 'Dost'na like the smell of rotten fish?'

'Did you throw that?'

She marched over to this red-faced woman of her own age who was standing in a wet and very smelly apron with a battered old bowler hat on the back of her head.

'Aye, and what if I did? It's all th'art good for.'

There was a burst of laughter from all about her and, whipping round, Sarah saw the women all staring at her.

In another second she delivered a good ringing slap to the face of the woman in front of her. She saw the surprise on her face as it changed to rage.

'Th'art a whore, and it's as good as tha deserves.' She struck Sarah in the face so hard that she staggered away, clutching her face as a sting of pain and rage flooded through her. As she did so, another woman caught her by the bonnet so that the ribbon pulled at her neck; she was dragged back off balance and half swung round. Another woman snatched the basket out of her hand and threw it to the ground. There was a confusion of voices in her ears – a muddle of shouts, jeers and laughter – as she struggled to gain her balance and free herself.

The ribbon snapped, she was flung unexpectedly free and as she turned she saw the woman throw the bonnet to the wet cobbles and trample it to a pulp of wet straw. She was outraged.

'How *dare* you!'

'How dare I? That's good – coming from thee! Comin' from a whore! Get along!'

She was pushed violently from behind and for a moment thought she was going to fall, but she staggered along and then, just as she managed to right herself, she was pushed again, and now there were hands in her hair, pulling at it so that the pain made her cry out and she twisted herself in a superhuman effort to free herself. As she turned she reached to one of the faces before her, took the woman by the nose and twisted it as sharply as she could. The woman screamed and broke away and a moment later Sarah stamped on the foot of another. This was useless. Her dainty shoe made no imprint on the stout boot soaked in fish oil.

She managed to free herself at last and

staggered away. It was as if the whole quay-side was laughing at her. Her bonnet gone, her basket gone, stinking of fish, she made her way back out of town.

Twenty-Seven

She was on her hands and knees, staring down at the grass, all the strength gone out of her. She could still hear the shouts and laughter ringing in her ears. She allowed herself to crumple to the grass and lay some time, her mind empty. Later – it might have been five minutes, it might have been half an hour – she managed to stagger to her feet again and found herself weaving along the cliff path like a drunkard. She kept wanting to cry; she stared about her, she felt she had gone crazy; she looked down at her clothes, torn, wet, stinking of fish. Her bonnet was gone, her hair everywhere tangled about her shoulders.

At length, after what might have been a hundred years, she was at the door and hanging on the bell pull.

Jenny opened it, and she staggered past her. Jenny said something but Sarah didn't hear it; she weaved her way upstairs clutching at the rail and slammed her bedroom door behind her. Immediately she began to undo her clothes, stripping off the wet dress as if it was polluted and at last, pouring water into her bowl, she washed herself. Like an automaton, she scrubbed at her hands and arms. As she leaned over the bowl, splashing water over herself, she could feel the tears beginning at last as the shock worked through her and, clutching the towel to her, sat on the edge of her bed and wept until her body shook.

At last, shakily she dressed herself in fresh clothes, and gathering the wet things went down to the kitchen where Mrs Hudson was alone. Sarah put the bundle of clothes on the table. Mrs Hudson looked round at her, immediately stopped her work and came across to Sarah.

'Art all right, lass?'

Sarah stared at her without speaking.

'Eh – sit down – summat's happened.'

Sarah nodded, sitting heavily on a stool, her hands lying in her lap, and stared across the room. Mrs Hudson laid her hand over Sarah's. 'Th'art as cold as death. What is it?'

'They attacked me,' Sarah stuttered, 'in the fish market.' She was nodding as if she had the palsy. 'Attacked me – called me a whore—'

'Tha'st had a shock, I can see. Stay theere and don't move.' She went out and Sarah sat alone in the silent kitchen. It was warm and Sam was asleep by the range, which was alight, even on this sunny day. Her mind was completely blank.

Mrs Hudson returned with a small glass of an amber liquid. 'Drink that.'

Without thinking Sarah took the glass and drank it off. She erupted into a fit of coughing; it was neat brandy.

'Aye – that's shaken some life into thee.'

'Mrs Hudson, I'm afraid,' Sarah said unexpectedly. Her hand was shaking as she set the glass on the table. 'It'll be the same everywhere! Everywhere. He'll follow me. He'll never give me a divorce.' She looked up wildly. 'I must leave Mr McMaster! How can I stay here? I'll ruin him!' She began to weep. 'I should go back, it's the only thing I can do. I'll go back, then Mr McMaster and Robin will be safe.'

Mrs Hudson was standing looking closely down at her. She now leaned down and looked carefully into Sarah's face.

'Art tha feelin' a bit stronger now?'

Sarah nodded puzzled by her manner. But in another moment she had seized Sarah strongly by the wrist.

'Then listen, and listen hard! Ruin him? Aye, tha's right! Tha'st brought shame on t'mester, *Mrs Bradley*!' she hissed in Sarah's ear. 'He were above reproach till tha come! And now there's folk whisperin', wi' scurrilous messages in t'paper. T'whole town's talking of thee and him! T'best-known barrister in t'north, and mebbe a judge too in a few years, and tha's dragged his name in t'mud. Thee and no one else. Tha'st the name of a whore! So get thee gone, go back to thee

297

husband and it'll be not a moment too soon!'

With a sudden jerk she shoved Sarah from her. For a second Sarah rubbed her wrist – for Mrs Hudson had a vice-like grip.

But in another second she reacted with a flare of anger. She stood up and confronted the housekeeper.

'Don't you dare talk to me like that! What business is it of yours? Mr McMaster loves me! I didn't ask him to, and I never seduced him. But he loves me, and I love him, and I will allow *nothing*, and *no one*, to come between us! Now get out of my way!' She pushed angrily past Mrs Hudson and out of the kitchen.

She let herself out of the house and set off at a fast walk along the cliffs. Her whole body seemed to be trembling and Mrs Hudson's words drove round and round in her mind as she strode sightlessly along the grass path. What if she was right? She *had* brought shame on John McMaster, it was true. It was true! The words went round and round in her mind.

And there was only one way to put matters right: she must leave. The more she thought, and the more she remembered the scene in the kitchen, the clearer it became. If she had never come, none of this would have happened. How could she calculate the effect of this scandal on John's career? It might ruin him. Surely, as a man of the law he must be above reproach, as Mrs Hudson had said?

What right had she to bring disgrace on him?

Even as she began to cool and to moderate her pace, as she began again to be aware of her surroundings, the thoughts refused to go away. Everywhere she looked, every way she turned them, the logic of Mrs Hudson's words was irrefutable. 'Allow no one to come between them'? What was she talking about? Sarah could never be John McMaster's wife. And so long as she remained in his house, she was a standing reproach to him, a stain on his character.

She could not bring herself to mention the matter to John, but two days later, when she was beginning to think that if she didn't discuss it soon with someone she must go mad, she decided to walk over to see Chrissie. The thoughts had gone round in her mind so many times that she could no longer think straight.

She set out after dinner, but after she had started on the path towards the town, she suddenly stopped. No, not that way, and she turned and struck away across a field. She did not wish to walk through the centre of the town. She did not think she could do that ever again.

Because of the long circuit she made, it was almost nine before she knocked at the door. Sampson opened it and she asked to speak to Chrissie. She was admitted to the hall and Sampson disappeared, only to reappear and to usher her into the drawing room. Mrs

Barrington was waiting. This time she was on her feet. She came forward and took Sarah by the hands.

'My dear, do come in, come – take a seat – here...'

Sarah was seated, and Mrs Barrington went on, 'You cannot imagine how we felt when we saw that scurrilous piece. Of course we didn't believe it, not a word of it!' She laughed gaily. 'But I must say, McMaster put them in their place; you saw the retraction, of course?'

Sarah nodded. 'You are very kind, and I cannot tell you how pleased Mr McMaster was when Chrissie called about it. Because – I confess it has been a strain. Actually, I was hoping to see Chrissie – if I may?'

'Oh – what a shame. Chrissie is out – staying with a friend.'

Sarah frowned.

'By the by.' Mrs Barrington leaned in. 'I believe I ought to thank *you*, Miss Shaw, for what has happened.' She raised her eyebrows.

'You mean – her breaking off her engagement?'

Mrs Barrington nodded emphatically. 'I was never so relieved in my life, I can assure you! It was a most unsuitable match and Christina was far too young to know her own mind.'

'I dare say you are right,' Sarah said quietly. She was annoyed – more than annoyed – to have missed Chrissie. 'Perhaps if I were to call again tomorrow? Would she be back?'

'Possibly. The girl lives with her head in the

300

clouds. I believe she doesn't know herself what she is going to do from one day to the next.'

Soon after this, Sarah took her leave and made her way home through the very last of the late-evening light. She was more upset than she could say. Chrissie was the only woman in the town with whom she believed she could be really intimate. There had been a real bond between them since their first meeting in the White Horse. And she badly needed to talk this matter through.

The following afternoon she was with Robin in the drawing room when she heard the front door open and close, and soon afterwards excited talk and calls through the house. In a moment Jenny appeared at the door.

'Hast heard, miss? There's been a murder! The whole town's talkin' of it! A body was found this morning on Collier Hope! They've tekken it to Town Hall!'

Robin looked up at Sarah but she was equally mystified.

'Collier Hope – what is that?'

'Tha knows, Miss, that bit of sand in t'lower harbour, on t'other side – right below church. Where the colliers beach when there's not space at t'quay.'

'Is it a man or woman?'

'Oh, a man, miss.'

Again Sarah and Robin looked at each other – but there was really nothing more to be said, so after a moment they continued with the lesson. And later she went with him up to his nursery for tea.

It was while they were eating tea together that Jenny reappeared.

'If tha please, miss, there's two gentlemen wish to speak with thee.'

Sarah followed her down into the drawing room where two men were talking to Mc-Master. They turned as she entered. Their air was respectful, sombre.

'Mrs Bradley?'

She nodded.

The man coughed but before he could go on John took Sarah by the hand. Sarah glanced up at him.

'Bad news,' he whispered, and tightened his grip on her hand. 'These two gentlemen are police detectives. Detective Inspector Iveson, and...'

'Detective Constable Matthews, sir.'

The inspector drew a breath. 'A man's body was found this morning in the harbour, Mrs Bradley, and we would be grateful if you could assist us in making an identification. We would be obliged if you would come with us now.'

Sarah turned instinctively to John. 'George?'

He said nothing, but still held her hand. She turned again. 'Very well.'

As they issued from the house, a four-wheeler was standing on the track. On the way into town the inspector told her what little there was to say – that the body had been discovered on the sand near Tate Hill

302

pier, and there were marks from knife wounds.

They arrived at the Town Hall and mounted the few steps to the door, where a police constable was on duty. He stood aside as they went in. In the half light, a body lay on the table beneath a cloth. Sarah stared for a long moment until the detective turned to her.

'Mrs Bradley, are you all right? I very much regret the necessity...'

She nodded, and approached the table. The inspector was before her, and at the far end turned the cloth back neatly – as if he had done it many times before. And there was George.

She nodded, and the inspector replaced the sheet, neatly as before.

'Thank you.'

He indicated the door, and a second later they were descending to the square again. The whole business had taken less than a minute.

'A surgeon will make his report and there will be an inquest on Thursday. Unfortunately we cannot release the body for burial before then. But of course you are free to go ahead with arrangements for the funeral in the meantime.'

It was all rushing at her. It was barely forty minutes since they had called at the house and already they were talking of the funeral. Sarah was still too shocked to speak.

John saw this and nodded to the two policemen. 'Thank you. I will take Mrs Bradley home now.'

They saluted, John helped her into the carriage and they swayed off down through the narrow street towards the bridge. Sarah said nothing, only held tight to John's hands.

They were nearly home before she spoke. 'John – I mean – who—'

'We'll talk about it later,' he said quietly.

He led her into the drawing room, and rang the bell. When Josiah appeared, he said, 'We'd like some tea, Josiah – and Josiah...' The servant turned. 'You've heard what has happened?'

'Yes, sir.'

'About Mr Bradley?'

'Yes, sir.'

'You'd better tell the others.'

Josiah nodded and went out. They sat facing each other for a minute, unable to speak. Eventually he said, 'It's so unexpected. I can't think who – I mean why should any-one— Stabbed, too,' he added, thoughtfully. The legal mind was coming to life. 'It looks like a robbery. Well, we'll have to wait for the inquest. Then we'll have a clearer idea.'

'Yes.' She had nothing to contribute. The enormity of it simply left her stunned. Then, 'George,' she murmured, staring vaguely out of the window, 'I had better write to his parents. And his brother. I wonder where Marcus Collins is? He wasn't there.'

There was another long silence, until Josiah appeared with a tea tray.

As she sipped her tea, a new thought came

to her.

'I brought this on him,' she muttered in a low voice, 'I did. If I had not come here in the first place, he would not have followed me, and this would not have happened.'

'Now!' He stopped her. 'Sarah! None of that! Whatever happened, and whoever is responsible, you have nothing to reproach yourself with. So stop that now!'

She thought further. 'Of course, there is no need for Robin to know. Of course he's going to want to talk about the murder – but we needn't mention George, need we?'

'No.'

This was a relief. But after another silence she went on, 'John, there is something else. After the inquest, I ought to bring George here – I mean – to prepare the body. But if I do, Robin will ask...'

'I'll go into town in the morning and speak to Oldsworth the undertakers – something can be arranged to avoid bringing the body here.'

'Thank you.'

Later they dined, and inevitably the subject of the murder was uppermost. Robin was full of questions. Had they found the murderer? Was the victim stabbed to death? Was he robbed? He took a bloodthirsty relish in the details, though there weren't any details except those he invented. In the end, Sarah tried to cool his excitement. 'A man has been killed, Robin. It's very sad. Just imagine if you were his papa or mamma.'

The following afternoon the two police detectives reappeared. They were quietly spoken and polite and were ushered into the drawing room. John had gone out for a walk.

'There are a few questions we'd like to ask, Mrs Bradley.'

She waited as the inspector took out a pocket book, opened it and carefully extracted a piece of paper. He unfolded it and flattened it on his knee. With a slight shock she recognized the letter she had written to George.

'We found this letter on the deceased's body, and would like to ask you about it.' He passed it over. 'Do you recognize it?'

'Yes. I wrote it.' She passed it back.

'We wondered. Would you be so kind as to explain in a little more detail what it means?'

She was mystified but drew a breath and marshalled her thoughts. 'Very well. Mr Bradley was my husband, as you know.'

'You say here, "you nearly murdered me". What did you mean?'

She realized immediately that she would have to tell the whole story – though what it had to do with the murder was beyond her.

'My husband was of a very erratic and unstable temperament. Unfortunately, he also had financial and other problems. Under these pressures he sometimes drank. And unfortunately, when he drank he would sometimes become violent.'

'Go on.'

306

'Well, last December, in a drunken rage he very nearly succeeded in murdering me. I only escaped with difficulty and fled here.'

'Why didn't you go to your parents?'

'My parents had disapproved of the marriage. My father would not have me under his roof.'

'Go on.'

'So – I came to Whitby, where I was fortunate enough to be engaged by Mr McMaster as governess to his son Robin.'

He nodded. 'As it says in the letter.'

'Then through an accident, my husband discovered my whereabouts and followed me here. He has been pestering me to return to him.'

'You refused?'

She nodded.

The inspector coughed. 'It also says here – ' and he read from the letter – ' "John Mc-Master means more to me than life itself. I love him and I will never return to you." '

There was a pause. At last Sarah said in a low voice, 'That is correct.'

'So ... what did you intend?'

'Mr McMaster is applying on my behalf for a judicial separation. It was the most I could hope for. My husband adamantly refused a divorce.'

'Oh?'

She nodded.

'He told you that?'

She nodded. The inspector glanced to his assistant, who was busy writing, then began again. 'Now then, Mrs Bradley, I must ask you where you were on the evening of September third last.'

'The third?'

'The evening your husband was murdered.'

'Oh. Of course.' She was bewildered. 'Well.' For a moment her mind was a blank. 'Well, what did I do? Oh, I remember now. I went out after dinner to visit Christina Barrington.'

The constable was making notes as she spoke. Her mind was distracted by the sight of his pencil on the pad. It made a faint scratching noise.

'Christina Barrington?'

'She is a friend.'

'What time would this be?'

'Well, let me see.' She had become intensely nervous, threading her fingers together. 'It was after dinner, and it was late in the evening. The sun had set – though it was still light – I suppose half-past eight or nine.'

'And did you see Miss Barrington?'

'No. She was out.'

'I see.'

'I spoke to her mother.'

'Ah. We can check on that.'

This puzzled her.

'How long did you stay?'

'I suppose...' She shook her head vaguely. 'Half an hour possibly.'

'Then what did you do?'

'I came back here.'

'So – that would be – around ten?'

'I really can't remember. It was dark by then.'

'Did anyone see you come in?'

'I know Mr McMaster was still up. I saw the light in his room.'

'Did he see you come in?'

'No. I didn't want to disturb him.'

'Did anyone else see you?'

'I went into Robin's room – Mr McMaster's son – to see that he was safely asleep, then I went to bed myself.'

'I see. So no one saw you come into the house?'

'No.'

'Thank you.' He looked at the constable, who was still writing. When he was finished the inspector rose and said, 'I think that will be all for the moment, Mrs Bradley. Thank you for your cooperation. We may need to come back, to interview the other occupants—'

At that point she heard the front door open. The inspector was folding up the letter and installing it in his pocket book as John stood in the doorway.

'Sarah – what is this?'

'There were just a few things we needed to clear up with Mrs Bradley, sir,' the inspector said casually.

McMaster was alert. 'What things?'

'Relating to a letter Mrs Bradley wrote to her husband.'

'Sarah? What have you been saying?' She was alarmed by his tone of voice. 'You should not have spoken to these men without me here.'

'No need to worry, sir. We've found out what we wanted to know. Oh, and since you're here, sir, perhaps we could put a few questions to you now?'

'What questions?'

'Concerning the evening of the third last.'

'What do you want to know?'

'Could you just tell us your whereabouts that evening?'

'I was here.'

'In this room?'

'In my study across the hall.'

'I see, sir. Did anyone see you there?'

'Yes. My servant Jenny brought me a drink at ten o'clock and at about eleven my servant Josiah looked in to ask if there was anything further before he went to bed.'

'I see. And at what time did you lock the front door?'

McMaster was thoughtful. 'I worked quite late. Probably around one o'clock.'

'Mrs Bradley tells us she went out that evening to visit a friend and arrived back around ten o'clock. Did you hear her come in?'

'No.'

'I see. Well, thank you, sir, for your co-operation. Sorry to have put you to any trouble. We'll see ourselves out.'

Twenty-Eight

Next day John disappeared into town and Sarah sat with Robin in his room making a pretence of going though his lessons. Robin was compelled repeatedly to jog her when her attention wandered.

When John returned he told her that the undertakers would take care of the body until the funeral, which would be on the Monday.

'Thank you,' she said wearily. 'I must write to his people.'

The following day the inquest took place and that evening they heard that a verdict of wilful murder had been returned. Also, a cloak had been found by a lady out with her dog, hidden beneath some boulders at the foot of the West Cliff. It bore bloodstains. There was also a knife found by a fisherman in the harbour at low tide which also bore bloodstains even though it had been in the water.

The morning after that, while she was upstairs with Robin, there was another visit from the inspector. This time he was accompanied by a uniformed constable. He was more formal.

'You are Mrs Sarah Bradley?'

311

'Yes?' He knew perfectly well who she was. But before she could say anything else, he went on, 'Sarah Bradley, I arrest you for the murder of George Bradley on the night of September third last. You are not obliged to say anything but I must warn you that anything you do say may be taken down and used in evidence against you.'

For a moment she thought she was going to faint.

'I must ask you to accompany me now to the police station.'

'I will come with her,' McMaster said immediately. The inspector glanced at him in surprise. 'I am her legal representative. Any interview she gives or any statement she makes will be in my presence.' He turned to Sarah. 'Don't worry. I will be with you. You have nothing to fear. Go up now and fetch a few things. They will be keeping you for a few days. I will explain to Robin.'

In a daze she thrust a few changes of clothes into a bag and returned to the drawing room. McMaster had meantime been talking to Robin. Within a few minutes they were in the four-wheeler on their way into town. He said, 'I will go and talk to Furniss. He's a good man and I believe I can trust him to act for us in this.'

The police station was in a busy street in the heart of the town, and as she got out of the carriage she was dimly aware of a few townsfolk watching her as she went inside.

It was a small, dingy stone building. The

312

window was dirty, there was the smell of stale tobacco, the walls had once been white-washed, but were dirty, and disfigured with scrawled words.

A sergeant was behind a counter, and she waited while he wrote in a book. She was escorted through a door and into a short corridor, through another door and then found herself in a cell. Before the door was locked, John repeated that he was going to speak to Furniss.

'You'll come before the magistrate tomorrow morning for committal proceedings. We'll both be there with you. You have absolutely nothing to worry about.' He took her hands and held them both for a moment in his strong warm hands.

'John—'

He turned.

'I shall need mourning clothes.'

'Of course. I'll send in a dressmaker this morning.'

'Also can you bring me some pens and paper? There are letters I must write.'

He nodded and was gone, and the door was locked behind him.

Strangely, after the shock she suddenly felt calm. She sat on the edge of the bed. She had passed the police station many times yet it never occurred to her that there would be cells in it.

Later that morning John returned with another man.

'Sarah, this is Mr Furniss. He's going to act

313

for us.'

Furniss was a youngish man, perhaps in his thirties.

'I've also spoken to the dressmaker. I told her to come this afternoon, around two. She says she will be able to get you fitted before Monday.'

'Thank you.'

'I'll leave you with Furniss for the moment. I'll come back and see you this evening. There are things I have to do.'

She sat with Mr Furniss for an hour telling him what she had told the police detective.

After he had gone she sat at the small deal table and began to write letters. The most difficult was to George's parents, giving them details of the funeral. She tried to explain how things had come to this but it was difficult. How had she got herself into this situation? And as she was writing, setting down everything she knew, she began at last to wonder – who had killed George? She knew no one who had any motive for killing him.

In the end it seemed the only reason could be robbery. As soon as she thought this it seemed clear. He had been robbed and his body left on the sands.

The cell window, which was heavily barred, looked out over the street, and she could hear the sounds of the citizens going about their business. It was a cheering sound. Life was normal; the fact that she was sitting in the police station was an aberration which would shortly be set right. Tomorrow morning, probably. Mr Furniss would explain to the magistrate that it was a mistake. Or they would interview Mrs Barrington. She was slightly vague in her mind about it, but she had got over her first terror, and it now seemed clear enough that she would soon be out again.

She was even more cheered when she heard footsteps outside, the door opened and a waiter with a napkin over his arm entered and bustled about her setting a tray on the table with a bottle of wine.

'Mr McMaster's compliments, ma'am, your lunch.'

'Who are you?' she asked, bewildered.

'White Horse, ma'am, at your service. I'll call again in an hour for the tray.'

She lifted a silver cover from the plate to reveal a substantial dinner of roast beef and vegetables. As she sat down before it, she found herself very hungry indeed. She demolished the meal, drank most of the wine and felt greatly restored.

Soon after the tray had been removed the door opened again and a woman appeared staggering under several rolls of black fabric.

'Mrs Bradley? Mr McMaster sent me. Most sorry to hear of your loss. A tragedy. Who could have done such a thing? The whole town's talking of it, of course. I understand your feelings, but I have been consulted by many ladies on such melancholy occasions and I assure you, you may repose complete

315

confidence in me. Lady Mulgrave was saying only last week how pleased she had been with the ensemble I created for her on the sad occasion of the death of the dowager countess. Now, Mr McMaster said the funeral is to be on Monday, so we must lose no time. I have taken the liberty of bringing a selection of fabrics suitable to mourning.' She threw a bolt of black fabric across the table in a skilled manner, and with a hand beneath it, brought up the cloth for Sarah's inspection. 'This is a bombazine, considered very suitable for a mourning day dress. I would recommend this for the funeral. Most becoming.' The bombazine was a dull, lustreless fabric. The dreariest cloth ever devised, but considered de rigueur for mourning. Seeing her expression of dismay the lady produced another and threw it across the first. 'This is a very fine merino worsted. The evenings are beginning to draw in a little, so a warm material would be a wise choice. And the quality is very fine – if you would care to feel the nap.'

Sarah tentatively ran her hand across the wool. But soon the dressmaker was throwing yet another bolt of fabric across the first, as if she were in a shop. Having a specific task to focus her mind on, Sarah was able to forget for a while the weightier matters which beset her.

She stood up as the dressmaker measured her.

'Mr McMaster said he would be taking care

of the account so there's no need to worry about that,' the woman prattled on, jotting on a notepad. Soon she was ready to depart. 'I'll make a start on the funeral gown immediately and will have something for you to try on by Saturday morning. Good afternoon.'

This air of bustle and the feeling that John was everywhere working on her behalf made her reasonably optimistic. After all the very idea that she would murder George was so absurd, it was obvious that she could not be here long.

In the evening John returned and they sat talking.

'I've had a long preliminary talk with Furniss and he's been speaking to Handley, the Crown solicitor. They'll be constantly in touch, so we should have an idea soon what evidence the Crown intend to present.' His manner as always was brisk and forthright. His energy alone was enough to cheer her. Even so, the words had an ominous sound.

'Evidence?' she asked tentatively.

He looked at her squarely. They had been sitting side by side on the edge of the bed, holding hands. 'The letter, mainly.'

'Oh, the letter. How stupid of me.'

'I've seen a copy of it. It was a bold and brave letter. I honour you for it, my darling.'

'Do you?' She looked up mournfully.

'I do.' He squeezed her hands encouragingly. 'Don't be downhearted. We are going to fight all the way.'

'All the way?' This too sounded less than

cheering.

'Wait and see. We'll take it one step at a time. Did the dressmaker call?'

'Yes. And, John, thank you for my meals.'

He smiled. 'Oh, I've had experience of prison food.'

'Prison? But this isn't prison, is it? Not yet?'

'Hold on, my darling. Everything is going to be all right.'

After he had gone, she put herself to bed. After the light was extinguished, and she lay in the near dark, listening to a few passers-by in the street outside, and seeing a faint light on the wall opposite her tiny window, the loneliness came down on her badly and fear rose in her throat.

At ten in the morning she was led up into the magistrate's court. Furniss was there and McMaster. The room was high and light and there was a relaxed everyday feeling to it. Other miscreants, too, were led in and out; a man with a black eye and a torn coat, who did not appear to have slept all night. Another suspicious-looking man in black, unshaven, was also led down.

When she found herself facing the bench, she thought she recognized the man facing her. He might have been someone she had seen at one of Mrs Barrington's events; however, he showed no sign of recognizing her.

The charge was read out by a clerk in the well of the court and a man who was afterwards identified as Mr Handley read out a short statement referring to the letter, a cloak which had been found and a knife. Then he said that two witnesses would be produced to testify that they had seen her on the night in question with the deceased.

This threw her into a panic.

Within a very short time the magistrate committed her for trial at York Assizes on the charge of wilful murder.

As she was led back to her cell her mind was still reeling. What witnesses? she repeated over and over to herself. And as soon as Furniss appeared, she blurted out, 'What witnesses?'

'He didn't tell me. But I shall learn very shortly, don't worry, and I shall get a copy of their statements. We shall have plenty of time to prepare our case. The assizes don't come on for a month.'

She was still looking about her in a daze. 'Witnesses? How could there be witnesses? I wasn't there! How could there—'

'Be calm, Mrs Bradley. I shall be in constant touch with Handley and I shall know as much as he does, I assure you. There is one other thing. They have agreed to postpone taking you to York until after the funeral.'

'Taking me to York?'

'Yes. Next Tuesday you will be taken to be lodged in York Gaol – in the castle.'

'In the castle?'

She sat heavily on the side of her bed. Her head was swimming. In the dungeons! In

York, away from John – she stared wildly about her.

'Mrs Bradley, calm yourself. You are in very capable hands, believe me. Mr McMaster is extremely well known. Perhaps the best-known barrister on the northern circuit. As soon as it is known that he is leading for the defence—'

'Leading? You mean—?'

'Mr McMaster intends to defend.'

'But – he is mentioned in the letter – isn't he – I mean – isn't he compromised?'

Furniss looked grave. 'I must admit, Mrs Bradley, I inclined to your opinion, but Mc-Master was adamant. So long as he is not under suspicion himself, there is nothing to prevent him undertaking the defence. I should state, however, that the choice lies with you in this matter. If you wish me to instruct another barrister to represent you, I will do so.'

'What is your opinion?' she asked hesitantly.

'It is a risk. We do not know what the prosecution may make of it. Since he is men-tioned in the letter, in a very compromising manner, they might hint that he had colluded in the murder. Or at the very least, that he is an interested party. But, so long as the police do not charge him, so long as he is free of suspicion ... All the same, as I said, the fact that he is mentioned – perhaps you should speak to him yourself.'

She was thoughtful and at last said in a low voice, 'Mr Furniss, I must trust Mr

McMaster's judgement in this.'

'To be sure.' The solicitor cheered up. 'There's no better man in the business, you may depend on it. If he undertakes the case, in my experience, we're three-quarters of the way there.'

Somehow the weekend passed. The dressmaker returned, Sarah was fitted, pins were stuck in, chalk marks made, and she was assured the dress would be ready by first thing on Monday in time for the funeral. All the other things – gloves, a bonnet, a short cloak to throw about her shoulders, a veil and stockings would also be supplied.

So on the Monday morning the dressmaker returned again with a parcel, helped her to dress and made last-minute adjustments; she also promised to make up a couple of other dresses and have them delivered. By ten Sarah stood in the centre of her cell in the bombazine gown; it was strange to smell the fresh fabric, strange to hear the different sound of it moving about her body, as she adjusted her gloves, her bonnet. There was of course no mirror.

John arrived, she let her veil fall, and together with a constable she went out into the street, on a cool September day, walked the short distance through the street to the foot of the 199 steps, and together made their long way to the church at the top. People turned to watch them pass.

'How is Robin?' she whispered. 'What have

you told him?'

'I said you had to go away for a while to visit your parents.'

Silence. She reached for his hand and he squeezed it briefly. As they arrived at last in the churchyard she was able to look about her at the panorama of the sea and the rooftops of the town huddled below her. She stopped again and took a deep breath as the veil flapped about her face in the light breeze. 'I don't know when I may be able to breathe the sea air again,' she murmured. 'I must make the most of it.'

As they entered the church it was almost empty. She saw Marcus Collins and a couple sitting near the front; they were George's parents. As Sarah was coming down the aisle, his mother turned to look at her. Neither woman made any sign. Sarah wanted to make some gesture but how could she? That other woman, that other Mrs Bradley, must think she was the murderer of her son.

Sarah had known them well. They had had no objection to George's wife; in fact his mother had been delighted. 'You're just what he needs,' she had told her. 'He's always been rather wild. A wife will help him to settle down.' This had made no sense to Sarah at the time. The last thing she wanted was to settle down. George had offered the prospect of high spirits, adventure and fun. That was what made him such intoxicating company.

Then, as she was settling into the pew, her gaze fastened on the coffin ahead of her on

322

trestles before the altar. She leaned for a moment on John's arm.

They made an incongruous trio – John on one side, the constable on the other. She could not stop staring at the coffin. It was a large coffin. George had been a large man, a large presence in the world. Now he was in that box. Not in the world any longer. He was in that box, and soon he was going to be in a hole in the ground. Unconsciously, tears started. Poor George. He hadn't deserved this. Why hadn't he stayed at home? Why couldn't they have just gone their separate ways? Then he would be still alive. Why couldn't he be still alive? It was so grossly unfair. She wanted to make it all not happen. She wanted George to be still alive. She did not sob, did not wipe away her tears; she simply sat upright in her strange new black clothes, between John and the constable, and the tears trickled down her face as she thought of the horrible injustice of everything. George there in that box, with all of his life to look forward to, and now just cut off. And she, accused of killing him.

Twenty-Nine

That afternoon in the coach yard she took her leave of John.

'It's a month until the trial. Furniss and I shall be working night and day to assemble the evidence. I'll come over to see you as often as I can. But I'll have to be here a lot of the time to interview witnesses. You understand. Don't worry. I shall be thinking of you always.'

'Thank you.'

With the constable standing beside her and the passengers milling about them, there was no proper chance to say goodbye, and finally they tentatively reached for each other's hand.

'Be of good cheer,' he murmured at last as he released her hand.

The constable helped her up into the coach and climbed in beside her. For a moment as she left the police station she had been afraid they were going to be chained together and was relieved to find they weren't.

The coach rolled out of the town and up onto the moor. Everything that had happened since her arrest had an unreal feeling as if it were happening to someone else and she were merely a bystander. Even so, leaving Whitby felt like a further step on a one-way journey, binding her more and more in the tangle of the law, driving her further and further into a web of destruction.

It was a fine soft September afternoon and as they got clear of the town she caught her last glimpse of the sea. She remembered the drive she had made with John to Scarborough. If only they had never gone! Then Marcus Collins would not have seen her, George would not have come, he would still be alive, and she would be safe with John and Robin. So what if they could not be married? She would have been his mistress! She didn't mind! She would have hidden in a little cottage somewhere and he would have visited her.

It was that trip to Scarborough which had started all the disaster.

She opened the window and forced herself to breathe deeply, and tried to enjoy the clear sky, and the breeze in her face.

The constable was a relaxed, middle-aged man who seemed to take things very much in his stride. He didn't find it strange to be in a public coach with a remanded prisoner. Eventually they got into conversation.

'Done it scores of times,' he told her. 'Though it makes a pleasant change to be escorting a lady. No need to lock thee up, lass.'

'Oh?'

'Oh aye.' Now he became talkative. 'Some-times–' he drew a long breath – 'but tha wouldn't want to know. There's *some* – rough diamonds, hard men – we've had the irons on *them*. Only it frightens the other passengers – that's why we don't like to do it unless it's necessary. But with a lady like thee...' He shrugged and smiled.

'You mean – I'm not likely to run away?'

He shook his head knowingly.

'You know I'm up on a charge of murder, don't you?'

'Oh aye.'

'Well then—'

'What – you mean – you might be dangerous?'

She waited. He went on, 'Sithee, lass. Them like thee – what tha might call, domestic murderers – them's always the gentlest ones. Th'art not a murderess by temperament, see? Tha were provoked to it, and—'

'I didn't do it!'

'Oh aye – ' he was unruffled though unwilling to concede the point – 'that's for jury to decide. But I've seen many a one. Ladies like thee an' all; you'd never call 'em the *criminal* type – not criminal by nature, tha sees – but it were just somehow they were provoked to it. Mind, I know what it's like. There's times I could murder my wife, I don't mind admittin'.'

Sarah clenched her jaw, crossed her arms and stared away.

It was after dark when they arrived in York. She was stiff and cold; there was an autumnal

326

chill in the air now, and although she was wearing gloves she felt it all through her. Having to sit still so long and be bumped and rattled too; she was glad to be standing on the ground again.

'What do we do now?' she asked wearily.

'Walk.'

They set off through a series of narrow confused streets. Houses and shops were long ago shut up, though they passed a public house or two. Eventually, they were passing a tower on a mound and came to a broad range of buildings, barely discernible in the last vestiges of light, and arrived at a large door.

It was opened, there was the feeble light of a lamp held high by a man in uniform, she was ushered through. Across a high hall, a mass of wavering shadows in the weak light of the lamp, and into a room. Here the man sat at a desk, opened a large book, took up a pen and unfolded the paper which the constable had handed him.

For some minutes there was no sound but the scratching of the pen across the paper. Eventually he sanded the paper, blew it off, shut up the book and rose again. On the wall there was a row of large keys hanging on hooks. He took one down.

'Follow me.'

Out in the hall again he unlocked a door. She was uncomfortably aware that it was thick and strong. They entered a narrow corridor of stone flags. Immediately a sour-sweet, fetid smell made her stagger slightly.

The man was in front of her, the constable behind.

They stopped before a door and it was opened. It was thicker than the first and of ancient timber, hard, blackened with grease and grime, and studded with large rusty iron nails. There was a tiny window in it.

He opened the door and went in holding up his lamp. She followed him. Stone wall, stone flags, a bare board along one side, a blanket folded on it, a small window high up and almost filled with bars.

Her skin crawled with fear and she thought she was going to faint.

'Slop out at five.' He indicated a bucket in the corner. There was nothing else.

Then he went out, the door was closed and the large old iron lock echoed in the tiny cell as the bolt was driven home.

She was left in darkness and it was only now that the full horror of her predicament descended on her. She stared at the door. She looked at the window.

She could never get out. No one could get out. Once you were in here, you were lost. There was only John and he was miles away in Whitby. If John could not rescue her she was lost, utterly, irretrievably lost. He must get her out, otherwise – her head swam, her hands and feet were cold, her hands sweaty, she ran them through her hair, staring wildly about her.

Utterly, utterly, lost.

★ ★ ★

The difficult thing was to keep herself clean. She was given a bucket of cold water in the morning and a rag of a towel. Then there was breakfast. A hunk of coarse bread, and a metal can of a disgusting, unidentifiable drink.

As the warder handed it in, she asked, 'Am I allowed out at all? For exercise?'

'You'll be allowed out after breakfast for an hour.'

Later that morning her door was opened and she was permitted to walk in a enclosed yard among a few other prisoners. They were all men, and none wore prison clothes. They were all awaiting trial – except for one, kept separate, who she was told a few days later was awaiting execution. He seemed the same as the others, and walked about, but when she heard this Sarah went cold.

She had been standing by the warder near the door as he told her this; she didn't like to venture out among all the men.

'Not long neither,' said the warder. 'Monday they turn him off.'

She couldn't take her eyes off the condemned man.

'They are going to hang him?' she asked breathlessly. 'What has he done?'

'Counterfeiting. Good workman too, they tell me.'

'Oh God,' she murmured at last and turned away, unable to see anything for a minute.

'Art all right?' the warder asked considerately.

'I don't know.' She sounded hoarse. 'Where do they – where—'

'The gallows? Just outside t'city – on t'Leeds road, by the race course. Oh, it's a famous gallows, is that. They hanged Dick Turpin there.'

For a moment she felt dizzy.

'What's the matter, lass; art took queer? Mind,' he went on a moment later, 'it's not a healthy place, this. It's a good thing th'aren't here long. Otherwise, it'd get thee down. What art in for?'

'Murder,' she croaked.

'Oh.' There was a silence. 'Oh. I see. Eeh, sorry, I spoke out of turn. Eeh! Murder!' He drew a long breath. 'I see what tha means. Murder! No joke that!'

'No,' she said briefly and turned away, but couldn't help stealing another glimpse at the condemned man.

The cell was partly submerged, so that the window barely looked out above ground. The walls were stone, which glistened as if they were perpetually sweating, and the air in the cell was a cold damp, which seemed to get into her clothes. At night she wrapped herself in every stitch she had and lay down beneath her blanket. It was difficult to sleep – not merely the cold and damp, not merely her thoughts, which were too black to bear looking into – beyond all this there was a strange, macabre hubbub, of rattling and knocks, the distant echoing of a door, or footsteps on the stone paving of the corridor outside her cell. She was never alone.

She would lie awake for hours, willing sleep to come, dazed with tiredness, as images ran through her mind. George mostly. She remembered the good times: George flirting, George flattering, teasing, herself dancing with him – and then the bad times, the shouting, the drunkenness and the violence. And then, George dead. Lying on the table in the Town Hall. That was so odd, it didn't seem right. George wasn't supposed to be dead; he was supposed to be alive. No one would want him dead, however bad he was.

At last she would fall into a light slumber, waking at intervals during the night, and finally as the brutal knock at her door came at five, before dawn, she had the disgusting and humiliating task of slopping out.

Two days later, to her inexpressible relief, John arrived. He had a large bundle with him, which turned out to include bedding, towels, soap and other things to make her life a little more comfortable.

'I'm going over to the White Rose to arrange about your meals. It's a hotel not far away – just over behind Clifford's Tower.'

'Thank you. I could hardly eat what they give me here. I ate nothing the first day.'

'Don't worry, you won't have to now. I'm sorry I wasn't able to get over sooner. We've had the witness statements from Handley, and I've been studying them. Two men claim to have seen you with Bradley on the evening of the third – around ten.'

'That's impossible.'

'Yes. That's what I am working on. I have to break their stories. You said you left Mrs Barrington around half-past nine?'

'I don't remember exactly. Between nine and half-past. What are you saying?'

'Don't be afraid. I'm only thinking what the prosecution are going to say.'

'I told you before. I left her and walked home.'

'Did anyone see you?'

'No. I walked a roundabout way to avoid going through the town.'

'Why?'

'Why? Don't you remember my little adventure with the fishwives?'

'Forgive me, of course. So you got home without seeing anyone?'

She nodded.

'Can you remember what time that was?'

'No. It must have been around ten. I let myself into the house quietly. I didn't want to disturb you – I could see you had your light on.'

He reached for her hand. 'Thoughtful of you.' He continued to hold her hand. 'That's the part I am going to have to concentrate on.'

'What?'

'Where you were between the time you left Mrs Barrington and arrived home. And who the person was with Bradley.'

She looked up.

'If you weren't with him, then someone else was. The question is – who?'

Stupidly, this question had never crossed her mind. 'I have no idea. He didn't know anyone in Whitby except us. Unless it was a thief? Do you think he was lured down on to the sands and then murdered and robbed?'

'He wasn't robbed.'

'Oh.' She thought for a moment. 'So there is the letter I wrote, and two witnesses who saw me with him on the night he was murdered. How can I possibly escape?'

He held her hands tight. 'You are innocent. Hold on to that. You're innocent and we are going to get you off. Be sure of it.'

She stared up into his face, and a moment later he took her in his arms. 'Have no fear,' he murmured.

Slowly she calmed. As they separated, she asked, 'John, the fact that you are named in the letter – will it affect our case?'

'I won't let it. In any case I don't want to hand the case to another man. I know plenty, of course. I could – if you'd prefer it?'

'No – I'd rather it was you.'

'I know the judge too. Forsyth. And he knows me. We've had a few run-ins in our time – ' he smiled – 'but he knows me. That's important.'

After he had gone, she busied herself with the things he had brought, and felt greatly cheered.

And that evening, as at Whitby, a waiter

appeared with a tray of dinner. It was nearly cold from its long walk, but still it was a vast improvement on the thin and greasy stew she had been served hitherto.

A few days later the door opened, and as she stood up her parents were ushered into the cell. As the door was locked behind them, they confronted each other. For a moment none of them were able to speak; they stared and stared, until at last her father muttered, 'We had your letter. This is a sorry business, Sarah.'

'Papa, I swear to you I am innocent!'

They were still unable to touch. Sarah wanted to embrace her mother; and she knew her mother wanted it too, but she was too afraid of her husband to move without his consent.

'Of course we came to see you. You are our daughter, in spite of all.'

Her mother was sending wordless messages of comfort and support, but would not speak.

They were still standing. Sarah looked round helplessly. There was no comfort, nothing she could offer them, no hospitality. At last she said, 'When did you come up?'

'Last night. Fortunately, no word of this has been published in London, so you are quite safe.'

'Quite safe?'

'Your name is quite safe,' he corrected himself.

Her mother unexpectedly disconnected herself from her husband, stepped forward and embraced Sarah.

'Oh my darling, you can't imagine how we felt when we had your letter! Murder! And not having heard from you for so long! Not having any idea where you were!'

'Charlotte!'

Her father sounded harsh in the little stone cell, but his wife did not seem to hear him.

'Why did you not write sooner?' she went on as they clung together.

'I'm so sorry, Mamma, I was frightened you would tell George! I did write once – did you get it?'

'Yes, we had it.'

'Charlotte!' Her father was sterner. 'Unhand her! Sarah!' He became strict. 'I vowed when you married George Bradley against my express wishes that I would never speak to you again. I have broken that vow – under these exceptional circumstances.'

'Yes, Papa,' Sarah said quietly.

'Who is your solicitor?'

'Mr Furniss of Whitby.'

'And your counsel?'

'Mr Johnston McMaster QC.'

'QC? He is well known? I have spoken to Mr Brownlow of Gray's Inn, who is willing to take the case—'

'Thank you, Papa. Mr McMaster is acting for me,' she said quickly.

'Has a date been set for the trial?'

'I believe the eighth of October.'

'And your solicitor – a Mr Furniss, you said?'

'Yes.'

'What is his address?'

Sarah hesitated. 'His address?'

'His address,' her father repeated brusquely. 'I wish to speak to him.'

'Papa, there is nothing you can do.'

'You are my daughter – do you think I am going to stand idly by when you are in danger of your life?'

'But what do you intend?'

'I shall know that once I have spoken to him. If it is a question of money—'

'You are very kind,' she said quietly.

'Kind? It is my duty, Sarah. No father could do any less. No man shall say I did not stand by you in your hour of need.'

All this time there was something rigid, inflexible in his conduct, his physical stance, the set of his features. Sarah saw all this, even as she saw her mother watching him, and willing him to unbend, to soften towards his daughter.

Sarah turned to the little table, sat and wrote out Mr Furniss's name and address.

As she handed it to her father, she asked, 'Where are you staying?'

'At the Railway Hotel. I shall wire to Furniss tonight and go up to see him tomorrow.'

'I shall stay here,' her mother added more gently, smiling encouragingly to Sarah, and reached to take her hand. 'We shall stay in York till the trial, darling. We shall be with you all the time.'

'Thank you, Mamma,' Sarah murmured, and the two women subsided into each other's arms.

Thirty

Early in the morning of the trial John sent in a lady's maid who dressed her hair, helped her prepare herself, and arrayed her in her mourning gown. John called in briefly, and recommended a bonnet and veil, and helped the lady's maid. The courtroom was in the same building and only a short walk from her cell. Severe in black, bonneted, with her veil lowered, she made a startling appearance as she emerged into the dock.

She raised the veil and looked about her. The courtroom was crowded. Jurymen were assembling in their box, barristers were arranging papers and documents before them, ushers hurried back and forth. The public gallery was full and she was acutely aware of the stares which greeted her. Her father and mother were among them.

John was in his barrister's robe and wig. He glanced up at her at one point and gave a brief smile. She sat for some time, waiting; all kinds of preliminary arrangements had to be gone through, it seemed. Officials in robes talked to each other. The court was filled with a hubbub which to her surprise had quite a genial tone. Men greeted one another; there was a laugh now and then. Obviously a lot of them knew each other. *This* was a regular affair for them; they had been here before, they would be here again, after she was gone. She was peripheral, a mere adjunct to their essentially private games. These observations were interrupted by a loud voice.

'Be upstanding!'

A door opened, and a judge, wigged and belted in his red robe, entered rapidly to his throne and bowed to the court. The court bowed back and the judge sat.

There was more discussion between the judge and a clerk in the well of the court. Then the usher produced a board and proceeded to the swearing in of the jury. Sarah had never been in a court of law in her life and in other circumstances there would have been much of interest here.

'I swear that I will well and truly try the issue joined between our Sovereign Lady the Queen and the prisoner at the bar and will a true verdict give according to the evidence, so help me God.'

Our Sovereign Lady the Queen. Sarah looked up at the coat of arms on the wall above the judge's head. It was large and splendid, carved in wood, and freshly painted. Sarah was in a personal combat with the Queen herself; that was what the coat of arms meant. It wasn't the judge or the jury. It was the Queen herself. Standing in the dock, with its row of spikes round her and the two warders behind her, she felt she was lost before the trial had started. How could she contend against the Queen?

It was terribly difficult to concentrate; her mind would keep running away to irrelevant issues. While she had been studying the coat of arms the clerk of the court had read out the charge against her. She was abruptly brought back to the matter in hand and was relieved to hear her own voice loud and firm as she replied, 'Not guilty.'

Counsel for the prosecution rose and introduced himself and his junior. John had warned Sarah about him. 'Harcourt. He's a bruiser, Sarah, I won't disguise it. I know him of old. Still, he won't get the better of *me*.' And he had smiled grimly. 'I have a few tricks up my sleeve for Mr Harcourt.'

Harcourt addressed himself to the jury. He was a heavy middle-aged man, with a bulbous nose, thick bushy eyebrows and the cavernous, growling voice of a fairground barker. A vulgar bully, it was immediately obvious that he did not intend her any crumb of comfort, nor allow for any shadow of doubt.

'The accused Sarah Bradley is the widow of the murdered man George Bradley. I shall show that she fled from him last December after he had attacked her so violently as to endanger her life. She went to Whitby where she was employed by my learned friend the counsel for the defence. I will show that she was in love with my learned friend for the defence!'

He allowed a pause here for the gasps and murmurs that ran round the room, and followed them with a heavy look. 'And I shall bring evidence,' he went on, 'that the accused was seen with the deceased between the hours of ten and eleven on the night of the murder. If, as I shall show, Mrs Bradley and my learned friend have been lovers, there can be no clearer motive for the murder.'

It was a voice of granite. Again he paused to allow a reaction in the court. But before he could go on, McMaster rose. Heads turned, and the prosecution counsel glanced up in surprise.

'It is alleged that I am Mrs Bradley's lover! Is he suggesting that I have colluded in this murder? No criminal charge has been preferred against me! Now – hand me the Bible and swear me!' He stretched his hand towards the usher.

The judge was scandalized. 'Mr McMaster! What is this? Do not interrupt counsel in his preliminary—'

McMaster ignored the judge. 'Hand me the Bible!' he roared in a voice of thunder. The usher terrified by his voice hurriedly handed the Bible across to McMaster.

'Now – ' he held the Bible above his head, as comments and protests erupted around him – 'I swear by Almighty God that the evidence I give shall be the truth, the whole truth and nothing but the truth!' The court was mesmerized as McMaster, still holding up the Bible, turned to the jury. 'Now,' he went on in a voice of thunder, 'I can state upon oath that this is categorically not so! Whatever Mrs Bradley's feelings may be, we are not lovers, nor have we ever been. And Mrs Bradley is innocent in this matter, which I shall prove to the satisfaction of every man in this room!'

He sat abruptly. Harcourt was still standing, apparently unmoved by this outburst, and watching McMaster with a cynically raised eyebrow.

The judge leaned forward and spoke with a voice like a sliver of ice. 'Mr McMaster, your interruption was gravely out of order, sir. I give warning that I shall not tolerate it.'

McMaster stood, bowed and murmured, 'Beg pardon, my lord, but I could not allow such a slur to pass unchecked.'

The prosecution continued, apparently unaffected by this hurricane interruption. But the entire court now understood that this was to be a contest of heavyweights, and that the defence counsel was heavily implicated with his client.

The letter was read out. Again there was a sharp reaction in court. McMaster did not look up during the reading but appeared to be studying his notes.

Harcourt did not waste much time on the letter; it spoke for itself.

Another item was produced: the knife. It was a large kitchen knife, the blade at least a foot long. Sarah could not help a gasp.

The judge looked up immediately. She caught his eye.

'I beg pardon, my lord, I had no idea ... poor George,' she murmured.

'Be silent!'

McMaster had glanced round but his face was expressionless. Prosecuting counsel motioned to the usher.

'Show the exhibit to the jury. This knife, gentlemen, was found in the harbour not far from the body. It was found at low tide a few yards from the Tate Hill Pier. It appeared to have been thrown in at high tide, and was found on the morning of the fourth of September by a fisherman.'

The knife was returned to the table, and the first witness called.

'You are Mr Hart? Member of the Royal College of Surgeons?'

'I am.'

'You conducted the autopsy on the body of the deceased and presented your report to the inquest?'

'That is so.'

'Mr Hart, when you made your initial examination of this knife, were there blood-stains on it?'

'There were.'

'Recognizably?'

'Yes.'

'Thank you. Now then, Mr Hart. You performed an autopsy on the body of the deceased. Would you say that the wounds in the body could have been made by that knife?'

'I should say so.'

'Thank you.'

Harcourt sat down and McMaster rose. 'Mr Hart. The knife was found during the morning of the fourth, at low water. It must therefore have lain in the water for at least several hours. Are you alleging you found bloodstains still remaining?'

'Definitely.'

'Can you be sure that it was human blood?'

'It is very difficult to say.'

'Oh? What other kind of blood could it be?'

'Almost any.'

'Any? What kind, for example? An animal?'

'Yes.'

'Name one.'

The surgeon shrugged. 'A cat.'

There was a slight laugh. McMaster took him up in a tone of utter disbelief. 'A *cat*? You are saying that could be cat's blood?'

'As I said, it could be the blood of almost any animal.'

'What about fish?'

'Yes. It could be fish blood.'

'Are you quite sure?'

'Yes.'

'So – beyond the fact that the knife is consistent with the wounds on the deceased, there is no proof that it was the murder weapon?'

'No.'

The next witness was a Mr Halliday. Harcourt rose.

'Mr Halliday, you keep a ironmonger's shop in Whitby, do you not?'

'That is so.'

'And how many years have you kept that shop?'

'It was my father's before me. It has been established forty-three years.'

'And how many years have you worked in it?'

'Twenty-seven years.'

'Twenty-seven years. Show Mr Halliday the knife, if you please.'

The knife was passed across to the witness.

'Do you recognize that knife?'

'I do.'

'Is it one you stock in your shop?'

'Certainly. It is a kitchen knife. We have many like it.'

'I should like you now to study this piece of paper, exhibit three.' He gestured to the usher. 'Do you recognize it?'

'Certainly. It is an invoice for purchases made in our shop.'

'Purchases made in your shop. And who made these purchases?'

'Mr McMaster of West Cliff House, Whitby.'

There was a burst of murmuring and comment at this.

'Thank you, Mr Halliday. Now cast your eye down to the fourth item on that list. Would you be so kind as to read it to the court?'

'One large kitchen knife, steel with a bone handle, four shillings and eight pence.'

'One large kitchen knife!' thundered Harcourt. 'Mr Halliday, do you see that knife in this room?'

Mr Halliday raised his eyebrows. 'I see one *like* it,' he said mildly.

'Where?'

'There.' He pointed to the knife lying on the clerk's table.

'That is the knife?'

'It's like it.'

'Thank you. Now, Mr Halliday. Let me ask you another question. To your knowledge when did you last sell such a knife – before that one?'

'Not for over two years before.'

'Thank you, Mr Halliday. You may stand down.'

McMaster looked up negligently. 'No questions,' he said casually.

'Call Mr Marcus Collins.'

Collins took the stand and was sworn. He did not look at Sarah.

'Now, Mr Collins, you were a friend of the deceased, were you not?'

'I was.'

'And how long had you known him?'

'Can't say exactly. Five years?'

'So you knew him well.'

'I knew him very well.'

'And you recognize the prisoner in the dock?'

'Of course I do. That is Mrs Bradley.'

'Quite. Mr Collins, when did you last see Mrs Bradley?'

'Eh? At the funeral.'

'*Before* the funeral, Mr Collins,' the lawyer said heavily.

'Ah.' Collins recollected himself and repeated, as if he had memorized it, 'I saw her going out of the White Horse around ten o'clock on the night of the third of September.'

Sarah felt the room shift round her. She reached a hand to the rail to steady herself.

'Describe the scene.'

'Well, I was upstairs, in my room. I had gone up early, wasn't feeling quite myself, something I ate, I think. And I was just closing the curtains when I saw Mr and Mrs Bradley come out of the inn and go off down the street together.'

'You are sure that it was Mrs Bradley?'

'Yes.'

'Thank you, Mr Collins.'

Harcourt sat down looking very pleased with himself. For a moment there was a hiatus. Everyone looked at McMaster, everyone was waiting to hear what he was going to say against what appeared to be such a damning indictment. When at last he rose, he did so slowly, looking down at his notes and only after a long silence looking up at Collins. He seemed very serious. The court was now quite silent.

'Mr Collins,' he said quietly, 'I will remind you first that you are on oath. And second, that a woman's life may depend on what you

346

say.' He paused, and Collins almost seemed to shrink before his gaze. 'You say you were up in your room at the White Horse?'

'Yes.'

'Standing in the street and looking up at the front of the inn, would you say your window was to the left or the right of the main entrance to the inn?'

'Eh?' He paused to think, and could be seen making little motions with his finger as he tried to work it out. 'Not sure...'

'Fortunately, Mr Collins, I can help you out. You were in room number five, were you not?'

'Eh?'

'You were. If necessary, I can call the proprietor of the White Horse to confirm it. You were in room five, and standing in the street and looking up at the front of the inn, your window is three along on the left side on the first floor. So you were looking down to your left. Do you recall *that*?'

'Yes,' he said brightly, 'by Jove, you're right.'

'Yes, I am right. You were looking down sharply to your left. Now, Mr Collins, in your testimony you state – ' here he consulted a paper – 'you state that Mr Bradley and a woman set off in the direction of the bridge. Is that not so?'

'If I said it...'

'Yes, Mr Collins?'

Collins shrugged. 'I suppose – I did?'

'You suppose you did?' McMaster took him up.

'Well, dash it, I did, then.'

'Mr Collins, if Mr Bradley and a woman left the inn and set off towards the bridge, that means that they left the inn and turned to their *left* – that is, they turned their backs on you, as they came out of the door.'

'By Jove, that's right. I remember now.'

'Very well. Let us be clear about this. You were upstairs, at a window three rooms along, so you were looking down at a sharp angle towards the front door. You then saw Mr Bradley and a woman come out and turn in the direction of the bridge – *away* from you.'

'Yes.'

'What was the woman wearing?'

'Er – a cloak.'

'And what colour was this cloak?'

'Dashed if I remember.'

'Very well. Now, Mr Collins. Sunset on the third was at twelve minutes before eight. What time did you see Mr Bradley and this woman?'

'Around ten, I think.'

'Around ten. That is over two hours after sunset. Was the street in darkness?'

'I don't think so.'

'Well, by what light did you see them?'

'Don't remember.'

'Try.'

'Well, it was sort of dusk.'

'How could you tell it was Mrs Bradley?'

'Who else could it be?'

McMaster waited. There was a silence. He was looking very serious and at last said quietly, 'Thank you, Mr Collins.'

Collins came down from the witness stand looking slightly perplexed. He seemed to realize he had done the wrong thing but didn't know what. Sarah felt distinctly cheered.

But the next witness was Marmaduke Hardcastle. Her heart sank.

'You are Marmaduke Hardcastle?' Harcourt began.

'I am.'

'Do you recognize the prisoner at the bar?'

'I should say I do.' His manner was what it had always been: breezy, confident, cynical.

'Mr Hardcastle, when did you first meet the accused?'

'In the White Horse, last Christmas.'

'Last Christmas? Describe the occasion.'

'Well, I'm a commercial traveller, and a regular at t'White Horse. They know me of old. Good old Hardcastle, well known there, I can tell yer. Well, I were stayin' at t'White Horse, and she were, an' all. And one night I were sittin' down to me dinner, when she comes in; next thing I know, she's sittin' at me table.'

Prosecuting counsel affected to sound surprised. He glanced round to the jury to make sure they were as surprised as he was. 'I see. And then?'

'Well, it were right embarrassin'. She's mekkin' eyes at me, she offers to buy me wine. I didn't know rightly what were goin' on. Couldn't mek out who she were. She *seemed* a lady, so naturally I weren't goin' to be rude to her. I didn't like to tell her to find her own table. But I were beginnin' to wonder. And then later, I could see she'd drunk more than she should have, so I offers to help her to her room, and as we're goin' up the stairs, she starts shoutin' the house down. I tell yer, I were that worried. I thought she were goin' to accuse me of molestin' her or some such. Any road, next day I complains to t'manager, and he soon showed her the door. Good riddance too.'

'The manager asked her to leave?'

'Aye.'

'I see.' Prosecution looked grave, and allowed a moment for this to sink in. 'Thank you, Mr Hardcastle. Now. When did you last see the accused?'

'On the night of the third of September.'

'Describe the occasion.'

'It were in Sandgate, just outside the Whaler's Return.'

'And what was she doing?'

'She were wi' a man, talkin' together.'

'Did you recognize the man?'

'Aye. He were George Bradley.'

'Did you know Mr Bradley?'

'Aye. I answered an advertisement in the Scarborough paper, when he were lookin' for his wife. I helped him find her.'

'You helped him find his wife?'

'Aye. I recognized her from the advertisement and I remembered her from the White Horse. So I wrote to Mr Bradley, and he come up to Whitby, and I told him she were livin' wi' Mr – wi' yon defence counsel, Mr McMaster.'

'Living with Mr McMaster?' Harcourt asked carefully.

'Oh aye, it were well known. A scandal in t'town,' Hardcastle went on casually.

McMaster rose. 'My Lord, I must protest. This is pure hearsay.'

Hardcastle shrugged. 'I can only tell what I've heered.'

The judge looked grave. 'Strike that from the record.'

Harcourt seemed quite relaxed about it. He went on, 'And you recognized the woman with him?'

'I did.'

'Do you see that woman in this room?'

'I do. She's standin' in t'dock.'

'Mr Hardcastle. I want you to think back very carefully to that night. Do you remember what Mrs Bradley was wearing?'

'Aye. It were a blue cloak.'

'Show the witness exhibit number six, if you please.'

A blue cloak was passed across. Sarah swayed as she stood. She recognized that cloak. It had a piece of embroidery round the collar. It was Chrissie's.

Thirty-One

It took her a second or more to recover as questions raced through her mind. But counsel was proceeding with his questions. She forced herself to concentrate.

'Would you say that was the cloak Mrs Bradley was wearing?'

'I would.'

'Show the cloak to the jury, if you please.'

The usher paraded it in front of the jury.

'This cloak was found the following morning hidden beneath some rocks at the foot of the West Cliff. I should like you gentlemen to take particular note of the bloodstains.'

Sarah could feel the blood draining from her head and there was a faint ringing in her ears.

Harcourt turned to the jury. 'According to the coroner's report, which is based on the surgeon's report, those stains were less than twelve hours old when the cloak was found.'

He sat, and again after a relaxed pause, McMaster rose to question the witness.

'Mr Hardcastle.' He paused again, studying his notes, taking his time and looking very grave. 'Let me take you back to that night last Christmas when you and Mrs Bradley dined together. It was Christmas Day, was it not?'

'Was it?' Hardcastle said vaguely.

'It was!' McMaster said in an unexpectedly loud voice. 'Mr Hardcastle, will you tell the jury *why* you were dining alone in a hotel on Christmas Day?' Glaring at the witness, he made this sound the most heinous of crimes.

Hardcastle was caught off balance. 'A man can if he wants, can't he? It's not a crime.'

'Mr Hardcastle, are you married?'

'Aye—'

'You *are* married, yet you were dining alone in a hotel on Christmas Day – that day of all the days in the year most consecrated to family life. Mr Hardcastle, would you describe your marriage as a happy one?'

Hardcastle looked bewildered to the judge.

The judge frowned at McMaster. 'Is this relevant, Mr McMaster?'

McMaster shrugged, and said nothing. After a moment he went on, 'Now then, Mr Hardcastle, you say the lady bought you wine. Plied you with wine, perhaps?'

'Aye. She did.'

'Show the witness exhibit number seven, if you please.'

The clerk passed across a piece of paper.

'What is that paper, Mr Hardcastle?'

Hardcastle was taken by surprise. 'It's a bill from the White Horse.'

'*Whose* bill?' McMaster said severely.

'Mrs Bradley's.'

'What is the date?'

'Twenty-eighth of December last.'

'Read it. Aloud. Let the gentlemen of the jury hear it. Loud and clear, if you please.'

Hardcastle drew a breath. 'To bed and breakfast, December twenty-second to the twenty-eighth, three pounds and six shillings. To dinners, one pound seventeen shillings and six pence.'

'Go on.'

'That's all.'

'Thank you. Pass that back to the clerk. Now show the witness exhibit eight, if you please.'

The paper was passed across.

'And what is *that* paper?'

'It's a bill, an' all.'

'Whose bill?'

'Mine.'

'Read it. *Aloud.*'

'To bed and breakfast December twenty-second to the twenty-ninth, three pounds and seventeen shillings. To dinners, two pounds twelve shillings and sixpence.'

'Go on!' said McMaster in a voice of bronze.

'To wine, five pounds five shillings.'

'Thank you. You may return the paper to the clerk.'

He paused and examined his papers for a moment as a slight hubbub arose in the court.

'Silence in the court,' shouted the judge.

McMaster looked even more grave than usual, exceedingly severe.

'Mr Hardcastle, I will remind you that you

354

are under oath. I will remind you further that perjury is a serious crime. You said earlier that Mrs Bradley offered you wine. Is it not in fact the case that you offered *her* wine?'

Hardcastle shuffled. 'Oh aye, well, maybe now I come to recollect—'

'Mr Hardcastle, you were a married man taking his Christmas dinner *alone* in a hotel. I will not enter into the reasons why you chose to be absent from the family home on Christmas Day. Then a single lady entered, to whom you offered wine. Is that not the case?'

'Aye—'

'Aye,' McMaster echoed in a very final tone. He studied his notes once more. 'Now, I turn to the night of the third of September last. You say you saw Mr Bradley in conversation with Mrs Bradley outside the Whaler's Return. That is an inn, is it not?'

'Aye. In Sandgate.'

'And that is a street in the centre of Whitby. A narrow street, is it not?'

'Aye.'

'Mr Hardcastle, would you say you knew Whitby well?'

'Oh aye,' he chuckled, his confidence beginning to return. 'I should say I do. I've been goin' theer nigh on twenty-five year.'

'How often do you go there – in the year?'

'Four or five times. I travel all over northeast, as far south as Sheffield, as far north—'

'Four or five times a year over a period of twenty-five years. So you must indeed know the town well. Thank you. That will be all.'

McMaster sat down, and after a moment Harcourt rose. 'No more witnesses, my lord.'

That was the end of the prosecution case and a recess was now announced. Sarah was now taken back to her cell, and dinner brought in from the hotel. As she finished, McMaster appeared.

'How are you?'

'Quite well – considering. Thank you for the dinner. I was starving. But, John – there is something I must tell you.'

He sat at the table. He had removed his wig and gown, but was in his dark suit with his white bands.

'That cloak. I recognized it.'

He was alert.

'Yes. I know whose it is.' She hesitated. 'I know for a fact that cloak belongs to Chrissie Barrington. Beyond a doubt.'

'You mean perhaps – the embroidery?'

'For a certainty.'

They stared into one another's eyes for a second. McMaster looked grave.

'So – the woman with Bradley was Chrissie?'

She shrugged, looking bewildered. There was another long silence as they both thought.

'You know her better than I do,' he said at last. 'Do you think her capable of murder?'

'Chrissie? It is impossible.'

'Yes.'

'Yet she said to me once – the last time I saw her – that she would do anything for me,'

Sarah went on in an uncertain voice. 'She knew more about – us – than anyone else in the town. I told her everything, John. On the night George died I went over to see her.'

'You realize, don't you, that if you tell the court whose cloak that is, it would free you from suspicion? And it would be the easiest thing in the world to prove it is Chrissie's.'

Sarah leaned forward, her head on her hand. 'Put Chrissie in the dock?' she whispered hoarsely. 'John, I cannot allow Chrissie to be caught up in this.'

'Even at the price of your own life?'

Sarah was silent. It seemed to go on for ever.

'Oh God, I cannot think,' she murmured at last. She reached for a glass of water.

'There may be a way round this. Leave it with me. There may be a way to show that it is not your cloak without implicating her.'

'How?'

'I don't know yet. We'll wait and see. There is a lot more evidence to get through yet. And things are going well so far.'

'Are they?'

He chuckled, 'Very well. Collins blew himself up. And as for Mr Hardcastle, he's made a bad showing so far. And it'll be a lot worse for him before I've finished with him. By the time I've finished with him he'll be heartily sorry he ever set eyes on you.'

McMaster exuded confidence; she reached for his hand. 'Oh, John, thank God I have you.'

'You have me, my darling. Fear not. Now there is something we have to discuss. I want to call you as a witness. I want the jury to hear you. Don't worry, it will count for a lot in your favour, believe me. Once they see you and hear you, they will find it much, much harder to believe you capable of murder. However, the drawback is that it will give our friend Harcourt his opportunity too. He will ask you about George's violence towards you. He will want to build that up – so as to provide the motive for murder. He will also ask about your feelings toward me. The letter. We cannot get round the letter. It is the strongest plank in the prosecution's case. You realize that, don't you?'

She nodded.

'But – since that letter is out in the open, it is better to confront it. I repeat: this is going to be the hardest part of all for you. You've heard Harcourt, you know what he is like. He will show no mercy. So be strong, my darling. There is no need to lie. We have done nothing criminal. You may freely admit you would have liked to marry me – you can't deny it – but that is a long way from a desire to commit murder. And that is the point.'

'Thank you. You make me feel so much stronger.'

'Have no fear. We are going to win. I feel it in my bones.'

Soon afterwards the court reassembled and McMaster rose to present the case for the defence. His first witness was Mrs Barrington. It was an excellent choice. Mrs Barrington's imposing appearance, her strong commanding presence and voice, immediately caused everyone to sit up and take notice.

McMaster took her through the events of the evening of the third. He was the soul of affability.

'Can you recall, Mrs Barrington, at what hour Mrs Bradley called?'

'I should say around nine.'

'And stayed – how long?'

'About fifteen or twenty minutes. She hadn't come to speak to me – it was my daughter Christina she wanted – but she was out for the night.'

'So – at around what time did she leave?'

'I think – perhaps twenty past nine.'

'Mrs Barrington, do you recall what Mrs Bradley was wearing that evening?'

'Oh – something light. It was a warm evening – though nearly dark by then. As far as I recall, she was in a light dress with a little jacket – a sort of pea-jacket.'

'Very good. Thank you, Mrs Barrington.'

He seemed in excellent spirits and very businesslike as he glanced round the court. 'Call the next witness.'

A middle aged man with a large walrus moustache, in a drab black suit, took the stand and was sworn.

'Now, Mr Friend, you keep an ironmonger's in Whitby, is that so?'

'More of a chandler's, actually.'

'I beg your pardon, a chandler's. What do

you stock?'

'What do we stock? We've got fifteen hund-red different lines. Where do you want me to start?'

'Ironmongery will do.'

'We have the completest range of ironmon-gery in the town.'

'Very good – show the witness exhibit two, if you please.' The knife was passed across. 'Do you recognize that knife?'

Mr Friend identified it immediately. 'Cer-tainly, it's a Webb and Peabody's, Sheffield steel. We stock it.'

'Oh, you stock it? How many do you keep in stock?'

'At any one time? It varies, goes up and down.'

'On average.'

'A dozen?'

'And how many do you sell in a year?'

'Well...'

'Have no fear, Mr Friend,' McMaster said cheerfully, 'show the witness exhibit nine.'

A hefty leather-bound book was passed to Mr Friend. 'Do you recognize this book?'

'I had better. It's my order book.'

'Indeed it is. I have marked a page, Mr Friend. If you would be so kind as to read the sixth line on the left-hand page?'

Mr Friend raised his eyebrows, and after a moment read out, 'To Webb and Peabody's Sheffield, re-order three dozen knives, bone handle, twelve inch, steel.'

'And the date?'

'July twenty-seventh last.'

'Was that a quarterly order?'

'It was.'

'A quarterly order. So let us be absolutely clear, Mr Friend. You reckon to dispose of three dozen of these knives four times a year?'

'On average.'

'Twelve dozen a year. A hundred and forty-four knives a year. Is that so?'

'It is.'

McMaster turned to the jury in case they hadn't been following the argument. 'A hundred and forty-four knives a year. *Every year.* Thank you, Mr Friend.'

He consulted his notes and looked up. 'Call Mrs Turner.'

A plump businesslike lady appeared and was sworn.

'Mrs Turner, you are the landlady and licensee of a public house, are you not?'

'I am.'

'And what is the name of your establishment?'

'The Whaler's Return.'

'That is in Sandgate in Whitby, is it not?'

'It is, sir.'

'Now, Mrs Turner, I want to take you back to the night of September third. Do you recall that night?'

'I do, sir.'

'At what hour did you close that night, Mrs Turner?'

'We didn't close.'

'I beg your pardon?'

'We didn't close, because we never opened.'

'Never opened?'

'No. Pub were closed all day, on account of a bereavement.'

'I beg your pardon, I am most sorry to hear it. You are saying the house remained closed all day?'

'All day. We were over at my sister's for the funeral.'

'There was no one in the Whaler's Return all day?'

'No one.'

'And the evening?'

She shook her head. 'We weren't back till gone midnight. Then we went straight to bed.'

'Mrs Turner, this is most important, and I must ask you to be very careful how you answer. You say that no one was in the house all day. Was any light on in the building?'

'How could it be? House were empty and all t'blinds down in mourning.'

'No lights were on. Mrs Turner, tell me about the street lighting in Sandgate. Where would the nearest street light be?'

'You're jokin'! What street lighting? There ain't any! At night it's dark as pitch.'

'Thank you, Mrs Turner.' He consulted his papers then looked up at the judge.

'My lord, I now propose to call the prisoner.'

There were murmurs in the public gallery, as Sarah was escorted to the witness stand. In her black dress and black bonnet, the black veil thrown back over it, she made a noble and arresting figure as she stood to take the oath. To her surprise her voice sounded strong and confident.

'Now, Mrs Bradley,' he said quietly, 'for the sake of absolute clarity I wish to take you back over some of the things mentioned in the letter. You say that your husband came close to killing you. Do you believe he intended to kill you?'

'No.' Her voice was clear and calm, she was glad to hear. 'He was so blind with rage that he was probably not conscious of what he was doing.'

'Have you any idea why he was in such a fury?'

'It was the consequence of a long series of disappointments and, I should say, miscalculations.'

'Can you explain?'

'My husband was always in hope of something better turning up, an appointment or post. He was often without employment. Then even when he had money he spent it unwisely.'

'Unwisely?'

'He was very gregarious, always surrounded by a group of friends, and as long as they were there, as long as there was a bottle on the table, he could forget his worries and disappointments. The next day it was another matter. He swung to the opposite extreme. So he took it out on me.'

'Why did you tolerate it?' McMaster said

delicately.

'I had no choice,' she said simply. 'My parents would not have me back. They had disapproved of my marriage.'

'I see. Now, tell us what happened on the night of the twenty-first of December last.'

'My husband had received a bill – from the grocer – and accused me of overspending – of wasting our money. Whereas in fact I had spent only what was barely necessary to live. The rest went on drink.'

'Yes?'

'We had an argument. I pointed out to him that the reason why we had no money was that he was never in work, and that whatever money we had he spent on drink. Whereupon he attacked me. Unfortunately he attacked me so violently that I realized that if I did not leave the house that night he might kill me. So I went to Whitby.'

'Why Whitby?'

'I simply flung myself upon the first ship I came to at London Bridge. It was pure chance.'

'I see. I should now like to take you through the evening of the third of September. Tell us what you did.'

'At about eight – or half-past eight – I set out to walk to Mrs Barrington's house.'

'Mrs Barrington – just tell the jury briefly, who the Barrington family are, will you?'

Sarah felt her confidence growing. She faced the jury and spoke out, clearly and simply. 'They are a very well-known family in

Whitby. Mr Barrington is a marine biologist, well known in his field, I believe, who has lectured to the Literary and Philosophical Society on more than one occasion. I believe he is to be proposed for the Royal Society.'

'Is he married?'

'Yes, he and Mrs Barrington have eight children.'

'And do you know the family well?'

'Yes. Fortunately I have been invited to the house a number of times, in company with your son Robin. I was asked to play the piano at Miss Barrington's coming-out ball.'

'Indeed. Go on.'

'So, I arrived at the Barringtons' and asked for Miss Barrington, but she was out. I stayed about twenty minutes talking to Mrs Barrington, then came home.'

'What time did you arrive home?'

'Just after ten.'

'Thank you. And what were you wearing on that walk?'

'A light jacket. It was a warm evening; I wore a pink and green dress and a jacket over it.'

'Let me be more specific. The Barringtons live outside the town, is that not so?'

'Yes.'

'And the walk to their house – how long would that take?'

'About forty minutes.'

'About forty minutes. And the walk into town from West Cliff House, where you were staying at the time?'

'About twenty minutes.'

'Thank you, Mrs Bradley. Is that your cloak?' he pointed unexpectedly to the cloak on the table in the well of the court.

Sarah stared down at it for a moment.

'That is not my cloak.'

'Thank you. That is all, my lord.'

Harcourt took his time to rise. He was looking very ponderous, very severe. John had warned her this was going to be the most difficult part of the whole trial.

'Mrs Bradley, you mention in your letter that your husband beat you.' He paused and went on quietly, 'Tell me about the beating.'

'What do you want to know?' she asked uncertainly.

'Everything,' said counsel heavily. 'I mean to have everything out of you, Mrs Bradley, you may depend on it. But for the moment, we'll confine ourselves to the night you fled from your home. Describe the beating.'

Sarah had to think. She looked down in an attempt to order her thoughts. 'He hit me,' she began.

'Where? I mean, where on your body?'

'On my arms, on my chest—'

'On your chest? You mean, on your breasts?'

'Yes. And on my face, and the side of my head.'

'Did he knock you over?'

'Yes, he did.'

'Did you hurt yourself falling?'

'I bruised myself.'

'Any bones broken?'

'No.'

'Nevertheless your husband beat you brutally; he struck you on your face and breasts. He knocked you over. What were your feelings during this beating?'

'What do you think?'

'Never mind what I think, Mrs Bradley; I want to know your feelings.'

'I was terrified.'

'Terrified. As well you might be. What else?'

'I was angry with him.'

'Very angry?'

'Yes.'

'Quite right. Your feelings were a mixture of intense anger and fear. Very natural. What else?'

'What do you mean?"

'What other feelings did you have? A desire for revenge?'

'I don't think so.'

'Your husband beat you to within an inch of your life and you had no desire for revenge?'

'Not at the time.'

'Not at the time? Do you mean you wished for revenge later on?'

'No. I only wanted to get as far away from him as I could. And never to see him again.'

'You fled from him in terror?'

'Yes.'

'So you went to Whitby. There you were employed by my learned friend here, Mr Mc-Master, as governess to his son.'

'His crippled son, Robin.'

'What is your relationship with Robin, Mrs

Bradley?'

'We love each other dearly.'

'And what is your relationship with his father?'

'I said in my letter that I loved Mr McMaster. That has not changed.'

'Have you been lovers?'

'No.'

He glanced down at his notes. 'On August seventh last you were seen in a theatre at Scarborough by Mr Collins. That same night at the Imperial Hotel in Scarborough you shared a room with my learned friend under the name Mr and Mrs McMaster. Is that correct?'

There was a long silence. She swallowed.

'Answer the question, Mrs Bradley,' said Harcourt quietly, glancing to the jury. 'Did you or did you not share a room with Mr McMaster?'

Another long silence as she stared at him, frozen by the unexpected question.

'Mrs Bradley,' he thundered, 'I will put the question to you again! Did you or did you not share a room with Mr McMaster?'

'We were not lovers,' she said hoarsely.

'You were not lovers?' he roared incredulously. 'When you shared a bedroom all night?'

'I have sworn an oath to tell the truth. We were not lovers,' she said stubbornly.

Counsel thumped his hand on the table and looked at the jury in disbelief. 'Well, I thought I had heard everything! Thirty years at the bar and I thought I had heard everything!'

'We were not lovers! I swear.' Her voice rang out.

'Mrs Bradley!' He took her up sharply. 'You have confessed in your letter that you are in love with Mr McMaster! I put it to you that you and he became lovers! I put it to you that you and he *are* lovers. You wrote to your husband that you would never return to him – and we have heard why! I put it to you that you and my learned friend plotted the life of your husband!'

'No!'

'I put it to you that you murdered your husband in order to marry Johnston McMaster!'

'No!' she burst out again. 'Never! I would never do such a thing! However bad George might have been I could never have killed him. I could never kill anyone! How could you!'

Her whole body shaking, she clasped her hands over her face and burst into tears. 'Never!' she repeated, over and over. 'Never! Never!'

'My Lord, I must protest!' McMaster was on his feet, but Harcourt had already sat down.

Thirty-Two

The next thing she was aware of was that she was in her cell again. How she had left the witness box, how she had been escorted down to the cell, she could never afterwards remember.

She stood staring at the wall, shaking, shivering, staring without seeing, still stunned by the force of Harcourt's attack, hearing his voice over and over again, echoing in her head.

McMaster came in a few minutes later. He found her still standing, white-faced. When he took her hands he could feel her shaking, and without thinking took her into his arms. Her whole body still quivered. He held her tightly, and for a long time they said nothing. At last she forced herself to look into his face.

'He knows about Scarborough,' she said hoarsely.

'Ssh,' he murmured.

'John—'

'I know.'

'What—'

'Hush,' he said again quietly, and made her sit on the side of the bed. They sat side by side, his arm round her shoulders, as she

370

gradually quietened.

'He took me by surprise,' John murmured at last. There was a silence as they looked into each other's eyes. 'And he will certainly make the most of it. It's our old friend Hayes all over again.'

'What do you mean?'

'Chapel folk. The jury, I mean. They take a dim view of adultery. A very dim view.'

'Will it count badly against us?'

McMaster did not reply for a moment but at last was forced to nod slightly. 'I shall have to work very hard to keep their minds on the evidence,' he said grimly. 'We're on strongest ground there.'

She was searching his face for some sign of hope.

He took her hands. 'The evidence is in our favour.'

'But?'

He drew a long breath. ''It's a question of appearances, Sarah. People will overlook a volume of evidence if things *look* bad.' He paused, and said at last quietly, 'We must do what we can.'

Sarah slept little, constantly waking during the night, that horrible moment going round and round in her mind. It had shaken her badly.

The following morning the prosecuting counsel rose to present his summing up.

'First of all, gentlemen, I remind you of the letter which Mrs Bradley wrote to her husband after he had followed her to Whitby and begged her to return home. Mr Bradley had promised to reform, to turn over a new leaf; her parents were begging her to return. Mrs Bradley refused to return. And why? Because she had entered into a clandestine and shameful affair with another man. With my learned friend here, who has taken it upon himself to defend her. I say clandestine! Why? Why else should Mr McMaster and Mrs Bradley have stolen away to Scarborough, where they were not known, and taken a room in a hotel? Why else spend the night together in a hotel room? What other reason can there be? And I say shameful! Why? Because she was a married woman who had forgotten the vows she made when she entered into the state of holy matrimony! Those vows, I remind you, gentlemen, contain the words, "For better, for worse"! What business had Mrs Bradley to be in a hotel room with another man? But she tells us the reason – she was in love with Mr Johnston McMaster, with my learned friend, and wished to become his wife.

'Now. A knife was found in the harbour near the body, showing traces of blood. That knife has been shown to be consistent with the wounds on the body. I suggest to you that that was the murder weapon. We know that such a knife had been purchased by Mr McMaster and would have been lying in the kitchen drawer of his house – available as a murder weapon! I put it to you that she plotted the murder of her husband with Mr McMaster. I suggest that she then went into the kitchen when the cook's back was turned and took that knife from the drawer. The work of a moment. Nothing could have been simpler! You have heard from her own lips of the horrific violence which her husband had inflicted on her – and which might drive any sane woman to thoughts of revenge.

'Now we have heard two witnesses state that Mr Bradley was seen with a woman at around ten on the night on which he was murdered. I repeat, *two* witnesses. One witness has positively identified that woman as Mrs Bradley.

'And I ask you this question: George Bradley was a stranger in the town. He had been in Whitby no more than a few days. What other woman could it be, if not his own wife? He knew no other woman. That woman could only have been his wife!'

He paused, and lowered his voice. The jury leaned forward to catch his words. 'I do not need to remind you gentlemen of your responsibility. You are all law-abiding citizens, who feel abhorrence at the thought of wilful murder, the murder of a man by his own wife. You are men who have families of your own. Now,' he straightened, and stretched out his arms in a gesture of mild reasonableness, 'every one of us has been tempted at some time or another to break the law – who can deny it? Every one of us has had moments when it might make our lives easier. But we resist those temptations! Why? Because we know that the fabric of our society depends on the responsibility and respect for the law which each one of us maintains day by day through our lives. That is why the law in its wisdom inflicts its fullest rigour on those who transgress, who forfeit the protection of the law by their crimes. It is a heavy responsibility, gentlemen, and I know you will discharge it. Mrs Bradley is clearly responsible for the wilful murder of her husband George Bradley, and I call on you to bring in a verdict of guilty.'

Mr McMaster had been studying his notes during this speech, and exuded a relaxed air, flicking over papers, picking them up, putting them down, making pencil notes here and there, taking out a handkerchief briefly and putting it back, and altogether taking as little notice of his colleague's harangue as could be.

When he rose to make his closing speech, he still exuded this relaxed air. His attitude towards the jury, however, was now very serious. He waited for complete silence.

'First of all, gentlemen,' he began quietly, 'I propose to take you through the farrago of assertions and suggestions which the prosecution has provided by way of proof of the guilt of the accused. Let us take the knife first. Undoubtedly I did purchase such a knife – and so have half the households in the town! We have heard from Mr Friend the chandler that he reckons to sell a gross of them every year. It was then suggested that the blood found on this knife was Mr Bradley's. Yet we have heard from the surgeon himself that that blood could be of almost any animal, including a cat! Whitby is a fishing port. It is full of knives! Fishwives are cutting up fish along the quay every day. How often does a knife get dropped into the harbour by accident? It is laughable to assert that that knife was the murder weapon. It may be or it may not be. But it is impossible to be certain. And, gentlemen, we must be certain! Nothing less will do.

'Now the witnesses. We heard first from the lamentable Mr Collins. Mr Collins himself admitted that he did not see the face of the woman leaving the White Horse with Mr Bradley. He merely "assumed" that it was Mrs Bradley. "Assumed"! Heaven help us! A woman is on trial for her life! And that man "assumed" he saw her with Mr Bradley! As for the second witness, Mr Hardcastle.' McMaster paused, and the climate in the room felt appreciably colder. 'What his motives for such blatant perjury may be I cannot say, but I shall be writing to the Chief Constable of Whitby to point out the gross fabrications in his testimony. He first had the impudence to suggest that Mrs Bradley had approached him in the White Horse and offered him wine – when the evidence from the hotel records shows clearly that it was he who paid for the wine. You saw Mr Hardcastle – his bulk, his flushed cheeks. I ask you – does he look like a man who enjoys his wine? I think he does! It is clear that he deliberately took advantage of Mrs Bradley, distressed and alone as she was after her ordeal. Then, on the night of the murder, he told us he had seen and identified Mrs Bradley with her husband outside the Whaler's Return, two hours after sunset, in a narrow unlit street. He told us he identified her by the light from the windows of the Whaler's Return. What a monstrous lie! We have heard from the landlady of the inn that no light was visible in the windows of that house.

'As to the cloak. There is no doubt that Mr Bradley was seen in the company of a woman in a cloak, around ten on the night of the murder. And a cloak was found at the foot of the West Cliff with marks of blood on it. It is possible that the cloak was worn by the murderer, possible that it was the cloak worn by the person accompanying Mr Bradley. Possible – but not certain. And we must be certain! Blue cloaks are ten a penny in Whitby! In fact there is not even positive proof that the person wearing the cloak was a woman! Mr Collins did not see the face of that person! But even supposing that it was a woman, there is still no proof that that person was Mrs Bradley. Not one shred of proof!'

McMaster had really got into his stride now, and there was no stopping him. He never hurried, he never stumbled; his brain was a cold machine as he demolished the evidence against Sarah item by item.

'We have heard from Mrs Barrington. The Barringtons are one of the leading families in the town, widely known and respected, on visiting terms with all the best families. And with the aim of benefiting my son, of introducing him to children of his own age, Mrs Bradley formed a friendship with the family. She is an accomplished pianist and was invited to play at their daughter's coming-out ball. Mrs Barrington has testified before this court that she saw Mrs Bradley at her home between the hours approximately of nine and twenty past on the evening in question. Her testimony coincides with that of the accused. They agree furthermore as to Mrs Bradley's dress that evening. They both state that Mrs Bradley was wearing a light summer dress with a jacket. Mrs Barrington has told us that Mrs Bradley left her to walk home at about twenty past nine, and we have heard that the walk would last approximately forty minutes. In other words Mrs Bradley would have arrived home at approximately ten o'clock. Precisely the moment when two men have sworn they saw a woman with Mr Bradley in the town!'

He paused, and then went on more quietly. 'As to the letter. You have heard the letter, and Mrs Bradley does not deny having written it. Now – Mrs Bradley came to my house to care for my crippled son. My son had never known a mother's love...' He paused, looked down at his notes, then went on very quietly, 'My wife died in bringing him

377

forth. I am myself compelled by my profession to be absent from home for long periods and my son, who has not the use of his legs due to that very difficult birth – the birth that took the life of my beloved wife – my son, I say, trapped in a chair, had suffered greatly from loneliness and lack of self-confidence. Mrs Bradley, through her loving care, through her thoughtfulness and patience, gradually brought him round, taught him to have confidence in himself, to take a pride in himself. It was she who brought him to the notice of the Barrington family with their eight children with whom he has become friends. And it was she who taught him to play the piano. My son, gentlemen, crippled, had at last found a means to assert himself in the world – had found something which he could do, and of which he could be proud. I say to you with no false pride, no father could ask more from a woman. I am not ashamed to say that I owe more to that woman than you can imagine. She saved my son.'

It was clear that McMaster was greatly moved. He paused and looked down at the notes for some time. The whole court, who had hung on his words, now allowed a low murmur of sympathy to escape them.

'Mrs Bradley and I have formed a close friendship, it would be useless to deny, and in any case neither of us is ashamed of it. And certainly we should like to be married. I do not deny it, nor should I be ashamed of it. But it is asserted that because Mrs Bradley

378

wished to marry me she therefore murdered her husband. That is a monstrous lie! Nothing in Mrs Bradley's character or behaviour, nor in the letter that she wrote, gives any grounds to believe she would be capable of such a dreadful thing. Does she look like a woman who would commit cold-blooded murder? Does she sound like such a woman? The very idea is grotesque! Grotesque!'

He paused again.

'Finally, I will remind you, gentlemen, that Mrs Bradley is on trial for her life. It is a heavy responsibility, to send a woman to the gallows. A heavy responsibility. A man will weigh the evidence very carefully indeed before returning a verdict of guilty in these circumstances. A man will want to be absolutely certain of the guilt of the accused. Nothing less will do. The proof must be absolute, unequivocal, cast-iron. And *unless* that evidence is cast-iron, absolute and unequivocal, she *must* be acquitted.'

Thirty-Three

There was a recess for lunch. Sarah was quite exhausted. The emotional heat in the court room had become almost unbearable and she was not surprised to find, as McMaster concluded his speech, that her face was bathed in tears. She pulled out a handkerchief to wipe her eyes and drew a shattering sigh. Until he had spoken those words she had not realized how deeply he loved her and how deeply she too loved him. It was something unbreakable, something between them for ever.

In her cell she had to lie down and close her eyes. Her meal was brought in, but it lay on the table untouched. John came in later, and for a moment they held hands without speaking. He was as moved as she, she knew. They held hands looking into each other's eyes.

'You were wonderful, my darling,' she whispered. 'I never heard anything like it. Thank you, thank you.' There was another silence until she asked uncertainly, 'What next?'

'The judge will make his summing up...'

'And then?'

'Then the jury retire.'

'Yes.'

By this afternoon she would know whether she was to live or die.

It was impossible to concentrate. The judge went through the evidence in an obtuse and pedantic way. Things which were so vital to her sounded in his mouth like examples from a dry textbook. He did not clarify the issues and dwelled on aspects which seemed to her irrelevant, dry and legalistic. Her innocence did not seem clear at all.

Her mind constantly wandered. Anything could distract her, a fly against the window-pane, the usher blowing his nose, an odd-looking man in the jury box who was staring at her.

With a slight jolt she heard the court rise. The judge retired then the jury filed out. There was a relaxation in the court. The public burst into life, while officers of the court chatted amongst themselves. Sarah watched them; tonight they would be going home. There would be a drink, a warm fire, a family to welcome them home. How could they imagine her feelings? She stared about her, taking in all these things, knowing them in a strange surreal way, as if her mind was perfectly lucid, while in her stomach there was a nest of seething, writhing anxiety.

Now the jury was returning. It was barely twenty minutes since they had left. Was that good? Was it bad? How could you tell? The judge returned, and she was ordered to stand as the foreman of the jury was asked whether

381

they had reached a verdict.

They had.

And did the jury find the accused Sarah Bradley guilty or not guilty of the charge against her?

Not guilty.

Her strength gave way and she fainted clean into the arms of the warder behind her.

When she came to she found herself in a chair and someone was administering a glass of water and saying, 'Just drink this, dear, just drink this, you'll be all right in a moment.'

As she tried to sit up a sharp pain shot through her neck into her brain. The light was too bright and her eyes hurt. She forced herself to concentrate and saw her mother kneeling beside her. She was unable to speak, felt utterly wrung out, utterly spent, as if she would never have the strength even to stand again. She could hear voices all round her; everyone in the court seemed to be talking at once, and as she slowly focused her gaze onto her mother's face, she could now make out her words, incoherent, repeating, 'Oh my darling, you are safe, you are safe,' and Sarah saw the tears running down her face. They embraced, and again she could not concentrate on anything, only conscious of a rushing of talk, the shuffling of chairs and clattering of feet on the boards of the courtroom floor.

Only very slowly was she able to think straight and, looking round at last, saw her father and McMaster. Her father was shaking his hand over and over and saying, 'My dear sir, my dear Mr McMaster, I can never thank you enough, not in a lifetime. My daughter, sir, my child. What can I say? No words can express my thanks. Never in a lifetime – my daughter – my child. What a speech. I never heard the like. It was masterly, my dear sir, masterly.'

Her father now turned to her and saw that she had recovered. He came and knelt beside her chair, where she still sat as weak as water, and took her in his arms. 'Don't say anything, Sarah,' he whispered. 'You are safe. I ask no more.'

'Papa...' She could not go on. Her mind was empty, only containing perhaps those distant memories of being held in his arms as a small child, and conscious all through her of a wonderful reconciliation after so many bitter scenes, so many things wished unspoken, since her marriage. 'And we are together; that is all I could wish.'

As he broke away at last he took his hand-kerchief to wipe the tears from her eyes, and she saw the tears in his, the tears running down his cheeks. 'Oh, Papa,' she whispered and embraced him again.

Only very slowly, as they were able at last to separate, she was able now to stand and, leaning on her father's arm, embracing her mother with her other, she looked round for John McMaster. The courtroom was nearly empty now, only an usher on the further side, busy at some task. John was shuffling documents together, apparently concentrating on the desk before him. As she looked at him he looked up at last, and for a moment they looked at each other, she standing between her parents, and he with papers in his hands. They both smiled, a slight, hesitant smile perhaps, a smile of knowing and understanding miraculously that all obstacles had been cleared away between them, and that they were free at last, free to pursue the course of their lives together.

There was nothing to say. They knew it all.

The following morning she travelled to West Cliff House with her mother and father. They were welcomed by Josiah, Mrs Hudson and Jenny, and Robin was brought down to be introduced to her parents. John had to remain in York to tie up some details of business and would join them the following day.

As soon as she arrived she wrote a note to Chrissie to share the good news, and that afternoon Chrissie arrived while she was sitting at the tea table with her parents and Robin. After kisses and hugs had been exchanged, Sarah suggested a short walk along the cliff.

Sarah wanted very much to get Chrissie alone. A small doubt, a fear, had been gradually growing in her mind. She herself had been acquitted but the identity of the murderer was still unknown. And the cloak still lay somewhere in the jail at York.

She explained what had happened at the

trial. 'Can you imagine my feelings when the cloak was held up, and I recognized it? Have you any idea how it came to be on the beach?'

Chrissie shook her head, but after a moment she said in a low voice, 'I confess, Sarah, I did go to see your husband.'

'You did?'

She nodded. 'It sounds very foolish perhaps, but I felt I owed it to you to do anything I could to help you. I went to see him in the White Horse.'

'What happened?'

'Nothing. Mr Bradley was determined you should return to him. I tried to explain that you and Mr McMaster were – you know – in love, but he would not hear it. He was fixed. In the end, when it had got quite dark, I was leaving and he said he would escort me to the cab rank. I had told my mother I was going to stay at my friend Susan's, and as it was dark, I took a cab.'

'You were seen leaving the inn. They thought it was me.'

'Oh no!'

'That still doesn't explain the cloak. Someone got hold of it. Have you any idea who?'

'No one. It's absurd – there is no one in our house who would do such a thing. Oh, Sarah – let's not talk of it – it is all so hateful. Do tell me – what are your plans? Will you be married?'

'We had better be,' Sarah smiled grimly, then lightened. 'Of course we are, as soon as possible. I cannot wait a minute longer. But,

Chrissie, let me ask you one other thing. When you and George walked to the cab rank, did you walk through Sandgate?'

'No, we went straight down Church Street to the bridge. And Sarah, Mr McMaster should have called me as a witness. I could have told the court that it was me outside the White Horse.'

After Chrissie had left, Sarah thought about this. Put Chrissie in the witness box? Leave her to the mercy of the prosecution? And if she had identified the cloak? It was out of the question.

And she was still left with the basic question: if Chrissie didn't do it, how did her bloodstained cloak get to the bottom of the cliff? And who was the woman Hardcastle saw? If he saw anyone. Perhaps he never did see anyone at all. That still left the question: who killed George?

Then as she was letting herself in at the front door, a thought struck her like a violent blow across the back of her head. She almost stumbled as she crossed the drawing room and dragged at the bell. A moment later Josiah appeared at the drawing-room door.

'Come in and close the door, please, Josiah.' She paused, composing her features and clasping her hands, and went on lightly, 'A few weeks ago Miss Barrington called here and left her cloak behind by accident. I asked you to return it to her. Do you remember?'

'Oh, Mrs Bradley!' He slapped his forehead. 'It went clean out of me head. With all that's happened, you can imagine – but I'll tek it tomorrow first thing.'

'It's quite all right, Josiah, it's not important. Only that Miss Barrington was wondering where it had got to. I'll take it over myself sometime. You may go.'

Josiah crossed to her, and took her hands. 'Mrs Bradley, before I go, may I say how glad I am that everythin's turned out alreet. We were all that worried for thee—'

'Thank you Josiah,' she said hurriedly, 'you may go.' She turned away and he let himself out of the room. In a second she was behind him, and had opened the closet in the hall where overcoats were hung. The cloak was not there, and everything was now clear. She went briskly into the kitchen; Mrs Hudson was at the table kneading pastry, and Jenny was tidying dishes onto a shelf.

'Jenny, will you go and lay the table now, please,' she said flatly.

'Very well, miss.'

Mrs Hudson looked up in surprise at the authoritative tone in Sarah's voice. But as Jenny went out, Sarah went quickly over and took her by the wrist.

'Now you listen to me. Listen and don't say anything. I want you out of this house tonight. I won't say anything to anyone, but you must be gone before morning. Don't speak to anyone. Just go.'

'What art tha talkin' about?'

'You know exactly what I am talking about.

It's no thanks to you that I'm not dangling at the end of a rope. I know whose cloak that was, and who took it from the closet, and I could tell the police too. You could be in a cell tomorrow morning, if that's what you want. Is it what you want?'

With a wrench Mrs Hudson freed herself. 'Tha don't know *nowt*!' she hissed. 'When that man come here, he were desperate. Him and his son both. The father hated t'son, son were in fear o' father. And there were no one to care for 'em but *me*! Do thee understand? It were my charge. T'mester had saved me and it were my charge to care for 'im and his son. Then tha come! No one asked thee, but tha come wormin' thee way into his affections, seducin' him, aye, and Robin too, that sweet boy. He were like a son to me!'

'What? There were other governesses before me. Miss La Touche—'

'Fools all of 'em, none of 'em worth the time o' day. It were a sacred charge to me, to care for 'em both. Dost tha think I were goin' to stand by and see thee ruin him? Drag 'im into t'mire?' She stepped back, contempt written all over her face. 'Hah! I'd do it again. I'm only sorry tha'st got off. So, do thee worst! Dost think I'm afeared o' thee?'

'I don't care whether you're afraid of me or not. But you're not staying another night under this roof. This night, out you go. Or *I* go to the police.' Mrs Hudson's expression did not change, and Sarah took another step closer. 'What do you think the master would say if I told him what I know? You haven't thought it out. I'm going to marry him and there's nothing you or anyone can do to stop it. Will he have you in the house if I tell him what I know? Now, if you go tonight, I promise I'll say nothing. But if you're still here in the morning, I swear he will know everything. *Everything!*'

The following morning Mrs Hudson was gone, no one had any idea where. She had told no one of her intention to depart, left no message nor forwarding address. When John arrived from York, Sarah had to explain how she had simply disappeared the previous night. It was a mystery, but not one that they were anxious to probe very deeply. Another housekeeper was procured.

Four weeks later she and John were married in the parish church at the top of the 199 steps. Robin was with them in his chair. It was a very quiet wedding and absolutely against all the proprieties, but after everything that had happened they were not prepared to wait a year for her to be out of mourning.

Then they set off on their honeymoon. Her parents were more than willing to stay on and take care of Robin. Her father in particular had become very attached to the boy.

They travelled to Menton on the Riviera. It was late in the season and some of the houses were closed up, so it was not difficult to find a villa overlooking the sea. A pink-washed villa set among Mediterranean pines, with a stone terrace sheltering beneath a vine-trellised pergola, sun-bleached steps leading down through a garden filled with aromatic shrubs, thyme and rosemary, and with large urns set on either side at intervals. It was November, a month of cool misty mornings, which gradually, as the sun rose higher, burned off to give three or four hours of hot sunshine through the middle of the day. During those warm afternoons they would sit over lunch on the terrace, watching the sea, mist-shrouded sometimes, the horizon lost in a haze, watching the tall sails of the fishing boats dotted here and there on the glittering waves.

Then they would retire, able at last to be alone together, and in a room where the sun cast long thin shadows through the blinds, John would take her in his arms, sit her on the edge of the bed, and they would both know that at last they had come into their kingdom. And he would lay her down gently, gently picking at the buttons on her dress. And then the chemistry would begin to work in them both, faster and faster, the eagerness to possess what was at last rightfully theirs, and as she emerged from a sea of underwear, like some classical nymph from the waves, and he naked now and over her like a god, so their love would be properly, fully, expressed. She would take him into her arms, into herself, with a feeling of completeness...

390

During the journey back to Whitby, she mentioned as they were travelling over the moors that it would soon be the anniversary of their meeting.

'Do you remember it?' she asked. His arm was about her shoulders as they sat looking out of the window.

'Remember it? I noticed you as soon as I stepped on the ship,' he said drily.

'And I noticed you,' she echoed dreamily. 'You looked very cold, and very frightened, and very determined.'

'And you looked very big, and very strong, and very determined.'

He chuckled. 'An infernal bully, in other words.'

'You ordered me about shamelessly.'

'Quite right. I thought you were trying to get yourself washed overboard.'

'Part of me was. If you could have read my thoughts just then...'

'Perhaps I could – just a little.'

'Could you?'

'A woman travelling alone? With almost no luggage? Not knowing where she was bound? You had desperation written all over you.'

'I had no idea it was so obvious.'

'The worst of it was you were so determined not to be helped. If you had come with me that afternoon—'

'When you offered me a lift?'

He gripped her a little tighter. 'But you were determined to be independent.'

'What a fool,' she murmured.

'It was what made you so memorable. It was what first drew me to you.'

'Thank you, my darling.' She rested her head against his chest.